PRAISE FOR *THE SEVENTH SUN*

"With a rich world and even richer characters, Lani's
The Seventh Sun will pull you in and keep you wanting more."
—KARA BARBIERI,
author of the Permafrost series

"This vivid, historic tale will transport readers to an ancient culture
and, along the way, will capture their hearts, as well."
—MERRIE DESTEFANO,
award-winning author of *Valiant*

"Lani Forbes delivers lush storytelling, vivid characters,
and heart-pounding drama in her compelling debut novel…
Lani Forbes now joins Leigh Bardugo and Alwyn Hamilton
in the ranks of the most talented fantasy authors of today."
—MARGO KELLY,
award-winning author of *Who R U Really?* and *Unlocked*

"With a blazing-hot romance and a world that rises and sets
with Aztec and Mayan legends, Lani Forbes delivers a story
as majestic as the sun itself."
—PINTIP DUNN,
New York Times bestselling author of *Forget Tomorrow*

"Mesoamerican mythology gets a long overdue epic
fantasy treatment…A page-turning adventure that…
highlights a rich and relatively unknown mythological
heritage that begs to be explored."
—KIRKUS REVIEWS

THE

JADE
BONES

THE
JADE
BONES

LANI FORBES

**BLACK
STONE**
PUBLISHING

Printed in the United States of America

First edition: 2021
ISBN 978-1-982546-10-6
Young Adult Fiction / Fantasy / General

1 3 5 7 9 10 8 6 4 2

CIP data for this book is available
from the Library of Congress

Blackstone Publishing
31 Mistletoe Rd.
Ashland, OR 97520

www.BlackstonePublishing.com

To Vicki, Alaina, and the other women who walked beside me as I went through my own version of hell.

THE PLACE WHERE SMOKE HAS NO OUTLET

THE CITY OF THE DEAD

THE FINAL RIVER

MARSH OF PUS

THE PLACE WHERE BEASTS DEVOUR YOUR HEART

THE RIVER OF SCORPIONS

THE RIVER OF BLOOD

THE PLACE WHERE BODIES HANG LIKE BANNERS

THE PLACE OF WIND LIKE KNIVES

THE PLACE WHERE MOUNTAINS CRASH

THE PLACE OF PATHS

THE PASSING OF THE WATERS

CHAPTER

1

The sun set in the world above, dying to the land of the living and beginning its journey through the land of the dead.

Not that Mayana of Atl could see its glowing light through the thick clouds swirling overhead. The only sign of day beginning in the underworld was that the darkness seemed to soften slightly, a pale comparison to the light of the Seventh Sun she had experienced only yesterday. She missed its warmth creeping across her skin and prayed she would be able to feel it again.

She was alive, and—considering she was sitting on the shores of the underworld while her heart still beat—it was a miracle. Her soul was supposed to be festering in the belly of the great crocodile, Cipactli, for even daring to enter this level of creation.

Mayana's wary gaze roamed the cove where they had washed up, taking in the tall black cliffs at their backs and the tiny crescent beach of dark volcanic sand. Far out in the churning gray waters, behind the finger-like rock projections lining the mouth of the cove, she swore a monstrous shadow lurked beneath the surface, waiting for them to return to the water. A tingle of fear crept down her spine.

She tore her gaze away and absently stroked her thumb across the smooth jade skull pendant hanging around her neck. It felt cold to the touch, despite lying against her flushed skin. Perhaps there was more to the unique gift from the Mother goddess than she knew.

Beside her, Prince Ahkin of Tollan sat in reverent silence. His own fingers traced the golden curves of the sun carved into the shield that had been worn by his ancestor, the sun god Huitzilopochtli. The faded light of the Seventh Sun barely registered on the dark waves of his short hair, equally as dark as the expression he wore. Mayana was getting used to the scowl that always seemed to shadow his features, but he had been unusually silent since the Mother's departure, as though he was afraid to speak.

Mayana, however, itched to be on her feet. Xibalba was not called "the place of fear" for nothing, and her nerves already felt as frayed as the end of an unfinished weaving. A distant, tortured scream echoed from somewhere above their heads, making her flinch.

"Should we get moving?" she asked, rubbing her arms vigorously. Her resurrected dog, Ona, leapt to his feet, large pink tongue lolling out of his mouth and smooth, dark-furred head cocked slightly to the side as though she had offered to take him on a walk through the city instead of a trek through the underworld. He whined and bounced in place, but his presence bolstered her courage. She still couldn't believe he was here, her dearest companion from childhood. She had been sure she'd never see him again. But thoughts of home reminded her of her father, her brothers. Of little Tenoch hearing the news of her fall into the underworld. Imagining his eyes filling with tears made her own burn. "We have to go."

Ahkin sighed heavily.

Mayana reached out and squeezed his hand gently. "Ahkin?"

Her touch must have pulled him out of wherever he had retreated to inside his head. He lifted his cacao-colored gaze to meet hers.

"I'm sorry. I'm still—recovering from the shock of it all."

Mayana chewed her bottom lip. Her skin prickled with the sensation they were being watched, but maybe she was being paranoid.

"It was definitely a lot to take in," she said, tucking a long, sand-encrusted strand of hair behind her ear.

Ahkin shrugged. "I can't believe my own sister tricked me into killing myself so that she could steal my throne. And then to learn that the rituals that define every aspect of our lives, including the one that took my own mother away from me, are unnecessary. I'm just . . . feeling a little unsettled." The depth of his scowl intensified. The Mother goddess had been gracious with her gifts, but she had also been harsh in her corrections.

Mayana grimaced. "I know. And I just found out I'm supposed to make a decision that will either save or destroy our world. That's not reassuring either." She placed a hand on his shoulder. "But at least we don't have to do this alone."

Ahkin's hand reached up to cover hers, squeezing it. They stayed like that for several heartbeats, standing together in silence on the edge of death. Unsaid words passed between them. Whatever came, they would face it together.

The prince of light sniffed and rose suddenly to his feet. "We need to make a plan."

"A plan?" They had only until the end of the Nemontemi, the last five days of the calendar stone, to escape the lower levels of creation, and only the gods knew if days passed the same in Xibalba as they did in the upper levels. There was no time to sit and strategize for hours. Were they even safe sitting here on this beach?

Ahkin furrowed his brow. "Of course, a plan. You can't charge into battle without a thorough understanding of—"

"We have a plan. Escape before the end of the Nemontemi. Which starts tomorrow." She spread her hands, as though that answered everything.

He narrowed his eyes at her. Something in that moment shattered. As if the magic and excitement which had encased them in a bubble during the empress-selection ritual suddenly popped. Maybe they didn't really know each other as well as Mayana thought.

But how well did she really even know herself anymore? So much had changed in the last few weeks. She had been forced from her home, thrown into a ritual where she had to win the prince's heart or lose her own, her royal blood sacrificed to the gods. So much had depended on Ahkin choosing her, she had made herself be who she needed to be. To become his wife. To become empress of the Chicome.

But did he truly her know *her*? The rebellious, passionate heart that everyone else in her life shamed? The nagging fear that it was her own selfishness that made her so? If she showed the truth of who she really was to Ahkin, would he still even want her to be empress?

The Mother goddess was right. They were dualities. Head and heart, passion and duty. She had said they would teach each other the lessons they needed to learn—but Mayana had a sudden uneasy feeling it was going to be much harder than either of them realized.

"What do we know about the underworld?" Ahkin said. She imagined he would be pulling out books and holy texts and preparing to study them if he could. Ahkin always viewed knowledge as power, as though it gave him a sense of control.

Mayana patted her hands nervously against her thighs and eyed the sheer cliff of obsidian rising behind them. She had no idea how they were supposed to climb the cliff . . . or what waited for them once they did.

"I know Xibalba has nine layers that are supposed to represent the nine months of gestation," she said. "It takes nine months for a soul to enter the land of the living, and nine levels to return to where life first came from."

Ahkin nodded in agreement.

Mayana let her gaze wander back to the eerily dark waters of the Sea of the Dead. Somewhere beneath its churning eddies lurked the massive crocodile that had almost devoured their souls. The rocks lining the cove should hold him back . . . in theory, anyway. In her mind's eye she could still see his enormous maw spread wide, the darkness within in it deep enough to swallow the cosmos, the razor-sharp teeth—longer than she was tall—lining his mouth, the additional mouths hidden at various joints, the spikes rising from his back as large as mountains.

She shook out her shoulders to dispel the memory. They had made it past him—barely. But that's all that mattered.

"What's in each layer?" she asked quickly.

Ahkin rubbed the back of his neck. "I don't know."

"How can you not know? You're the one who's read all the codices on creation."

Ahkin turned away from her. He kicked at the black sand with a sandaled foot, and shoved the round, leather-and-gold shield of his ancestor onto his forearm. His other hand opened and closed as though feeling empty without a weapon.

"I've read them all, but the codices aren't very clear on matters of the underworld. I only know vague descriptions. Very few have ever returned to describe it. Certainly not anyone from the age of the Seventh Sun."

Ona whined and licked Mayana's hand with a warm, rough tongue. She absently scratched his ear but didn't take her attention off of Ahkin. "What are the descriptions, at least?"

Ahkin turned back to face her, his eyes squeezed shut in concentration as he recited from memory. "'The passing of the waters, the place of paths, the place where mountains crash, the place of wind like knives, the place where bodies hang like banners, the place where beasts devour your heart, the final river, the City of the Dead, and finally, the resting place of souls, where smoke has no outlet.'"

Something cold slithered down Mayana's spine as she listened. Crashing mountains? Wind like knives? Beasts that devour your heart? How in the nine hells were they supposed to survive this journey? At least there was no mention of scorpions. She would probably curl into the fetal position here on the beach if there had been any mention of those armored little demons.

"How—" Mayana coughed as her throat went dry in the stale air. There was no moisture here on the beach, only the musty stench of death, decay, and rot. "How long is the journey supposed to take?"

Ahkin grimaced. "It's supposed to take a soul four years to complete."

A slow moan came from behind them and they both whirled to see the spirit of an elderly man waft past their crescent of beach. He eyed them mournfully, as though he had heard their conversation and was not looking forward to a four-year journey.

Mayana waited until the spirit slowly drifted to the top of the cliff behind them, a silvery cloud of mist ascending the smooth obsidian like a bird caught in an updraft. The moment he disappeared over the edge and out of earshot, she turned back to Ahkin.

"*Four years?*" she hissed at him. "We only have a week!"

"Kind of. From what I've read in the codices, time works differently in each layer of creation. A single day here might be several days or more in the land of the living. So, four years in Xibalba is very different than four years above."

Mayana rubbed her temples. "So, if we escape by the end of *Xibalba's* Nemontemi, more than a week will have passed back home?"

"Likely we would emerge several weeks after we fell. It seems like a long time, but don't forget we have Ona to guide us. The Mother goddess wouldn't give us an impossible task."

Mayana hoped that was true. As if responding to his name, Ona barked impatiently, the sound echoing around the cove. He loped over to Ahkin and instead of licking his hand, nipped it.

Ahkin yanked back his hand. "What is wrong with your dog?"

Mayana folded her arms across her chest and stuck out her hip, a smirk pulling at her lips. "I told you, he wants to get moving. I don't think he cares about making a plan. We don't even know what those vague descriptions mean anyway."

Ahkin stuck his finger in his mouth and sucked at the pinprick of blood that had appeared, eyeing Ona with distrust. "Fine. Show us the way to go then, beast, because unlike that spirit, there's no way we are floating up to the top of the cliff."

An idea slipped into Mayana's head at Ahkin's words, and she felt her smirk spread into a genuine smile. Her eyes went back to the ocean stretching out into the distance. "Actually, we can."

Ahkin gave her a flat look. "Mayana, no. I know what you're thinking. You lost a lot of blood even getting us to this beach."

"It worked before. Besides, Ona healed us—"

"No. Based on how I felt after he healed my wounds, Ona doesn't replenish blood lost. I have to figure something else out. I just need a little time."

"Time is the one luxury we don't have." Yes, she was a little dizzy from the blood she'd had to supply in order to access her powers and bring them safely ashore, but they didn't have a choice. They couldn't stay on this beach forever.

She picked her way over to the foot of the cliff. Boulders and shards broken off the cliff's glossy black wall littered the beach at its base. The blade her brother had given her was gone, lost somewhere in the depths during their escape from the beast, Cipactli, so she kicked at the debris until she found what she was looking for—a shard of obsidian fire glass as big as her hand. And sharp enough to slice through skin.

"Mayana—" Ahkin started toward her, obviously guessing what she was doing. "Please don't. Just let me think."

Ahkin stopped before her, his eyes pleading. He bent and picked up a shard of obsidian of his own and shoved it in the waistband of the filthy, once-white wrap around his waist.

Mayana felt that familiar rebellious streak she always tried to subdue flare to life within her. She wasn't going to let him tell her what to do, not when she had been right about everything—from the rituals to his sister. If he wanted to stuff away his own shock and grief and mask it by pretending he was in control, then that was his problem. She was so sick of everyone telling her not to trust herself.

She fixed Ahkin with a glare that said, *Go ahead and stop me,* before she straightened her spine and sliced the length of her palm. The blood of her ancestor, Atlacoya, goddess of drought, oozed through the cut. A cool awareness spread across her skin, the way it always did when she was close to water. The sensation called to her, summoning her to the element that allowed her to unleash the power contained within her divine blood.

Ahkin threw his hands up in defeat as Mayana threw out her own hand toward the Sea of the Dead. A geyser exploded from its depths and shot toward them, enveloping them in salty, swirling water.

The current surrounded them and pushed them against each other, Ahkin grunting slightly as Mayana slammed into his bare chest. Their sudden closeness sent a flash of heat across her skin. He wrapped his arms around her, grasping her tight as the mass of water lifted them off the sand. The rushing sound of the water filled Mayana's ears. Her heart thrummed with excitement, as it always did when she used her godly gift. Her stomach dropped to her feet, but she told herself it was from the sudden weightlessness and not from being pressed against the warm, solid chest of the young man she had thought she was going to marry. Her mind chose that moment to bring up the memory of the night he came to her in her chambers, the night he had told her he was choosing her, when they were pressed against each other in a very different way . . . but she shoved the memory away. Whatever life they could have had together was probably gone—assuming they lived to the end of the calendar year.

Ona barked in excitement and paddled against the buffeting water, keeping his smooth head above the surface. His pink tongue lolled out of his mouth as though he were having the time of his life.

The mass of water carried them up toward the cliff's edge, and a sliver of fear lanced through her. What would they find at the top? Were they ready for whatever it might be?

She willed the water carrying them to crest the ledge. Ahkin's arms released her as they crashed on the ground in a massive splash. The ripped remains of her long loincloth skirt stuck to her soaked legs and her hair hung in a matted sheet over her face. She flipped the hair back and scrambled to her feet.

Ahkin was already standing, his eyes as round and wide as the shield strapped to his arm. She felt her own eyes widen in fear as she took in the landscape that stretched out before them.

A field of tall, dead, gray grasses sloped up and down in small rolling hills. Black, twisted trees with no leaves curled toward the clouded sky like tortured, screaming souls. Far in the distance, the sloping hills rose into pitch-black mountains, craggy and broken like shattered fire glass. But it wasn't the dead field that made Mayana's stomach twist like the tortured trees.

The place of paths.

The clearing where they stood was smooth soil. Narrow dirt paths wound through the grasses ahead of them, branching out in a maze of complicated patterns and punctuated with dark, gaping sinkholes large enough to swallow a house. Mayana didn't want to know what lurked inside those sinkholes, because the hundreds upon hundreds of snakes writhing across the paths were bad enough.

Snakes of every color and shape, from poisonous yellow to bloody red to venomous green, covered the paths that stretched as far as they could see. Some of the snakes were small and as thin as her finger, while massive brown-spotted pythons as big as branches fixed them with bulbous yellow eyes. The faint hissing she had assumed was the wind rustling the tall grasses wasn't wind at all.

The musty, dead smell of the air was suddenly too much. Mayana stumbled sideways. Ahkin caught her and steadied her.

He frowned. "I told you, you've lost too much blood."

Mayana didn't feel like arguing. She held out her hand to Ona, who licked the wound clean. The skin healed instantly, thanks to the unique gift the Mother goddess had bestowed upon her furry friend.

"I'm fine." She tried to stand again and felt a sudden swooping sensation in her head. Nine hells, he was probably right, but she didn't want to tell him that. "I was shocked by . . . well, I'm sure you can see." She motioned toward the impossible obstacle before them.

"Right now, I'm kind of wishing Zorrah had jumped in after me," Ahkin breathed.

Mayana laughed bitterly. She knew Ahkin had no interest whatsoever in the brutal princess from the city of beasts, who had the ability to control animals with her divine blood. She had tried to kill Mayana more than once.

"We'll have to step over them, I guess. Some of them aren't venomous, I can tell by the markings. If we can get a branch from one of those trees, we can move them out of our way too." He stared at one of the trees that rimmed their little clearing of dirt with a glimmer of hope in his eyes.

He stepped toward the tree, but before he could move any farther, the ground beneath their feet rumbled. It roiled as though a gigantic snake moved beneath the very surface. Mayana dropped to her knees to stop from falling on her face. She screamed.

"What? What happened?" Ahkin rushed back to her side, kneeling beside her.

Mayana lifted a shaking hand and pointed to the nearest sinkhole—where a gigantic snake was rising from the stinking black depths. But no, it would be unfair to call it a snake. The diamond-backed monster was thicker than the fattest ceiba tree, big enough that ten men couldn't wrap their arms around it. It arched high above their heads and smelled the air with a lashing forked tongue. Behind them, smaller snakes blocked Mayana and Ahkin from moving so that they would have no way to escape the monster before them.

It turned its massive head toward them, bearing curved fangs even more terrifying than the crocodile's had been.

Ahkin wrenched Mayana to her feet.

"Run!" he screamed.

With an almighty hiss that made Mayana's blood run cold, the monster snake lunged right for them.

Yemania of Pahtia had never thought she'd see her home again. It wasn't a home she wanted to return to, but she had expected her trip to the capital to be a one-way adventure. After all, everyone knew that Prince Ahkin would never choose someone like *her* to be his wife.

Her father had known, which was exactly why he had sent her in the first place. If there's only a one-in-six chance that your daughter won't be sacrificed to the gods, you pick the daughter it would hurt the least to lose.

She grabbed a red skirt and shoved it roughly into her basket. There weren't many belongings left to pack, but she couldn't wait to get out of this palace. She wanted to get away from every reminder that she wasn't good enough for anyone. Mayana had been the only one to show her kindness, the only one to treat her like she had worth, and now she would never see her again. Mayana had jumped into the underworld with Ahkin and they were as good as dead—if they weren't dead already.

She reached for a red-jeweled necklace, but her eyes suddenly burned with tears. She pressed her fists against them. She couldn't think about Mayana right now. There were many maladies and ailments her divine gift of healing could cure, but a broken heart was not one of them.

A soft knock echoed off the doorframe to her room.

"Come in." She sniffed, not even bothering to see who had come to visit.

"Hey, Yem."

Yemania turned and her heart leapt at the sight of her older brother, Coatl. Until she remembered that he had helped Metzi betray Ahkin—then her heart curled back into its fetal position. She didn't have the courage to confront him on his actions right now.

"What do you want?" she snapped, stalking past him to grab a feathered headpiece and add it to the basket.

"Don't be mad at me, Yem. I did what I had to. I love her."

"Enough to betray your best friend? Enough to help his sister convince the empire that the Seventh Sun was dying and that Ahkin needed to sacrifice himself to save it?"

Coatl leaned against a painted red pillar and frowned at her. The gold-and-ruby pendant lying against his bare chest glinted in the torch light. The earth-colored curls that clung to his head matched her own, but that was where their similarities ended. Where he was tall and lean and handsome, she was short and round and plain. Somehow, he'd even escaped the large nose that she'd inherited from their father. He fixed her with the same exasperated look he always gave her when they were children and she would critique one of his healing remedies. "Yes. Enough to be with the woman I love instead of seeing her bartered like a clay pot for the sake of keeping the peace."

Yemania snorted a laugh. "You really think she's going to marry you and make you emperor of the Chicome?"

Coatl pushed himself off the pillar and spread his arms wide, a wicked smile spreading across his face. "That's the plan."

She froze, her hand hovering in disbelief over the lid to her basket. She turned slowly to face him. "You can't be serious. There is no way on Ometeotl's great green earth she'd be that foolish."

"What's harder to believe, that Metzi already sent a messenger to break her engagement so that she can marry me? Or that your brother is going to become emperor?" His arrogance filled the room, making Yemania feel as though there was no room left for her. But Ahkin's sister wouldn't possibly do something so dangerous, would she?

She dismissed his claim with a wave of her hand. "Ehecatl would be furious. She's supposed to marry their storm prince."

"And what are they going to do? Kill the only descendant of Huitzilo-pochtli left? Doom us all to die in darkness when the sun can no longer rise?"

Coatl was drunk on the power of his new position, on the possibilities finally within his grasp. He had always been ambitious, begging their father from the time he was ten years old to allow him to work as a healer in the palace at Tollan, the glittering golden capital of the empire. But he had never before been so *selfish*. This was not the same brother that had been willing to jump between her and their father's raised fist. The same brother that used to take the brunt of that anger on himself to save Yemania and their younger sisters from their father's rage.

"Well, I don't want to be here when Ehecatl marches on Tollan. I will be happily secluded in the jungles of Pahtia where I can work on new remedies and—"

Coatl sucked in a breath through his teeth, slowly shaking his head. "Actually, Yem, you won't be going back to Pahtia."

She slammed the lid to the basket down, cracking the basket's fibers. "What do you mean? The other princesses are already packing and leaving as we speak. The empress selection ritual is over."

"Remember how I said Ehecatl wouldn't dare attack us since Metzi is the only descendant of the sun god left?"

Yemania narrowed her eyes at him. "Yes . . ."

"Well, I'm the official healer for the palace, but I can't be with her all the time. Especially not if the council gives her any grief about our marriage. But still, if anything happens to Metzi, the sun will never rise again. We need her blood for the morning sun sacrifices, and until more heirs are produced, she wants a healer with her at all times."

Yemania quickly put the pieces together. "You want me to be with her at all times? Like her personal handmaiden?"

"When I can't be with her, and only until we have a dozen or so little nieces and nephews for you to chase around the palace." He cocked his head playfully.

"Do I have a choice in the matter?" Yemania's voice remained flat.

"Not really," Coatl said brightly, swiping aside the curtain and leaving her room with a flourish.

Yemania cursed and upended her basket of belongings. Act the servant to the young woman responsible for killing Ahkin and Mayana? Maybe she should have jumped in that sinkhole after them.

An hour later, after she couldn't possibly stall another moment, Yemania stood outside the white-and-gold woven curtain of Metzi's room. She curled and uncurled her fists several times before finally gritting her teeth and knocking on the frame.

"Come in," chirped Metzi's melodious voice.

Yemania pushed aside the curtain and entered the new empress's chambers. She had never been impressed with Ahkin's sister, not after she humiliated the other princesses in the steam baths to prove herself above them—and that was before Mayana had told her about Metzi and Coatl faking an apocalypse to steal her twin brother's throne.

Metzi lay sprawled across an ocean of luxurious furs and cushions, a bowl of succulent fruits overflowing at her side. She plucked a berry from the dish and licked the juices off her dainty, polished fingers. Her long flowing hair reminded Yemania of a waterfall of ebony—thick, dark, and waving down to the subtly curved hips that attracted the attentions of every male member of the palace residence. Yemania dropped her gaze to her sandals, a twinge of disappointment mixed with jealousy at the thought that she'd never be considered beautiful in the way Metzi was.

"My future sister!" Metzi sat straight up and reached with welcoming hands, motioning for Yemania to join her. "I would love for us to become better acquainted. All I have heard about you is your prowess with remedies, and I didn't get to spend much time with you during the selection ritual."

Yemania gingerly lowered herself onto the furs. Metzi's tone sounded sweet and innocent enough . . . like the poisonous flowers that used their nectar to lure insects into their deadly traps.

"Ahkin was never going to choose me, so it would have been pointless for you to make the effort." Yemania shrugged.

"I disagree." Metzi scooted closer, and Yemania felt the need to lean back. "Coatl tells me you are exceptionally valuable, which is why I requested you. I would love the opportunity for us to get to know one another, given that I plan to become a part of your family, after all."

Yemania pursed her lips slightly. "I'm flattered, Your Highness, but are you sure it is wise to marry my brother so soon . . . so soon after . . . ?"

Metzi's sweet smile became fixed. Her honey-colored eyes hardened into petrified amber.

"After canceling my engagement to the storm prince?" Her tone was calm, but Yemania swore a swarm of angry bees raged within her hardened gaze.

"It's not—I didn't—I'm sorry." Yemania fumbled with her hands and fought the urge to run from the room.

Metzi lounged back and withdrew a dagger from the golden belt secured around her waist. She twirled the blade several times in her hand before gripping the handle with a fierceness that matched her eyes.

"How did you feel, Yemania of Pahtia, the moment you found out your father was forcing you into the selection ritual?"

Yemania blinked several times, fighting back the surge of emotion that came along with the memories of that day. She remembered with painful clarity. Her father calling her into the throne room of the white stone palace in the city of healing. Jungle vines blooming with flowers encircled the towering white pillars, releasing a calming scent that had done little to ease the tension in her stomach as she approached him. The Lord of Pahtia hadn't looked at her, just picked absently at his nails as he informed her she was going to Tollan as his sacrifice to bless the emperor's marriage. He hadn't even told her that she would be trying to earn the emperor's affections. Coatl had told her about that later. She was written off as a sacrifice and that was that.

Metzi must have read the anguish on her face, because the hardened look in her eyes softened.

"I know that pain, Yemania. To feel as though you are property, someone else's to barter or toss away at their slightest whim. To feel as though you have no control over your own life." She rose to her feet, still holding the dagger, and approached the open golden window. Beyond it, the canopies of the lush jungle stretched out below the volcanic plateau upon which the city of Tollan was perched. "I swore to myself the moment my father arranged my marriage for the sole purpose of securing Ehecatl's loyalty that I would not be a piece in his political games. If there was a game to be played, I would be the one playing it. I'm smarter than any of these pompous rodents who refuse to see me as anything more than a pretty face with good hips for bearing children."

Yemania's heart twinged with pity, but only for a moment. "There's still a difference between strength and cruelty. You didn't have to kill your own brother," Yemania whispered.

"I did what I had to do!" Metzi turned around and drew herself up to her full height. "The only way to get control of my fate was to take it, and I don't regret it. No one will tell me what to do ever again. And if they do," she sliced her palm and held it out toward the glowing orb in the heavens, "I'll show them who really has the power."

The light filling the room turned suddenly orange and bronze, the color of a brilliant sunset, before Metzi lifted her hand and the light returned to normal. The slightly manic gleam that edged Metzi's amber eyes made Yemania's stomach turn. Would the princess of light take the whole world down with her before she'd be willing to give up her power?

Before Yemania could respond, one of the elite Eagle warriors burst through Metzi's tapestry, panting heavily and searching the room for their new empress. He carried a flint-tipped spear, and large eagle feathers protruded from his wooden helmet. Metzi turned to face him, irritation flickering across her features.

"What is it?" she barked.

"Your Highness." He coughed slightly to catch his breath. "It's Ehecatl. They've declared war on Tollan."

●●●

CHAPTER

3

Ahkin thought he understood fear, but the moment the monster of a snake lunged toward Mayana, he swore he had never truly experienced it before. He couldn't let anything happen to her—it was his fault she was even here.

He should have chosen her and ended the cursed selection ritual. He never should have tried to sacrifice himself. He should have seen what his sister was planning. Mistake after mistake, every single one of them piled on his head like stones. He would be damned to a thousand layers of hell before he let her down again.

Ahkin threw her to the side, and the snake's head collided with the pale dirt between them. A cloud of dust rose from where it struck, and the snake arched back again, ready for another attack.

"Get to that tree! I'll distract it!"

Mayana opened her mouth to say something, but Ahkin didn't have time to listen. "Go!"

He steadied the shard of obsidian he had picked up from the cliff's base in his hand. The edges of the fire glass cut into his palm, but all the better for exposing his divine blood, for unleashing the power of his ancestor. He willed the faded light filtering down through the clouds to bend around him, hiding him from view.

The snake lashed out with its whiplike tongue, tasting the air for what it could no longer see. It opened its mouth and exposed its fangs—then lunged again.

Ahkin dodged, knocking the head of the snake to the side with his shield. He whipped his hand around and sliced into the side of its head with the makeshift knife. The ground beneath his feet rumbled. The snake writhed away from him, its hiss loud and agitated.

He looked behind him to make sure Mayana had hidden herself behind the giant dead tree. A flash of black hair disappeared behind the trunk. He breathed a small sigh of relief that she was safe . . . at least for the time being.

"You can't kill it with such a small weapon, you'll only make it mad," she yelled.

"You stay safe," he yelled back, but at that moment, something thick and heavy slammed into his back, knocking him face-first into the dirt. The taste of blood coated his tongue. He looked up, and the snake's head was directly above him, its diamondback tail slowly curling around his chest. Ahkin pushed at the powerful, muscled body, trying to keep it from trapping him within its grasp. But its strength was too much. Desperate panic started to creep its way up his chest along with the snake's smooth scales. He'd seen too many creatures die in this exact same position in the jungles. He couldn't fail Mayana again . . .

"Ahkin!" Mayana's voice was far too close.

"Get back, Mayana. I don't need your help!"

"Yes, you do!"

With enormous effort, he turned his body against the snake's tightening grip just in time to see the spear hurtling through the air. A single crooked stick from the blackened tree, a shard of obsidian secured to its base with a piece of cloth torn from her ruined skirt.

He didn't have time to marvel at how she thought to create such a weapon so quickly. Instead, his fist closed around the spear's shaft as it hurtled past. He cast up a prayer of thanks to the gods for his years of battle training. The snake lunged toward him again. Combining his strength with the snake's momentum, he drove its tip directly into the bulbous yellow eye of the great snake. A surge of victory flowed through his veins at the sight of its diamond-shaped head arching away.

The grip around him loosened as the snake thrashed. Its defenses were down. He took the opportunity and drove the obsidian shard back into the side of its neck. Hot, sticky blood coated his hands and arms as he ripped the blade downward.

Its head finally thumped against the ground in another cloud of dust, its body twitching and writhing as it fought back against the claws of death. Ahkin darted toward the head and wrenched the makeshift spear out of the ruined eye socket. Time to finish it for good. The massive fanged mouth opened in a last-ditch effort to attack, but Ahkin dove forward and drove the spear through the roof of its mouth. More hot blood flowed over his arms and down over his chest. He couldn't hear anything above the pounding pulse in his ears. Finally, he yanked the spear back and used his sandaled foot to kick the now lifeless head away from him.

"Ahkin!" Mayana screamed, running forward.

He stumbled away from the snake's body, an overwhelming dizziness slamming into him harder than the snake tail. He willed the light to stop bending around him so that she could see he was okay.

"I'm f . . . f . . ." he slurred, unable to finish forming the words. He was fine and needed to tell her. He needed to ease the panic painted all over her face. Why couldn't he speak? His tongue felt swollen and numb.

Her face tilted sideways, and he found himself staring up at her from the ground. A sound like a war drum pounded painfully loud in his ears. He tried to reach for her, but his arms now tingled as though they had fallen asleep.

A sharp pain in the muscle between his shoulder and neck, above his collar bone, registered right as Mayana knelt beside him. She looked at his shoulder and gasped.

The pain intensified to the point that he leaned to the side and vomited. Mayana didn't even flinch away. When the wave subsided, he focused enough to see a sliver of a curved snake fang grasped in her fingers. Did she pull that out of his shoulder? Had the snake bitten him when he stabbed it?

He tried to apologize, but he couldn't make his mouth move anymore. The edges of his vision went dark as Mayana whistled a sharp sound that made his head throb . . .

———

Mist clung to top of the jungle canopy, hovering over the band of warriors like the spirits of those who had perished generations before them. The warm air hung heavy with the scent of the recent rains. The barren field, barely visible through the line of trees, stretched wide, scattered with flat stones rising from the mud like the faces of sacrificial altars. Soon more than rain would coat the stones.

"Don't be afraid. Focus on your skills and what you know." The deep voice came from his right.

That was easy for Yaotl to say. He was Ahkin's mentor and the leader of the Jaguar warriors, the most elite fighting force in the empire. The jaguar pelt he wore supposedly imbued him with the strength of a great jungle cat. There was nothing on this level of creation he feared.

Ahkin shifted his sandaled feet in the dirt, his muscles tensing. Sweat slicked the palm of his hand beneath the grip of his macana sword. The watery sunlight filtering down through the storm clouds reflected off the shards of obsidian lining a wooden club. This would be the first time his newly crafted weapon would taste Miquitz blood.

And the first time Ahkin would enter a real battle.

Yaotl lowered his wooden helmet over his narrowed eyes. "You have an advantage the other initiates do not. Use it to protect them. They are your brothers. This is your divine responsibility."

Ahkin glanced to his left, where the other young men he had trained with since he was a boy stood ready to enter the field. Though many of them tried to appear brave, their hands trembled as much as his own. Throats bobbed with heavy swallows. The stench of fear hung as heavy as the mist. A fierce wave of protectiveness swept over him. He was to be their leader, their emperor. It would be his responsibility to keep not only them, but the entire empire safe. He would not fail. "Yes, sir."

Ahkin knew what would happen next. The battle horn would sound, and the newly initiated group of warriors would charge. Many of them would not leave the field. He had not been able to protect his brothers, the young men he'd sparred and laughed and lived with for almost a decade, from the time they were barely old enough to hold a weapon . . .

But instead, everything around him stilled, freezing in place as though suddenly turned to stone. Even a passing butterfly hung unmoving in the air. Ahkin lowered his weapon, inspecting the scene around him with disbelieving eyes. This wasn't what had happened that day. Was his memory lapsing?

He stepped forward and turned back, only to see his own body frozen in place along with everyone else. It was as if he were a spirit that had just stepped out of himself.

What in the nine hells? Was this some kind of dream?

"I remember that courageous young man," said a voice suddenly.

Ahkin nearly leapt from his skin, but considering he seemed to already be outside of his skin, he wasn't sure that would even be possible. But he at least recognized the elderly woman who had come to stand beside him. She was dressed in geometric patterns of white and black, and her equally contrasting light and dark hair was swept up into a knot atop her head. Her lined face crinkled even further as she smiled at him. The motherly form of Ometeotl, the duality, the Mother, creator of everything. Her eyes gazed fondly upon his younger frozen form.

"I—you—I don't understand. How can I be there and yet"—he looked down at his body, surprised to see it wasn't as translucent as other spirits he'd seen—"here at the same time?"

"There are many things you do not understand, son of the sun," she cackled.

Ahkin frowned. Yes. They had already covered that thoroughly on the beach.

"We are inside one of your strongest memories. There is something I want you to see." She snapped her brittle fingers and the scene around them shifted. Ahkin's stomach rolled unpleasantly.

Before him, the battlefield raged. Around him, animal costumes whirled and slashed, while the death demons from the Miquitz Empire, dressed in black and bones, dodged between their obsidian blades like shadows. Ahkin watched his younger self flicker in and out of sight, his royal blood bending the light around him and hiding him from sight. He and the other initiates sliced through enemy Miquitz with impressive ferocity. Pride bloomed hot and full inside his chest at the sight. They had thought themselves gods, invincible, untouchable . . . until the first of them fell. The young man's name still sent a barb through his heart. Pech. They had been fighting side by side until he took an obsidian blade to the stomach that had been meant for Ahkin's back.

Ahkin remembered it clearly enough without Ometeotl showing him the memory in whatever bizarre dream this was.

Pech fell to his knees, his common blood coating his hands as he grabbed at his abdomen. Ahkin watched his younger self fell the Miquitz soldier with a single strike, his macana sinking into the man who had stabbed his friend. He hadn't heard the man's scream above the rushing sound in his ears. Panic had overtaken him as Pech's lifeblood drained onto the jungle floor. Because he had taken the blade for his prince. Ahkin cradled the body of his friend in his arms, roaring his agony to the heavens. Pech's eyes grew as glassy as the smoothest obsidian . . . and the scene froze again. The agony on his younger self's face lanced through him to the point that he had to finally turn away. He had lived that moment once. He didn't want to live it again.

"You never forgave yourself for letting him die," Ometeotl stated matter-of-factly. "For letting any of them die that day."

Ahkin's throat constricted and his chest tightened. He could not answer. Would not answer.

"Sometimes there are moments that define a human for the rest of their lives," she continued thoughtfully. "This was one such moment for you. You took the loss of those lives onto your shoulders, blamed yourself for not being able to save them. For Pech taking the blade meant for you. You have done nothing but add to the burden on your shoulders ever since."

Ahkin finally cleared his throat. "Did he . . . did his spirit . . . ?" He couldn't finish the question.

The Mother goddess nodded in understanding. "His spirit found peace in paradise. He rests with other men fallen in battle and women fallen in childbirth. The bravest of warriors among you."

Though he was happy to hear it, the news did little to ease the aching wound in his soul. The guilt, the feeling of failure. Ahkin dropped his gaze to his feet. "What is the purpose of this, Mother? Why are you showing these memories to me?"

She stepped closer and cradled his cheek in her withered hand. He lifted his eyes to hers, to the eyes of the creator of the very universe. Inside them swirled *endless depths of love he couldn't even begin to fathom.* "Because, my dear child, I need to warn you before it is too late. This journey before you is fraught with many dangers, and I fear that one of you will not survive. You must prepare yourself."

The words were a knife to his stomach. One of them would not survive? A million questions flooded his tongue.

And Ometeotl did not give him the chance to ask. She reached up and touched his forehead, and once again, all went dark.

———

"You're an idiot."

Those were not the first words Ahkin expected to hear upon waking up. His head felt heavy, but judging by the ache in every muscle of his body, he didn't think he was a spirit yet.

He tried to sit up and instantly felt Mayana's ice-cold hands steady him. "W-what happened?"

"You almost died. You should have let me help you." Mayana's voice trembled with a mix of anger and relief. He lifted his gaze to hers and saw moisture rimming her eyes. He automatically reached up to find her hand. Their fingers wove together upon his shoulder.

She made a small choking sound and threw herself toward him. Their bodies collided and Ahkin fell back into the dust, Mayana's arms tight around his neck.

He grunted in pain as she landed on top of him. She immediately scrambled back, sniffing and wiping her nose with her arm. "I'm sorry! I was so worried, I—"

But Ahkin reached out and pulled her back toward him, this time wrapping his still-heavy arms around her. He pressed his face into the gritty strands of her hair. She was here. She was alive. *He* was alive.

Her arms held him equally as tight as she let out a sob.

He would have held on to her forever, except that Ona growled a warning from somewhere nearby. Ahkin pulled back slightly and found the dog standing not even an arm's length away, his stance protective. They made eye contact, and Ona barked an angry, sharp sound.

"It's all right, boy, I'm okay." Mayana chuckled and reached out a hand to rub him gently on the side of his head. Ona leaned into her touch, instantly relaxing. Mayana pulled her hand back, and Ona's gaze hardened on Ahkin again. He had never seen a dog act so protective of someone. And though he could relate to the feeling, he still felt intimidated by the stupid beast. Ahkin loosened their embrace, as though he had been scolded by his father.

"What happened?" he asked her again.

Mayana settled back onto her knees. "I ripped the snake fang out and you went unconscious. I thought you were dead." She placed a hand against her forehead, as if the memory caused her physical pain. "I couldn't remember if you were supposed to take them out or not. I'm not good with healing like Yemania. But then Ona came and licked your wound clean and it healed, but you still didn't wake up for a long time. I was so scared."

Ahkin fell silent for a moment, trying to remember the details of the dream he'd just had, of everything Mother Ometeotl had told him. Wondering if it had been real at all. He looked sideways at the dog, nodding his head in thanks. Ona curled his lips and bared his teeth. Ahkin almost laughed. He'd have to win the dog's trust somehow.

He placed a hand on Mayana's cheek. "I'm okay now. You don't have to worry."

She placed her hand over his and pressed it harder into her cheek. "I know, I just . . . I don't want to do this alone." She turned her head and pressed a kiss against his palm. His heart ached in response.

I fear that one of you will not survive. You must prepare yourself.

Ahkin's chest tightened painfully. He refused to believe it was true. He would not let her die here. He couldn't leave her alone in this place. Mayana's large brown eyes were so tender and full of concern. His own eyes focused on her full, slightly trembling lips. The need to kiss her overwhelmed him.

"You won't have to do it without me, I promise," Ahkin whispered fiercely, leaning forward to close the distance between them.

Before their lips could meet, Ona wriggled between them like an obnoxious toddler and ran his fat tongue across Mayana's face.

She laughed—a beautiful, joyful sound that Ahkin swore he could listen to for the rest of his life. She hugged the irritating creature that had interrupted his plans. Ona snuggled into her embrace and looked back at Ahkin with a satisfied smirk.

This isn't over, dog, Ahkin mouthed at Ona, pointing a warning finger.

"Ahkin, look!" Mayana rose to her feet.

Ahkin jumped up to join her, half expecting another monster snake to be lunging toward them. He swayed slightly, grabbing Mayana's shoulder to steady himself. She slid an arm around his waist and hugged him, her touch like blazing fire against his skin.

"They're gone," she breathed, pointing to the winding dirt paths that had—an hour before—been covered with writhing snakes of every size and color.

Sure enough, the dirt paths were clear, meandering away through the tall dead grass like little rivers of pale dust. Not a single serpent was anywhere to be seen.

Ahkin narrowed his eyes at the jagged obsidian ranges in the distance. "Each layer must be a test of some kind."

"And now we have to make it to the mountains?" She didn't sound very enthusiastic, but he couldn't really blame her. He didn't want to think about what they'd find waiting for them there.

Ahkin pulled her tighter against him, and Ona growled in response. They would survive this. They had to.

She looked at him with such tenderness in her eyes, and Ahkin was grateful they were in this together.

That fierce protectiveness swept through him, the same he'd felt for his brothers on the battlefield. He pulled her in and pressed a kiss against the top of her head. The Mother's warning still sent a chill down his spine. If one of them would not survive, he would make sure it was him. But it was also just a dream. Perhaps it had been induced by the snake's poison, and the Mother hadn't visited him at all. No, he'd make sure they *both* escaped the underworld if it was the last thing he did.

And with all the dangers waiting for them, it very well might be.

CHAPTER

4

"Where are we going?" Yemania whispered to Coatl. She leaned toward him over the edge of her wooden chair.

Her brother bobbed along beside her, suspended in his own chair carried by servants, and gripping the arm rests until his knuckles were white. Around them, the heat and moisture of the jungle pressed in as though someone had covered them all with thick, suffocating animal furs. At least with the heat came the fragrant smell of fresh earth and jungle blooms. Yemania always cherished the smells of the various flora, hidden treasures of possible remedies waiting to be found. Dappled light filtered down through the thick canopy above their heads, while the shadows of monkeys twitched amongst the branches.

"Millacatl," Coatl answered, his mouth tight. He had hated being in the jungles ever since they were children. He was bitten by a spider that made his whole hand swell up to the size of a pineapple, and he had avoided the trees ever since. A loud bird call echoed somewhere above them, and Coatl flinched, turning around in his chair as though he was about to be attacked.

"Relax, Coatl. Birds are not venomous, and even if they were, I can heal you as fast as I did when you were bitten by the spider." Yemania rolled her eyes at her brother's unease.

"What spider?" Metzi trilled from where she lounged in her golden chair, several servant heads in front of them.

"Nothing. Nothing about spiders," Coatl said quickly. He glared at Yemania in warning.

Yemania turned away and stuffed her fist in her mouth to keep from laughing. When she gathered her composure, she turned back to face him. "So why are we going to Millacatl?"

But Metzi cut in to their conversation and answered for him. "Millacatl is the wealthiest city-state in the empire. They grow all of our food and the cacao beans we use for currency. If Ehecatl is declaring war on Tollan, we are going to need Millacatl's financial backing for any military campaigns."

Of all six city-states ruled by Tollan, Millacatl was perhaps the most essential, and maybe Metzi's cleverness would be enough to keep them loyal.

Yemania had never visited the rolling foothill farms that graced their eastern border, but she knew they lay at the base of the Miquitz Mountains. A shiver ran through her. She'd never been so close to those cursed mountains, the home of the Miquitz Empire and its terrifying death worshippers. Legend said Miquitz even housed its own cave entrance to the underworld like the sinkhole in Tollan. All Yemania knew was that they often came into the valley to capture enemy soldiers for use as sacrifices—though more recently they had begun kidnapping innocent farmers and peasants from Millacatl. She made a mental note to stay as far away from those mountains as she could.

Their trek through the jungle took an entire day, so by the time they finally reached the rolling farmlands, the Seventh Sun flirted with the horizon, staining the sky a faint orange. The great stone city perched on the hill beckoned them with the scent of freshly baked flatbreads and the sweet smell of cooked maize. Yemania couldn't wait to collapse onto a bed mat overflowing with rabbit furs.

Though the city was not made of gold like Tollan, it exuded an ancient, if somewhat eclectic, elegance, from the intricate carvings along the stone walls to the trees and greenery incorporated into the structures as though they were part of the buildings themselves. Tree trunks wound their way through curving walls inlaid with different colored stones and tiles. Gardens in the various homesteads overflowed with every kind of flower and fruit imaginable, making the air thick with their scents.

Somewhere close by Yemania could hear the bustling and chatter of an active marketplace.

The households of Millacatl greeted their traveling caravan at the entrance to the city, throwing flower petals and cacao beans at their feet as they passed. Yemania wrinkled her nose at the dull brown beans bouncing across the paved stone walkway. Were they really so wealthy that they could throw money in the streets? Such abundance and affluence often lead to a sense of superiority, something she had seen clearly in their Princess Teniza during the empress-selection ritual. Her stomach soured at the thought of having to see the princess again, let alone her nine other brothers and sisters, who were likely to be just as spoiled.

"How long are we staying?" she whispered to her brother as the servants lowered them to the ground in the stone palace's lush courtyard.

"A few days. Metzi wants to be back in Tollan before the start of the Nemontemi," Coatl said.

Metzi had left several blood-soaked strips of sacrificial maguey papers back in the capital so that the priests could raise the sun for the next few days without her. The whole situation still made Yemania nervous. The survival of their world now depended on this egotistical young woman, who had only seen eighteen cycles of the calendar.

They focused their attention on the towering lord of Millacatl, who approached them with outstretched arms. His cloak was a dark emerald green, exactly matching the color of his eyes. Were the princess Teniza's eyes that startlingly green? Yemania couldn't remember. For a man blessed by the gods with ten sons and daughters, he had relatively few creases marring his face. Her own father had only five children, but his face was as deeply lined as dried cracks in a riverbed. But then again, the lord of Pahtia was not known for his kindness, just as the lord of Millacatl was not known for his humility.

He swept right to Metzi and bowed before her, a considerable act given his impressive height. "My dear princess of light, welcome to Millacatl. We are so fortunate that you have blessed us with your benevolent presence."

Yemania bit back a snort. "Benevolent" was not a word she would use to describe Metzi. But the new empress bowed in return with an elegant flourish, and Yemania was forced to follow them into the banquet chamber of Millacatl's elaborate stone palace.

The palace at Millacatl wasn't as glorious as the palace in Tollan, lacking in size and the shine of gold, but it certainly surpassed the beauty of her palace back home. It was as if Millacatl had been built to complement the nature around it instead of interrupt it. At first, she couldn't tell what the dark curving walls of the banquet hall were made of, but as she stepped closer, she realized the entire room seemed to be made of manipulated tree trunks, bending to the will of their masters. The ceiling itself mimicked the jungle canopy they had traveled through, and the throne at the top of the room looked as though it had simply grown out of the earth. The scent of fresh earth and newness hung in the moist air. Yemania suppressed a giggle at the sight of Coatl eyeing the hall with distrust as though spiders lurked within the very walls, waiting to ambush him. But it was the feast that made her mouth drop open. The floor was covered in bowls of every dish imaginable, from rare fruits she had never seen before to multicolored flatbreads to a succulent roasted deer rubbed with various spices.

Yemania settled onto a cushion on the other side of Coatl. She glanced at the gathering of Millacatl's royal family and caught the eye of Teniza, the daughter of plants who had been sent to the capital for the selection ritual. She was as regal as ever, towering above most of her siblings in both height and regal grace. Though she and Yemania had not become well acquainted in the capital, Teniza bowed her head in recognition. Yemania nodded back, her stomach tightening.

The lord of Millacatl rose to his feet and led the assembly in the sacrifice of a bird to bless the meal. Yemania never used to mind the ritual sacrifices laid out in the holy codices of their people—they were a way of life—but that was before Mayana had shown her the original codex sheets in the temple at Tollan. Even Yemania couldn't deny the fact that they appeared much newer in comparison to the older historical texts—as though they had been written by man and not set forth by the gods. With the new knowledge that these sacrifices might not be entirely necessary, Yemania flinched at the sight of the obsidian blade slicing through the bird's throat. Blood covered the lord of Millacatl's hands, and he threw the small beast into the flames of the brazier burning in the sunken pit in the stone floor. She watched the smoldering remains of the bird crumble into ash and her throat felt suddenly tight with emotion. She didn't want to think about Mayana right now.

"Well," the lord of Millacatl announced after settling himself down beside Metzi, "I am excited to solidify the alliance between our two great cities, especially given our recent treatment in the selection ritual."

Metzi took a sip of pulque from a bowl and pursed her lips. "I am sorry, my lord, that my brother gave so little attention to your daughter. I'm sure if he had, the results would have been very different."

The lord of Millacatl waved a dismissive hand. "The boy was inexperienced, far too young to assume the throne. It was to be expected, perhaps."

Metzi's eyes suddenly hardened into amber. "My brother and I were twins, my lord, meaning that I, too, have seen only eighteen cycles of the calendar. Perhaps you are insinuating that I am too young to assume the throne?"

Yemania swore she saw the color drain slightly from the lord of Millacatl's face. "Of course not, Your Highness. I—I think that Prince Ahkin was putting his heart above the needs of his people, and you seem much wiser than—"

"Except that I am here because I need funding for a military campaign. I canceled an engagement to a prince that I did not love and now his city-state has declared war on the empire." Metzi's tone was as hard as her eyes.

The lord stumbled over his own tongue. "I did not mean—I am sorry if I—"

Metzi sat up straighter, and her eyes bore into his. "Let me be very clear, my lord. I am young, yes, but every member of this empire is alive because of the power that I alone can wield. I will not tolerate anyone speaking down to me, whether to my face or behind my back. If you have allowed us to come here under the impression that you will be able to lord your power and influence over me like you did to my brother, you are sorely mistaken. I am *not* Ahkin. I will be either respected or I will be feared, and you may choose which it will be for Millacatl."

The lord of Millacatl drew back slightly, his emerald-green eyes suddenly shrewd and calculating. "I will not be spoken to like that in my own home. If you wish to maintain the support—"

But Metzi cut across him. "By all means, run to Ehecatl. Join their side if you think they stand a chance against the blood of Huitzilopochtli, god of war. Because that is who I am descended from, Lord of Millacatl. Not a god of farmers. I have been underestimated my entire life, and that is something I have learned to use to my advantage. See how well your plants grow without the light of the Seventh Sun—and that is only *one* of the powers at my disposal. I am not here to play games. I am here to see where Millacatl stands in the coming months and if they will be contributing financially."

The silence that followed her announcement was heavy and thick with unspoken words. Yemania's stomach felt suddenly full, as though she were going to be sick. What had she meant about the sun being only *one* of the powers at her disposal?

The lord of Millacatl surveyed the princess of light, his face unreadable. After several moments, he lifted his bowl of pulque and rose to his feet.

"I would like to drink to the long and prosperous reign of our new empress, Metzi of Tollan. Millacatl will always stand behind and support her as a member of our united Chicome Empire. May the gods bless her with their favor." He drank, unsmiling, from the bowl, never taking his eyes off Metzi's face, and motioned for everyone else to join him.

The voices around the hall echoed his sentiment, and then the entire room drank to his blessing. Metzi smiled in triumph and lounged back on her cushion. Coatl leaned over and started feeding her berries in a manner far too sensuous for a public gathering. The sight of them almost upended Yemania's stomach.

"I'm going to step outside if it's all right," Yemania said to her brother. Metzi was slowly sucking the juice of a bright-red berry from Coatl's finger and he didn't even bother to acknowledge that Yemania had spoken. "I'm taking that as a yes," she mumbled in frustration.

The earthy air now felt suffocating, as though she was stuck underground. She needed to get outside. She slipped quickly from the banquet hall and out into the courtyards of the palace. She needed to clear her head before she actually got sick from the overwhelming feeling of powerlessness she felt coursing through her. Mayana was gone. Ahkin was gone. The empire had no choice but to yield to Metzi, someone clearly as obsessed with power as Yemania's own father was. She hated to be stuck with Metzi, but she couldn't go back home either. Everywhere she turned, she felt more trapped.

The jungles? Maybe she could go into the jungles and gather some herbs for remedies? Yes. That's what she could do. Nothing cleared her head more than when she was lost in the rhythms of grinding a pestle. Metzi had Coatl for now, so she would be fine if anything happened.

Her eyes went to where the Seventh Sun slowly set over the mountains, casting the sky in brilliant shades of purple and orange. Yemania hesitated. It was bad luck to be out at night, everyone in the empire knew that. Creatures and demon spirits lurked in the jungles at night, waiting to devour souls foolish enough to venture out after dark.

Yemania chewed her lip. It wasn't *dark* yet. She didn't need to be out in the jungles for long, just long enough to clear her head and keep her from having to watch her brother feed berries to that selfish, murderous—Yes, she was definitely going. She would be back before the sun had fully disappeared into the underworld for the night.

She stomped forward and made her way toward the city's gate.

"Where are you going, miss?" A soldier with a flint-tipped spear spoke as she passed the stone pillars engraved with glyphs.

"Um, I'm going to gather some plants. In the jungles. For remedies." She nervously fingered the red woven dress she wore, the mark of her status as a healer from Pahtia.

The soldier narrowed his eyes, but finally nodded. Perhaps he could see the desperation in her eyes, the heaviness weighing on her shoulders. "Be careful. Please be back before darkness falls. If you don't return by then, I'll send someone to look for you."

"Thank you," Yemania breathed. She rushed past him and onto the dirt road they had taken into the city earlier that day. Behind Millacatl stretched miles and miles of rolling farms along with villages that tended to those farms, but the jungles they had traveled through skirted the mountains themselves. If she wanted to venture into the jungles, she would have to risk getting closer to those misted peaks.

Yemania took a deep breath and threw back her shoulders before she marched toward the trees.

The moment she passed into the jungle, she felt as though she could breathe again. Almost immediately she spotted a white sapote tree, the round green fruits hanging from its branches inviting her to pluck one. The fruit was an excellent sedative. She collected several in her bag and then noticed some epazotl roots. They would be perfect steeped in water for someone having difficulty breathing or suffering from headaches. The thoughts and worries of the day melted away with each new plant she collected, her excitement growing with each new find. Mecapatli, small red berries used for joint pain. Yellow guava, good for digestion. Every so often a small creature would scuttle through the underbrush, making her jump, but as soon as she recognized it, her fear would ease.

The light around her started to fade, and she realized that if she wanted to make it back before darkness truly fell, she needed to head back. Her bag, propped open on a boulder near a thick, rushing river, was bursting with treasures from the earth, and she paused to make sure everything was packed in properly. Every single leaf was precious. She adjusted the contents to fit before rising to her feet, her heart lighter and more joyful than it had been in weeks.

Yemania turned to head back, but a smudge of darkness along the riverbank caught her attention. It was several yards away from where she stood, but she couldn't make out what it was. She blinked several times to clear her vision, but the moment she realized what she was seeing, she screamed and jumped back.

The body of a young man lay sprawled on his back, half submerged in the water. Bodies were not something to fear, merely empty vessels void of their souls, but this young man was dressed in inky black fabric and wore a necklace of what looked suspiciously like human finger bones.

He was a soldier from Miquitz.

CHAPTER

5

Mayana wrinkled her nose. When Ahkin stabbed the snake, he'd been coated from head to toe in the creature's blood. Now the blood was dry but sticky, and the dirt from the paths clung to them both like a second skin. They had been wandering the dusty paths through tall, dead grasses for what felt like hours, yet the looming mountain range still seemed so far in the distance.

They kept a careful, awkward space between them as they walked. The silence itched at her like the swollen bite of a mosquito. With each dusty step the urge to say something, *anything*, became overwhelming.

"You look disgusting," Mayana finally complained. Perhaps she could have found something more eloquent to say, but at least it broke the silence.

Ahkin shrugged, as though being coated in dirt and the lifeblood of another creature were a common occurrence for him. As he was an accomplished warrior, Mayana supposed that wasn't far off from the truth.

She remembered when her eldest brother, Chimalli, had returned from his first battle. He'd been quiet, but his eyes were screaming. She'd teased him until finally he smiled. Once she'd broken through his shell, he'd finally shared his burden with her, telling her of the horrors of the battlefield. Perhaps if she lightened the mood, Ahkin would be more willing to talk.

"No wonder you got the doll so dirty," she teased. The little worry doll she had chosen for Ahkin as part of the empress-selection process had returned from his battle in Millacatl as filthy as Ahkin was now. He had tied it to his macana sword for luck. He said it had saved his life that day.

"In my defense, cleanliness is the least of my concerns when I am in the middle of a battle." He closed the distance between them and bumped playfully into her shoulder. Mayana's heart fluttered in response. Somewhere beside her, Ona growled softly.

"Have you captured many enemies in battle?" she asked.

The Chicome considered the number of enemies captured a sign of your prowess as a warrior. Chimalli had explained the whole process to her when their father secured him a battle mentor. All boys were required to register with their city-state's army, and usually the wealthiest could afford to hire the best mentors to train their sons.

Ahkin grimaced and kicked absently at the dirt. "I've only captured two."

"That's still pretty impressive for someone who's only seen eighteen cycles of the calendar."

"I guess." But the corner of his mouth ticked up. He suddenly walked a little taller too.

"I don't think I could ever kill someone. I mean, you saw me with the animal sacrifices. I think I'd die before I took a blade to another person."

Ahkin swung the shield on his arm back and forth absently. "I didn't think I could either. My mentor, Yaotl, is the leader of the Jaguar warriors, so I had the best training available. But something changes the moment you step onto the battlefield. It's almost like your heart stops beating, and you cease to be a person outside of what you've trained for. Your survival instincts kick in and you realize you don't have a choice unless you want to be killed or captured."

Mayana shook her head slowly. "I don't think I could ever block out my heart like that."

"That's why you would be a horrible warrior."

Mayana stuck out her tongue at him. "I'd probably be better than you think. Having a sensitive heart doesn't mean you're weak. It takes more strength to care than it does to not care."

Ahkin considered her. "Perhaps. Weak is definitely not a characteristic I would use to describe you."

Mayana tilted her chin up. "Thank you. After all, if it weren't for me you'd probably be devoured by Cipactli in the Sea of the Dead right now."

Ahkin gave her an amused look. "Definitely not weak, though *stubborn* might be more accurate."

Mayana fished a maize kernel out of the bag the Mother goddess had given her and flung it at his head.

Ahkin batted it away with his impressive battle reflexes. One of his eyebrows arched playfully. Mayana took a step back. He lunged forward and rubbed some of the gritty, bloody mess coating his arms on Mayana's shoulder.

"Yuck! Ahkin! You're a beast!" she shrieked and shoved him away.

Ona barked a warning, but she shushed him while she tried to wipe the muck off her skin. Ahkin grinned at her like her younger brother, Tenoch, always did after playing some sort of mischievous trick. She wished she could wash the grime off, but the thought of water reminded her of how dry her tongue felt.

"Is there a sign of water anywhere?" She looked around the billowing grasses hopelessly. The tall reeds reached only to her chest, so she could still see the hills that continued to roll and ripple out from their current path in every direction. But there was no sign of a river anywhere in the sloping fields. There was one way for her to find water, but she was sure Ahkin would disapprove of her using any more of her blood.

"Maybe there will be some kind of stream or river at the base of the mountains?" Ahkin narrowed his eyes in the direction of the dark peaks.

"If you'd let me—"

"No." Ahkin cut across her. "No more blood. You've lost enough."

Mayana frowned. His tone was laced with a panic she didn't understand. It wasn't as if he needed to protect her from bleeding to death. And if they didn't find any water soon, she'd pretend to accidentally cut herself and use her divine senses to find some anyway.

Several more hours passed, and finally the mountains appeared to be getting closer. They reached another fork. As they approached, two spirits materialized out of the grasses. Just as they had at every fork in the paths.

"Come this way, for that way leads to certain death!" wailed the spirit of a woman wrapped in a shawl.

"No! This is the only way to find your destination. If you go that way, you will wander for all eternity!" cried the spirit of a young man dressed in a servant's cloak.

The first time this had happened, Mayana had nearly leapt into Ahkin's arms. Spirits materialized every time they reached another fork in the paths, determined to keep them lost for all eternity. She tried to judge which of the two spirits seemed the most trustworthy. But Ahkin decided that the path to the left seemed the most appropriate. The spirit of the woman wailed warnings after them, leaving Mayana with a sick feeling of unease.

At least until the next fork, when two more spirits appeared with similar warnings.

"They are trying to misdirect and confuse us. I think it's part of the challenge," Ahkin said, scratching at his chin.

"How do you know which way to go then?"

"We don't listen to them." Ahkin directed them to the right.

"Why not the left path?" Mayana asked, only now realizing that Ahkin had been making every decision so far.

"Simple strategy. I'm marking an *x* on the ground with every turn we take so that if we run into a mark, I'll know we've already been that way. If any path is marked twice, I know it leads to a dead end. We don't have to pay attention to the spirits at all."

Mayana blinked at him. "I—I guess I was going whichever way felt right."

Ahkin shook his head. "No, having a strategy is always best. You can't follow your heart with a maze or trust these spirits to direct us."

"You certainly like planning things out, don't you?"

A shadow darkened his eyes. "I like things to be predictable, that's all." The spirit of an old man wailed after their latest choice of path. Mayana struggled to drown out his warning cries.

"Like with the rituals," she whispered.

A muscle in his jaw tensed. "I used to think so. Now, I'm not so sure. I thought if we followed the rituals, it would make everything as it should be. So, for the Mother goddess to tell me that they are only our way of trying to gain control . . ." He didn't finish.

Mayana shrugged a shoulder. "I never liked the rituals."

Ahkin snorted. "I've noticed. Though I never really got a chance to ask why."

She'd had a thousand conversations with her parents, her siblings, Yemania. Every time she was accused of disrespecting the gods, being ignorant or selfish, or worse—putting their entire world in danger. No one had given her the freedom or space to just be herself. The rituals outlined in their holy codex texts governed everything from religious ceremonies to the proper way to prepare a meal. The instructions were supposedly passed down from the gods themselves, a way to honor and remember the sacrifices that were made each time another god had to sacrifice him- or herself to save their world from destruction. Blood had been paid and so blood was owed, regularly returned by the descendants of those gods and the creation that benefited from their gifts.

"I don't know," she said. "It's hard to explain. Something about the blood sacrifices never felt *right*. Not when I think about the love required for self-sacrifice—the kind of love my mother always showed to everyone around her. That kind of love is selfless, undemanding, freely given. It doesn't require repayment."

Her belly began to squirm. Perhaps he wouldn't understand her either. She let her gaze wander far in the distance, the mountains looming like the dark clouds of a coming storm.

She sighed. "I could never reconcile gods that supposedly loved us enough to die for us with the beings depicted in the codex sheets, the ones ordering such strict and brutal obedience. Love and power don't mix well together."

But no one ever believed her. Not when fear dominated their minds and hearts. The codex stipulated that if the rituals were not followed, the same disasters that destroyed their world six times before would repeat, dooming the Chicome to floods, or plague, or beasts, or fire. Fear is a powerful and controlling thing, but her mother taught her that true love casts out fear. That's where she chose to focus her energy—on her love of the gods, not her fear of them.

Ahkin didn't answer her at first, just stared at his feet as his sandals stirred little bursts of dust with each step. She tried not to let his silence proclaim judgments over her. She could practically hear the hum of his brain working through everything.

"What was your mother like when she was alive?" he finally asked.

His thoughts must have drifted to his own mother—the mother the rituals took away from him after the early death of his father.

Mayana shifted the bag on her shoulder, warmth spreading from her chest out to her fingertips at the thought of her mother. It filled the cold space her fear of his rejection had left behind. "The thing I remember most about her is her smile. She could brighten any day by smiling at me. I have five brothers—three older, two younger—and being the only girl wasn't easy. Rivers are everywhere in Atl, and we spent so much of our time fishing and swimming. My brothers always teased me or left me out of games, and I would cry because I couldn't keep up with them. My mother never let me quit or give up, though. She'd throw me right back in the water and tell me to keep swimming, that I could be as strong as they were if I was willing to practice. I eventually learned to swim and climb as well as any of them. She believed in me when no one else did. That's why I loved her smile so much. It was a smile that whispered encouragement, that told me she knew I could do whatever I set my heart to.

"But my father . . . I don't think he knew what to do with a girl. He could teach my brothers to fight or discuss religion and politics, but he'd leave me out of everything. I never understood why. I still don't. Look at the women of Ocelotl, they learn to fight as well as any of the men. It used to make me so angry, but my mother would discuss those things with me. She tutored me in the codex sheets, even if she wasn't allowed to teach me to fight. We'd talk about politics and the rituals while we weaved or made flatbreads. We raised litters of puppies together, training them and finding homes for them in the city. She loved animals as much as I do, and she never saw the point of the sacrifices either. She didn't have to lead rituals because her blood was common, but she knew that I would have to. I was twelve when I—I wouldn't perform my first animal sacrifice. It was the month of the lizard and I had the blade in my hand but I . . . couldn't. My father slapped me in front of the entire city-state. I fell to the ground and he lifted his hand again, but—" Mayana stopped at the sudden tightening in her chest. The memory washed over her and burned at her eyes, as though she were peeling an onion root.

She could still see it all in her mind's eye. The hundreds of faces, blurred and blank, watching her from around the stone banquet hall in Atl. Her father standing over her, the fear and anger in his eyes burning as hot as the fire in the brazier beside them. The throbbing ache in her cheek where he had struck her, the smooth wood of the handle clutched tight in her sweaty grip. He had hissed something as he gestured to the lizard wriggling in her brother's hands. The burning defiance, the rebellious stubbornness that lived deep inside her soul and refused to bend to his will. She shook her head, positioning her hands onto the stone floor to push herself back up. But then, icy fear gripped at her heart as she saw his fist rise again, pleading in his eyes . . .

"But my mother ran in between us and took the blow for me," she finished quietly. "That's when I knew that real, sacrificial love looks nothing like what the codex demands."

Ahkin winced. "What did your father do after he struck her?"

"He was horrified. The room was deadly quiet. He carried my mom out of the banquet hall. I don't know where they went. My brother ended up doing the sacrifice for me, and I ran to my usual hiding place."

Ona pressed his head against her thigh and Mayana stopped walking to bend down and pet him. "Ona always knew where to find me."

Ahkin stopped walking too, though his eyes darted to the horizon before he asked, "Where did you like to hide?"

"Always the same place. In Atl, our temple is stone, but my family's blood keeps the rivers and canals flowing from the underground well that flows through the temple and out into the city. If you climb the temple's steps, you can slide behind the main waterfall and find a little nook between the water and the stone. I would sit there and listen to the waterfall and watch the rainbows dance on the rock walls." She rose to her feet and rubbed her arms.

"Rainbows." His mouth curved into a smile. Mayana wondered if he, too, was remembering the rainbow they had made together when she was first introduced in the capital. *Water and light can come together to make something beautiful,* she'd said.

Ahkin's eyes met hers, and the squirming feeling in her stomach intensified. She'd laid herself bare, exposed such deep parts of herself she always tried to keep hidden. But instead of disapproval, his eyes held something softer. As if he was seeing the real her and he actually *liked* what he saw . . .

She wanted to linger there, in that tender moment of allowing him to truly see her. But it made her so vulnerable. And vulnerable was the last thing she wanted to feel in a place filled with such danger. It was hard to imagine the beauty of light and color when you were trapped in a world of darkness and shadow.

As if to make her point, the dark clouds rumbled threateningly. A dry wind rustled across the dead grasses with a soft hiss, like unseen spirits whispering warnings in her ear. The back of Mayana's neck tingled. The constant wailing spirits already had her nerves teetering on a precipice.

The moment between them dissipated like fading smoke. "But then she died last year. Fell down those horribly steep stairs of the temple and no one found her until it was too late. I still have trouble going up and down those same steps for the sacrifices. I miss her so much sometimes. Even now. I can't imagine such a loving soul trapped in a place like this." She waved a hand skyward.

"I know what you mean," Ahkin said quietly. He blinked his eyes several times in quick succession.

Before she could ask if he was okay, thunder rumbled again, and a fork of eerily green lightning arched across the sky.

She blinked up at the angry clouds. "Does it rain in the underworld?"

"No idea. I wouldn't mind washing some of this off though." Ahkin gestured to his filthy arms.

Another gust of wind swept across the dead plains, stronger this time. It pulled at Mayana's sand-encrusted hair, whipping it into her face. Ona whined and stepped closer. Several wayward spirits took flight out of the grasses and flitted from view.

"I'm sorry about your mother, Mayana. I miss mine too. I can't imagine her spirit making this journey, and to think that the ritual that demanded she take her own life—to think that she didn't need to—" He stopped and looked away.

Mayana reached out and grabbed his hand, her heart twisting at the pain she could see lurking beneath the surface. He squeezed back, but then pulled his hand away just as quickly, as though he didn't want to admit how much he appreciated it.

Thunder tumbled overhead. An icy drop smacked into Mayana's forehead, then her nose, her shoulder. The drops increased in intensity, and soon the skies unleashed themselves. Mayana was familiar with the torrential humid rains of the jungles, the summer storms that could blink into existence and swell the rivers to overflowing. That was her family's main responsibility in the empire, to assist the other city-states in avoiding disasters of drought or flooding, to make the regular sacrifices that would appease otherwise angry gods that would punish with water.

But she had never experienced a rain like this before. It was chilling, unforgiving. Icy rivers ran down her back in torrents, plastering her hair to her head and rinsing it clean of caked sand. They both opened their mouths to try and catch some of the freezing drops on their parched tongues. It would have been refreshing, if it weren't for the frigid cold. The blood and grime flowed off Ahkin's arms and chest, pooling into brownish-red puddles at his feet.

Ahkin shook the water from his hair. Ona mimicked him to the point that Mayana bit her lip to keep from laughing. At least, until her teeth started chattering so hard, she feared she would bite right through.

"We need to find some kind of sh-sh-shelter," she said, looking around and seeing nothing but the sea of grass, now thrashing in the wind like a turbulent tide.

Ahkin pulled her close, his bare chest slick and cold beneath her hands. She snuggled into him, seeking what little body heat he had left. With one arm tight around her shoulders, he lifted the other with the round shield above their heads, holding off some of the downpour. Ona whined and fidgeted between their feet.

"This isn't going to be enough," Ahkin shouted, his voice hard to make out over the sound of the storm. Mayana's ears began to throb from the roaring of the wind, so she covered them with her hands. Perhaps the wind wouldn't be so brutal if they could find a way to keep themselves dry, but Ahkin couldn't hold up his shield for long. Already she could see his arm shaking with the effort.

Mayana slipped her hand down to where the obsidian shard was wedged in the waistband of her skirt. She didn't even bother asking his opinion, knowing what his answer would be.

Her finger ran briefly across the sharp edge, exposing barely enough blood for what she planned to do.

"Ahkin, you can drop the shield," she said, looking up to where his jaw was clenched tight with the effort of keeping his arm up.

"No, we have to stay dry or else . . ." but he slowly lowered the shield. His eyes went wide with wonderment and then flat with suppressed annoyance.

Mayana beamed an innocent smile as Ahkin's head swiveled, taking in how the sheets of rain now parted around them, as though a dome of air was protecting them.

He sighed and pulled her closer. "I'd be angry, but I'm too exhausted and freezing to argue."

"Good, because I'm insanely thirsty, and there's another little trick I've picked up."

Mayana pricked another finger and pointed it toward the rain outside of their bubble. Some of the rain condensed into a perfect sphere and she summoned it toward her. It hovered over her hand like a butterfly waiting to land.

"Open your hands," she instructed him. He did, and she let the orb splash into his cupped palms. He brought his hands to his lips and promptly sighed in relief.

Mayana summoned another orb of water for Ona, and lastly for herself, savoring the cold wetness across her parched, dry tongue.

"Thank you," Ahkin said. He eyed her bloodied finger with dark worry creasing his features. "But please promise me you didn't inherit too much of your mother's self-sacrificing tendencies."

Mayana pursed her lips. Was she self-sacrificing like her mother? She did jump into the underworld to save him, after all. But it felt like more than that.

"I think I care so deeply about things it moves me to act. I can't *not* do something."

Ahkin tightened his arms around her. "I know. That's what scares me."

She laid her cheek against the smooth muscles of his chest, savoring the sound of his steady heartbeat. It was such a blessing he survived the snake. What would she have done without him?

She couldn't think about that now, not when they were both here and very much alive.

Before your journey ends, you will have to make a choice that will destroy your world or mine.

Mayana's stomach twisted as she remembered the Mother's words to her. The warning that she would make a choice. A choice that could possibly destroy *her* world. She peeked up at Ahkin. Would she be willing to destroy her world to protect the greater world around them? Maybe that wasn't what the Mother's warning had meant. But could it . . . ?

Their bodies slowly started to warm the longer they pressed themselves together. Ahkin laid his cheek against the top of her head, which of course made Ona growl. Ahkin's chuckle lightly shook them both, before his head snapped back up.

"Mayana, do you think those snakes from the first test are gone for good?"

"I hope so. It seemed like once we actually killed the biggest one, we passed the test. Why?"

"Because I think we might be able to take shelter in one of the burrows inside of that hill." He lifted a hand and pointed to where the shadow of a hill loomed ahead of them, an even darker shadow of a hole gaping in its side. It looked large enough to fit the snake that had attacked them, but perhaps they would be safe if they stayed within the mouth of the opening? They didn't really have any other choice.

Their sandals slapped against the pale mud as they splashed their way toward the hill. Ona darted ahead of them to reach the opening first. The dog sniffed around and finally barked an excited yelp. He sat back onto his haunches, pink tongue lolling lazily as he waited for them to join him.

"Well, if the dog says it's safe . . ." Ahkin laughed, his hand still gripped tight around his own shard of obsidian.

As they stepped inside the rounded, earthy opening of the hole, several heads taller than even Ahkin, the damp smell of decay overwhelmed her. The air was still and heavy, as though the opening were a great mouth of the earth holding its breath. But at least it was dry and protected them from some of the relentless wind. The burrow curved down and away from them, deep into ominous darkness. Ahkin walked in small circles, still inspecting for safety. Her eyes followed his movements, her head swirling with thoughts. He hadn't criticized or attacked her thoughts on the rituals. He'd taken them for what they were. Her heart swelled at the memory of the moment they'd shared—when his eyes had met hers and she didn't see disgust or rejection hidden within them. He'd just seen the real her and didn't turn away. It was a heady feeling, intense. She felt almost raw with it.

Yes, they hadn't really known each other during the selection ritual. But perhaps they were starting to.

A small smile tugged at her lips as she and Ahkin settled in to wait out the rest of the storm.

Yemania knew she should run. Where there was one Miquitz soldier, there were sure to be more. She knew she should—and yet she couldn't.

Because his chest still lightly rose and fell with shallow breaths.

If there was one thing to stop her from running, it was her instinct to heal. Yemania wasn't sure if it was something she'd been born with because of her divine ancestor, Ixtlilton, god of healing, or if it was something she developed later, but she *had* to heal. If there was someone in pain, especially someone so close to death, it was an impulse, as if she were living out her divine purpose. There were so many things she wasn't—beautiful, brave, strong—but she could heal. And she did it well.

His tanned skin was tinged with blue, almost ghostly in appearance. He had lost a lot of blood. If he had washed up on the shore of the riverbed, he would have copious amounts of water in his lungs as well. Yemania chewed the inside of her cheek, but her mind was already made up.

She pulled out the stingray spine she always carried with her and pricked her thumb. The moment the blood of her ancestor was exposed, a knowledge washed over her, whispering gently to her like a sixth sense. He was inches from death; if she was going to heal him, she had to hurry.

Her bag hit the dirt, and she ran to his side, dropping to her knees on the riverbank. She needed to get him out of the water—his body temperature was already so low.

Up close, she could see the defined line of his squared jaw, his full, rounded lips, parted and tinged blue, his thick dark brows. Sweet Mother Ometeotl, he was handsome for a death demon. But that was unimportant—he was soon going to meet the god his people idolized so much.

But he was so much bigger than she was! He probably cleared her own modest height by two heads, and his shoulders were twice as wide. Moving him would be a massive undertaking. Yemania wedged her hands beneath his arms and pulled with every ounce of her strength. She thanked the gods above that the mud beneath him was so slick, or she never would have been able to manage it. Her sandaled feet slipped as she inched him away from the water, falling several times and coating her backside in mud in the process.

By the time he was safely away from the currents, she was panting heavily and wiping sweat from her eyes. She was filthy too, which she'd need to take care of quickly if she was going to address the gaping wound in his chest. His lack of blood immediately made sense.

She lunged back to her feet and washed her hands in the river. The prick on her thumb had healed, but she'd likely need a lot more blood for a wound as severe as his. Yemania sliced across her palm with the stingray spine and quickly went to work. She moved her hand over his chest, sensing where something had pierced his waterlogged lung. Willing it to heal, she forced out the water and paid close attention to the intricacies of his internal wounds before turning her attention to the open skin. Someone or something must have stabbed him between the ribs.

Once the wound itself healed, she reached for the bag of herbs she had collected. His pulse felt somewhat stronger, but not at all where she wanted it. His skin was still so cold.

He needed to replenish his blood supply and get warm, or the new blood would never circulate. She dug through her bag until she found the leaves she was looking for. Hissing in frustration that she didn't have her usual supplies, she quickly scoured the riverbed for two flat rocks to grind the leaves into a paste. She mixed the paste with some of the water from the river and dribbled what she could into his slack mouth with a folded banana leaf. What she really needed was a pestle, a bowl, and some fire.

That would allow her to make the tea he needed to regain some of his strength. It would still likely be another day or so until he would be strong enough to leave, and that's if she could get him warm enough to get his blood moving.

"Gods above," she whispered to herself. "What am I doing?"

She assessed her surroundings for a place to get him situated, and her gaze fell on a hollow within the trunk of a kapok tree, its twisting roots creating a kind of burrow probably used by a deer—hopefully not a wolf or a jaguar. The soldier did have an obsidian knife strapped to his waist, but perhaps she should relieve him of it . . . just in case.

Why did the soldier have to be so big? She'd never drag him across the dry ground on her own. Yemania leaned back on her heels and blew the stray strands of hair out of her face. It was definitely getting dark now, but she couldn't leave him like this. The soldier would die sometime in the night without her help. If she brought him back to Millacatl, he'd die anyway as a battle sacrifice. Something about the peaceful stillness of his face made her heart twist at the thought of him tied to the sacrificial platform.

She'd have to stay out here all night if she wanted to save him. Which meant everyone back in the city would panic when she didn't return. Could she pretend she got lost and slept in the jungle? It was a risk to be sure. Was she willing to take that risk for an enemy soldier she didn't even know? An enemy soldier who would likely capture her and take her back to Miquitz as his own sacrifice, given the chance?

She ran her hands roughly through her hair and grabbed her scalp in frustration. Gods, how did she even get herself into this position? This was not how her life was supposed to go. She was supposed to have found someone quiet and meek, a humble homemaker that would marry her and get her out of her father's home. He was likely going to be portly, balding, and not at all the type of man that would make a girl's heart flutter, the type of man her father would have scoffed at for his lack of health. But he would have been kind and given Yemania the sort of home she'd always wanted, where she could open her own little shop of remedies for the commoners, the ones the blood of the gods could not be "wasted" on. That's what she always imagined for her life anyway.

Certainly not this. Stuck in the jungle covered in mud and trying to save a dying enemy because she was escaping the company of her arrogant brother and his soon-to-be-empress, unable to return home and stuck as that same empress's personal handmaiden. She was not supposed to be sent to Tollan as a *sacrifice* to bless Prince Ahkin's marriage to her best friend, chosen to die by her father as the most worthless of his four daughters.

Her eyes burned at the reminder that no matter where she went, she was never enough. She looked down at her hands, the hands that had healed so many wounds and saved so many lives. At least there was that. It was something her father, the rituals, Metzi and Coatl—none of them could take away from her. Her calling to heal. That was what she was born to do, and thirteen heavens above, that was exactly what she would do.

Yemania stood, her mind made up, and found some long palm fronds attached to a low tree. It took her several minutes of pulling and hacking with the soldier's knife, but she finally managed to break away one of the larger branches. She laid it down beside the soldier and heaved with her entire body to roll him onto the fanned-out leaves. That would make it easier to pull him, at least.

The smooth surface of the leaves between his body and the ground allowed her to pull him ever so slowly toward the burrow. When she got him close enough, she rolled him several more times until his body was safely tucked inside the little cave of roots.

He still needed to be warmed, but she couldn't light a fire, not if the soldiers at the gate came looking for her like they promised. She had no furs, no cloaks. She groaned as she realized the only option she had left.

Her own body heat.

"Stinking, filthy, death-worshipping—" she muttered as she slowly stripped off her red dress. *He better live after this*, she thought savagely as she rolled him onto his side and draped the fabric across his back. Blood rushed to her cheeks and flushed across every inch of her skin at the thought of lying down naked beside this beautiful dying soldier, but she knew what she had to do.

Yemania gently lay down and wormed her way toward him like a caterpillar, facing him and making her heart rate raise even higher. Thank the gods he was still unconscious. She pressed herself against him, hissing slightly as his almost frozen skin met her own. Hopefully her blush would help heat him up that much faster.

Once the initial shock of what she was doing wore off, she pulled him tighter against her own chest and began rubbing his back in long sweeping motions with her hands—movement to create more heat. Definitely not to touch the sculpted muscles of his back.

Night had completely fallen by now, the Seventh Sun beginning its journey through the underworld. Yemania briefly wondered if there was any chance Mayana was still alive to see it as day began in Xibalba. She wondered what her friend would say if she could see what she was doing right now. But that was a fool's hope. She and Ahkin were both gone. They were never coming back.

The thought brought tears to her eyes and she blinked them back. She let herself nuzzle her face into the chest of the soldier, to be close to some- one, to not feel so alone in the world.

But she couldn't hold back the tears no matter how hard she tried. Because with Mayana gone, and her brother so enraptured with Metzi, she truly was alone.

By the time the clouds finished their furious tantrum, Ahkin was ready to be on his feet again. Mayana had fallen asleep, her head in his lap. Restless, he watched the darkness of the tunnel curving down and away from them. He couldn't shake the feeling that something was watching them, just outside the range of his vision. It was enough to set his nerves on a blade's edge and prevent him from getting any rest.

He looked down at Mayana's peaceful, sleeping face and gently ran his thumb down the length of her cheek. Gods, she was so beautiful, even if she was foolishly risking herself over and over to keep them safe.

She would not die for him as Pech had. What a horrible emperor he was if he couldn't even protect and take care of this single young woman. And he was supposed to take care of an entire empire? He'd obviously already failed at that, getting himself stuck in the underworld while his sister sat upon his throne. His treacherous, backstabbing . . . He reached for the bag of maize. A sour feeling roiled inside his stomach. He needed to nibble on something to settle it. But the maize kernels didn't help, and the longer he sat alone with his thoughts, the more anxious he became.

He thought about Metzi, now the only remaining descendant of the sun god, the only one with the power to raise the sun if he didn't make it back. How she had stolen his throne and faked an apocalypse to convince him to sacrifice himself. Anger burned its way up his throat. How could she have done this to him? Hadn't she loved him at all? And worse, how could he have been stupid enough to let it happen? How had he not seen her plot as it unfolded? Mistake after mistake after mistake. If he ever did make it back, he'd . . .

But what would happen if, by some miracle, they did both make it back? Would he march into the palace in Tollan and demand she step down? He knew how determined Metzi could be when she set her heart on something. And he would not be fooled by her again. Ever.

But Metzi was only one of the worries that plagued him. He still needed to father more descendants to protect the empire, and the one bride he actually wanted was the one bride Toani, the head priest, would never approve. An empress that didn't believe in the rituals? Despite what the Mother had told them, there was no chance the rest of the empire would willingly give up their centuries-old traditions. Especially when they believed those traditions protected them from another apocalypse.

That didn't even include Miquitz and their death priest, Tzom. Ahkin had faced him once before on the battlefield, and the escape had been a narrow one. The enemy empire was certainly more active at their borders than usual, and there had to be a reason. But now he wasn't even there to protect his people from their raiding parties.

Shame burned hot inside his chest as he thought of the peasants he hadn't been able to save on the misty morning battlefield in Millacatl. Tzom and his death demons had whisked them away into the mountains, and their families probably mourned them as sacrifices. He prayed he wouldn't meet their souls somewhere here in Xibalba. Would they shame him and mock him for his failures as well?

Maybe staying in Xibalba would be easier after all.

And then there was the warning from the Mother goddess, if in fact that dream had been real. One of them would not survive this journey. He dropped his gaze to Mayana's sleeping face again, and his stomach contracted. No. There was no way. If only one of them was going to survive, it was going to be her. But he would make sure to take her as far as he could before that happened.

Tired of being alone with only his darkening thoughts to keep him company, Ahkin gently shook Mayana awake.

"Let's get moving, the storm has cleared."

Mayana arched her back and stretched in a way that made the back of Ahkin's neck grow hot. He lifted his gaze to meet Ona's, who eyed him with a slightly curled lip.

"Were you able to get any rest?" Mayana asked, worry pulling her eyebrows together.

"A little," Ahkin lied. Ona's other lip curled to reveal his teeth.

Don't you tattle on me, Ahkin warned the dog with his eyes.

Mayana reached into her bag and grabbed a few maize kernels to pop in her mouth. He wanted to urge her to eat more, but he knew she'd stubbornly refuse if he tried to tell her what to do. He'd seen that defiant blaze in her eyes when she felt someone trying to control her. And he was lying to himself if he didn't admire the hells out of it.

Mayana reached back into the bag, but instead of pulling out more kernels, she brought out the tiny worry doll the Mother had given them before they began this journey. In addition to Mayana's jade necklace and Ahkin's shield, both treasures of their ancestors, she had also given them some rather odd gifts. The bag of maize made sense, but the little worry doll the size of his thumb with a yellow dress? A walnut shell housing a worm that painfully bit Ahkin when he tried to open it?

"Why do you think the Mother gave us these?" Mayana's brow furrowed as she studied the reed pattern woven into the doll's tiny dress.

"Who knows? Maybe she's gone senile over the last few millennia."

Mayana slapped him on the shoulder. "You're lucky she doesn't smite you. For someone supposedly so reverent of the gods . . ."

But Ahkin shrugged. He had a feeling the Mother goddess had a rather twisted sense of humor. A warm breeze gently blew past them, so unlike the icy winds of the storm. Ahkin felt he had his answer. The thought lifted his spirits. Slightly.

"I'm sure there's a reason," he told her. Mayana didn't look so sure as she stuffed the doll back into the bag and rose to her feet.

"I wish I understood. She gives us these random gifts, tells me I've been right about the rituals all along, warns me I'm going to make a decision that could possibly end the world, and makes us promise to bring her the bones of Quetzalcoatl. You'd think she could be a little clearer, or at least a little more specific. Where are we supposed to find these bones? What decision will be the right one to make? And what in the hells is the stupid worm for?"

"You're asking me to explain the mind of the creator of the universe?" Ahkin gave her an amused look. He couldn't bring himself to tell her about the possible warning *he* had received. He couldn't place that burden on her shoulders.

"Good point. Part of me worries she's using us, like we are just pieces in some bigger game we don't see." She sighed, squinting into the semi-brightness of the world outside. The dark clouds hadn't cleared, but mercifully the storm had stopped. Now that they could see more clearly, Ahkin was both thrilled and terrified to realize they had nearly reached the base of the mountains.

Jagged black peaks curved over them like a massive cresting wave, hiding unknown terrors within their wickedly dark crevices. But forward was the only way, and the "mountains that crashed together" was one of the layers of Xibalba, even if he wasn't entirely sure what that meant.

Thunder rumbled again somewhere in the distance, and Ahkin eyed the sky with distrust. Hopefully they could make it into the crags before another storm hit.

His body dragged with exhaustion, but Ahkin forced himself forward, leading the way over the last few rolling hills of grasses. By the time the pale dust of the dead grasslands transitioned into dark pebbles and stone, a twitch had developed over his right eye—something that only happened during those long nights he had studied texts and star charts, sometimes until his father had performed the ritual to raise the sun. It seemed a lifetime ago that his only worries were to impress his battle mentor on the training fields or his tutors with his knowledge of the star charts. That had been before his first battle. Before the reality set in of how many lives truly rested in his hands.

Perhaps he should have tried to get some rest, but the thought of leaving Mayana unprotected had forced the idea from his head.

He'd have to push himself away from the ledge of exhaustion and shoulder that burden on his own. He refused to let Mayana carry the weight of his mistakes.

———

Boulders littered the base of the mountains like rubble from a collapsed house, making their climb slower, but also more dangerous. Ahkin watched the progression of the Seventh Sun across the sky, or at least where it appeared to hide behind the clouds. Had it really been an entire day since they fell? How long would it take to cross a mountain range like this?

Eventually the boulder field transitioned to steeper rock ledges, stretching high above their heads. Ahkin's stomach clenched with anxiety as a cold wind roared in his ears.

"Are you any good at climbing?" he asked Mayana. Hopefully there would be some kind of path to follow. Climbing these uneven surfaces was sure to become more perilous the higher they ascended. Ona leapt onto the nearest narrow ledge and yipped at them to follow. Mayana secured the bag around her shoulder and pulled herself up with incredible ease.

"You forget, Your Highness, I had five brothers to keep up with and a stone temple that was perfect for climbing adventures." She scrambled up another ledge and gave him a playful smirk as though to say, *Aren't you coming?*

Ahkin looked down and immediately regretted it. His head swam as he took in the distance between them and the ground far below, but he curled his fingers over the coarse volcanic stone and heaved himself up after her. He'd show her how well *he* could climb.

The scratchy stone bit into the flesh of his hands. He wedged his sandaled feet into every crevice they could reach. Each time, he feared a scorpion or snake would emerge from the dark cracks and startle him into losing his grip. Mayana managed to stay ahead of him, and a swell of pride swept over him. He loved the sight of her slender yet strong legs, bare in the winds that whipped at the tattered remains of her loincloth skirt. The muscles of her back worked each time she reached a hand up higher. A small smile of satisfaction pulled at her cheeks as she proved herself to be the excellent climber she had claimed.

Thunder rumbled again, shaking the stone beneath his hands and pulling his attention away from watching her. He frowned, a thrill of fear fluttering in his stomach. Thunder shouldn't be strong enough to shake the stone. Not like this. Now that he thought about it, he had never heard thunder like that before . . .

"Mayana, wait. Stop climbing."

Ona noticed something was wrong the same moment Ahkin did. The dog hunkered down, his ears flat against his head. He let out a warning bark not a moment too soon. A boulder taller than a ceiba tree flew toward them, hurtling out of the sky like an earthbound comet. It smashed into the cliff face just above Mayana, rattling Ahkin's teeth and raining down an avalanche of debris upon them.

Ahkin flattened himself against the face of the mountain, clinging to the stones and squeezing his eyes shut. Shards of rock cascaded onto his back, slicing as the sharper edges found his exposed skin. He gritted his teeth, sure the tips of his fingers were bleeding with the effort to hold on.

Ona's piercing howl echoed off the walls of the ravine, reverberating in Ahkin's eardrums.

Along with the sound of Mayana's scream.

Ahkin's eyes flew open. Time itself seemed to slow. Mayana tumbled past him, her arms and legs flailing to find a foothold. He lunged. Their fingers barely brushed, but when he closed his hand, he was holding empty air. Her large brown eyes widened with terror, her hand reaching desperately for him.

"Mayana!" Fear ripped its way up his throat, a scream of anger and frustration, a scream of failure. He had been so close. He had *touched* her fingers . . . and he hadn't been able to catch her.

Helplessness overwhelmed him as she fell into the open air.

CHAPTER

8

Yemania must have fallen asleep at some point during the night. That alone was a miracle, considering every twitching leaf she heard was likely a wolf coming back to its den. She slowly opened her eyes, noticing that the soldier's body, still pressed tightly against her own, was much warmer than it had been last night. She breathed a sigh of relief. His heart beat strongly against her own, and joy flooded her at the thought that she was the cause. She had saved his life.

But after the joy came utter terror, as she realized the soldier's arms were wrapped tightly around her, holding her against him. Her eyes immediately shot to his face, but he was still sound asleep.

Nine hells!

Yemania moved her hands to his chest and tried to push gently away, only to have him grunt slightly and pull her tighter against him.

She slammed her fists against his chest, trying to wrench herself free. Frustration and fear mingled together inside her until she did the stupidest thing she could think of: she screamed.

The soldier's eyes flew open as he scrambled away from her, bumping his head loudly against the rooted roof of their burrow. Yemania skittered back, grabbing her dress off the ground where it had fallen and holding it over her naked chest. The soldier held a defensive pose against the back wall, one hand reaching for the weapon Yemania had relieved him of while the other rubbed the top of his injured head.

Yemania launched herself toward the hole where she had stored his knife. She brought it up with one hand, pointing it warningly at him, while the other held her dress in place.

Both of their chests heaved as they stared at each other, each assessing their peculiar situation. The soldier looked thoroughly bewildered, but Yemania felt panicked. She had wanted to save him, yes, but she hadn't thought about what to do once he actually woke up.

His gaze dropped to his knife held firmly in her hand, and he frowned. "You stole my knife."

Yemania sputtered. "What? That's the first thing you notice? That I stole your knife?"

"Well, that's not the first thing I noticed, but I also didn't want to be rude." His gaze dropped suggestively to her chest, but darted back up to her face, a sheepish smile spreading across his face. His defensive pose relaxed, and he settled himself on the ground, leaning against the wall for support as he rubbed at the nonexistent wound on his chest.

Yemania tightened her grip on the dress covering her own chest. "How dare you! I saved your life and—"

"And unless you're planning on ending it, can we put down the knife please?"

Yemania harrumphed and lifted the knife slightly higher. "Why? So you can take me back to Miquitz and sacrifice me to the lord of Xibalba?"

The soldier snorted. "No. I am not planning on taking you back to Miquitz."

She lowered the knife. "Why not?"

"Well, frankly, I have no plans to go back to Miquitz myself, so it would be rather counterproductive to take you there."

Now it was Yemania's turn to frown. "What do you mean, you aren't going back to Miquitz? Aren't you one of their soldiers?"

He dropped his head and ran his hands through his long, black hair several times. She hadn't noticed before the beautiful way it waved down to his shoulders. She shook her head to make herself focus as he wound his hair into a knot at the back of his head.

"Yes, I'm a soldier," was all he said.

"But—"

"What's your name?" he asked suddenly.

"Yemania," she whispered quietly. "Of Pahtia."

"Ah," he nodded in acknowledgment. "So you're a healer. I'm guessing that's why my spirit is still with us in the land of the living?"

"Unless you'd rather it wasn't, which I can still make happen, I assure you." She lifted the knife again.

But to her surprise, the soldier laughed and lay back down on the ground, as though he wanted to take a nap.

"Go ahead, Yemania of Pahtia. But if you are a true healer, I'll bet my life on the fact that you wouldn't be able to take a life even if you wanted to."

Bitterness coated her tongue. This death demon was as arrogant as her brother, Coatl.

"Well, you seem to be feeling well enough. I think I'll—" She moved to crawl out of the burrow, but the soldier reached out a hand toward her instead.

"Please don't go," he said, his tone softening. "I'm sorry if I offended you."

Yemania scoffed. "Why? So you can laugh at me again?"

"I'm not laughing at you, daughter of healing. I was paying you a compliment. You healers are the most valuable asset the Chicome Empire has, and you don't even realize it."

Yemania blinked at him. "No. The sons and daughters of light are the most valuable asset we have. Without them, we have no sun."

"If you say so," he smirked, putting his hands behind his head and closing his eyes as he relaxed against them.

Yemania took advantage of him looking away and put her dress back on. When she pulled the fabric down over her head, she noticed he was peeking at her with one eye half open.

She gasped in indignation, which only made him chuckle.

"Nothing I haven't seen before, daughter of healing."

Yemania narrowed her eyes at him. "And what's your name, soldier? You've conveniently forgotten to tell me."

He closed his eyes again. "Ochix."

"Ochix of . . . ?"

"Miquitz."

"Well, obviously you're from Miquitz, but—"

"Are you going to tell me why you saved me, Yemania?"

Ochix was blatantly avoiding talking about himself, which made Yemania even more suspicious.

"You were hurt. So I healed you."

Ochix opened one eye, this time in disbelief. "That's it? I was hurt, so you healed me?"

Yemania leaned back slightly, feeling embarrassed. How was she supposed to explain? "Yes. That's it."

Ochix rolled onto his side and studied her, both eyes open and narrowed as though he didn't understand. "But I'm the enemy."

"Doesn't matter to me. If someone needs to be healed, I heal them. That's my gift, and I use it to the best of my ability."

"Why were you lying naked next to me, then?"

Her face went hot again. "Your body temperature was low, and I needed to bring it up to get your blood circulating better. My body heat was the quickest way to do that." She wrapped her arms across her chest as if she still weren't wearing her dress. But even with it on, she felt suddenly exposed, like she needed to protect herself.

Ochix didn't say anything for a long time. He continued to stare at her as though he'd never seen anything like her before.

Yemania felt suddenly flustered. "You probably need to eat something. I have some yellow guava in my bag or I can try to find you something else."

Ochix tried to sit up, but swayed slightly before lying back down against the soft earth. Yemania was on her knees beside him in an instant.

"Why am I so—so dizzy?" he asked, bringing a hand to his forehead as though he could stop his head from spinning by holding it in place.

"You lost a lot of blood. I healed your wounds, but your body needs to replenish what it lost. That might take a little while." She dug in her bag and pulled out the small round fruit. "This helps with a variety of ailments, but I think the sustenance is what you need most right now."

"Thank you," he said, his eyes intensely focused on her own. "Yemania of Pahtia."

"You're welcome." She smiled, feeling a little arrogant herself. "Ochix of Miquitz."

Mayana was falling.

What had thrown that boulder? She knew it hadn't been an accident. It was sheer dumb luck it hadn't splattered her across the face of the mountain.

But she'd have to worry about that later. Because the more pressing issue was that she was careening through the air like a flightless baby bird falling from its nest.

She slammed against the side of the mountain's slope. Her fingers scrabbled for a grip, the rough surface of the volcanic rocks ripping open her palms. Warm, sticky blood coated her hands.

Her stomach collided painfully with the lip of a jagged edge, and she threw out her hands as she tumbled across it. The muscles of her arm screamed as she caught a handhold. A shooting pain shot down her shoulder and back, but she didn't dare let go. Her other hand flew to join the first, securing her hold. Her sandaled feet scrambled helplessly against the rock. Her pulse pounded in her ears as panic overwhelmed her.

"Ahkin!" she screamed.

Her stomach continued to feel as though she were falling, bringing back horrible memories of her initial plunge into the underworld. She pressed her face into her arm and fought back a sob of terror.

"I'm trying to get to you. Hang on," Ahkin yelled from somewhere above her.

How far away was he? Mayana tilted her face up to see. He was still a good ten body lengths above her. Ahkin delicately inched his way down, his balance precarious. But her arms began to tremble with the effort of holding on. She knew the truth deep in her bones.

He wouldn't reach her in time.

She frantically assessed her surroundings, seeking any possible way to steady her hold. A root, another rock ledge, anything. But that was when she noticed it. Far to their right and high above their heads, the dark slash of a crevice whistled in the whipping wind. There was some kind of cave or passage there. If they could find a way to make it all the way up . . .

But first, she couldn't fall. She tightened her grip, blood slippery beneath her fingers. Her heart pounded against the jade skull necklace on her chest, as though begging the goddess Atlacoya to help somehow. It still felt so cold, icy almost, not unlike . . . Mayana gasped in realization.

Not unlike the same coolness that swept across her skin in the presence of water.

Hadn't there been a legend about her ancestor? That the first sun, the sun Ahkin's ancestor had sacrificed himself to create, had been destroyed by a great flood. Atlacoya, goddess of drought, used her jade skull pendant to withdraw the waters, to capture them inside the skull and end the flood that had destroyed the world. Then she sacrificed herself so that her blood might be used to resurrect the bones of humanity and usher in the age of the second sun, Water Sun.

The flood waters. They were still trapped within the amulet of Atlacoya. The same jade skull used to save the world must be the pendant hanging around her neck. And surely the power of Atlacoya, housed in the blood that flowed through Mayana's veins, could summon them forth. Blood that now coated the rocks under her hands. How had she not realized it before?

Mayana closed her eyes and called to the waters, willing them to emerge. At first she feared nothing would happen, but then, through the gaping mouth of the jade skull, water burst forth as though it had been waiting millennia to be freed. She commanded the freezing waters to surround her, to embrace her, as they had so many times before.

Ahkin still clung to the rocks some distance above her, his eyes wide as he beheld the miracle of water emerging from the amulet.

"Ahkin, let go," she called to him, but she didn't give him a choice as she willed the waters to sweep him up with her. His body pressed against hers, arms wrapping around her shoulders as he held on. Ona barked in excitement as he bounced along the rock face, following after them like he might have chased a cart back in the marketplace of Atl.

Her focus remained on that dark crevice, the hollow she prayed would offer them some sort of steady ground where they could recuperate. It wasn't terribly wide, but as they neared she could see that it led into some kind of internal cave, winding away deep into the mountain.

Ona barked in warning and darted inside. Mayana turned her head to see another massive boulder careening through the air toward them. But this time she saw where it had come from.

A creature unlike any she had ever seen or imagined materialized out of the far wall across the ravine. It let out an almighty roar that shook her eardrums as effectively as it did the walls of the canyon. It reminded her of the camouflaged moths that hide against the bark of a tree, completely blended into their surroundings and impossible to distinguish until they moved. This creature was roughly humanoid in shape, though it was gigantic, taller than the temple back in Atl. It was made entirely out of stone, as though a part of the mountain itself had broken free and come alive. The name "mountains that crash" suddenly made perfect sense. These mountain giants were as large as mountains themselves, and they did not seem to enjoy trespassers in their realm. It reached a rocky hand to break off another boulder to continue its attack.

On their own side of the ravine, another creature made itself known to their right. Its rough-hewn face roared in anger, a sound like thunder, and it lifted a rocky arm longer than the tallest trees of the jungle canopy back home. It swung toward them, intent on crushing them against the side of the mountain.

She threw every ounce of her strength and concentration into making it into the crevice. As they swept into its opening with a large splash, the thrown boulder and the other stone giant's arm smashed into their side of the ravine. With a boom that made her ears throb, solid rock covered the crevice opening. Remnants of the mountain showered over them. Mayana curled into a ball on the stone floor of the small cave, arms over her head to shield herself. Dust burned inside her lungs. She curled in tighter, sure she was being buried alive as the cave opening collapsed.

A faint ringing in her ears grew louder as the clatter of the last few rocks settling into place faded. Tendrils of light slipped in through cracks, barely illuminating the wreckage. She shifted her body to sit up, kicking off the debris that covered her legs. Ona whimpered somewhere. She turned, but the words to ask Ahkin if he was all right froze on her tongue.

Terror overwhelmed her senses as she beheld Ahkin's steadily paling face. Shock had kept him from crying out, but now that the shock was wearing off, the scream ripped out of him. It tore Mayana's heart in half. She slipped over the rocks as she stumbled toward him, all thoughts of her own safety diminished to nothing.

Ahkin's right hand, his sword hand, was trapped beneath a large chunk of the shattered boulder. The shield still strapped to his left arm appeared to be the only reason the rest of him had not been crushed. He pulled and pushed at the stone, which was about the size of Ona when he curled into a ball. But it would not budge.

Another scream escaped him, raking along Mayana's nerves and sending her heart rate even higher. He beat the shield uselessly against the rock. She fell to her knees beside him. Tears poured down her cheeks and a sob escaped her, despite her efforts to keep her fear in check. She worked furiously to help clear away the debris around the boulder trapping him, shoving and kicking to push away the smaller stones. Ona whimpered again, his ears flat against his head as he watched them work.

Ahkin panted, growing paler with each passing minute, a sickly greenish hue replacing the blood in his face. He vomited once, twice. Mayana worried that he would lose consciousness from the pain.

Finally, she cleared enough to wedge her feet underneath the bottom edge of the boulder. She used all the force her exhausted body could muster to try and lift—but it wasn't enough. It settled back down with a crunching sound. Ahkin screamed again.

"I'm trying! I'm trying!" she sobbed.

She grabbed the amulet around her neck and summoned more water, willing it beneath the rock to help her lift as she wedged her feet back beneath it. She focused the magic of her blood and the strain of the muscles in her legs. His whimper of pain shot through her tender heart and gave her another burst of strength. The boulder inched upward, so slowly it felt like an eternity, but finally, *finally*, Ahkin pulled his hand back from beneath it.

She released her strength and the boulder collapsed back down. Ahkin fell onto his back, cradling his wounded hand against his chest. She whistled for Ona, whose ears perked up at once. The dog lightly leapt toward them and began licking at the split skin and bloody mess that was once Ahkin's hand. The blood began to fade, and the skin began to close. But the misshapen *wrongness* of his hand did not change. His fingers bent at strange angles, and parts of the bone looked crushed entirely.

"Why isn't Ona healing it?" she whispered frantically.

Ahkin continued to pant, as though he had just climbed to the top of the Temple of the Sun. A sheen of sweat glistened on his bloodless face. "He's . . . he's stopping the bleeding, but it seems he can't heal the bone."

"W-what? What does that mean?" Fear kept its cold claws wrapped around her heart, so she knew she wasn't thinking clearly, was having trouble understanding.

"It means my hand is crushed, Mayana!" he yelled suddenly.

Mayana arched back as though he had slapped her, tears burning in her eyes. "Ahkin, I—"

"What were you thinking?" His voice filled with a rage that didn't feel fair. "You basically screamed our location by summoning the water like that! You made us shining targets for whatever those . . . those . . . stone things were! You should have waited for me to get there and help you!"

Shame burned through her chest, sending her cheeks flaming. "If I hadn't, I would have fallen into the ravine! Besides, they already knew where we were. It didn't change anything."

"You never think, never plan anything out. You just act. And now this!" He waved his mutilated hand in her face. "This is what happens when you act rashly, Mayana. People get hurt."

Mayana bit at her lip to keep it from trembling. "I saved us," she said quietly. Where was this hostility coming from? He wasn't seeing her heart anymore. Not at all.

"Well, now I'll be lucky to ever hold a sword again. Some emperor— unable to even defend myself, let alone anyone else. That's what *I* get for trying to follow my heart. For choosing the lying heretic. None of this ever would have happened if I had done what Toani wanted and picked Teniza as my bride from the start."

Something sharp lanced through Mayana's chest. She'd opened herself to him, exposed deep, painful parts of herself, and he . . . he called her a heretic. He should have chosen Teniza, the princess of plants from Milla-catl. The throbbing pain in her chest transitioned into something hard and cold. She immediately shoved it away, shoved it deep into some dark place inside of her where no one would ever touch it again. She rose to her feet, the coldness now spreading out and slowly creeping into her limbs. She imagined when she finally met his eyes, the ice in her gaze would be enough to freeze him to *his* core.

Mayana didn't even bother to respond. Without another word, she turned and marched straight into the dark interior of the mountain without him.

chapter 10

Ochix might be injured, but that didn't mean Yemania had to be nice to him. No, the sooner he was strong enough to be on his way back into those cursed mountains, the better. Foraging for food to help bolster his energy seemed to be the best way to avoid the dark, intense gaze that seemed to follow her as she moved around their makeshift little camp.

What had she been thinking in healing him? She hadn't thought what would happen *after* she saved his life. Would soldiers from Millacatl be looking for her? Surely. She imagined Coatl would be terrified to realize that she hadn't come back to the city. Being so close to the Miquitz Mountains, the logical conclusion would be that she had been abducted. If the soldiers found her with Ochix . . . well, she doubted he would live much longer after that. Captured enemy soldiers were always sacrificed. And to lose his life so quickly after she saved it . . . her spirit recoiled at the very thought.

Yemania told herself it was purely her healing instinct that made her so concerned for his well-being.

Plump yellow fruits spilled onto the ground by Ochix's feet as she emptied her arms. She didn't meet his eyes, quickly turning to start a small fire. Now that the darkness of night had lifted, the fire wouldn't attract as much attention. It would warm him as effectively as her body could.

"I wish I could get you some meat to help rebuild some of the damaged muscle, but trapping is not a gift I possess. I could try fishing, but . . ." She let her gaze wander to the rushing river. She'd never been gifted at fishing. He'd just have to do without it.

Ochix gingerly lowered himself to the ground beside her, wincing. He wrapped an arm around one knee and extended the other leg with a groan. The bones of his necklace rattled slightly as he settled. Yemania's heart lurched in response.

"I'm sorry. You'll be sore for a while still, until your body recovers. Those were some major wounds."

"How bad were they?" he asked her. "I remember—" but he stopped himself.

Yemania narrowed her eyes ever so slightly. "Remember what? Being stabbed?"

His square jaw tightened, but he remained silent.

Yemania rolled her eyes. "Fine, don't tell me how you got stabbed, but you are a fool if you think I can't recognize a knife wound when I see one. My life has not been as pampered as you might imagine." She arranged the kindling she had shaved off a white cedar tree in a small dirt pit.

The corner of his mouth twitched. "Fine. I was stabbed."

"By who?" She piled the kindling higher.

He smirked, but again remained silent.

Yemania threw her hands up in frustration. "You don't make for very pleasant conversation."

"Well, ask easier questions."

"Fine, what's your favorite food?" Yemania said, exasperated.

"That's a boring topic of conversation. Surely you can come up with a better question than that."

Yemania groaned and reached for his knife. She struck it repeatedly against a flat stone she had found, praying a spark would catch. "Nothing says we have to talk," she grumbled. Sweat started to bead along her hairline, but she continued to try.

"Why don't you let me—?" but he stopped with a small chuckle at the seething glare Yemania gave him. He lifted his hands in surrender. "Fine, healer, do as you must to take care of your patient."

The blade of the obsidian knife continued to scratch at the stone with no success. Irritation flared and got the better of her. "I'm fairly certain that using your voice is taking up energy that you could be conserving."

Ochix boomed a laugh that sent several birds into flight from the surrounding trees. "You are not what I expected from a healer."

Yemania shrugged a shoulder. "You certainly aren't what I expected from a death demon."

Ochix's face fell slightly and he cocked his head to the side. "Death demon? Is that what you call us down here in the valley?"

Yemania wiped a hand across her sweaty forehead and leaned back. Maybe she should let him start the fire after all. "That's what you all are. You worship Cizin, god of death and decay." She gestured to the necklace of human finger bones around his neck.

"How does that make us demons?"

"Aren't Cizin's minions called demons? How are you any different? You sacrifice our people to him, innocent farmers, not only captured soldiers like the gods decree. You kill your own citizens if they get too old. You glorify death and destruction."

Ochix frowned deeply at her. "There is a difference between glorifying something and respecting it, sun worshipper."

"Sun worshipper?"

"Your people are entitled to use nicknames and we are not?" Ochix arched a brow at her.

"I never said that. What do you mean by respecting death instead of glorifying it? How is there honor in killing your sick and elderly, or inno-cent farmers?"

Ochix leaned back against the thick trunk of the kapok tree, its expan-sive canopy casting them in dappled shadows. Behind them, the dark outline of the Miquitz Mountains loomed as a deadly reminder of how close they resided to his home. The darkness fell across his face in a way that made Yemania shiver with foreboding. "You Chicome believe that how you live affects what happens to you in the afterlife—where you are able to start your journey through the underworld or whether you get to enter straight into one of the paradises. In Miquitz, we believe it is based on how you *die*. Anyone who falls in battle or acts as a sacrifice joins the paradise in the east with the rising sun. Women who die in childbirth are considered warriors fallen in battle. If you die from water or lightning or certain diseases, you go to Tlalocan, the paradise with the god of rain. We believe only those who die of old age or most illnesses go to Xibalba, where they must be tested to earn their right to rest in a paradise. We believe in helping them avoid the excruciating journey, ensuring they find their place in a paradise with a death that brings honor."

Yemania threw the dagger down in the dirt and balanced her elbows on her knees as she studied him. The Miquitz believed they were helping their sick and elderly escape Xibalba? That the farmers they sacrificed made it to the highest levels of Paradise? She wasn't sure how she felt about that, but it definitely made her question what she knew about the enemy empire. This was not the first time she had had her core beliefs about her world challenged. Mayana had succeeded in making her question the very nature of her reality, the way in which her people worshipped the gods. Was it possible they were mistaken in other ways as well? That maybe like with Ehecatl, always at odds with the rest of the empire because of their different beliefs, Tollan and Miquitz faced tensions because of their religious differences?

"I don't know," she said after a few minutes of thoughtful silence. "What is the point of life, then, if how we die is all that matters? To me, that cheapens life more than it respects death. And wouldn't you be trying to control your own fate by controlling how you die, the way we control how we live with the rituals?"

Maybe it was a trick of the shadows, but Ochix's face seemed to darken further. He studied her with a gaze as black as onyx, made even more intense by the white stripe of paint smeared across his eyes. He certainly looked like a demon to her, a smoldering fire of deadly embers that longed to devour her if she wasn't careful.

"You fascinate me, Yemania of Pahtia. You may be a sun worshipper, but you seem to think for yourself instead of merely believing everything you are taught to be true."

"Is that what you think of us as in Miquitz? Mindless sheep that do as we are told?"

Ochix gave her a wicked smile. "It is an effective way to maintain power, you must admit. Frighten your subjects into submission, convince them that if they do not obey, they will all perish. But you, at least, don't seem to be mindless."

"How kind of you," she spat, her tone dripping with venom.

Ochix threw back his head in laughter again.

Yemania guessed she had Mayana to thank for that, to opening her eyes to the possibility of things being different. Had she been a mindless follower before that? Accepting everything the way it was as truth? How was she supposed to ask questions when they were taught that the rituals themselves saved them from the end of the world?

She crossed her arms across her chest. "You never answered my question, death demon. How does your focus on death not cheapen the value of life?"

He considered her for a long moment with that intense gaze of his. The way he devoured her with his eyes sent a thrill up her spine. When he finally did speak, it was not at all what she expected from his answer. He began to recite a poem,

> *"Oh, only for so short a while you have loaned us to each*
>   *other,*
> *because we take form in your act of drawing us,*
> *and we take life in your painting us, and we breathe in*
>   *your singing us.*
> *But only for so short a while have you loaned us to each*
>   *other.*
> *Because even a drawing cut in obsidian fades,*
> *and the green feathers, the crown feathers, of the quetzal*
>   *bird lose their color—"*

Yemania took a deep breath and finished the final two verses,

> *"—and even the sounds of the waterfall die out in the dry*
>   *season.*
> *So, we too, because only for a short while have you loaned*
>   *us to each other."*

Tears stung the corners of her eyes. Ochix's gaze seemed to burn a little hotter as he smiled at her.

She recognized that ancient poem from another age: the time of the fifth sun, perhaps? She couldn't remember exactly when it had been written, but she recognized it because it had always been her favorite. It was a love poem, talking about the fleeting fragility of life. How when we love, we are only together for a little while, that nothing lasts forever, so savor it while you can. Before it's gone forever.

He tilted his head. "To answer your question, life is not meaningless, daughter of healing. Because the gods designed us for love. To love them and worship them, and also to love each other. We respect death and honor it, yes, but that does not mean we do not also value life."

A death demon lecturing her on the importance of love? The value of life? The absurdity of such a thing almost had her in a fit of laughter. Perhaps she would believe such a thing if love were ever a possibility for her. Certainly not from her family, and she doubted she'd ever be able to marry for anything more than convenience. Perhaps that was why the poem always meant so much to her. It reminded her of what love *should* be, had the possibility of being, if you were lucky enough to find it.

She had felt the love of a friend from Mayana, however brief their friendship had been. But wasn't that the point of the poem? The gods only loaned them to each other. She took a shuddering breath and said a quick prayer of thanks to the Mother for the gift that Mayana's friendship had been through such a terrifying time.

Then she thought of Mayana and Ahkin. Though it was far too soon to call it love, the excitement they felt for each other certainly seemed to be heading in that direction. The memory of Mayana's face when she talked about him was bittersweet. How truly short-lived their romance had been. But maybe that brevity was what made it so much sweeter. Their relationship had been a flash of brilliance, like a falling star from the heavens, before it was extinguished. Just like her friendship with Mayana had been.

Yemania swallowed, a lump forming in her throat. "Yes, I suppose love would make life feel as though it has value if you are lucky enough to find it," she said quietly, not lifting her eyes to meet Ochix's. She was afraid that if she did, he'd see the sorrowful longing in her own heart. "You fascinate me as well, death demon. I didn't know your people held such beliefs."

"Most of us do, anyway. We are not all one and the same, as your existence among the Chicome so clearly proves."

Yemania gave a watery chuckle and turned her head so that Ochix could not see her wipe the wetness from her eyes.

"Here." Ochix hissed in pain as he leaned over and held out another obsidian dagger. "It's easier to get a spark if you strike two flints together instead of striking the blade against a rock."

Yemania sniffed and took the offered weapon. "Where were you hiding this? I thought I took all of your weapons."

"If I made them easy to find, I would be a horrible soldier. But it would be more fun to make you search for them."

She dubiously eyed the plain black wrap around his waist. The corner of her mouth twitched at his irreverent humor. Then, bending over the fire pit, she struck the two obsidian blades together, over and over above the bark shavings.

Ten minutes later she huffed in frustration, about to throw the stupid knives back in the dirt. They would have to forgo fire, she supposed.

"Keep going. Don't give up on yourself so easily," Ochix said. He didn't offer to take the knives from her or do it himself. His complexion was still tinted with shades of gray, and though he tried to hide it, his breathing was labored. Maybe he was too tired to exert such an effort himself, but Yemania got the sense that it wasn't his reason. He wanted to give her the chance to do it herself.

A not-unpleasant warmness formed in her chest as she tightened her grip on the daggers' bone handles. She could start this fire, and she would.

Clack. Clack. Clack. The strike of obsidian against obsidian reverberated through her like the steady drum beat of a worship song. *Clack. Clack.*

"You're close," he said, his tone low and encouraging. They both watched the kindling with tense expectation.

Clack. Clack. Clack.

A spark suddenly jumped from the blades into the scraps of bark. Yemania yelped, so surprised that she had made a spark big enough that she completely forgot to coax the ember into something more. It sputtered before her eyes, and her excitement faded along with it.

"Try again," Ochix said. "Now you know you can."

A spark of something like pride now burned inside of her. She might have forgotten to coax the ember on the bark, but perhaps she could coax this ember inside her heart. She set to work again, her hands striking with more and more confidence. *Clack. Clack. Clack.*

Finally, a wisp of smoke appeared and the end of a scrap of bark glowed with white-orange light. This time, Yemania was ready. She bent down and used her hands to lovingly shelter the fledgling flame. She blew, watching the ember grow brighter. She carefully added another piece of kindling, blowing and watching her labor finally come to fruition. A tongue of orange flame licked up the side of the bark. She added bigger and bigger pieces until the small, hollowed-out pit was filled with life-giving fire.

Sweat drenched her back and dripped into her eyes, but when she leaned back, arms spread wide with success, she knew she had fed the ember inside herself as well. Pride filled her and warmed her, and she sat up a little taller than she had before. She did it! She had made this fire completely on her own.

She turned to Ochix, joy bubbling out of her so much that she couldn't contain her squeal of excitement. "I did it!"

Ochix gave her a smile unlike any she'd ever received. It was a smile that said, *I see you.* "Never doubted you could, daughter of healing. Anyone with enough courage to heal a wounded enemy alone in the jungle, enough of a mind to question and discuss life as you do, and enough of a heart to appreciate a poem like that, I knew you'd get that fire made eventually."

Something wriggled inside her stomach, and Yemania couldn't decide if she wanted to cry or laugh. She settled for a meek "Thank you" whispered at the ground. "I wish I could catch some fish or something to help you get your strength back. Meat would be so much better than fruit."

"Don't change the subject away from your own success so quickly. Enjoy it for a moment." He winked. "Besides, I can handle the fish."

Yemania blanched and perched her hands on her hips. "You do *not* have the strength to go fishing. As your healer, I insist—"

But Ochix rolled his eyes and waved her down. "Keep your dress on, sun worshipper."

Yemania's cheeks blazed at his comment, but that wriggling in her stomach started again.

"And how exactly are you going to fish in your state?"

Ochix's mouth curved into a wickedly teasing smile as he reached for one of the blades she had left in the dirt. His jaw tightened slightly as he moved, the only sign of pain he allowed to show. Yemania's heart flickered in fear for the briefest of moments, but before he could do anything else with the knife, he sliced a small cut along the edge of his thumb and held it toward the river.

His coal-black gaze, which was already so intense they made Yemania's toes curl, focused on the churning current. A ghostly mist seemed to cloud over his eyes.

Her flicker of fear solidified into something closer to terror as two fish leapt from the eddies and threw themselves onto the shore. The fish did not flop and fight as she expected them to. Instead, they lay obediently on the muddy bank, their mouths gaping in suffocation.

Their eyes were clouded with the same misty sheen that shone in Ochix's. Ghostly. Otherworldly.

Yemania had heard only rumors of that power, a power that grabbed hold of a creature's life force and bent it to the will of the wielder. It was the power contained in the blood of the descendants of Cizin, god of death. There were horror stories of death priests in Miquitz using their gift to control sacrifice victims, causing people to walk themselves right into the pit of the underworld. Or stab themselves in the heart. For Ochix to use such an ability could mean only one thing . . .

Ochix was not just a soldier of Miquitz.

He was a prince.

CHAPTER

11

Ahkin knew he'd gone too far the moment the words escaped his mouth. He didn't even believe those horrible things he had said, that he should have chosen Teniza instead of Mayana. That she was a lying heretic. That everything was *her* fault.

It was the furthest thing from the truth, and he knew it. He was in pain and he'd lashed out at the one person who didn't deserve it. This was all *his* fault. Everything. He never saw Metzi's plan, fell right into her trap. He let his own insecurities lead him to plunge that knife into his own stomach. It was his fault they ended up in the underworld.

Mayana never told him about her aversion for the rituals, but how could she have, with her life depending on his opinion of her? No princess in her right mind would have willingly told him something so damning. She tried to keep her true self hidden—until she couldn't any longer. Then she had been brave enough to stand up for what she believed in. When he was challenged, he hadn't had that much faith in himself. He was so ready to believe that his blood wasn't enough to keep the sun fed in its journey across the sky. That *he* wasn't enough. That his self-sacrifice was necessary to save his people.

He still wasn't enough. Strong enough. Clever enough. All the things a legendary emperor was supposed to be. What his father had been. He looked down at his hand, his lip curling in disgust. The one area where he had actually felt confidence—and now he couldn't even fight anymore. How was he supposed to defend his people from the Miquitz if he couldn't even hold a weapon? The truth was as cold and decisive as the edge of a blade. He couldn't save anyone.

He stretched out his fingers the best he could, but lightning bolts of pain shot down the tendons. It wasn't bleeding anymore, but the wounds to muscle and bone could not be fixed by Ona. He needed a healer. But by the time they got to a healer, the scar tissue and damage might already be done. Would there be anything left to fix?

He couldn't entertain the thought right now. Not if he wanted to find the strength to continue. To follow Mayana into the depths of this cave.

He pulled himself to his feet using his good hand. The cave's roof stretched high above his head. At least, he assumed it did. He actually couldn't see it. The walls seemed to reach up into gaping nothingness, like the maw of a beast waiting to swallow him. The wide passageway wound into the mountain itself, and if they wandered too far away from the cave's opening, darkness would envelop them entirely.

Mayana must have realized this too, because when he cleared the first bend, he found her waiting for him, half turned away and arms crossed tightly across her chest. The look in her eyes cut him deeper than a macana sword. Ona stood beside her with his hackles raised, growls echoing off the stone. He certainly hadn't earned any favor with the dog.

"You'll need to summon light for us to continue." Her tone was as cold as her eyes.

Ahkin rubbed the back of his neck with his left hand.

"I don't know how far I can bend the light into the caves. I could try starting a fire. Can we find something to use as a torch?" His eyes swept the floor of the cave for any scrap of wood.

Mayana, however, narrowed her eyes at his shield. "I wonder . . ." She stepped toward him and inspected the sun carved into the golden metal surface. The back of it was made of wood, but surely she didn't expect him to burn the shield.

"Cut your finger," she commanded.

Ahkin stiffened, feeling defensive. "Why?"

Mayana made an impatient noise in the back of her throat. "I want to see something."

Ahkin debated whether or not it was worth it to argue, but his curiosity got the better of him. He used his obsidian shard and pricked the finger of his ruined hand, not wanting to damage the only good one he had left. "Now what?"

Mayana fingered the jade skull pendant around her neck. "The Mother goddess gave me this necklace. I didn't understand why at first, but it's the amulet Atlacoya used to capture the flood waters that destroyed the first sun. I can summon the waters with my divine blood. Your shield is the Shield of Huitzilopochtli. I'm wondering if you can summon the light of the sun with it."

Ahkin's eyes went wide at the possibility. Holding his hand over the carved, golden sun, Ahkin called the light to him, urging it to obey his will. Almost immediately, the image of the sun began to glow, surrounding them in brilliant sunlight and illuminating the passageway. A little surge of pride swelled through him at the thought that his light would allow them to keep moving. Finally, he could contribute something of worth.

Mayana shielded her eyes. "I'd say it works. Can you dim it a bit?"

Ahkin obliged, willing the bright light to fade to a glow just bright enough to let them see the path ahead.

"Let's keep going." Mayana turned away from him without another word and marched forward.

Ahkin reached for her arm. She yanked it away.

"Mayana . . ." he pleaded. "I'm sorry. I shouldn't have said the things I did."

At first she said nothing. He wondered if he should repeat himself, but then she finally found her voice.

"And why wouldn't you? If that's how you truly feel, then by all means express it. Better than letting those thoughts fester inside you."

"I don't actually think those things."

"Don't you, though? From the moment we ended up on that beach, you've fought me every time I tried to do something to help. You think you know so much better than me, Ahkin. Your arrogance astounds me."

That word felt bitter on his tongue. Arrogant? How could he be arrogant when he was so insecure? When every waking second, he worried about how he was never enough? "No, I don't think I know what's better than you do. I just think more logically and—"

"Arrogance!" Mayana turned back to face him and stomped her foot. "You are so convinced that because I *feel* things, because I actually have a heart, that it is somehow inferior to your *logic*. Do you know how I've learned the truth, Ahkin? Through following my heart and not only listening to my head. The rituals are a creation of man, not the gods. My heart knew the truth all along, and I let my family, people like *you*, constantly tell me how wrong I was. You all tried to control what I thought and felt, to drown me with duty and rules and 'knowledge.' But guess who was right in the end? So don't you dare pretend that your way is better than mine."

The silence that hung between them was dry and crackling. It felt like tinder ready to catch—the right words would ignite the tension between them. Ahkin blew through his nose in heavy bursts, his good hand curling into a fist at his side. She had no idea. No idea the burden he carried on his shoulders, the pressure he felt to make sure everything and everyone in the empire was safe. He was a soldier. This is how he had been trained from the time he was little. Assess all possible scenarios. Study and know your enemy. The more you know, the more prepared you will be. On the battlefield, there is no place for *feeling* anything. Those who did were the first to fall, the fellow soldiers who didn't make it home. That was why he loved to study the stars as he did, because the gods communicated through the signs in the heavens. The more you knew, if you could know what to expect . . . it gave you a greater chance of success. Of survival.

"Making decisions based off emotions never ends well. To blindly run into something without a well-thought-out strategy—"

Mayana stuck out her hip. "And how well has that worked out for you so far, Your Highness? Did you *plan* to end up trapped in the underworld?"

Ahkin's face flared with heat, and he stumbled over his tongue for a response.

"Arrogance," Mayana repeated, resuming her trek into the darkness. "You think you can control the outcome of something simply by thinking it through. But someday, Ahkin, you are going to realize you don't have a shred of the control you think you do. And when that day comes, you will be a terrified little boy with no idea which way to turn. All the people who tried to help you, that you shrugged off because you thought you knew better, will be gone."

Ahkin tried to open his mouth to argue, but Ona growled. He took a step back, fearing the beast might lunge at him. He lifted his hands in surrender and settled to seethe in silence. Let her think what she wanted. She had no idea that inside his heart, he *was* a frightened little boy. All the time. It's why he tried so hard to make up for it.

Her words stirred something deep within him. He fought back against the beast that slowly roused to wakefulness, knowing that if it did, it would devour him whole. It would make him have to face the truth.

If he had followed his heart that fateful morning, he would have ripped the dagger out of his mother's hand. He would have told her to forget the rituals that demanded she take her life simply because her husband had died. She would still be alive. Instead, he did as he was always taught. Turn off all emotions, turn off all thought. Trust. Trust in the rituals. Trust in what he knew as opposed to how he felt.

And then the Mother goddess told them on the beach that the rituals were not what the gods demanded. They didn't want to be honored with more suffering and death, but to be honored and worshiped with love and life. Ahkin hadn't wanted to face the truth of that, either—that his mother's death hadn't been necessary. The rituals had been his security. His way to avoid the unpleasantness of what he was feeling and *do* what he knew he had to. Life was a lot safer when the heart had no place in it.

And then he thought of Metzi. His sister. His twin. His blazing anger dimmed slightly. How miserable had she been when she was betrothed to the storm prince of Ehecatl? How intensely had her heart raged against their father's decision, a decision made out of duty and logic? It was the right political move to secure the loyalty of the rebellious city-state. He had sensed it in her every time her marriage was discussed—the anger, the bitterness. He himself had lectured her over and over about the importance of following through with her duty, no matter how she felt. He essentially told her to divorce her own heart. Did that create the very monster he now faced? A sister willing to trick her own brother into killing himself so that she could take her life back? If he had listened to her heart from the beginning, would he have ended up in Xibalba?

He didn't know what to think anymore. He didn't know what to feel. If he acknowledged the truth of what Mayana said, he would have to admit that he had no control over anything.

And perhaps that was the most terrifying thought of all.

———

They wandered the caves for several hours, steadily climbing upward through the mountain. The temperature started to drop the farther they went, and soon their breath rose in clouds before their faces. They were fortunate to have the shield. Without it, they would be wandering the caves in total darkness, feeling their way hopelessly forward. He wasn't sure how common men could make it through such a test. No torch would last this long.

Spirits, and hopefully nothing worse, seemed to hover just outside of their bubble of light, waiting for the moment the light would be extinguished. Dark spirits feared the light, which was why the Chicome Empire imposed a strict curfew. No one ever went out after dark. Ahkin couldn't see anything, but every so often a flicker of something in the corner of his vision would make him jump. For extra protection, Ahkin bent the light around them as well, hiding them from the view of watching eyes. His instinct told him something lurked inside these caves. He had no desire for whatever it was to find them.

Mayana had stopped speaking to him again, but it was probably for the best. He was too jumbled in his own thoughts to try to say anything back. He'd probably make her angrier if he tried. She stayed close, though, if only for the heat and light provided by the shield.

They eventually stopped for a meal of maize kernels and water from the amulet of Atlacoya, not acknowledging each other beyond what was necessary. Mayana went around a corner for a few minutes of privacy, so he bent the light of the shield toward where she had wandered so that she wouldn't get lost. Ahkin realized with a sinking feeling in his stomach that even if they did both survive this journey, they probably wouldn't end up married after all. They were too different. Opposite dualities that couldn't find harmony. He stared down at his mutilated hand. She wouldn't even want to be married to someone that couldn't protect her. He solidified his plan to be the one to die if necessary. The beast inside his chest stirred again, and he ordered it back to sleep. He didn't want to feel anything right now. He couldn't. He blinked back the burning that started behind his eyes.

But that was when Mayana screamed.

12

Ochix was a prince of Miquitz. A descendant of the god of *death*. He was the antithesis of everything Yemania stood for. Death and decay, compared to life and healing. His power craved to control and destroy, while hers craved to free and rebuild.

Ochix gently got to his feet and collected the fish he had summoned using his ability to possess their life force. Yemania shrank back. Using such a power to ensure they had lunch was one thing, but that power could easily take over her soul—and force her to slice her own throat, if he chose.

He offered the fish to her, a half smile forming on his lips. But when he saw the look on her face, the smile faded.

"I'm sorry, but I'm sure you are as hungry as I am, and this really was the quickest way."

"You're . . . you're a royal. A prince of Miquitz," Yemania breathed, not taking the fish.

Ochix grimaced. "I guess there's no point denying it."

Yemania spread out her hands to him. "What are you doing here? Alone? Who stabbed you? Why don't you want to go back?"

Ochix set the fish down and settled back onto the ground with his legs crossed. He rubbed his hands together and looked away from her as though he was nervous to explain. "I confronted my father on . . . on . . . something I didn't agree with him on. He's the head priest of Miquitz. The

Father of Skulls. And you don't really . . . challenge him. Or get in the way of his plans. He has this nasty habit of killing anyone who disagrees with him, which I imagine does not help us lose our 'death demon' description." He smirked, but Yemania didn't think it was remotely funny.

"Anyway, I confronted him, and he possessed me and . . . well, made me stab myself. I remember falling backward into the waterfall that flows behind our temple. I can't remember anything past that."

Yemania was silent for several heartbeats. "You stabbed yourself," she repeated, her tone flat.

Ochix rolled his eyes. "Not by my own choice, I assure you."

"Your father killed his own son?"

"*Tried* to kill," Ochix corrected. "I obviously survived, thanks to you. But I am stronger than I look."

Yemania let her gaze rove over the defined planes of his bare chest beneath the bone necklace, the thick bands of muscle that coated his arms. If he was stronger than he looked, then holy gods above.

"Well, my father tried to have me killed too, so I can relate."

Ochix's lips pressed so tightly she thought his mouth might disappear altogether. "Your father tried to have you killed?" His tone barely masked his disgust. "Why?"

"Not by his own hand." Yemania shrugged. "When our emperor selects his wife, each of the city-states sends a daughter of godly descent to the capital for him to choose from. The daughters that aren't chosen . . . well, their blood blesses the marriage to the daughter he picks and brings the favor of the gods upon his reign."

"And you were sent as your city's hope to be chosen?"

Yemania laughed bitterly. "No, I was not their hope. I was their chosen sacrifice. My father didn't even tell me it was a selection ritual, that I had a chance of being named empress. He told me he was sending me as a sacrifice and that was that. I am nothing like the rest of my family. I never looked like my siblings, the epitome of fitness and health. I was more shy than outgoing. My mother couldn't look at me without curling her lip in disgust. He chose me because I was the easiest to . . . the one he was most willing to . . . lose." Her voice broke at the end. She absently ran a hand across her middle, her mother's continual criticisms, suggestions of foods to eat or exercises to try stinging in the back of her mind.

Ochix closed his eyes as though he were in pain.

Yemania immediately leapt into action. "Are you all right? Is the pain getting worse? I can get you some—"

Ochix gave her an amused look. "My pain is for *you*, Yemania. It's not my injuries."

Yemania's brows pulled together in confusion. "For me? Why would you hurt for me?"

"Do you really think so little of yourself?"

She frowned, but didn't want to answer the question. "Wouldn't your people say I should be honored to die in such a manner?" she countered.

"True, but I'd rather you not die before getting to experience what makes life so worth living."

The memory of the poem he recited, about love being the reason for living, made her pulse flutter.

"Well, I never got much of that from my family, so—"

"You can find love in many places, trust me," he said with a wink.

Yemania imagined that being a prince would let him find "love" in a variety of places. She didn't even want to know how many girls he had trapped with those burning looks of his.

"I would like to think that love is more than *that*," she said, absently adjusting her dress to make sure it covered her full chest. Her cheeks blazed.

Ochix chuckled and skewered the fish on a stick to start preparing their meal. "Yes, love is much more than *that*."

"Have you ever been in love?" she asked, but immediately regretted such a forward question. What was she thinking, asking this enemy prince something so personal after having just met him? Even if it did surprise her how easy it seemed to talk with him, how comfortable she felt in his presence . . .

"Now that is finally an interesting question. Much better than 'What's your favorite food?'" he teased.

She narrowed her eyes. "You aren't going to answer, are you?"

"I said it was an interesting question, not that I would answer it."

Yemania felt the urge to slap him. "You're infuriating."

"Obviously my father thought so too." He smiled playfully and pointed to the newly healed skin on his abdomen. "Otherwise he wouldn't have made me stab myself."

Yemania rolled her eyes. "Would such a death have gotten you into a paradise? Someone forcing you to take your own life against your will?"

"Well, luckily, thanks to you I didn't have to find out." He saluted her with the roasted fish and then ripped off a bite with his teeth.

Yemania smiled despite herself and fiddled with the hem of her dress. A howler monkey screeched somewhere in the distance, surrounding them with his echoing call. It reminded her that they were still sitting in the middle of the jungle. "Are you going back to Miquitz?"

Ochix chewed thoughtfully and swallowed before answering. "I wasn't planning on it, but to be honest, I haven't given it much thought. I didn't have time to map out a plan while I was bleeding and plummeting down the waterfall."

Yemania laughed harder than she'd let herself before, and Ochix beamed a smile.

She finally gave in and ate some of the fish, even if she didn't approve of the way he had caught them. She was incredibly hungry.

The Seventh Sun made its way across the brilliantly blue sky, and they continued to talk, hours slipping by, the conversation flowing as easily as the river during the rainy season. They discussed their religious practices, differences in the daily life of their respective empires, their dreams for the future.

Yemania told him about Pahtia, the jungle paradise filled with white stone temples and blooming with every kind of herb and flower imaginable. How their royal family mostly traveled to the other city-states to protect and heal the royal families descended from the different gods. How the blood of the Chicome royal families was essential for the ritual sacrifices they made to ensure continued protection from the various natural disasters that had destroyed their world in the past. Pahtia's sacrifices protected them from plague.

Ochix described Miquitz's capital of Omitl, a city built of stone and set high on the jagged ranges of the Miquitz Mountains. Precarious rope bridges spanned the gaps between the pointed peaks, dangling over canyons that never cleared of mist. They grew their food in terraced gardens and kept herds of alpacas and goats on the steep mountain slopes. A cave in the center of the city, the entrance protected by a temple and amphitheater built around it, led into Xibalba itself. Their legends said that at times when Cizin's realm was underpopulated, he would emerge from the underworld to harvest more souls. This was only possible when the layers of creation were unstable, like during the Nemontemi or a solar eclipse. Cizin supposedly hadn't appeared for more than a hundred years, but the Miquitz always had a selection of the finest sacrifices available, ready to appease his lust for souls. This would ensure he spared the city from total destruction should he ever choose to emerge again.

Yemania sat with her mouth open in wonder and horror at all he described. She couldn't stop herself from asking question after question. He drank in all she described too, his eyes wide with amazement.

She hadn't noticed that they had slowly scooted closer to each other the longer they talked, until they were sitting so close, she could reach out and touch him.

And part of her wanted to. Desperately. It felt so long since she had talked to someone without feeling like she was a burden, or that they had something more important to be doing. Mayana had been the only one since—well, since her aunt had left for the sea to serve the royal family of Ehecatl. Her heart had broken at losing such a caring mother figure. Coatl was always kind to her to a point, but then he left home to train in the capital, obviously caring more about himself than he cared about her. Yemania had seen only fifteen cycles of the calendar stone when he left. The gods above knew how cold and judgmental her mother was, not a shred of compassion to be found anywhere in her perfectly fit body, especially for a daughter who was never able to keep the shape her mother valued.

She told Ochix about her Aunt Temoa. How she had trained Yemania in the healing gifts offered by the earth itself, ways to heal commoners on whom they weren't allowed to use their divine blood. Yemania had memorized all of her aunt's recipes and remedies and had even started trying some of her own combinations.

"You are not allowed to use your healing gifts for those with common blood, yet you still try to find ways to help them?" Ochix said, his features crumpling in puzzlement.

Yemania explained how her instinct to heal was not limited to helping descendants of the gods. That the gods created all of humanity, and therefore, all had inherent worth and dignity. She shared her dream of someday creating a booth in her city's marketplace to offer free remedies and medicines for those who needed it most.

"Your face lights up when you talk about healing," he said, those eyes burning right to the core of her. "It's beautiful."

Her stomach didn't just wriggle that time, it felt as though it turned itself completely inside out.

"Ochix, I know this probably sounds crazy, but—"

Ochix suddenly went as still as a predator. He held up a hand to silence her. Yemania clamped her hands over her mouth and inched herself closer to him.

To her surprise, Ochix wrapped a protective arm around her and pulled her against his chest, a knife in his hand pointed at the jungle's underbrush.

"Shh . . ." he whispered in her ear. His eyes darted back and forth, assessing for the danger he obviously sensed was approaching.

Yemania tried to calm her rapidly beating heart. The sun above was tipping into sunset, the sky turning orange and gold. Had they really spent the whole day talking to each other? Her brother would be frantic—at least when he wasn't distracted in Metzi's arms.

Panic clenched her heart at the thought of Millacatl's soldiers finding her here with Ochix. She imagined him tied to the platform used for gladiatorial sacrifices, saw his blood spilling into the sand, the intense fire that burned within his eyes snuffed and empty. She clenched her own eyes shut to dispel the image. No, she would not let that happen. Not if she had any choice in the matter.

But it was not soldiers from Millacatl that slinked out from between the trees and shrubs into their riverside clearing. These soldiers wore black costumes with vibrant splashes of pink, red, yellow, and blue. Some wore masks made from human skulls, while others pulled bows notched with arrows made of human arm bones. Some wore white paint across their eyes like Ochix, contrasting starkly with their black attire and tanned skin. Jewelry of bones or fangs dangled from some of their ears and clattered around their necks.

No, these soldiers were not from Millacatl.

They were a raiding party from Miquitz.

CHAPTER

13

Mayana needed to get away from Ahkin. His very presence was like wet sand rubbing into her raw skin. What was the Mother goddess thinking, sending them on a journey like this? Why hadn't she taken them home? She had the power. Instead she was making Mayana suffer through challenge after challenge, all with an arrogant prince she longed to punch in the teeth.

Lying heretic. I should have chosen Teniza.

The words echoed in her head, painfully loud each time she thought of them, but then fading to throbbing pulses. Stupid, arrogant, son of a sun god . . .

It wasn't like picking someone else would have made a difference anyway. He would have chosen to sacrifice himself regardless of which princess he took. They both knew that. He had only said those things to drive a barb into her heart, to tear her down. But why? What was going on inside that thick head of his? Was he really so afraid to let her in? To trust another person to lift some of the burden of responsibility off his shoulders? Perhaps if he could make himself think she couldn't handle the responsibility, then he wouldn't have to.

It all came back to control for him. Controlling the fate of the world through deciphering the stars or following the rituals. If he couldn't let go of his control, it would destroy him.

She stomped through the darkness, slightly surprised that the light followed her as far as it did. Maybe Ahkin was shining the shield more brightly than he realized. She found a private corner to see to her needs. As she made her way back, a glimmer of light caught her eye. The light radiating from Ahkin's shield illuminated some of the darker crevices of the cave, and it was within one of those crevices that a twinkling light shone. Mayana rubbed her arm nervously, but she stepped closer to peer inside.

And she screamed.

The glimmer had been a reflection off a golden necklace—a golden necklace hanging around the neck of a decaying corpse.

Mayana jumped back and screamed again as Ahkin and Ona scrambled toward her. When Ahkin rounded the corner, the obsidian shard was already in his uninjured hand, waiting and ready to meet any threat. Ona, hackles raised, scanned the empty cave.

Ahkin's eyes roved over her. His brow creased in confusion. "What happened?"

Mayana pointed a shaking finger toward the dark crevice. Ahkin lifted his shield to project the light inside.

Two shriveled corpses sat huddled inside the small opening. Sagging, long-dead skin barely clung to their frames beneath dust-covered cloaks. What was left of their dark hair had become thin and brittle. Tiny worms wriggled in several places, scavenging what remains they could. One of the figures had a plated golden necklace hanging over a collapsed chest, the item that had caught the light and drawn Mayana's attention. The skeletons' hands appeared to be clenched together, as if they had died holding on to one another.

Mayana swallowed hard at the sight of their entwined fingers. "Who—who were they?"

Ona slowly padded forward and sniffed tentatively. The dog snorted in disgust before shaking his head and taking a seat beside her, ever the alert guard.

"No idea," Ahkin said, bending lower to inspect them. He lifted their cloaks and examined the bodies. Mayana turned away, unable to stomach it any longer.

"They were injured; I can see broken ribs and hundreds of tiny slashes in what remains of the skin. There are dark stains all over the rocks beneath them. They lost a lot of blood. They were dying and must have taken shelter here. How fortunate."

"Fortunate? That's horrible!" She didn't want to think about what in these caves could have sliced their skin to bits like that.

"Fortunate for *us*. Not them, obviously."

Mayana turned back around to face him. "How is this fortunate for us?"

"We aren't freezing because of the warmth my shield is omitting, but those cloaks will still come in handy."

Mayana sucked in a breath with a hiss. "You would steal from the dead?"

"Well, they certainly don't need them. Their spirits must have traveled on after their bodies failed."

Mayana tried not to think about what would happen to *their* bodies if they failed at some point during this journey.

"And there are some weapons here, look." Ahkin pulled out an obsidian blade from one of the skeleton's belts. It was as long as her hand, with a simple carved wooden handle. The other body held a similar knife. Ahkin handed it to her, and Mayana reluctantly slipped it into her waistband. She didn't like taking their possessions, but she couldn't deny that having a real knife would be a blessing.

Ahkin eased their cloaks off, and Mayana tried not to gag at the crunching and snapping sounds the bodies made as Ahkin moved them. She had no idea how long they had been dead, tucked away inside these mountains. She was even more anxious to know how they had gotten those injuries, or how they had ended up in the underworld at all. Whatever the reason, she was grateful for their sacrifice so that she and Ahkin might continue.

"The fabric is thick wool. That should help us to stay warm. We might want to use some of their other clothes to wrap around our feet. I don't think our sandals are going to be much use in the mountains." Ahkin draped the heavy, dark-blue cloak across her shoulders. Tiny geometric patterns of yellow and gold embroidered the fabric.

Mayana tied the corner of the cloak into a knot at her shoulder to secure it. It was too big for her, but bigger would be better to wrap herself in. She tried not to notice the decayed smell of it, reminding herself that the warmth would be worth it. Ahkin threw the deep-green cloak with similar embroidery over his own shoulders. His ruined hand fumbled with the corners at his shoulder. Mayana got tired of watching him struggle and tied it for him. His mouth pursed into a thin line of frustration, but his "thank you" sounded gracious enough. His frustration was obviously with himself. She stubbornly ignored the way her hand warmed wherever it brushed his skin.

Mayana ripped the woven fabric of one of the tunic shirts into strips to wrap around their feet. She hadn't realized how frozen her toes were until they were wrapped in the thick woolen fabric. A sigh of relief escaped her. She tied the strips around Ahkin's feet too, a muscle in his jaw flickering as he watched her work. His fingers twitched toward her nimbly tied knots, as though they itched to be helping.

"Let's keep going," Ahkin said, standing up and testing his traction on the rock. He patted his leg and whistled for Ona to follow.

"Wait." Mayana took a few tentative steps toward the stripped bodies. Her chest felt full of gratitude at these unknown strangers. They deserved her thanks.

"Mayana, we don't have time to—"

But she held up a hand to silence him. Ona immediately trotted back to her, eying Ahkin with a mischievous curl to his lip.

She closed her eyes and began chanting a prayer her father had taught her, the prayer to bless those who had recently departed the land of the living. The same prayer she and each of her siblings had chanted over her mother's earthly body before it was sealed in the royal tomb of Atl. It was a prayer of thanks for what they had been, for what their life had given to those around them. For the loan of their lives from the gods. *We do not live for ourselves*, her father had said. *A life well lived is a life that has been used to bless others.* Though she had not known these people when they were alive, their deaths had given her gifts that would help her and Ahkin survive. She would not leave them without showing her respect.

Ahkin worried his lower lip between his teeth, but when she finished, she noticed him bow his head in the direction of the crevice.

A warm sensation crept across her skin, as though a phantom hand of flame had rested against her cheek. She smiled slightly and continued her march into the steadily sloping passageways.

Their breath still rose in clouds of mist before their faces as they climbed. After several more hours, the darkness began to press in, suffocating her with its completeness. She had just begun to wonder if they'd ever escape the caves when they turned onto another sloping cave path. The first thing Mayana noticed was the sound—a violent screaming that sounded as though a thousand spirits were wailing all at once. Ahead of them, pale watery daylight trickled into the darkness. She raised her brows at Ahkin, who stepped closer, his blade held high. The screaming grew louder. Mayana wanted to cover her ears with her hands. Up they climbed until an opening grew larger, the light filling the tunnel enough to see without the shield.

Mayana ran ahead, craving the sight of the Seventh Sun after being trapped beneath the mountain for what felt like days. The light was so close, just through the mouth of the cave, but where there was *light*, there was an opening . . .

"Mayana, wait!" Ahkin ran to catch up.

Ona barked.

Mayana stopped dead in her tracks. Her arms flailed to catch her balance and she tipped precariously over the steep ledge. Ahkin grabbed her arm and yanked her back so hard that they both tumbled onto the rough stone floor.

Her breath came out as sharp, panicked gasps. She lay sprawled across Ahkin's body, her hands on his muscled chest. His heart beat painfully hard beneath her palms. She laid her cheek against it, trying to calm her own.

His arms wrapped around her and held her. She didn't even fight him. Instead, she savored the stability after almost tipping into nothingness. Ona whined with concern from somewhere nearby. The whistling cries of the spirits still made her eardrums throb. As she finally disentangled herself from him, she realized the screaming was not coming from ghosts. It was the sound of a powerful wind whipping up the side of the mountain, rushing across the opening of the cave like the breath of a musician across a reed flute. Tiny specks of white floated in the wind like bits of feathers, too soft to be called rain. It was something she had never seen in person, only heard stories of from merchants and travelers who had dared venture into the mountains of Miquitz and beyond.

"Is that—snow?" she asked, stepping carefully toward the ledge.

"Snow?" Ahkin repeated.

It seemed like such an impossibility, frozen water falling from the sky, like legends of star demons or talking deer.

She peered over the edge, down the steep sloping side of the mountain. Snow covered the ground completely, as though the cliff was coated in white rabbit furs. Far below them the snow blew through winding canyons in a whirlwind of white. The sight brought back memories of the storm princess Itza's demonstration with flower petals at the beginning of the selection ritual.

Mayana yelped and drew herself back into the cave. For where her face had met the wind, tiny shards of ice pelted her, like bone needles piercing her skin. She lifted a hand to her cheek, expecting to withdraw it and find blood, but her hand was clear.

"Wind that cuts like knives," she breathed. "The next level of hell indeed."

Though as sharp as the ice was against her skin, it still didn't compare to the damage Ahkin's sharp words had done to her heart.

CHAPTER

14

"My prince?" One of the masked demons spoke in a raspy voice, tilting his head to the side as he considered Ochix. "What are you doing here in the jungles? Your father told the city you fell from the terrace waterfall."

"Oh, right," Ochix mumbled in Yemania's ear. "I like how my father forgot to mention he made me stab myself first."

"Did you wash up here?" the soldier continued.

Ochix cleared his throat. "Yes, I did. And fortunately, this young woman found me and healed me."

"Then we will escort you back to Omitl. Your father was most grieved after the accident."

Yemania heard Ochix snort softly behind her. "I'm sure he was. Fine. I will go back with you. Just let me ensure that this young woman finds her way to—"

But the Miquitz soldiers around them suddenly tensed, pointing spears and obsidian macana swords in her direction.

The closest death demon spoke with contempt as he assessed her head to foot. His painted eyes lingered on her red dress from behind his skull mask. "This woman is Chicome. And a royal healer at that. You mean to *release* her?"

Ochix tightened his arm around her ever so slightly as he pulled them both back a step. "She saved my life. I intend to repay the debt."

"You know your father's orders. We must collect as many as we can

before the Nemontemi. If we can add the blood of a royal to the sacrifice . . . can you imagine!" The warrior let his skull-like smile widen as he
leered at her. His eyes danced with bloodlust.

Ochix lifted his blade a little higher. "No. This one will not be taken to
Omitl for the offering." His voice thrummed with the power and authority of a prince.

The warriors exchanged nervous glances, but did not lower their
weapons.

Yemania whimpered despite her best effort to remain silent. She had
narrowly escaped being sacrificed once already, and she wasn't about to
go through that again. Having the blood of the gods had its benefits,
but it certainly had its risks as well. Her gaze darted to the trees as she
weighed her options. If she ran, they would hunt her down easily. But
if she stayed, she would be dragged into the mountains and given to
the god of death. She wished for a moment that she was descended
from any other god but Ixtlilton, any deity that could give her the
power to do something offensive. She could bind their hands with vines
like Princess Teniza, turn a flock of birds against them like Zorrah, or
whip them into a whirlwind like Itza. Her eyes caught the gleam of the
setting sun against the ripples of the river, and her heart lurched with
grief. Or even summon waters to drown them like Mayana.

But she couldn't do anything the other Chicome princesses could do.
She could heal. And that was the last thing she needed: to make them even
stronger.

"I'm sorry," she mumbled to Ochix. "I wish there was something I
could do to help."

Ochix whispered against her ear, his breath warm on her neck. "Never
apologize for being yourself, and like I said before, you have no idea the power
you possess, daughter of healing. Now when I say to run, you run, understand? Do not look back. You run until you reach the gates of Millacatl."

She shivered slightly but nodded.

Before she could ask what he was doing, there was a flash of obsidian.
Ochix used his blade to cut the length of his palm and threw his hand
out toward the gathered raiders. Yemania watched with horror as their

eyes clouded with mist, weapons dropping to the dirt as their hands and mouths went slack.

She turned and looked up at Ochix, his own eyes clouded with mist. His teeth clenched in concentration.

"Go," he ground out. Every muscle in his body seemed taut with the effort of restraining his companions.

"But what about you?" Yemania asked, tears building behind her eyes. "Come with me."

But Ochix shook his head and let out a strangled laugh. "I can't go to Millacatl. I'd end up on one of your sacrificial platforms faster than you could blink."

"Then run somewhere else. Don't let them take you back to your father. What if he tries to kill you again?"

One of the warrior's faces tightened in anger as he let out a roar of frustration, his eyes clearing as he pushed against Ochix's possession. Ochix gritted his teeth and groaned with the effort of holding him. The warrior's eyes misted over again.

"I have to hold them, Yemania. To give you time to get back. I can't hold this many for very long. If I'm taken back to Omitl, so be it. But I have to give you"—he grunted again—"the chance to escape. You saved my life, and now I give you yours."

It shouldn't be this way, not when they were just planting seeds that could bloom into something beautiful. Yemania drank in the sight of him—his tall, muscular body, the dark hair waving around his strong-jawed face. He intrigued her and confused her, and yet there was something about him she admired. And here he was risking himself to make sure she could escape.

She looked behind her, down the path that would take her back to Millacatl—back to Metzi and Coatl—torn over leaving him or finding a way to stay. Then her eyes instinctively went to the newly healed skin on his abdomen.

"But your injuries, I still need to—"

"GO!" he yelled again. The warriors around her twitched and contorted their faces at the fight raging inside their souls.

Yemania leaned up and kissed him swiftly on the cheek. "Thank you,

Ochix. For everything. I pray the Mother allows us to see each other again." She wiped a single tear from her eye. For a moment, she wondered if she saw one in his as well.

"'Because only for a short while have you loaned us to each other,'" Ochix quoted softly. She wasn't sure she was meant to hear him.

Yemania swore the act of turning her back on him fractured a piece of her heart she would never get back. She would leave it here with him, a shard that could have eventually encompassed her whole heart if they had had the time. Like Mayana's friendship, some things were too vivid and bright to last for long.

She did not turn around, didn't watch him battle against holding the spirits of her would-be pursuers. Afraid that her conviction would falter if she did.

So she ran.

The tears flowed freely down her cheeks and her legs burned, but she kept pushing herself. She fell once, then twice, tripping over roots and branches strewn across the jungle floor. But she scrambled to her feet again, refusing to let Ochix's sacrifice be for nothing.

The forest thinned and transitioned into the rolling foothill farms of Millacatl, but still Yemania did not stop running. She reached the stone gates carved with hieroglyphs, Chicome soldiers positioned at either side.

She threw herself into the arms of the closest soldier, gasping "Miquitz" and "raiders" with each panting breath. The soldier steadied her in his arms. Then he ordered his fellow to notify the palace.

"Are you Princess Yemania of Pahtia?" the older soldier asked, his eyes roving her face, assessing for injury. "We've been searching the jungles for you since yesterday!"

"Yes," Yemania panted, clutching at a stitch in her side. "Yes, I ran into a raiding party from Miquitz. I barely escaped."

He squeezed her tighter and growled. "Filthy death demons. Don't be afraid. You are safe now, my lady."

———

"What in the nine hells were you thinking, Yem?" Coatl's temper could rival that of their father if he was pushed far enough. Her disappearance for an entire day and night had done just that.

He picked up a small clay pot of yarrow root and smashed it against the wall of his guest room. The tiny dried buds scattered across the floor mat like ants. Like the walls of Millacatl's great hall, the walls of this room were one with the rocks, trees and vines, acting as much a part of the structure as the stones. Multicolored tiles inlaid into the stone reflected a rainbow of colors across the dark spaces between the leaves. Coatl kept his distance from the trees, always afraid of the insects lurking within, as he continued to pace and rant. "You could have been captured, you could have been sacrificed!"

"Oh, *now* you're worried about me being sacrificed?" Yemania crossed her arms and turned up her nose. Her nerves were still raw from the events of the day. Where was this concern during the selection ritual?

"I was always worried about you being sacrificed. You think I didn't care that Father picked you as the tribute to the emperor?" Coatl's nostrils flared as he stopped pacing to glare at her.

"You seemed a little distracted, wrapping your legs around Ahkin's sister, to care much about your own."

"I did what I could to save you. Metzi and I were carrying out our plan to make sure she wasn't forced to marry the storm prince, and I was making sure that there wouldn't need to *be* a selection ritual. Once Ahkin sacrificed himself, you were free, weren't you?"

"You still killed your best friend," Yemania snorted. She tried to hide her shock at the realization that part of his plan had been intended to save *her*.

"To save my sister and the woman I love! What would *you* do, Yem?"

She ran a hand through her hair. What would she have done? She wasn't sure, especially with what she knew now about the rituals. Would she have found a way to fight against such an awful tradition? The past was the past and impossible to change. It did no good to dwell there.

"I'm sorry I scared you, Coatl. Believe me, I wasn't planning on running into anyone from Miquitz." Yemania closed her eyes at the pain of those words. No, she had not planned on encountering one of Miquitz's death princes. Nor did she plan on caring for him as much as she did now.

Coatl sat beside her on the bed mat. "Why did you go into the jungles, anyway?" His tone was kinder now, more comforting than accusatory.

She sighed and pinched the bridge of her nose. "I was gathering herbs and fruits. That's all. I wanted some time to myself. I was sick of watching you and Metzi and how much you seem to love each other. I hate feeling like I don't matter to anyone."

Coatl draped an arm around her shoulders and hugged her tight to him. His voice sounded strained as he said, "You matter to me. You always have. I was so scared I lost you. Who would save me from spider bites?"

Yemania gave a watery chuckle and turned to embrace her brother fully. He buried his head into her thick, dark hair, a weight seeming to lift itself off his shoulders. The memories of all the times he took the brunt of their father's anger to spare her washed over her. The agony she'd felt at his decision to leave Pahtia and train in the capital. How it had felt like a betrayal.

"Then why did you leave for the capital all those years ago?" she asked, her voice trembling. "You left me alone with them, after you knew Aunt Temoa had left me too." She couldn't help the tears that pooled in the corners of her eyes.

"I'm sorry, Yem." Coatl hugged her tighter. "I never should have left you. I let my desire to escape numb me to everything else. And then I found Metzi and I . . ." but he stopped, unable to continue.

Yemania sensed the sadness and worry that hung around him like a second skin. Coatl was good at acting as confident as a puffed-up quetzal bird, but she knew what the pain of growing up with a family like theirs did to the soul. Unrealistically high expectations of perfection, brutal retribution when it was not achieved. Never, never feeling good enough. While she hid it by withdrawing and curling in on herself, Coatl handled his by trying to earn approval from everywhere else.

She pulled back from their embrace and laid a hand against his cheek. "What is it, brother? I can tell something more is bothering you."

Coatl kept his gaze low, sniffing slightly as he leaned into her warm hand. When he finally lifted his eyes to meet hers, the fear and brokenness within them shattered her fragile heart, but also sent a thrill of unease up her spine.

He blinked several times in quick succession. "I'm worried about Metzi."

Ahkin had never been so cold in his entire life. Having lived most of his calendar cycles in the capital and its surrounding jungles, coldness was not a sensation he was familiar with. He would gladly trade his other hand for a few moments in the steam and heat of a temazcalli bath house.

The back of the mountain where they had emerged was steep and slippery with ice. Their wrapped feet slid across the frozen ground, sending them both onto their backsides so many times that their cloaks soon became soaked. His teeth chattered together, and his limbs shook uncontrollably as he tried to hold his shield steady in front of them. Its rounded metal surface was their only source of warmth, as long as he kept a drop of his blood exposed. At least the shield's heat was efficient at melting the ice pelting them in the harsh wind. Mayana had offered to part the water around them, but he refused to allow her to lose more blood. He would do this on his own.

Mayana pressed tightly against him as they marched together through the onslaught of ice. Though he imagined she loathed their closeness, he was secretly grateful for it. Even as angry as she was with him, having her close meant more than he wanted to admit. The air around them was thick with white, making it increasingly difficult to see where they were going. Every so often a knifelike shard of ice would hurtle through the air and strike the shield. Ahkin was grateful for the protection, imagining the damage the larger ice shards could do to exposed skin.

"I don't like this layer," Mayana said, her teeth chattering.

"I don't either," Ahkin said into her ear. "But we have to be getting close to the base soon."

Ona, however, didn't seem to mind the snow. The dog leapt around, biting at the wind as though each ice crystal were a fly he wanted to catch. A few times he slipped or slid on a sheet of ice, but was quickly up again, tongue lolling and bounding with joy.

Ahkin rolled his eyes. He wished he could be enjoying himself half as much as the dog was. He gritted his teeth as another knife of ice slammed into his shield.

Mayana's head suddenly snapped up. "Did you hear that?"

"Hear what?" He had to yell to make himself heard over the incessant *whoosh* that was making his ears ache. "How can you hear anything over the wind?"

"It sounded like . . . never mind." She shivered and tightened her grip on her cloak.

"Like what?"

"Like . . . a child crying."

Ahkin strained his ears, but again, heard nothing but the howling of the wind.

"I probably imagined it." Mayana shrugged. But her eyes continued to dart back and forth, searching for something she could not see.

They continued on for several more minutes until Mayana stopped.

"Tell me you don't hear that."

Ahkin closed his eyes and listened harder. Sure enough, he could hear it. The sound of a child crying somewhere nearby.

"I do," he said, breathless. "I hear it too."

Ona had stopped, his ears erect and twitching. Without warning, the dog bolted into the blinding whiteness, his barks echoing off the mountainside.

Before he could stop her, Mayana whipped the knife out of her waistband and cut into her finger. He ground his teeth. She had used so much of her blood so far. If she wasn't careful, she was going to weaken herself too much.

Mayana broke away from him and threw out her arms. Just as the rain had parted around them in the dead field of grasses, the ice parted around her as if it were a crystal curtain she had pushed aside with her hands. Ahkin supposed he shouldn't be surprised; ice was water, after all.

"Mayana, wait . . ."

She pushed her hands out farther, and the ice pelting through the wind parted more. She chased after Ona through the tunnel of her own making, following the direction of his barks.

Ahkin cursed and followed after her.

His frozen feet were so numb he was surprised he was able to run, but at least the frigid air reduced some of the swelling in his crushed hand. He squinted through the pelting ice, holding his shield up to protect his face.

"Mayana!" he called, still following the sound of Ona's barking.

"Over here!" she called back. Her dark silhouette stood framed against swirling white. He ran toward it.

"There." She pointed to a small figure, shaking and huddled in a cloak in the snow.

Ahkin put a hand in front of her. "Careful, you don't know what it is."

"It's a child! Can't you hear him crying?"

Something nagged deep within Ahkin's gut, an instinct he had always learned to trust on the battlefield. And Xibalba was the biggest battlefield of his life.

"Something doesn't feel right," he said slowly, never taking his eyes off the huddled form.

"Oh, *now* you trust your feelings?" She pushed against his arm.

"It's different than a feeling. This is an instinct, something isn't . . ." But Mayana threw his arm off completely and approached the sobbing child.

"Are you all right, little one? Are you lost?"

The child, a boy no older than six calendar cycles, slowly lifted himself out of a curled fetal position. His cloak fell off his shoulders into the snow as he sat up. When he turned to face them, Ahkin immediately reached for the knife in his waistband.

The boy's eyes glowed as red as burning embers. Embers that were set in a face not of a child, but of an old man. Wrinkled, sagging skin so out of place on the body of a child.

Mayana scrambled back as the—Ahkin didn't know what to call it, but it definitely was *not* a child—rose to its feet and leered at them with a smile full of sharp, pointed teeth. Ona growled, and the fur on his back stood on end.

From the swirling, white winds behind him, at least six more pairs of eyes suddenly glowed red. More "children" stepped in to join the first, little boys and little girls dressed in simple cloaks and tunics, all with faces aged well beyond their bodies and eyes like lit coals.

"Mayana, get behind me," Ahkin ordered. He angled his knife, terrified about how to handle them all without his good hand.

"You trespass on our mountain," the little boy said with a voice that did not match his face. It sounded young and innocent, eerily high-pitched. He lifted his hands to expose curled claws at the tips of his fingers. "You must pay."

Ahkin lifted his knife higher.

The children crouched as if about to pounce.

"Wait!" Mayana said. "I think I know what these are."

"Demon children?" Ahkin guessed, still not lowering his knife.

"No, they are chaneque. Drop your defensive pose, or they will attack us."

"What? No! If drop my defensive pose, they will *kill* us."

"Ahkin! Listen to me!"

The first little boy leapt at them with the agility of a cat. Ahkin's shield came up and knocked him aside with a sickening *thud*. His broken hand might not be able to grab a knife, but his forearm could still hold a shield. He felt awkward switching his shield and knife hands, but it was better than nothing.

"Run!" Ahkin commanded as Ona leapt on one of the next children to stop it from launching itself at Mayana.

Mayana slipped on the ice as the other children let out horrible screeches like monkeys and attacked all at once.

Ahkin ran directly toward them, taking their attention away from Mayana. Sharp teeth sank into his arms and legs, but he shook them off, hitting with both shield and knife. They shrieked and growled like feral beasts intent on ripping him apart. Every time he managed to dislodge one, another appeared. Fear lanced deep into his heart each time he locked eyes with their glowing red gazes.

"Stop!" Mayana yelled suddenly. "We give you an offering to allow us to pass in peace." She dug her hand into her bag and then threw out a handful of maize kernels. They scattered across the snow like tiny stones.

The demon children stopped, their glowing eyes focused on the kernels.

"We do not wish to offend you. Please take the offering and accept our apology." She held her hands in the air in submission.

One of the demon children who had been gnawing on his arm looked up at Ahkin, devilish little head cocked as if in question. Blood dripped from his pointed teeth.

"Ahkin, drop the gods-damned knife!"

He looked at the sheer determination on Mayana's face and loosened his grip. The knife fell into the snow—along with his pride.

The children finally released him and crawled toward the kernels. They scooped them up and then scurried back into the whipping white winds.

Ona was already licking the bite wounds on his arms and legs by the time Ahkin realized what had happened.

"I told you." Mayana now stomped toward him. "They are chaneque. Nature sprites. They must guard the mountain."

"Chaneque?" Ahkin rubbed the back of his neck. He had never studied such creatures.

"Yes. They are lesser gods that often guard cenotes and swimming holes in Atl. They sometimes guard forests, meadows, or *mountains*. As long as you are respectful and give them offerings, they will not harm you. But if you offend them, well . . ." Mayana motioned to where splotches of his blood coated the snow beneath his feet.

"I—I'm sorry. I've never encountered chaneque."

"Now you know. And next time, I hope you can trust me. Instead of almost getting us both killed."

Ahkin wanted to argue: he could feel his pride bursting to remind her of exactly how *she* had almost gotten them both killed climbing the mountain. But he silenced it. Because she was right. He hadn't listened. And he had almost been eaten alive by demon children because of it.

He lifted his face to meet hers. "Fine. You're . . . right," he ground out.

The corners of her mouth twitched. "That wasn't so hard, was it?"

He fought the urge to grimace.

"Now come on," she continued. "We still have to see what lovely treasures the next level of hell has waiting for us." She marched back into the pelting ice. "And since my hand is already bleeding, I'm using it to part the ice the rest of the way down, whether you like it or not."

He smiled to himself. He wasn't going to argue this time.

The trek back to Tollan seemed to go much faster than their outward journey to Millacatl. Yemania wondered if it was because her gaze kept wandering to where the new empress bobbed along ahead of her.

She thought over all Coatl had said. "I'm worried about her," he had told Yemania. At first she thought he was about to reveal that Metzi was ill, that they might lose their last descendant of the sun god. But no, Metzi was as healthy as could be. Coatl was concerned about her heart. He said he feared that the power she had acquired was going to her head, that she might have plans that didn't involve him anymore.

"But you were all over each other at dinner two nights ago," Yemania protested. Perhaps her brother was getting paranoid.

"I thought things were fine too, but she sent me out of her room that same night. Today she kept a careful distance between us and would barely talk to me. I'm afraid the council might be getting in her head and convincing her I'm not the best option for a husband."

Yemania gave him a flat look. "You aren't."

Coatl puffed up his chest. "Why not?"

"Well, you helped her kill her brother. And her parents. That's hardly a good quality in a husband."

Coatl gave an exasperated groan and threw himself back onto her bed mat. He put a hand over his eyes, rubbing them with exhaustion. "We've been over this. I did everything—"

"To save her—yes, I know. And luckily the council doesn't know anything about what you or Metzi have done, or else you'd be sacrificed as a criminal faster than the snap of a crocodile jaw."

Coatl ignored her. "They're still pressuring her to complete her marriage to the storm prince. They think it will end this war with Ehecatl. I know that's what this is about."

"Didn't she do all of this to avoid marrying him? You really think she'd give in that easily? From what I've seen of Metzi, she won't let *anyone* tell her what to do." Yemania frowned at him. She remembered how Metzi had put the intimidating lord of Millacatl in his place with a few well-chosen words . . . and threats.

Coatl's eyes flew open, as though he realized something. "You're her new handmaiden! You could watch her and find out what's going on!"

"I don't know, Coatl. Can't you ask her yourself?"

He fixed her with eyes bigger than a pleading puppy's. "Please, Yem."

She sighed in defeat. "Fine. But I can't promise I'll find out anything that will help you. I still think you should talk to her about it."

And that had been that.

Yemania had no idea what she was supposed to be looking for. Evidence that Metzi wasn't interested in Coatl anymore? That she had other plans that didn't involve him? If she did, Yemania was sure they'd all find out soon enough, whether they wanted to or not.

The volcanic plateau of Tollan slowly came closer, until they were winding their way up the paths and through the golden gates carved with ancient hieroglyphs. Though it was night, the city glowed with the otherworldly light of torches reflecting off so much gold. Yemania expected to feel some sense of homecoming when they arrived at the palace, but it still felt as foreign to her as Pahtia had been. Perhaps home was more about those who dwelled within, the people who gave you a sense of belonging, as opposed to a literal place. Yemania wasn't sure where she felt her home was now. Misted mountains and dark, intense eyes lingered at the edge of her thoughts, but she forced them away. Ochix was gone, and she would never see him again.

Metzi gracefully disembarked from her chair and swept up the steep staircase, servants swarming behind her like a hive of bees following their queen. Coatl stumbled out of his chair and made to follow, but with a wave of her hand, Metzi dismissed him.

"I'm retiring for the night. I'll send for you if I want you," she said without looking at him.

Coatl stopped as though he had run into a wall. His eyes slid to meet Yemania's, and her heart broke at the pleading within him.

Yemania stepped down beside him and squeezed his hand gently. "I will watch her and see what I can learn."

Coatl tightened his jaw and nodded stiffly. She watched his retreating back disappear into the winding palace hallways, likely to the room that had been his for the last few years as Tollan's High Healer.

She let out a long breath, threw back her shoulders, and followed Metzi up the stairs.

Though it was night, the palace was bustling. Servants hurried past, balancing stacks of bowls and buckets of cleaning water. Cooks carried baskets of freshly baked breads to the storerooms or gathered their supplies to begin preparing for tomorrow's meals. Animal keepers led monkeys on thin tethers down a hallway or strode past with colorful macaws perched on their arms. Various nobles and government officials hurried by with tablets and scrolls, oblivious to the world around them.

Yemania made her way across one of the elegant courtyards. She took her time enjoying the lush blooms of various flowers hanging in bowls and overflowing from the tiled planters. Waterfalls trickled into a system of pools that wound through the garden like a glittering snake. She wished she could linger in such a beautiful place a little longer, but her promise to Coatl pushed her along like a phantom wind at her back.

"Oh, good, you're here," Metzi said the moment Yemania gently pushed aside the beaded curtain leading into the empress's chambers. The bead hangings rattled behind her as they fell back into place.

The room was surprisingly dark, lit by the single fire now crackling in the pit carved into the center of the floor. The flickering light danced across the colorful depictions of the gods painted and carved onto the walls and pillars—reds, blues, yellows, and blacks blending into beautiful geometric patterns and scenes. Metzi herself was already lounging on her raised bed mat, stretched across the luxurious animal furs.

"My head is throbbing. I need you to make something that will take the edge off the pain." Metzi threw an arm across her forehead for emphasis.

Yemania fiddled with one of her many bracelets. "Coatl is technically the High Healer. If you'd like me to, I can summon him to—"

"No," Metzi barked. "Don't summon him. You're here, and you made that tea for me before. Just make whatever that was."

Yemania chewed her lower lip and gave a small bow. "Yes, Your Majesty. I will get started right away."

Her curiosity was now piqued even more strongly by the empress's strange reaction to summoning Coatl as she left to gather the supplies she'd need to make the tea. When she returned, she worked in silence, carefully watching Metzi out of the corner of her eye and wondering how she was supposed to bring up her brother again without earning Metzi's rage.

"Is your brother much older than you?" Metzi asked after several more minutes of silence.

Yemania continued to grind the red chalalatli root into a powder in her small bowl. According to her aunt Temoa, mixing the root with tobacco did wonders for headaches. "He's two years older than I am."

"Do you have other siblings?"

"Yes, we have three more sisters, some older, some younger."

"Hmm," was all she said in response.

Yemania took a deep breath, preparing to ask about her brother, but Metzi interrupted her.

"How would you feel about becoming the High Healer for the palace here in Tollan?"

The bowl in Yemania's hands clattered to the floor. "The High Healer? But what about Coatl?"

Metzi sighed heavily. "I no longer wish to have Coatl reside in the palace."

The air in her lungs whipped out of her. "I don't understand. I thought you and Coatl . . . I thought he . . ."

Metzi cracked open an eye and smiled in amusement. "You thought I loved him?"

Yemania blinked at the unexpected tears that formed in her eyes. "Don't you? Isn't that the entire reason you've done what you've done?" She bent down to retrieve the bowl and began grinding a new piece of chalalatli root.

Metzi slapped her arm down with such force that Yemania flinched. "You think I did everything I did for *him*? That any action or decision I make couldn't be for any reason other than a man?"

"No!" Yemania said, opening her palms to the princess of light. "No, of course not. I thought that you cared about each other."

"Coatl had his uses. He has exhausted his purpose."

"Is this about what happened in Millacatl? Because the lord there challenged you?"

Metzi sat up and eyed Yemania with a look that could wither a flower. "No one will take me seriously as a ruler as long as they think I am a love-sick child making my decisions purely for the purpose of following my own heart. I had fun with him, yes, but I am the empress of a mighty empire. I will not let anyone, *anyone*, tell me how to live my life!"

Metzi's chest heaved with emotion, and Yemania's heart ached for the wound she sensed deep within the princess of light.

"But how does being with him—?"

"The priests, the other lords and noble families, no one wants to bend the knee to someone they view as weak. I've had a taste of what it feels like to be in control of my own life for once, and I will never give that up. Even for Coatl. If they somehow think they can delegitimize me for following my heart instead of doing what is best for the empire, then my heart be damned. But I will make the decisions on *my* terms. I will decide who I will marry, and I will make the alliances that I see fit. Ehecatl be damned. And once I've saved the empire from their greatest enemy, then maybe they will think twice about whether or not I'm fit to rule . . ."

Yemania could see a thousand conversations swirling in the empress's mind: the words of her advisors, the Tlana priests, the other royal families. The words haunting her and eating away at her. But it also sounded as though Metzi had a plan of some kind, that there was a method to what she was doing . . .

"What do you mean, save the empire from its greatest enemy?"

"Do you want the position or not, daughter of healing? If not, then I will offer it to someone else."

Several tears fell into the chalalatli powder, as Yemania thought about how Coatl would take the news. How would he handle having to return home to Pahtia, to their abusive father? "You do not have to marry Coatl or even have him tend to you, but please do not force him out of the palace. At least let me keep him on as my assistant? I promise that I will keep him away from you."

Metzi seemed to consider it for a moment. "Fine, I don't care what he does. I don't want him moping after me everywhere I go, or I will tell the priests who is responsible for the death of my father."

Yemania blanched, but held her tongue. She feared what she would say, so she only nodded in agreement. She combined the red powdered root with tobacco leaves and steeped the whole mixture in hot water from the clay pot beside the fire. Once it was strong enough, she ran the mixture through a clean cloth to strain the dregs and put the red tea in a new bowl before handing it to Metzi.

"This will ease your head pain, Your Majesty."

Metzi took the bowl and eased herself back into a comfortable position, sipping from the fresh tea. "Thank you, my new High Healer of Tollan." She winked, but Yemania's stomach roiled with nausea.

What on Ometeotl's great green earth was she supposed to tell her brother?

——

It was still dark when Yemania awoke that night. The moon was almost full as it hung over the city like a bulbous, ripe passion fruit from the branches of the heavens. At first she couldn't tell what had awoken her, just that a warm breeze had roused her to wakefulness. Perhaps it had been a mosquito buzzing in her ear again.

She fluffed the rabbit fur beneath her head. As she did so, the bowl of the leftover chalalatli powder caught her eye on the windowsill. It had been several hours since the empress's tea. She should take her another bowl, or else Metzi might have difficulty sleeping.

Damn her healing instincts. She scooted herself off the bed mat and started preparing another bowl.

When she arrived outside the empress's chambers, the guards that usually stood outside the doorway were absent. Yemania frowned. It wasn't safe for her to be without her guards, but she knew Metzi had a reputation for sending them away when she felt "smothered." Well, if Metzi was indeed in such a mood that she felt the need to send the guards away, then perhaps it was best to be quick and quiet about putting the tea somewhere the empress would find it.

Yemania pushed aside the beaded hanging and used her hand to gently guide it back into place, minimizing the sound. Her bare feet padded across the dark room, the faces of painted gods eerily following her in the faint light of the embers of the fire.

But Metzi was not in her bed. Perhaps she had retreated to one of her bathing chambers to cleanse? Yemania set the clay bowl down close to the remaining embers in the fire pit. There, that would ensure the tea remained warm until Metzi was ready for it. Yemania smiled a little at the satisfaction of her job well done and stood to leave.

"I made sure to break off any attachment with the healer."

Yemania froze. Metzi's voice was coming from the side chamber. She continued, "Are you're sure that it's essential? I really do love him."

The voice that responded was a woman's, but somehow as cold and ancient and empty as the void between the stars. Utterly inhuman. "If you wish to find the true freedom you seek, my dear, then it is essential."

A shiver went down Yemania's spine and she took several steps back. Who was Metzi talking to? And about her brother?

"I did exactly as you asked. I sent the message before we left Millacatl. I imagine the delegation will be arriving by tomorrow. But I'm still not sure how this will help me find my true freedom."

"Do you trust me, child?" the voice purred. "The gods work in ways unfathomable to mortal minds. You see only a tile, whereas I can see the whole mosaic. You do not yet see how the masterpiece shall come together. But I promise that if you do as I say, you will find the freedom you are searching for."

"Thank you, great Obsidian Butterfly. And what of the complication we discussed?"

"The complication has worked itself out. We will proceed as planned."

Yemania couldn't explain it, but something about that voice terrified her. There was a *wrongness* to it that the healing spirit within her recoiled from. She retrieved the tea from beside the fire and, parting the beads as silently as she could, inched herself into the hall. She prayed with every pounding beat of her heart that Metzi and . . . whoever that was did not hear her or know she was ever here.

When she was far enough away, she broke into a sprint. Her only thought beyond finding her brother was . . .

Who in the nine hells was the Obsidian Butterfly?

CHAPTER

17

The mountain sloped downward into rocky gorges, the temperature rising with each canyon they passed through. Mayana was grateful to be out of "the place where wind cuts like knives," but she couldn't get excited about entering a layer called "the place where bodies hang like banners." Irritation flickered that the Mother goddess couldn't have given them a little more preparation about what to expect.

They spent the night under a rock outcropping in the last gorge, Ona snuggled against her to keep her warm. Come morning, Mayana was surprised by the drastic change in scenery. Instead of rocky and jagged, the sands smoothly rolled in gentle dunes, the black volcanic sand as dark as glittering beetle eyes. The frozen, blasting winds were replaced by the dry, still air of the desert that stretched out before them, as if the land were holding its breath. The utter silence unnerved her. She could hear the whisper of the shifting black sand beneath her blistered feet with each step. Ona's panting beside her seemed loud and disturbing.

"Are you as terrified of facing this layer as I am?" Mayana kept her voice as quiet as possible. Above their heads, the ever present angry clouds of gray continued to obscure the Seventh Sun.

Ahkin tensed his jaw. "I am."

They walked without speaking for another hour, trudging their way up and down each of the dunes. Her legs ached and burned with each sinking step, sand spilling into the space between her feet and sandals and scraping her skin raw. Sweat began to bead along her hairline. But the silence dragged claws down her nerves. Maybe they could discuss something that had been biting at the back of her mind since they started this journey. "Can I ask you something?"

"Of course." She could tell by his eager compliance that he was trying to make up for how difficult he had been.

"Do you ever question the will of the gods?"

Ahkin pursed his lips. "I hate to admit it, but if I'm honest with myself—then yes."

"I do too."

"That doesn't surprise me in the slightest," he said with a playful smile. "What part of their will?"

Mayana wondered how to put it into words. "I've been thinking since the beach. If the Mother didn't approve of the rituals we created for ourselves, why didn't she intervene? Why did she—" Let her suffer constant degradation from her family because of her beliefs? Almost let the princesses of the various city-states lose their lives? There were so many questions Mayana couldn't answer. Why would the goddess let her mother die . . . ?

"That's a difficult question," Ahkin mused. "I wish I had an answer."

Mayana removed her weathered sandals and dug her toes deep into the warm sand with each step. Her feet still hadn't recovered from the ice of the previous trial. Just as her heart still hadn't recovered from the dagger he'd jammed into it.

"Sometimes I wonder if the Mother really cares about us at all. If she isn't just a selfish being who wants our praise and worship but doesn't actually care about us as individuals. That we are pieces to be played across the board of her creation."

Ahkin stopped. "Do you honestly think that about the Mother of creation?"

Mayana chewed on her thumbnail, her pain at his previous rejection rising back up. "I don't know. I know I'm not supposed to think those things, but I do. These are the thoughts running through my head. I don't control them."

He met her eyes with intense sincerity. "If we are being used as players in a game too big for us to understand, can you at least trust that the bigger game is for your good?"

"The collective good, or my individual good? Is that selfish of me to even wonder?" Mayana felt horrible even giving these thoughts a voice. He probably would think her a heathen if she shared all of what she really thought.

"I think that's something you have to discover for yourself. Maybe start by asking yourself, do you trust Ometeotl? *Really* trust that she is good?"

She didn't know how to answer that. Not yet, anyway. They continued to trace their way across the sands, both lost in contemplation.

"Thank you for discussing this with me, even if you think I'm a heretic," she said at last.

He sighed and ran his fingers through his hair. "Mayana, I don't think you're a heretic. I might have thought you were before everything that's happened, but I've seen how close your heart gets you to the truth of things."

Mayana wanted so desperately to believe him. "Do you really mean that?"

"I do. I was an idiot back in the cave. I was in pain and scared and—" He stopped, choking on the rest of the words.

"I know. I could have told you that." Mayana was proud he was at least trying. His heart seemed to be a little more difficult to access than hers was. But that didn't mean it wasn't there. And with all he'd been through, she suspected there were reasons he'd put up such strong defenses around it.

"In fact," Ahkin continued, "I wonder why the Tlana priesthood never allowed women to participate in religious discussions. I'm amazed by how much I keep learning from you."

Mayana frowned, remembering all the times she tried to discuss religion with her father and brothers. She was always banned from having a voice in the discussions because it wasn't "her place." But Mayana wondered if it was because she asked questions they didn't want to think about. "It's tradition. You won't find a commandment forbidding women anywhere in the original codices, only in those added by man."

Ahkin creased his brow. Mayana wondered if he was searching through the memories of his studies. "Actually, I think you're right. I don't remember anything in the older texts about forbidding women to study."

Elated that someone was listening to her for once, she boldly continued, "Notice it's not only the male gods that sacrificed themselves to create
the sun?" She lifted the amulet around her neck for emphasis. "There were
goddesses as well."

Ahkin nodded, following along.

Mayana plowed forward. "Look at Ometeotl herself. We refer to her
as the Mother, but she is technically the Father as well. The duality. The
divine coupling. Two equal parts. Balance. I don't think one was meant
to rule over the other. They are complements. There is no hierarchy in
Ometeotl's being, and yet we have created a hierarchy amongst ourselves."

Her chest heaved with excitement, the opportunity to give voice to the
thoughts and questions she and her mother had discussed—the conversations she missed more than anything now that there was no one left to have
them with. Excitement at the possibility that someone else could let her be
herself without condemnation. That her thoughts and opinions mattered.

"And yet you still struggle to trust Ometeotl's will?"

"I didn't say I had it all figured out."

Ahkin bumped his shoulder against hers as they walked. Mayana's
skin felt warm again where he had touched her. "It's all right. I'm beginning to see that I don't either," he said.

Her heart sang in response. He wasn't shaming her at all. He was *listening*. There was more to this prince than she knew. Or perhaps she had
always sensed something different about him, even if he didn't yet himself.
"When you get back, will you run the empire the same way as your father?"

Ona noticed a beetle of some kind scuttling across the sand and leapt
after it. Ahkin watched him frolic across the dunes before answering.

"In some ways. He was so respected. The servants cried when he began
his journey through . . . well, here." Ahkin waved a hand around the sands.
"He was a fearsome warrior. He captured dozens of enemies, and yet he
was not cruel. My mother loved him fiercely. And he loved her the same."

"You miss him."

Ahkin cleared his throat. "Yes. I do. He always knew what to do. The
council never questioned him. He never doubted himself—"

"Like you do," Mayana whispered.

Ahkin swallowed hard, his gaze dropping to the sand. "I'm not the man my father was."

She knew he had been acting like a fool since they arrived in Xibalba, but Mayana's heart lurched at the deep wound he was exposing to her. His own vulnerability began to soften the shell she had built around herself. As far back as she could remember, she couldn't watch the pain of others without experiencing it with them. It was as if she took their spirits onto herself for a moment, enough to touch her own soul with theirs. At least she could do the same with others' joy too. Tears welled at the anguish she sensed him straining to hold back.

"No, you're not the man your father was," she said finally. He flinched at her words, and Mayana reached out and held his good hand. "You are Ahkin, son of Huitzilopochtli, prince of light. You are a warrior. You are the emperor. You will be your own man and create your own legacy separate from his. You will be remembered for many things, and you have the freedom to choose what those things will be."

Ahkin squeezed her hand back. She could tell he didn't entirely believe her. "It seems like so much of a burden to bear."

Mayana dimpled her cheek. "I think it's too much of a burden to bear *alone*."

Ahkin's gaze shot up to meet hers again, hope trying to shine within them. "Perhaps you're right." Then he rolled his eyes. "Again."

"Get used to it." Mayana smirked and crested the next sand dune.

Whatever Ahkin was about to say in response must have stuck in his throat.

A flat expanse spread out between them and the next dune, sparse shrubbery dotting the tiny waves of the sand field with wind-blown hollows surrounding them. The small bushes were void of any greenery. Instead, black charred branches curled like fists cursing the heavens.

Tall poles like trimmed trees stripped of all their branches punctuated the landscape as well, and each pole seemed to have something shaped eerily like a limp human body hanging from it. *Bodies that hang like banners*. Mayana's stomach felt sick.

"Don't look at them when we pass," Ahkin said. "It will make it easier."

Her heart rate rose the closer they got to the first pole. She did as Ahkin suggested, keeping her gaze firmly on the shifting sands at her feet. The pull to look tugged at her, but she knew it would only taint her nightmares. Beside her, she assumed Ahkin was doing the same.

"I'm sure you're used to seeing bodies butchered on the battlefield." She fought the urge to look at him, fearing what she might see if she did.

"Less often than you'd think. Our main goal in battle is to capture enemies, not simply butcher them."

"But you've seen human sacrifices before."

"I have." He didn't elaborate.

Ona stayed close as they made their way across the barren field of death, ears back and tail tucked between his legs. Perhaps even he mourned the bodies hanging on the trees.

With every step she took, the thought tapped on her shoulder like an incessant child needing attention. Who are they? How did they get here? *Who are they?*

The sound of rope creaking against wood made her jump and almost look up. "What's that sound?"

Ahkin took a deep breath beside her. "The bodies are hanging from ropes tied around their wrists."

Tied like banners hanging from a city's gates. She finally voiced the question plaguing her. "Who are they?"

Ahkin didn't answer.

"Ahkin, who are they?"

Still he did not answer. Her self-control ached like an overused muscle close to fatigue. The need to know overwhelmed her.

"Keep your eyes on the ground, Mayana. Trust me. Please."

The anguish in his voice undid her. She couldn't stand not knowing another minute. If whatever he saw upset him this much, she had the right to join him in his suffering instead of letting him experience it alone. He didn't have to shoulder the brunt of everything.

She peeked up through her eyelashes to one of the nearest posts, her eyes grazing along the bare, bloodied feet of a young man. She lifted her gaze higher, across the deep-blue fabric tied around his waist, the chest piece of jade and gold hanging across the plane of his fit chest. To the face—the achingly familiar face that had teased her and supported her through so much, including giving her a beautiful jadeite-handled knife on the eve of her departure to the capital.

"Chimalli!" Her brother's name ripped out of her with the force of a scream.

She ran to the post suspending his brutalized body. Bruises and bloody gashes covered every inch of his skin. The gaping wounds to his head told her all she needed to know.

Her brother was dead.

"Obsidian Butterfly?" Coatl asked again, running his fingers across sheets and sheets of papers lining the stone shelves in his rooms. "You're sure that's what she said?"

"Yes," Yemania repeated for what felt like the thousandth time. "She said, 'Thank you, great Obsidian Butterfly.'"

"Hmm." Coatl frowned and continued his shuffling through the maguey paper sheets while Yemania waited nearby with crossed arms. "I know I've heard that name somewhere, but all the scrolls and codices I have in here are on healing. I think we might need to go to the library in the temple."

"She also said something about a delegation arriving tomorrow."

"And she didn't say from where?" Coatl turned around to face her. "Only that I am no longer needed?"

Yemania winced at the hurt in his voice. She could see the raw pain of how that rejection raked against his ego. He had been disposable to her. That was a feeling Yemania could relate to.

"At least she said she did love you."

Coatl looked out the window toward the towering Temple of the Sun and sighed. "Not enough."

"It's late, brother. You don't have to go back to Pahtia, at least. In the morning, when I accompany Metzi to the daily sun ritual, I'll see if I can slip into the temple's library. But let's get some sleep for now."

Coatl pursed his lips. "That's right. I forgot. I won't be accompanying her to do the daily sun ritual anymore. I'm no longer the High Healer of Tollan." His voice broke at the end.

Yemania blinked back tears. "Coatl, I'm so sorry. You know you are the best healer in the empire." She placed her hand on his arm, unsure of how to comfort him.

"We both know that's not true." He fingered the ruby pendant the size of a chicken egg that lay against his bare chest: the mark of the most distinguished healer in the empire. He seemed to think for a few seconds, but then he lifted the golden chain from around his neck. His eyes met hers, and he slipped the chain over her head. The heavy ruby settled against her chest, a weight unlike any she had felt before. "Tollan now has the greatest healer in the empire as its High Healer."

Yemania made a sound somewhere between a sob and a laugh. "You know *that's* not true."

"Well, at least you're the only one better than me." He gave her a roguish wink.

Yemania slapped his arm playfully.

"I know this is something you've never heard from anyone in our family, but I'm proud of you. I'm terrible at showing it, but I really am."

Yemania fidgeted, a hot uncomfortable feeling flooding through her. "Thank you," she said.

———

Yemania had never witnessed a sun ceremony before. All she knew was that every morning, a descendant of Huitzilopochtli had to climb the thousands of narrow steps leading to the top of the golden Temple of the Sun. There they must offer a sacrifice of their blood. Every night the Seventh Sun died and traveled through Xibalba, and could only be reawakened through the blood of Huitzilopochtli.

And with Ahkin gone, Metzi was the last remaining descendant.

Yemania followed along in the empress's wake, excited yet nervous to see such a legendary event take place. She supposed that to Metzi and the people of Tollan it was life as usual, but to Yemania it was a beautiful opportunity to appreciate the miracle of life granted by the gods.

A Tlana priest dressed in robes the color of blood adjusted his necklaces of glittering gemstones as he waited for them beside the massive brazier. Yemania stared in wonder at the flame within the bowl. It had been kept continually burning since the last New Fire Ceremony, years before she was born. Behind the brazier stood the altar, where strips of maguey paper waited for Metzi's daily blood offering. Yemania readied the stingray spine in her hand, her gaze darting to the pinkish glow behind the mountains where the sun waited like an anxious baby bird to be fed.

Metzi approached the altar and lifted the ceremonial knife to her palm. A slice, a wave of her hand, and raindrops of blood coated the strips of paper. Metzi gathered them in her hand and tossed them into the burning flame. The papers curled into dark smoke, and Yemania sucked in a breath as the brilliant face of the sun peeked over the distant mountains. The freshly birthed sunlight warmed her face.

Metzi cleared her throat, and Yemania jumped. The empress gestured impatiently with her bleeding hand.

"Oh! I'm so sorry. I got distracted watching the ceremony," Yemania mumbled, piercing her thumb with the stingray spine. She waved her thumb above the cut on Metzi's palm, healing the shallow wound almost instantly.

"Thank you, Yemania. Now if you'll excuse me, I have preparations to see to back at the palace."

A chill swept through her at the memory of that voice.

"Oh, are we preparing for something in particular?" Yemania tried to make her voice sound casual, indifferent.

"We have some guests arriving this evening, and I want to make sure their accommodations are ready. I'm also thinking of preparing a small feast in honor of their arrival."

Yemania stashed the stingray spine back into the pocket of her tunic dress. "Who will be visiting, if I may ask?"

"Oh, it's a surprise," Metzi said with a wink. She looped her arm through Yemania's and steered her back toward the stairs. "We'll have great fun tonight, I'm sure."

"Actually," Yemania said, easing her arm out of the empress's grip. "I was hoping to visit the temple library before I return to the palace. I wanted to do some research on . . . previous High Healers of Tollan."

Metzi narrowed her eyes, sending Yemania's pulse racing.

She stumbled to make an excuse the empress would believe. "You know, we've never had a woman as the High Healer before, and I want to make a good impression. Make sure I know my history and expectations and such." Yemania threw a prayer toward the Mother goddess, begging for Metzi to believe her.

To her surprise, Metzi's smirk softened into a genuine smile. She placed a hand on Yemania's shoulder and squeezed gently. "You do whatever you need to. Show them all what you're really capable of."

Yemania's heart lurched at the shared camaraderie in being underestimated. She watched the empress sweep back down the stairs with a deep sense of sadness. Such elegance and beauty, and yet such a sharp and clever mind to go with it. Metzi was a gifted young woman, and it broke Yemania's heart to see the bitterness and fear of losing control take away from her natural potential. But Yemania still believed what she had told Metzi before they went to Millacatl: that there was a stark difference between strength and cruelty. She worried that the empress's fear might take her too far over that ledge.

With a deep breath to steady herself, Yemania turned away from the stairs and into one of the dark doorways leading into the bowels of the temple.

The massive structure was the size of a small mountain, and it certainly felt like climbing a mountain to reach its peak. The temple housed storerooms filled with religious costumes, supplies for various rituals, residences for the highest-level priests, and stacks and stacks of codex sheets recording histories and stories and knowledge accumulated by the Chicome Empire through the various ages. But perhaps the most precious of all the items the temple contained were the original codex sheets. The rituals. Guidelines supposedly passed down from the gods about how to serve and keep themselves safe from another apocalypse destroying their world. The same codex sheets Mayana had shown her weeks ago—that had not appeared as aged as the creation accounts. As though they had been created much later . . .

But Yemania didn't have time to worry about that now. Her goal today was not to find the holy ritual codices, but the lesser-known histories.

She hurried along a hallway, the light of numerous torches reflecting off the patterned red walls. She roughly remembered the location of the library from her visit with Mayana, so she headed in that general direction. She had to ask a lower-level Tlana priest once for directions, but eventually she found the section of the temple that housed the library.

The room was as large, if not larger, than the banquet hall of her home palace in Pahtia. Light of the freshly risen sun flooded in through the wide windows cut along the wall. Torches would be too dangerous to keep near such an extensive collection of maguey paper and animal-skin codex sheets. She wondered how the many scribes bustling between the stone tables and shelves studied and painted at night, but perhaps they only worked during the day for that reason.

She approached a young man hunched over a sheet of paper spread out across a stone table. His nimble fingers painted the pictures of whatever event he was recording with a long, thin brush. A dark knot of hair rose above his angular face, and the crisp white tunic he wore was belted at the waist with a strand of rope the color of red cinnabar.

"Excuse me," Yemania asked. "Do you know where I might find histories on the lesser-known gods and goddesses?"

"Is there one in particular you are hoping to find?" He didn't bother looking up from his work as he continued to fill in the small image of a hummingbird.

Yemania chewed her lip, unsure if she should ask about the Obsidian Butterfly directly.

"Uh, I heard—someone—in passing—mention a goddess of butterflies or something like that, and I was curious—"

The paintbrush tip paused on the paper as the young man lifted his gaze to meet hers. "Goddess of butterflies?" he hedged. "Do you mean Itzpapalotl?"

Yemania's hands twisted behind her back. "Maybe that's what she's called, I'm not sure. If you point me in the right direction, I can always go look for myself and see if anything helps me remember exactly what I heard."

The scribe's eyes went wide. Yemania swore he shivered slightly. "You are not the first to inquire. But if you are curious about the lesser gods, I would research any but her."

Yemania didn't say anything for the length of several heartbeats. "Why?"

This time, the scribe shook out his arms as though he was dispelling an unpleasant feeling. "I'd research ones that are a little less . . . likely to haunt your nightmares."

A chill swept through the room. She shivered. Maybe Yemania didn't want to know more. Some part of her spirit whispered for her to leave and not press any further. But Yemania glanced down at the ruby around her neck, running a finger across its smooth glassy surface. This goddess had demanded that Metzi break her brother's heart. She owed it to Coatl to at least find out who she was.

"Maybe it wasn't even her I am thinking of. Probably some other lesser goddess. Where can I find the history sheets about them?"

"The histories of the lesser deities—the ones that did not sacrifice themselves to create one of our suns—can be found by the back wall there." He waved a hand to the left corner and returned to painting.

"Thank you."

Yemania made her way past several stone shelves containing various supplies for rituals, knives and measurement tools, jewels and masks, ritual costumes, and even the blue paint used on human sacrifice victims. Her eyes lingered on an empty shelf coated with dust everywhere but one small shining circle, as though whatever used to sit there had been removed. A whisper of wind blew across the back of her neck, making her skin prickle. Her heart seemed to pound a little louder. She tore her eyes away from the shelf.

Long stone tables were piled high with yellowing, aged sheets, all folded and stacked in neat rows. Each of the codex sheets could be unfolded and laid out to decipher the pictures if there was room enough to do so.

"Oh, Mother help me," Yemania whispered to herself as she took in the sheer volume of codex sheets, some stacks stretching high over her head. She blew away a strand of hair that had escaped from her braid and set to work.

The identity of the Obsidian Butterfly was hidden somewhere in these stacks, and she was going to find it.

CHAPTER

19

Fear spider-walked down Ahkin's spine when he had noticed the bodies hanging from the wooden posts, but then sank in with venomous fangs when he noticed exactly *whose* bodies they were.

His mother. His father. His general and mentor, Yaotl. The young men he'd trained for battle with since he was a child. Even Metzi and Coatl. Everyone he had ever loved or cared about now surrounded him, as dead as the sacrifices who painted the altar in Tollan with their blood.

It took every bit of his strength not to cry out when he first saw them, logic telling him that this shouldn't be real. It couldn't be.

When he saw Mayana's hanging body, he knew. This was a fantasy created by this layer of Xibalba. A deeper level of horror—beyond monstrous crocodiles and snakes, beyond death-filled caverns and demon children. All of those had been designed to torture the body, incite fear of destruction.

But this layer? This layer tortured the heart and soul. The girl he loved walked beside him and yet also hung from a post with her heart ripped from her gaping chest. It was the reality of what might have happened to her had he chosen another bride instead. The thought winded him like a blow to the stomach. A lump formed in this throat. He never could have chosen someone else. He couldn't have watched that heart of compassion ripped from her body, to beat no more.

One of you will not survive.

He made a vow that he would never see that image again as long as he lived.

He needed her heart to beat like he needed the air in his lungs. She made him feel a little less alone. She had painted his world with color, and he could never go back to seeing everything in shades of gray.

He also knew he could not let her see what hung from the posts. If he was right in his suspicions, she wouldn't see his loved ones, but her own. Her own family and friends, all tortured and murdered and hanging before her eyes. He was already struggling to contain how he felt, and he had seen death over and over again. How would such a sight affect her? She shouldn't have to experience that agony.

"Who are they?" she asked.

Panic clenched his heart. What could he tell her? How could he explain? This wasn't fair. These images would burn themselves into his memory for the rest of his life. He would never be able to unsee them.

"Keep your eyes on the ground, Mayana. Trust me. Please."

But he should have known. There was no holding back a spirit like hers.

"Chimalli!" she screamed, bolting for the nearest pole. To him, the pole hung with the body of Yaotl, his mentor. He had to look away from the massive limp body, which bore a vicious wound across chest and abdomen. To her, it held someone different.

She fell to her knees at the post's base, hugging her hands between her knees as she rocked. Tears left shining silver trails down her cheeks.

Ahkin ran after her. "Mayana, it's not him."

"What do you mean? He's right there!" She flung her hand at the hanging body.

"Who do you see?"

Mayana's face crumpled. Then she glared at him as though he was trying to play a sick joke. "It's my oldest brother, Chimalli. Can't you see that?"

"No, I see Yaotl. My general and battle mentor."

Understanding dawned on her face. Mayana sniffed and ran a hand under her nose. "It's not really him?"

"No. I think all of them look different to whoever passes through.

Each body is someone different you care about. Our worst fear in many ways. I imagine many spirits get stuck here, unable to move on."

Mayana cradled her head in her hands and kept rocking. "This is cruel. *Cruel.*"

It was. He couldn't argue. They sat there for several long moments. He wanted to give her the chance to collect herself, but he also wanted to keep them moving. Judging from the pale glow behind the clouds, the Seventh Sun was already starting to set.

"Why didn't she give us any warning?" Mayana burst out, her voice heavy with emotion. "No preparation beyond shallow words. She could have told us what we were facing. Or better yet, she could have saved us from ever having to go through this in the first place."

"The Mother goddess?"

"Yes, the Mother goddess! What kind of Mother allows her children to suffer through anything like this?" She gestured again to the hanging body of her brother. "She could send us home with a snap of her fingers, but she didn't. She wouldn't. I will be haunted by this, all of this, for as long as I—" She shuddered and didn't finish.

"She must have a purpose," Ahkin said. "She gave us a mission to save the bones of Quetzalcoatl, but I think there's more to this journey than that."

"What? What more could there be? She allowed your hand to be mutilated by stone giants, a monster snake to nearly devour us, demon children to chase us down the side of a mountain. And all she gave to help us are cryptic, meaningless worms and dolls."

And obscure warnings that one of us would not survive the journey, but without saying which one of us she means, Ahkin thought bitterly. But despite everything, he trusted the Mother goddess. If it was her will for him to die to save Mayana, he would do so without hesitation. He frowned. "The shield and the necklace have had their uses."

Mayana groaned in frustration. "That's not my point." She rose to her feet and trudged forward.

Ona whined with concern and followed after her, licking at her hands as they went. Mayana stopped and bent down to scratch his ears. "I am grateful she brought you back to me," she told the dog. She reached forward and embraced him. "But you never should have been taken away in the first place."

Ahkin felt lost. He had no idea what to say or how to help her wrestle through whatever battles she fought inside her mind. But perhaps it wasn't his job. She could fight them for herself. At least he could support her as she did.

He jogged to catch up and stretched out his stiff hand. He felt so exposed and raw without the ability to hold a knife or sword. But she didn't need his physical strength right now. She needed something else from him.

"I'm sorry you are struggling," he said.

Mayana crossed her arms and did not slow her pace. "Thank you."

"And I'm sorry for being an ass. Before."

"Thank you." Her answer was brief and curt. He could see her chewing on a question she longed to ask him. "Why wouldn't you tell me what the bodies were? Did you think I couldn't handle it?"

"I—I didn't want you to have to. It wasn't . . . personal against you."

That made her stop and face him. "What do you mean by that?"

"Ever since we fell, I haven't been trying to protect you and make all the decisions because I thought you couldn't. Not really. I feel like it's my fault we are down here, so it's my responsibility to make sure we escape. Like a sin I have to pay penance for. Time and again, you keep having to be the one to save *me*. I have to protect you because I'm supposed to be able to protect everyone in the empire. If I can't even do that . . ." He swallowed hard. She would understand his meaning.

Her face was a mask as she watched him. He wished he could read the emotions simmering within her.

He opened his palms to her. "I can't answer the questions you're asking about the Mother. I'm just trying to say, I think you need to find them for yourself. But I have the faith that you will. And I'm sorry if it has seemed like I didn't believe in you before."

Her mask softened. Slightly. "Thank you," she said again, but this time her tone was warmer.

For the remainder of their trek through the field of hanging bodies, they both tried to keep their eyes low. What they had seen would already be enough to follow them in nightmares. They didn't need to add more.

But Ahkin still couldn't help but look up every so often. Each body he saw left a new wound, but also solidified his determination never to see them dead again. He could not fail them.

Finally, they cleared the last post. But as they did, an evil whisper hissed in his ear to look back. Without thinking, he listened to whatever lurking spirit or internal impulse tempted him. And what he saw ripped the very air from his lungs. The posts no longer hung with various bodies of those he loved.

Every single body hanging from the posts were Mayana's.

They stretched out before him, a sea of death and gaping chest wounds, all perfect replicas of the young woman marching ahead of him.

Panic clenched his heart to the point he nearly lost his stomach. He forced his gaze away, chanting to himself. *It's not real. It's not real.*

But it could be, said the evil whisper in his ear. *That could be her future . . . One of you will not survive . . .*

No. It would not be her future. He would give his life if he had to, to make sure that vision never became a reality. But even after he refocused on the path ahead, on the Mayana that was still alive, the sight of her dead bodies burned behind his eyes like a phantom dark spot after looking too long at the sun.

When the flat field finally sloped up into more dunes, they continued in mutual silence, Ahkin trying and failing to get the images out of his mind. He couldn't forget seeing her dead body over and over and over again. With each step, he answered the image with his own promise. *She will survive. She will survive. She will survive.*

Eventually, the sound of rushing water filled his ears. There was some kind of river nearby. Sure enough, over the next dune, a wide river materialized to block their path.

But it was unlike any river Ahkin had ever seen before. Instead of cool, rushing waters, the currents ran as red as blood flowing fresh from a vein.

Because the currents *were* blood.

CHAPTER

20

Yemania's fingers were stained with dried paint from hundreds of codex sheets, and she still hadn't found any mention of an "Obsidian Butterfly." She was avoiding looking for the name the scribe had mentioned, the goddess Itzpapalotl, but some part of her knew that she couldn't avoid it anymore.

Steeling herself, Yemania set aside the recent stack of papers she had been poring over and located the correct stacks. The whisper of pages sliding against each other filled her ears. She unfolded sheet after sheet until finally, an image caught her eye.

A shiver ran down her spine.

A terrifying skeletal woman looked up at her, dressed as a warrior and holding a human femur bone in her upraised hand. The fingers wrapped around her trophy were tipped in claws as sharp as knives, as were the toes at the end of her decorated feet. Flowing obsidian hair ran down her back. Lines of black paint ran across her pale face from her forehead to her mouth, where blood dripped from luscious red lips. Yemania felt a thrill of foreboding as she took in the black-and-red butterfly wings sprouting from her back, tipped in flints. The Obsidian Butterfly. It had to be her.

Yemania snatched the codex sheet toward her and unfolded the pages within, drinking in any detail she could. The Obsidian Butterfly oversaw a paradise reserved for victims of infant mortality but was also a protector of all things feminine. She was the patron goddess of midwives and women in childbirth. Usually depicted as a butterfly or a moth, she also produced a cloak that made her invisible to the eye. Yemania immediately understood why Metzi felt an attraction to such a deity, why she would seek out her counsel. The goddess that was a warrior for women.

But what terrified Yemania was what she read next. All gods and goddesses existed in duality, with a positive and negative aspect. The Obsidian Butterfly was also the leader of the Tzitzimime—star demons and monsters of the celestial realms of creation. During times of cosmic instability, such as the end of a calendar year or century or during an eclipse, the star demons could descend to earth and devour mankind. They thrived in darkness and could be seen as the stars attacking the sun during a solar eclipse. Yemania remembered the horror stories her siblings loved to whisper after their parents had gone to sleep. The Tzitzimime supposedly waited for the day when humans and gods could no longer keep the sun alive, when darkness would devour the world. Then the Tzitzimime could descend and attack. When she was a child, if Yemania heard the sound of shells rattling, she would scream and run, convinced it was the shell-lined skirts of a star demon come to consume her.

Protecting the world from the star demons was the purpose of the New Fire Ritual, which took place at the end of every century—perhaps the most important ritual the Chicome performed. All fires in the empire were extinguished, and the priests sacrificed a member of a royal bloodline by ripping their heart from their chest. The heart was burned, and a fire was built inside the empty chest of the victim. From the new fire, the priests carried torches to the different city-states to light the braziers on the top of their temples. All households then went to their city-state's temple to retrieve the fires for their hearths. The last New Fire Ritual had been several years before Yemania was born, when the victim chosen had been Emperor Acatl's brother—Ahkin's uncle. According to those in her family who remembered, it was the most terrifying experience to live through. For if the priests were unable to light the fire in the sacrifice's empty chest, the sun would not rise. The darkness would descend, and with it the Tzitzimime. Yemania couldn't imagine waiting in the darkness of her home to hear whether the world was ending or not. Whether the sounds outside the door would turn out to be her father returning from the temple with a flame or a star demon prowling for victims.

She pushed the codex sheet away, unable to stomach the blood dripping from the mouth of the Obsidian Butterfly for another moment. What was Metzi thinking, consulting with the mother of the star demons?

Coatl had been right to worry.

———

Yemania stepped out from the temple into the fading sunlight. She lifted a hand and squinted toward where the Seventh Sun hung low in the sky. Her stomach growled. Had she really spent the entire day poring over the codex sheets in the library? She shifted the bag on her side, guilt and shame nipping at her heels with each step she took back toward the palace. No one was supposed to remove codex sheets from the library, and yet the sheet detailing the identity of the Obsidian Butterfly crinkled with her every movement. Her hand pressed against the side of her bag to silence it, her eyes refusing to make contact with anyone she passed.

The palace was bustling with activity when she returned, but the atmosphere crackled with negative energy. Harried-looking servants ran past with baskets of fruits and meats. Various high officials whispered to each other with dark looks clouding their faces. Something was wrong. Worry and unease seemed to hover in the air like the moths starting to flock around the burning torches.

Yemania stepped toward a young woman balancing a jug of water against her hip. "Excuse me, what's going on?"

The girl met her gaze with eyes swimming in anxiety. "We—we have guests, my lady."

Oh. Metzi's "surprise" visitors. The thought of the star demons had driven all else from her mind. "Who are the guests?"

The girl leaned close, as though it were a great secret. Obviously with the way the royal household was responding, it wasn't a secret to anyone anymore.

"They are a delegation from . . . from . . . *Miquitz*!"

Yemania felt like her head was underwater. She couldn't have heard the girl correctly. "I'm sorry, from where?"

"Miquitz!" she squealed. "Actual death demons, here in Tollan! Not as captured sacrifices. As guests of the empress!"

Yemania took a step back and let the girl rush past.

Miquitz? Metzi's visiting delegation was from Miquitz? What in Ometeotl's name was she doing? Did she want to be removed from power by the council?

But at the same time, a bruised and beaten piece of her heart stirred. If the empress was able to soothe tensions with the Miquitz, she might see Ochix again.

She was afraid to hope for such a thing, but if they really were here . . .

Yemania sprinted the rest of the way to Coatl's room.

———

"The Obsidian Butterfly is the leader of the Tzitzimime?" Coatl repeated. He stood before the polished mirror in his room, smoothing his dark curls into place. Yemania knew he was trying to look his best for Metzi before the feast. "That explains why I can't remember much about that legend. Mother and Father always banned us from talking about them because it scared the younger cousins."

"They scared *me*," Yemania added from where she sat on his pillows. "I hated when you and Tepi told stories after bed."

Coatl smirked at the memory, but Yemania stuck out her tongue in response. "And don't think I've forgotten the prank you both pulled."

Coatl loved playing tricks almost as much as he loved his own appearance. When Yemania had seen eight cycles of the calendar, he and their older sister, Tepi, had tied shells around the neck of one of their dogs. They let the beast loose in her room—and Yemania swore her scream had awoken the entire palace at Pahtia.

"So why do you think the goddess advised her to invite the Miquitz?" Coatl lifted his red feather headpiece and placed it on top of his curls, turning his head side to side to admire it.

"Maybe she wants to negotiate peace with them."

Coatl turned from the mirror and scowled. "Why would you want us to make peace with the death demons that steal and sacrifice our innocent peasants?"

"What makes you think I want to make peace with them?" she asked quickly.

Coatl narrowed his eyes. "Your tone made it sound like you were excited about such a prospect."

Yemania shrugged. "Well, would it be so bad to end the tensions with them?" *And allow me to see Ochix again?*

"I don't trust them," Coatl said, turning back to adjust his headpiece again. "Any of them."

"Regardless, we are expected downstairs to welcome them with the rest of the nobility." Yemania rose to her feet. "I'm hoping Metzi will explain her intentions at the feast."

Coatl threw back his shoulders. "I have to find a way to talk to her tonight. The guards won't let me anywhere near her rooms. I know she still loves me. If I can get a chance to ask her—" Yemania let him ramble but did not respond. None of his plans were going to convince Metzi to take him back. If she was acting on orders from a goddess like Itzpapalotl, a few well-chosen words from her brother would accomplish nothing.

She glanced at her own reflection in the mirror. Curving crimson feathers from her headpiece framed her round face. It was her favorite adornment of those she owned. She had added swirls of red paint beneath her eyes and outlined them in dark kohl, making them much more pronounced. The ruby pendant of the High Healer glittered around her neck along with the other necklaces she had added for the occasion.

"Do I look all right?" she asked her brother, a tremor of uncertainty trickling into her voice.

Coatl pretended to assess her from head to foot. "There's one thing missing." He reached forward and pinched her chin between his fingers. With a tiny jerk, he lifted her chin from her chest until her head was held high. Held with pride.

"Perfect," he said with a smile.

Yemania's cheeks warmed, but when he released her chin, she didn't let it drop.

She had attended several major feasts during the selection ritual but had been too terrified to really enjoy them. This would be her first feast where she could eat a meal without worrying it would be her last.

She and Coatl entered together, Coatl of course strutting into the banquet hall like a jungle bird preening in preparation for a mating ritual. Yemania bit her lip to keep from laughing. Towering columns painted and engraved with images of the gods overlooked the gathered crowd. The room buzzed with the nervous energy of hundreds of nobles seated on reed mats and cushions around the central fire. Servants bearing elegant dishes waited in the wings for the rituals that would signal the beginning of dinner service.

At the far end of the room on a raised dais, Metzi sat upon the golden throne that once belonged to her twin brother. Behind the tall-backed chair, sharp points shot out from the center like rays of the sun.

To her left sat members of the royal council, including the ancient head priest, Toani. Yemania's lip curled as she remembered the last time she had seen the man. He had tried to humiliate Mayana and then stop her from following Ahkin into Xibalba. He looked like an aged turkey, deeply creased skin surrounded by a feathered headdress bigger than any Yemania had ever seen before. His bloodred robes swept to the tiled floor, and the many gemstones strung around his neck rattled as he leaned over to talk to one of the generals of the elite Jaguar warriors. The general himself was a mountain of a man, with a face that looked to be carved from stone. The skin of an actual jaguar was draped across his expansive shoulders. Yemania did not envy those who faced him on the battlefield. Behind them, other generals and religious leaders from the temple watched Metzi with expressions that ranged from bored to suspicious.

But it was the guests seated to Metzi's right that drew not only Yemania's eye, but almost every gaze in the room. The delegation from Miquitz was six men, all but one clearly warriors, judging from their builds and postures. To Metzi's right sat a man in long black robes, a necklace of tiny bones around his neck and a single fang hanging from one of his earlobes. The man wore a strip of black paint across his eyes as Ochix had, but his head was entirely smooth, like a polished tree nut. He had not a single strand of hair. His frame was thinner than those of the warriors sitting beside him, more willowy and graceful than brawny.

Yemania worried for a moment that he might be the Father of Skulls, high priest of the Miquitz, but he looked far too young to be Ochix's father. A lower-level priest, perhaps.

Her eyes raked along the other warriors seated beside the death priest, but when they landed on a certain young man, Yemania swore the earth below her swayed.

Coatl caught her as she stumbled. "Yem, are you all right?"

No. She was not all right. He was here. *He was here.*

Her heart beat a frantic tattoo within her chest as she took in his defined jawline, the dark intensity with which he surveyed the room.

Ochix had come to Tollan.

Mayana had no desire to swim across a river of blood. She prayed there was another way. Ona bounded forward to the sandy shoreline, sniffing carefully. The moment his nose touched the surface he snorted and withdrew, scampering back as though the river had stung him. On the other side of the river, a forest of dark trees stretched into the distance. Mist hung thick between the trunks, making it impossible to see how far the forest spread.

Or what lurked inside.

Ahkin stumbled toward the riverbank and collapsed onto the smooth black sand. He mopped the sweat off his face, leaving behind dark trails of sand like bruises. "Can we rest for a while?"

Her stomach ached with hunger, and the haunted look in his eyes made her feel even more uneasy. He couldn't seem to shake the effect of seeing the dead bodies. Perhaps a break would be a good idea. For both of them. "How many days have we been down here?" she asked, plopping herself down on the sand beside him. Ona, of course, snuggled in between them. Ahkin gave an exasperated sigh but didn't say anything. Ona snorted, as if he was proud.

For a moment, she could pretend they were enjoying a lovely evening on a riverbank with her squirrelly pup. Not that they were trapped within the realm of the dead, camped out beside a river of rushing blood. She fished out several maize kernels from her bag to fill her stomach. She handed a few to Ahkin as well.

"Overworld days, I am not sure. But here in Xibalba, I think this will be our third night. So, there are two more left before the end of Xibalba's Nemontemi."

Mayana groaned. "How many more layers are there until the City of the Dead?"

Ahkin leaned back on his elbows. "We passed through where bodies hang like banners. So next should be the place where"—he coughed and lowered his voice—"beasts devour your heart."

Mayana felt her jaw drop. Beasts? What kind of beasts? And how did they "devour" your heart? Mayana flopped back onto the sand beside him. "I love how specific the descriptions are."

Ahkin laughed, but without real humor. "I know. After that, we have the final river and then the City of the Dead. I think the passage back will likely be there in Cizin's palace. We can retrieve the bones from him and go home. At least we don't have to go to the place where smoke has no outlet, the final resting place of souls that do not enter a paradise."

Mayana threw her arm across her eyes and let her sarcasm deepen. "At least we have that."

"I'm proud of us, Mayana. We've made it this far, which is a miracle itself. If we weren't descended from the gods, I don't know how we would have survived."

He was right. Mayana had been thinking about that since the cave. How many times had her ability to manipulate water lifted them or cleared the way? And they'd still be stumbling around the caves without his ability to light the way through total darkness.

Mayana grabbed another maize kernel from the bag, her hand brushing against the doll the Mother goddess had given her. So much for the other "helpful" gifts. Mayana slammed the pouch closed. She knew Ahkin believed the Mother had a purpose, but what if she didn't? Or worse, what if she was using them and didn't care about them at all?

"I think it would be safer to rest here for the night instead of waiting until we cross into a layer where beasts are waiting to eat our hearts. Would you agree?" Ahkin flashed her a crooked smile that made her stomach flip. Last night, he'd kept a careful distance from her, respecting her anger and need for space. But since his apology, she was starting to feel that familiar ache to close the distance between them.

Mayana studied the prince of light as he lay back against the volcanic sand, his hands behind his head. His eyes were closed. Deep crescents of darkness swept beneath each eye, and his lips were dried and cracked from the stale desert air. He tried to hide it, but Mayana could tell how exhausted he was. Had he slept at all since they arrived here? She was exhausted too. This journey had already pushed them so hard. They'd tasted death so many times, only to spit it back out. And that didn't count the emotional exhaustion she felt. And it had been only three Xibalban days.

Ahkin's chest lightly rose and fell, and Mayana took in the defined muscles of his stomach, which moved with each of his breaths. Even battered and bruised, he was beautiful. He always looked so serious. His breathing slowed and steadied as he slipped into sleep, and as he did, the tension in his jaw lessened. His features softened. It lightened the burden on her own chest to see him find a moment's peace.

"What do you think, Ona?" She ran her hand down the dog's back several times. His short dark fur was soft and comforting. "Should I forgive him?"

Ona growled low in this throat in way that sounded like *no.* Mayana giggled and nuzzled the dog's face with her own. "He's getting closer though, right?"

Ona grunted again, this time sounding doubtful.

She wrapped an arm around the dog, snuggling into him to let herself find a little rest too. "Bark if there's any danger, all right, boy?"

Ona yipped once, which she took as a *yes.*

A warm breeze off the desert dunes behind them swept across her face, like the gentle caress of a hand. Her eyes had barely started to slide shut when she heard it.

The sound of a woman crying.

She was getting used to the occasional wail or scream of agony in the distance. Wayward spirits were trapped and lost all over the layers of Xibalba, but something about the crying tugged her away from sleep. It was an anguished cry of heartbreak. Of loss. After losing her mother, it was a cry of grief that Mayana was all too familiar with.

She sat up. Ona immediately sat up too. "It's okay, Ona. Stay here."

The dog whined after her, but she motioned at him to stay. He lay down and lowered his head to the sand, ears flat against his head. After she had gone several yards, he rose to his feet and trotted along behind her anyway. It wasn't worth the fight, and perhaps it *was* safer to have him with her. The crying was coming from somewhere close by. She couldn't explain it, but she needed to find this spirit. She knew it could be another trap like the demon children in the mountains, but some instinct deep within her told her that was not the case. The warm caress of the wind pressed against her back, as though it was encouraging her to go.

Maybe it was a sign from Ometeotl. But maybe she was just a fool.

She climbed down the low sand dune, Ona creeping along behind her. There, at its base, the silvery, semitransparent outline of a middle-aged woman sat hunched on the sands of another little crescent beach along the river's bloody bank. The spirit wore a simple dress woven with a pattern of rushes. Something about that pattern tugged at Mayana's memory, but she couldn't quite place it. The woman was on her knees, long braid hanging over her shoulder, gripping at the sand as if her grief were causing her physical pain.

"Are you lost?" Mayana asked, cautiously taking small steps down the dune. She didn't want to get too close yet. The light around them was fading, casting an ominous shadow over the landscape.

The spirit ignored her and continued to wail. Mayana's heart twinged, and she put a hand to her chest to soothe the ache. She cursed her ability to feel what others felt. She took several steps closer. Could she put her hand on the spirit's shoulder? Would it go right through her ethereal form?

"Are you all right?" she asked a little louder.

The woman took several shuddering breaths but stopped. She raised herself to sitting and turned to look at Mayana with mournful eyes.

"I've lost her," the woman said. "My baby. She's gone. I thought I would find her spirit here, but children don't come to Xibalba. They ascend to the paradise with Itzpapalotl. Now I am separated from her forever." Her lip began to quiver, and she let out another anguished wail.

"Can you see her again if you complete your journey? Can you earn your way to a paradise?"

The spirit sniffed. "I'm trying to earn my way! That's how I became trapped here!" She threw herself face-first into the sand, beating her fists against the ground.

Mayana's arms itched to embrace her. There had to be something she could say, something she could do to help. She closed the distance between them, Ona sticking close to her heels. "How are you trapped here?"

"I am the Weeping Woman, the guardian of the River of Blood," she cried. "The Lord of the Dead told me that to earn my place, I had to serve. So now I am serving, protecting the bones of the mothers who perished before their time."

Mayana's heart lurched. The bones of the mothers who perished before their time?

"I don't understand."

"Many spirits become trapped here. Many mothers like me who anguish over their lost children, children left behind in the overworld. They wait. They wait for them to join us here. But mine never will, because she did not get the chance to grow up. I will not see her again until—"

"Until you earn your way to the paradise," Mayana said to herself. She curled her legs beneath her and sat down beside the Weeping Woman. Tears built and began to fall from her own eyes. She knew the pain of being separated from her mother . . .

Mayana sat beside her as she cried. Ona whined and forced his nose beneath her arm until he was almost curled in her lap. She wished there was something she could do. Her eyes roved the poor woman's sloped, defeated shoulders, her clawed hands digging into the sand, the pattern of bulrushes on her tunic dress . . .

The warm wind caressed her face again like a loving hand. She'd definitely seen that pattern of rushes somewhere before. Mayana suddenly gasped with understanding. "I have something for you," she said. How could she not have realized it before?

The spirit hiccuped and sat up again, her expression now dubious, as though she thought Mayana might be fooling her somehow. "You have something for *me*?"

Ona sat up, ears erect, and Mayana reached over and opened the flap of her bag. She dug inside and withdrew the tiny doll the Mother goddess had given her on the beach—the tiny doll with braided hair—and a white dress with *a pattern of bulrushes.*

"I think this is meant for you," Mayana said, holding the doll out in her hand.

"Meant for—for me?"

"Yes, I think the Mother goddess intended me to give it to you."

The woman sucked in a breath, awe and wonder filling her silver eyes as she appraised the doll. She reached out and grabbed it, bringing it to her see-through chest and cradling it as though it were a real child. The woman's eyes swam with some unreadable emotion.

"The great Mother has not forgotten me. She hears my prayers and blesses me. For she knows the pain of losing her children, and she has taken pity on my broken soul." She rocked back and forth as she cradled the small doll in her hands. "I will reach my paradise and see my daughter again. The doll is a symbol of her promise to me."

Mayana's eyes again burned with tears—but this time, tears of aching joy. "No, of course she hasn't forgotten you."

"Nor has she forgotten you, daughter of water." The spirit appraised her with a knowing gleam in her eye.

Mayana blinked. "You know me?"

"You are Mayana of Atl. I can feel the power of water within you."

"I—I am." This meeting had not been by chance. Mayana knew that now; she felt it deep within her bones. She had been meant to find the weeping spirit that guarded the River of Blood.

"I have seen your mother, daughter of water. Her spirit called to you."

At first, it took a moment for the words to sink in. Then Mayana felt as though her heart might burst through her chest. Her words came out in a torrent swifter than the river beside them. "What? You met my mother?"

The spirit nodded slowly and rose to her feet. "She waited for you here. She knew you would come for her someday."

A sob built in her throat, and Mayana looked around as though expecting to see her mother's ghost walking toward her. "Where is she?"

"Her bones are here." The woman motioned to the sand beneath her feet. "Waiting for you to retrieve them."

Mayana knew the legends that said once a body's bones were buried in the earth or thrown into a sacred cenote, they sank into Xibalba. The bones of all of humanity, from every age before them, rested *somewhere* beneath her feet. Broken remains of empty vessels, their souls either trapped or resting in a paradise.

"Her bones? What about her spirit? I want to talk to her." As quickly as her heart had soared, it plummeted back to the ground.

"Her spirit has moved on. But she left her bones for you to find. She said that you would know what to do with them."

Mayana's body felt heavy with grief, as if she had lost her mother all over again. She had been foolish to think the Mother goddess would allow her to see her mother again. Bitterness settled onto her tongue. No, the goddess's plan was for them to retrieve the bones of her son Quetzalcoatl, not for Mayana to see her mother again, even for a brief moment. They had to retrieve his bones so that—

Mayana's hands flew to her mouth as realization washed over her. The Mother goddess intended to bring her son back, to resurrect Quetzalcoatl from his bones. That was how the legends said humanity was resurrected after each apocalypse. Their bones were rescued from the underworld and taken to the caves of creation, where they were brought back to life with the blood of the gods.

The Weeping Woman said that Mayana's mother had told her to take her bones. Her bones! The very thing that would allow her to be brought back if Mayana could get them to the caves of creation! That had to be it. The Mother goddess didn't want her to see her mother's spirit for a fleeting moment; she was giving her the gift of bringing her mother back from the dead!

That *must* have been the reason she was given the doll—so that she could give Mayana back the thing she wanted most in this world.

Her mother.

The woman who showed her what love truly looked like.

The woman taken away from her far too soon.

Mayana could bring her back!

"Yemania, are you sure you're okay?" Coatl asked again.

She fanned herself with her hand. "Yes, I'm—I'm fine. I'm just a little nervous to meet the—uh—death demons, I guess."

Coatl narrowed his eyes toward the dais. "I don't blame you."

His hand remained a steady source of comfort on her arm as she followed him to some empty cushions along the side of the room. She couldn't tear her gaze away from Ochix's face. His dark eyes seemed to smolder with something like anger, and there was a certain rigidity to his jaw, as though he was irritated to be here. She wondered what he might do if he noticed her. Would he acknowledge her? Or pretend they had never met? Her stomach went sour at the very thought.

During the selection ritual, she had sat on the dais with Ahkin and the other princesses who were competing for his hand. She much preferred to be down among the crowd, not worrying about how many days she had left to live. Her only regret now was that Ochix might not notice her among the throngs of nobles. However, the moment she settled down beside Coatl, a servant dressed in white and gold materialized beside her so quickly she started.

"Excuse me, my lady. You are requested at the throne."

Yemania blinked. "What? Why?"

Coatl released a breath in a huff. "Oh, that's right," he said. "As the new High Healer of Tollan, you'll be expected to sit with Metzi."

"What about you?"

Coatl's eyes lit like a lightning bug. She could see an idea forming in his mind. "May I join my sister bedside the empress?" he asked the servant.

"Coatl, you can't beg her to take you back at a public feast like this," Yemania hissed out of the corner of her mouth.

Coatl looked affronted. "Beg? I don't beg. She needs to be convinced to see reason," he whispered back.

Yemania rolled her eyes.

The servant dropped his chin and refused to meet either of their eyes. "Actually, my lord, the empress specifically requested that the princess Yemania join her. And *only* the princess Yemania."

Coatl's mouth opened and closed, like a fish gasping for breath on the floor of a boat.

She squeezed his hand before rising to her feet. "I'm sorry."

Yemania marched up the cleared walkway through the center of the crowd. She couldn't help but remember the first time she took these same steps. The princesses had been presented before Ahkin to demonstrate each of their divine abilities. With a pang of sadness, she thought of Mayana. Grief never seemed to let her forget the daughter of water, always assaulting her with memories when she least expected it. Mayana had volunteered to help her with her presentation. She had been a friend when Yemania needed one most.

This time when she approached the golden-pointed throne, she felt the heated gaze of another young man. Ochix's eyes passed over her, but then they snapped back as though he didn't believe what he was seeing. His lips parted in surprise and she could have sworn the corner of his mouth ticked up into half a smile for a moment before his mask of composure returned.

He *had* noticed her. Yemania stood a little taller. She met that gaze for the briefest of moments before returning them to Metzi. *I see you too.*

The empress looked nothing short of regal. A white dress trimmed with purest gold hugged her feminine curves before flaring out from her hips, her thighs exposed by cuts in the dress's skirts. A thick golden necklace arched from shoulder to shoulder, while more white fabric flowed down to golden cuffs around her wrists, hanging beneath her bare arms like wings. *Like the wings of a butterfly*, Yemania thought bitterly. Her thick, dark hair fell to her waist and a pearl-encrusted circlet crowned her head.

"Ah, Sakatl, I'd like to introduce you to our newly appointed High Healer," Metzi purred, directing the death priest's attention with an elegant wave of her hand. "Yemania of Pahtia."

His eyes were like sinkholes, cold and dark. "So young for a High Healer," the death priest mused, angling his head as he considered her. "And a *woman* as well?"

Metzi's fingers tightened on the armrests of her throne. "Yes. I make my appointments based on skill and merit, not merely what is politically appropriate."

Yemania's chest bloomed with warmth at such a compliment from the empress.

"I can see you rule in a manner very different from your forefathers, daughter of light," Sakatl replied in a voice as slimy as an eel fish. Yemania didn't like the slight curl to his lip.

"Indeed." Metzi's answering smile was tight.

Yemania didn't have the faintest idea why Metzi had invited them here. The tension between them was as thick as cold honey. She inclined her head toward the death priest in greeting, her eyes darting to meet Ochix's before seating herself on Metzi's other side. Perhaps they were all about to find out.

Metzi signaled for one of the royal naguals, the animal handlers from the city-state of Ocelotl, to begin the animal sacrifice that would start the feast. As it was the month of the bird, a green parrot had been selected. Yemania averted her eyes as the bird's blood was spilled and cast into the fire. Another memory of Mayana washed over her, making her chest tighten with grief.

When she looked up again, Ochix was watching her with an eyebrow arched. She gave a small shake of her head, as though to say, *Don't ask.* His answering smile lessened the ache in her chest and made her stomach swoop.

Metzi rose to her feet and spread her arms as wide as her smile. A hush swept across the room like a brisk wind.

"I'd like to thank you all for joining us this evening as we welcome my personal guests, a diplomatic delegation from the Miquitz Empire." She nodded toward the priest Sakatl, who returned the gesture. "I'm sure many of you are wondering why I would invite such . . . *unusual* . . . guests into our palace. I would like to answer that for you."

Out in the crowd, Yemania could see Coatl hanging onto Metzi's every word, his arms crossed tightly across his chest.

"Long we have dealt with the rebellious nature of the citizens of Ehecatl. They challenge our right to rule in Tollan and question our methods of worshipping the gods." Mutterings filled the silence as Metzi took a breath. "Like angry children who have been left out of a game, they have declared war on us simply because I did not wish to marry their prince. The truth is, I did not wish to give them any more power or influence than they already possessed."

The council members seemed to lean forward the longer she spoke, some of their faces twisted with distrust.

"Instead, I wish to secure an even more productive alliance, not only to put Ehecatl in their place once and for all, but to put an end to a threat that has plagued our empire since the age of the Seventh Sun began."

A flicker of intuition made Yemania uneasy. A more productive alliance? Whatever she was about to announce would not be taken well . . .

"After my discussions with Miquitz, they have agreed to halt hostilities against our borders and aid us in the coming months against Ehecatl. In exchange, I have agreed to marry one of their princes."

Yemania felt the world slip away again. No. Metzi couldn't be marrying a prince of Miquitz. The only prince, she assumed, in the delegation was . . . She looked to Ochix for confirmation, begging him with her eyes to say it wasn't true. This time, Ochix would not meet her gaze. He looked determinedly at the low stone table before him, a grimace pulling at his lips.

To Yemania's horror, Metzi then motioned for Ochix to stand and join her in front of the crowd. Ochix grunted slightly as he got to his feet. Yemania couldn't help it; she immediately assessed the pinkish scar across his abdomen. A healer never rested.

Ochix slowly paced to stand beside the empress. He held his head high, but the muscles of his back were taut, as though tensing for battle. His face was as cold and blank as granite. She grabbed his hand and lifted it before the assembly. A show of unity, a mark of their apparent betrothal.

Dizziness suddenly overtook Yemania. This wasn't right. Metzi couldn't be marrying Ochix. Her heart raged against the possibility. It wasn't fair. The gods wouldn't torture her in such a manner, would they?

"We will be married after the Nemontemi is over. Wedding preparations will begin in the morning, and I look forward to celebrating such a momentous occasion in our empire's history." Metzi lifted her and Ochix's clasped hands higher. The tightness in his jaw intensified, and Yemania felt another piece of her heart crack apart.

Her attention shot to the crowd, to find the one person whose heart would be equally as broken by this sudden news. Sure enough, Coatl's mouth had fallen open, rage and disbelief mingling on his face.

"Let the feast begin!" Metzi called out.

Yemania had to remember how to breathe. And it appeared she was not the only one. The head priest, Toani, and most of the generals and military leaders looked as though they had bitten into an unripe passion fruit.

The council obviously didn't approve of Metzi making this decision without consulting them first.

———

Yemania forced the flatbread and spiced deer meat down her throat, despite how difficult it felt to swallow. Metzi was marrying Ochix. *Her* Ochix.

Well, technically he wasn't hers. It wasn't as if they had made any promises to each other. In fact, now that she looked back, how could she be sure Ochix had really felt anything for her at all? It was probably in her head. He was a handsome, strong warrior prince, and she was—well, he had no reason to pick someone like her.

Except, she was the High Healer of Tollan now. She had that to be proud of. And although it was an appointment by Metzi, Yemania knew she deserved it. She was a talented healer, and her tender nature made her that much better at it. Healing didn't always involve the body alone. As brilliant of a healer as Coatl was, he had always struggled to see those he healed as more than whatever ailed them. They were challenges to him, puzzles to solve. To Yemania, they were souls to save. Mothers to return to their children. Sons to return to their fathers. Lovers to return to . . .

She clamped her teeth down hard on her lip and then hissed at the blood she tasted.

"Are you all right?" Metzi asked from beside her, dropping a luscious blackberry into her mouth.

"Yes, I'm sorry, I bit my lip. I'm fine."

Metzi chewed and then pouted her own lip. "Well, luckily you can heal yourself, can't you?"

"Actually, no. The royalty of Pahtia can't heal themselves. We can heal others by drawing on the spirit within us—the presence of Ixtlilton's spirit within our blood. In a sense, we're gifting it to them. It is the self-sacrificial act of giving to another that allows them to receive the gift of healing. Without the self-sacrifice, there is no healing. So, another descendant can sacrifice their own blood to heal me, but it is not true sacrifice to help myself." Yemania swirled the pulque in her bowl before taking a sip. "At least, that's how my aunt Temoa explained it to me."

"And what is your role as High Healer of Tollan?" a deep voice said from Metzi's other side.

Yemania's gut twisted as she recognized the voice.

"Um." She swallowed hard. "I am the personal healer to the royal family of Tollan. As Metzi is the only living descendant of the sun god left, my job is less demanding at present. But I'm sure that will change after . . ."

"After my family grows." Metzi smiled at Ochix suggestively.

Yemania choked on her pulque. "Sorry," she sputtered. "The . . . pulque burned the cut on my lip."

"What if something happens to you?" Ochix asked. "Since you cannot heal yourself?"

"Well, I've given that some thought." Yemania turned to Metzi. "Your Majesty, as your life is of such crucial importance, I think it might be best if there are two healers living in the palace. In case something happens to me, there is always another who can heal me but can also be available should you—"

"You're going to ask if Coatl can be your assistant permanently, aren't you?" Metzi heaved a sigh.

"He is a gifted healer, Your Majesty—"

Metzi waved a hand, as though Yemania's next words were an irritating gnat she wished to swat away. "All right, all right. But I don't want him attending to me unless it's absolutely necessary. You are my appointed healer, not him."

Yemania let a breath of relief escape through her nose. "Yes, Your Majesty. I will keep him busy with other tasks."

It broke her heart how quickly Metzi seemed to be dismissing her brother, but the sheen in her eyes suggested Metzi was not as indifferent to him as she appeared. Maybe she gave in because some part of her wasn't ready to let him go quite yet.

"So what other tasks do you have in mind, Yemania of Pahtia? You seem like the kind of young woman that would have many ideas to help your empire." A slight smirk tugged at Ochix's lips as he took a sip of his own pulque.

Yemania's cheeks warmed. He was teasing her. Even now, he was finding a way to remind her that he remembered.

She sat up higher. "I do, actually. It was something I was hoping to bring up to the empress when the moment presented itself."

Metzi popped another berry into her mouth. "Well, the moment has officially presented itself. What ideas do you have?"

Yemania blinked. Metzi wanted to hear her ideas? "I—I've always dreamed of creating remedies for commoners. Perhaps even utilizing drops of my royal blood in combination with other natural remedies that can be sold or distributed in the marketplace. I think their lives are just as valuable, and if I can use some of my gifts to bless more, I think there would be many benefits."

"Hmm," Ochix said, lowering his bowl. "I almost wonder if such a thing would help to bolster public opinion and mood. You know, in times of war and transition, the masses can become restless and difficult to manage. Especially when so many of them have been conscripted into the army."

His eyes twinkled with mischief as they met Yemania's.

Thank you, she mouthed to him, heat spreading from her cheeks down her neck.

Metzi's eyebrows pulled together. "I hadn't considered something like that before. Sharing some of our divine gifts with those of common blood to help gain their support." Her mouth stretched into a smile. "Showing them that their new empress cares about them as she asks them to fight for her."

"Excellent idea, Your Majesty." Ochix lifted his bowl in salute.

Metzi beamed. "Yes, I think that would be an excellent idea." She faced Yemania again. "Have your brother get to work on that venture starting tomorrow. That will keep him busy and out of my way."

Yemania couldn't stop the surge of gratitude that swelled up within her—for Metzi, yes, but also for Ochix. He'd known this was her dream; she'd told him so back on the riverbank. He was trying to help influence the empress to make that dream a reality.

A cacophony of drums sounded as dancers took to the floor, signaling the beginning of the celebratory dances.

Metzi leapt to her feet and pulled Ochix up with her. "Let's see how well my future husband can dance."

Ochix let her drag him into the center of the room, but not before he looked back for the briefest of moments, flashing Yemania a conspiratorial grimace.

The air grew stifling as incense burned her nose. She felt slightly light-headed, perhaps from the pulque. But perhaps not. The tears stinging behind her eyes suggested it wasn't the fermented drink.

"Excuse me," Yemania said, rising to her feet. She squeezed behind the head priest and the leader of the Jaguar warriors.

The open doorway leading to one of the massive pleasure gardens outside beckoned to her.

She needed to get as far away from Ochix dancing with Metzi as possible.

23

When Ahkin awoke, Mayana was gone. He sat up, brushing sand from his arms and sleep dust from his eyes. He twisted around, but all he saw were the rolling sand dunes surrounding their sliver of beach beside the bloody river. Even the damn dog was gone.

"Mayana?"

Where was she? He scrambled to his feet, brushing shards of black fire glass from the once-white wrap around his waist. He hadn't intended to fall asleep, but exhaustion had pulled him under. Now she was gone. Had some terrifying beast snatched her away while he slept? Was it already devouring her heart?

The image of dozens of her lifeless corpses, hearts ripped from their hollow cavities, flashed behind his eyes again. His own body felt hollow and empty. How could he have failed her again? His mistake brought them both down here, and now because he was foolish enough to fall asleep . . .

"Ahkin!"

His head snapped up. Mayana slipped down the side of a sand dune, Ona on her heels.

"Mayana! You're okay!"

She jogged to his side, clutching her bag to her chest as though it contained a precious treasure. "Of course, I'm okay. You won't believe what happened."

He pulled her into an embrace. "I thought you were gone."

She laughed, squirming in his arms. "I'm fine. I promise. I was talking to a spirit."

Ahkin stiffened and pulled back. "A spirit?" he asked. "How do you know you can trust it? It might have been trying to deceive you."

"I just know. Please trust me."

Ahkin chewed his lower lip. He wanted to trust her judgment. He knew he should. But he wished he could have been with her to be sure. The circumstances raged against all he had been trained for. He took a deep breath. Details. He needed details. "What happened?"

Mayana launched into an explanation of how she gave Ometeotl's doll to the spirit of a weeping woman. The spirit in turn gave her the bones of her mother. Mayana hugged the bag tighter as she spoke.

"I just finished digging them all up and washing them off."

Ahkin's head was spinning. "But—what's the purpose of having her bones?" He didn't want to sound indelicate, but he failed to see why she would be so excited about them.

"Because I can bring her back," Mayana declared simply.

Ahkin swallowed. "Mayana, we can't bring back the dead."

It didn't deter her in the slightest. "Haven't you heard the legends of the caves of creation? Where the gods resurrected humanity with their own blood. *Our* blood. The blood of the gods.

She couldn't be serious. "Are you saying that if you take her bones to the caves of creation, you can use your godly blood to resurrect her?"

Mayana shrugged her shoulders. "I don't see why not. That's Ometeotl's plan for the bones of Quetzalcoatl, isn't it? Why can't I do the same for my mother?"

Ahkin rubbed the back of his neck. "I don't think we are supposed to disturb the dead, especially if her spirit has already reached the place where smoke has no outlet. Or if she made it into a paradise."

Excitement crept into every inflection of her voice. "This is the Mother goddess's plan. I'm sure of it. She has given me an incredible blessing. It all makes sense. It's why she gave me that doll back on the beach."

"I don't doubt she gave you that doll for a purpose. But are you sure it's her will for you to resurrect your mother? How do you know it's not your own will?"

Mayana scoffed. "I'll show you when we make it back to the over-world. I know this is a gift from the Mother."

There was no arguing with her. And maybe she was right. He was no better at deciphering the will of the Mother. Hadn't his mistakes that got them here proven that?

"Before we start planning a trek to the caves of creation, let's focus on escaping Xibalba before the end of the Nemontemi. We only have two more days. And we need to find a way to cross the River of Blood."

Mayana's lip curled in disgust as she turned to face the red current, oozing like an open wound. "We'll have to go through it."

He was afraid there was no other way. But they'd wait until morning. Because if he had to cross a river of blood, he'd rather not do so in the dark.

———

Ahkin didn't know why, but part of him expected the River of Blood to be cold.

He was deeply mistaken.

He gagged the moment he took his first step and realized the blood was as warm as his own body, as though the land of Xibalba had been sliced and its lifeblood now flowed fresh across the surface.

"I'll wash us with water from the amulet when we get to the other side," Mayana promised. She'd offered to float them across, but Ahkin didn't want her using the amount of blood it would take to carry them.

The river was not deep, running only up to his waist so far. Had it been water, he would have been swept off his feet, but the blood was thick and sluggish. Ahkin's tongue tasted as though he had bitten it, but he knew it was likely from the red droplets tossed into the air when he moved against the current. He spat the saltiness out of his mouth, but it didn't help. Mayana stayed close behind him. Ona whined from where he lay across Ahkin's shoulders, and Ahkin tightened his grip on the beast. Once he thought he felt another warm liquid running down his back, underneath where he had strapped his shield. He told himself it was splashed blood, but the dog snorted as if it knew exactly what it had done.

Mayana's promise of water once they reached the opposite shore was the only thing keeping him going.

The stones beneath his sandals were smooth and slick. Twice he almost slipped and dropped the dog, but he managed to keep upright. He was glad they had removed their heavy cloaks and stashed them in Mayana's bag. They would have bogged them down the moment they were soaked. She carried the bag above her head to keep everything dry.

About halfway across, something long and gray and scaled slithered past them before sinking back beneath the surface. Ahkin's skin crawled, but he remained steady. Mayana, on the other hand, screamed and jumped. Her foot must have caught on a slick stone, because her hands suddenly flew into the air and she lost her balance completely. She submerged and disappeared from view.

Ahkin yelled, his heart leaping into his throat. He thrashed through the bloody currents, trying not to dislodge the dog as he reached with his foot, feeling for any sign of her. Finally, his toes brushed up against something solid and warm, nudging her back to the surface. She flailed, trying to get her own footing as she gasped for breath, not unlike a newly birthed fawn trying to stand on untested legs.

"My bag!" She mopped soaking hair away from her red-stained face as she frantically checked to make sure nothing had been lost. The bag was soaked, but firmly closed. She sighed in relief.

Ahkin felt relief flood through him as well, though more for her safety than the bag.

"I won't tell you how disgusting you look right now," Ahkin said, his mouth twitching at the corners.

"You're too kind, Your Majesty," Mayana replied scathingly, spitting blood out of her mouth. But the corners of her mouth twitched too. "Keep going. I don't know what in the nine hells that was, and I don't want to find out."

They waded through the remainder of the river at a much faster pace, the tangy scent of the blood winding into Ahkin's nose until he thought he would be sick. A horrible thought occurred to him, making the hairs on his arms raise. "Do you think the purpose of the River of Blood is so that you are coated in blood when you go through the forest?"

Mayana's eyes went wide in understanding. "So the beasts can smell and track you."

Ahkin suppressed a shudder. "We will definitely need to wash off as much as we can when we reach the shore."

"What do you think the beasts are?" Mayana slipped again but caught herself before she went under.

"I wish I knew." Ahkin hated the thought of facing unknown foes. He always studied everything there was to know about his enemies before he engaged them. Without any knowledge of what to expect, his stomach churned with unease. The beasts could be anything.

Mayana groaned. "I don't want to face beasts that devour your heart."

Ahkin laughed. "I don't either. But I promise that whatever happens, I will protect you."

This time it was Mayana's turn to laugh. "And who has protected whom down here, prince of light? When will you realize that we are doing this *together*?"

Ahkin ground his teeth together and did not answer. He didn't want to be reminded of how many times he had failed her.

The river deepened so that Mayana was up to her chin in blood before the riverbed slowly began sloping upward. Ahkin stayed close beside her, though he struggled to balance the dog on his shoulders. They finally stumbled onto the opposite shore, drenched in both crimson and sweat. Ahkin eased the dog off his shoulders and back onto the ground. His back was definitely wet with more than blood. He glared at the dog, and Ona cocked his head to the side with a smirk that Ahkin swore said, *What?*

"That was awful." Mayana coughed several times and wrung thin red streams out of her long hair.

Ahkin shook out his shoulders. "I think it would be best to wash off before we enter the forest."

Mayana wrinkled her nose. "I agree." She withdrew her knife and cut the end of her thumb. Her eyes slid shut as she held her hand out in front of her, palm up. Water burst from the jade skull pendant hanging around her neck.

It surrounded her like an embrace, her hair swirling high above her head. The water turned from crystal clear to murky brown as it swept the remnants of the River of Blood off her body. She closed her fist, and the water fell back to the ground in an almighty splash. Ahkin tried not to look at how the water dripped off the smooth curves of her waist and the defined muscles of her legs. She turned her back to him and adjusted the fabric tied around her chest. Her hair hung down her back like a waterfall of ebony. The back of Ahkin's neck grew hot, and he swallowed hard. He mistakenly dropped his gaze to the dog. Ona watched him with suspicious eyes, so he cleared his throat and quickly diverted his gaze toward the trees. Mayana summoned more water to wash the surface of her animal-skin bag, though it would likely stay stained as red as the tattered remains of her loincloth skirt. He mistakenly let his eyes linger on where the cut along the side of her skirt exposed the skin of her thigh. Ona growled, and Ahkin was tempted to do that same right back at him.

She turned to face him and jutted out her hip. She opened her fingers again and summoned more water from her necklace. A shining silver snake emerged from the skull's mouth and curled around her hand, like a pet waiting for its owner's command. "Hold your breath," she said, arching an eyebrow.

Gods, she was so beautiful.

Ahkin sucked in a breath and Mayana opened her hand toward him. The water surrounded him with its current. It was biting cold compared to the warmth of the blood from the river. But he definitely needed it to wash the heat from his skin. By the time she closed her fist and the water collapsed to his feet, Ahkin's skin felt almost frozen. His teeth began to chatter, and bumps rose across his arms.

"Better?" she asked, a smile curving on her lips.

"Much," Ahkin agreed. He shook out his hair like a dog and wrung out some of the water from the wrap around his waist.

They both turned to face the twisted black trees. Their trunks stood within the mists like pillars of stone, welcoming them into the temple of the beasts. The sun that shone behind the clouds above did little to light the dense canopy. Whispers seemed to hover in the air, as though the spirits of those who had perished in this place were begging with the last of their strength for Ahkin and Mayana not to enter.

"Keep your knife out," he warned. He balanced his own in his left hand, feeling like a shadow of his former self—the warrior who could cut his way across a battlefield.

"I'm not good with a knife," Mayana complained.

"We'll need to remedy that. I can show you some basic skills. But at least keep it out in case you need to need to summon water. It can be as powerful as any blade."

"True, I've taken out a jaguar with water before."

Ahkin raised an eyebrow but didn't ask. There was a lot about the daughter of water he needed to learn, but oh, Ometeotl, if he was honest with himself, he still *wanted* to. He didn't care that they were so different. Mayana had shown him exactly how brave and strong and resourceful she was. She was tender, so tender, but that didn't take away from her strength. It gave her a different sort of strength, one he was beginning to worry he sorely lacked.

But in every challenge they'd faced so far, he seemed to have come up short of what she needed from him. But perhaps there was a way to prove, brutalized hand or not, that he could at least show her the strength of *his* heart. How everything he was, from his obsessive planning to his tendency to take everything onto his own shoulders, was because he *cared* as much as she did. Deeply. Passionately. He cared about protecting his people. And protecting her. Even if that meant she escaped this place and he did not.

He just wished he had what it took to succeed at fulfilling those deep desires. He wished he had what it took to earn back her favor.

"No matter what happens in this forest, promise me you'll run if I tell you to."

Her eyebrows dipped down, and she opened her mouth to argue.

"Promise me, Mayana."

She narrowed her eyes at him but didn't respond. It didn't sit well with his stomach.

"Mayana—"

"You know I won't," she snapped.

Ahkin sighed in defeat. "I know."

They strode with purpose toward the line of dead trees, and the mists enveloped them.

Stars blinked into existence above Yemania's head, and she wished she could go to bed and forget this evening ever happened. The stone seat of the bench was cool beneath her, but her skin felt as though it were on fire. Even the sweet aromas of blooming night flowers and the trickling water of the tiled fountains did little to ease her spirit. At least she had gotten permission from Metzi to start preparing remedies for the commoners of Tollan, even if it was Ochix who had been the one to help her make it happen.

She stared up at the twinkling specks of light, wondering if the gods that lived there were laughing at her. Of all the men in all the empires of the world, she had to care for a death demon. A death demon prince. A death demon prince now engaged to her empress. Were the gods playing a cruel joke? They had to be. There was no other explanation.

The sound of sandals slapping against the stones of the garden's pathway pulled her out of her negative prayers. She looked up to see who else was walking through the gardens during the feast.

Of course. It was Ochix.

Her heart skipped a single beat before thundering on harder than it had been all night. "What are you doing here?"

"Here in the garden? Or here in Tollan?" he asked, the corner of his mouth curving up.

"I know why you're here in Tollan." She clasped her hands in her lap. "The entire empire probably knows by now."

"News travels that fast here in the valley?"

Yemania laughed humorlessly. He had no idea . . .

Ochix stopped just before the bench and lowered himself beside her. Heat radiated off him. Beneath the bone necklace, his bare chest glistened slightly from the exertion of dancing. She tried not to look at the planes of his stomach. When she failed, she told herself it was purely to assess his injury.

"Your stomach seems to be healing nicely."

Ochix boomed a laugh. "Of course, you'd notice that."

Yemania shrugged. She couldn't muster the playful spirit she'd had in the jungles. The events of the night had crushed it out of her.

Ochix seemed to sense it because his demeanor shifted to one that was more serious. "I'm sorry, Yemania."

"What do you have to be sorry for?"

"That you found out this way."

Yemania scrunched her eyebrows together. "How else could I have found out?"

Ochix sighed and ran a hand through his dark, flowing hair. "I should have told you in the jungles. The reason my father and I got into a fight. What I had confronted him about."

"That was about marrying Metzi?" Yemania felt breathless.

"The entire arrangement was his idea. He dispatched the offer as soon as the empress canceled her engagement and the storm lords declared war. He saw it as his chance to get one of his sons on the throne in Tollan."

Yemania nodded slowly. "And Metzi finally agreed."

"Two days ago. I knew if I returned to Omitl that my father would press the issue again. I am the oldest of my three brothers. And by far the most handsome."

Yemania snorted. "You're impossible. Why didn't you stand up to him? Just say no?"

Ochix gave her an amused half smile, pointing to the scar on his abdomen. "I tried. Remember? The stabbing? The falling? The washing up on the riverbank half dead?"

"Right," Yemania whispered, her cheeks warming.

Ochix chuckled to himself, crossing a leg over his knee.

"Shouldn't you be back inside? Dancing with your . . ." but she couldn't say it.

"Dancing isn't my idea of fun." His dark eyes glittered like the shining shell of a beetle.

"You seem to dance well for someone who doesn't enjoy it."

"Were you watching me, daughter of healing? Or should I say, High Healer of Tollan?"

Yemania smacked his shoulder. "No, I wasn't *watching* you. I just noticed. In passing. In fact, maybe it wasn't even you I'm thinking of."

"Sure," Ochix said, rolling his eyes. "And why weren't you dancing? Surely there are many young men eager to join a woman of such talent and beauty in the ritual celebratory dances?"

Yemania gave him a flat look. "Really? Do you actually say those things to girls?"

Ochix's smile turned wicked. "Only the special ones."

"Ha," Yemania scoffed. "Save them for your soon-to-be wife then, prince of death."

"Prince of death," he mused. "That's better than death demon, at least."

"Ugh," Yemania groaned. "Why do you have to be so irritating?"

"I can't help it. You're fun to tease."

Her heart couldn't handle another minute of this. "Well, the teasing has to stop. You are betrothed. To the *empress*. It probably isn't even wise for you to be seen out here with me."

Ochix shrugged his wide shoulders. "I don't care what people think."

Yemania closed her eyes tightly. She couldn't look at him, at the burning fire she knew was smoldering in his eyes. "Well, I do. Trust me, Metzi's wrath is not something I want to bring down on either of us."

"Who says Metzi has to know? Who says anyone has to know? I haven't been able to stop thinking about the beautiful, caring healer who saved my life even though I was her enemy. The girl who talked with me for hours about life and love and matters of the spirit. All I could think when my father told me I was going to Tollan was that I might get the chance to see her again."

Her breath came sharp and ragged. It stung to even hear these words on his lips.

"How can you say those things to me? Do you have any idea how hard—" She couldn't do this anymore. She stood up to stomp away from him, away from her own breaking heart.

But she couldn't. It was as if he had become a dark moon pulling her into his orbit. She couldn't force herself away. She turned, and he took a step closer. His arms reached up and gently traced her shoulders. He was so close her heart practically threw itself out of her chest. His warmth seeped into her. His hand moved up to trace the side of her face.

She tried to turn away, a single tear trailing down her cheek. Ochix wiped it away with his thumb.

"Tell me you don't feel anything for me, Yemania. Tell me and I'll go back inside right now."

She couldn't say it. She couldn't even look him in the eyes.

"Tell me you feel nothing."

A shiver ran through her, more tears joining the first on her cheeks.

"You know I can't say that," she whispered finally.

"I know," he said.

Maybe it was the husky tenor of his voice, or the desire burning but restrained behind his eyes. She knew he wouldn't go any further than she wished. He truly would walk away if she told him to . . . but she couldn't stand the thought of it.

She leaned up on the tips of her toes, and kissed him.

It was unlike anything Yemania had ever experienced. Ochix responded to her enthusiasm in kind, claiming her mouth as though it would only ever be his. She'd never kissed a boy before but had always dreamed of what it would be like to have soft lips against her own, that sense of desire, of urgency, of *needing*. Her heart swelled to capacity, filling parts of herself she hadn't even known were empty. He tightened his arms around her, a soft groan escaping his throat.

Her arms slid up and around his neck, pulling him closer. She gasped as he broke the kiss and trailed his lips along her jaw, his fingers now digging into her back as though he couldn't hold her tight enough. Her toes curled against the stones beneath her feet, savoring the new sensations, the feelings coursing through her—

Somewhere nearby a monkey howled so loudly, it broke through the barriers of whatever world they had created for themselves. Yemania wrenched herself out of his arms. And not a moment too soon. A servant appeared from behind a row of bushes, rushing past with a basket of fruits balanced in her arms. She paid them no mind as she hurried past, but it was enough to bring Yemania down from the euphoric clouds she had been dancing on.

"I'm sorry," she said, pressing her fingers against her now throbbing lips. "I have to go. I can't—Ochix, I'm sorry."

Then she ran. Just as she had when he held the raiders in place so she could escape. She ran as hard as she had then, sure her very life depended on it now as much as it had that day.

She reached her room and stopped before her hanging red curtain. Her hands gripped the doorway to steady herself, her breath coming in gasps.

What was she thinking, kissing him like that in one of the palace's gardens? Anyone could have seen them. A servant almost did. For all she knew, someone else *did* see them, and Metzi could be planning to have her punished at this very moment.

Yemania pressed a hand against her chest, as if she could hold the pieces together if she pushed hard enough. She gave herself a few moments for the pain to wash over her and ebb back to where she could contain it. One deep breath. Two. Three.

Straightening finally, she threw aside the curtain to her room. She'd get started on some simple recipes to show Coatl in the morning. Then he could begin replicating as soon as possible. That should distract her mind enough.

But she wasn't alone in her room when she entered.

Coatl was already waiting for her, sitting on her bed. His curled hair was unruly, sticking out at odd angles from where he'd likely run his hands through it. His eyes were as red as the wrap around his waist and swimming with ghosts. She was not the only one trying to hold the pieces of their heart together.

"She's marrying someone else." His voice was hollow, void of the usual swagger. "After everything we—" His head dropped back into his hands. Yemania knew he was grieving the loss of not only Metzi's love, but the future he had envisioned for them. For himself. He would no longer rule the Chicome by her side. Part of Yemania thanked the gods above for that.

She barely had the strength to keep herself together, let alone Coatl. So instead of consoling him with words, she did the only thing she could think of. She dropped down beside him and wrapped her arms around him. Her healer's heart knew he didn't need words right now.

Coatl did not make a sound. He embraced her back, shaking at the effort to keep his emotions contained. Yemania let her own tears leak out onto her cheeks.

They held on to each other, her broken heart finding solace in knowing she wasn't alone anymore. Coatl hugged her tighter, finally letting the agony wash over him.

And perhaps her heart was not the only one finding healing.

The forest made Mayana's skin crawl. She felt as though thousands of tiny millipedes were running across her arms and legs. She swore the beasts, whatever they were, were watching them, lurking beyond the range of her vision. Every sound, every snapping twig beneath Ahkin's sandal made her jump, sure that claws or fangs were about to dig into her back.

Ona hunkered low, prowling as if he, too, knew the dangers of what waited for them in the mists.

A long, drawn-out scream of agony sounded in the distance, and Mayana wanted to scream herself. Were they tortured spirits trying to make their way to the City of the Dead? Or other living souls trapped down here like they were? It was possible. Legend said that if you dove too deeply in a cenote, you might accidentally fall into Xibalba. That water connected the layers like doorways. The sinkhole in Tollan and the cave entrance in Miquitz were the only direct entrances she knew of.

"What happens if we reach the city?" she whispered. She stayed close enough behind Ahkin that she could reach out and touch his back with her fingertips.

"We will likely meet with the Lord of the Dead and his council," Ahkin whispered over his shoulder.

"His council? He doesn't rule Xibalba by himself?"

"No. Cizin, sometimes called One Death or Ah Puch, is the leader, but there are eleven other lords that all oversee a different form of human suffering."

How pleasant. Mayana grimaced. "Different forms of human suffering?"

Ahkin held up a hand for silence. Ona tensed, his ears erect. Mayana's pulse pounded faster. Was it a beast?

He looked around, and after several tense moments, must have decided they were safe. "It's said that each of the lords of Xibalba has dominion over the different types of suffering and can actually inflict them. Sickness, starvation, terror, destitution. Cizin himself inflicts the final death."

Mayana swallowed hard. "That sounds lovely. And we have to negotiate with them?"

Ahkin shrugged. "I'm guessing. I don't really know. I've read they like to humiliate those who make it to the city, that they can sometimes challenge them to prove their worthiness to escape. But again, there aren't many details. Very few have ever—escaped."

"Maybe they're scared of worms," she teased, referencing the tiny worm in the walnut shell the Mother goddess had given Ahkin. After she had realized the purpose of the doll, Mayana was confident the worm would somehow play an equally essential role in their escape. She just had no idea how yet.

They continued on through the mist, trees materializing in front of them as the mist grew into a thick fog, making it impossible to see more than a few steps ahead at a time.

Mayana's breathing became shallower, panic clenching at her stomach. She rubbed her throat, as if that would help her draw in more breath.

Something dark and shining scuttled across the forest floor in front of them. Mayana froze. It appeared so quickly out of the fog, then disappeared equally as fast. *No. It couldn't be.* It must have been a creation of her own mind. Of course wandering Xibalba, "the place of fear," would bring thoughts of her greatest fear of all.

But then another appeared. Ona barked and snapped at it with his teeth bared. A barbed tail angled up over the shell of its armored body. Eight long legs, two tipped in pinching claws. A scorpion. A black one as big as her hand.

Mayana screamed and launched herself into Ahkin's arms. Not a scorpion. Anything, *anything*, but a scorpion.

She could feel the memory of the piercing pain in her leg, the poison burning its way through her veins, the numbness of her tongue, and the loss of sound and sight. The scorpion Zorrah had sent to her room to kill her had come so close to succeeding. The only reason she survived had been Yemania. She felt a jolt of sadness at the thought of her friend. Yemania had saved her, gotten her to Coatl so that he could drain the poison. Yemania apologized later that she only healed Mayana enough to get her to Coatl, thinking him the superior healer. Yemania always lacked confidence. All it had done was trap the poison in her system. But Mayana didn't fault her. She knew Yemania could have healed her on her own had she believed in herself. She had saved her life, and for that, Mayana would be forever grateful. Did Yemania think her dead now? She wished there was some way to tell her she wasn't.

But when it came to scorpions, Mayana would rather have her heart eaten out of her chest by an unknown beast. Or even drown in a river of blood. Giant snakes. Mountain monsters. Demon children. None of them terrified her as much as this wicked little creature. She felt all her strength dissolve into sand.

She buried her face into Ahkin's chest. His solid strength steadied her. But the memories of that night flashed over and over again in her head until she was sure they'd drive her to insanity.

"Mayana, what—? Oh." He must have seen the scorpion too. His arms instantly wrapped around her, holding her together as sheer terror washed over her in waves. She wanted to cry, scream, run. But at the same time, it was embarrassing to fear such a small threat. She tried to remind herself that at least this one wasn't possessed by the spirit of another princess who wanted her dead.

"I'm—I'm—" Her teeth began to chatter, and she couldn't finish.

"I'm here. You're okay." Ahkin rubbed her back in long, smooth strokes.

"I—hate—scorpions."

He pulled her back into a tight embrace. "I know." His wrecked hand gently cupped the back of her head.

She breathed in the scent of him, somehow rain and sun and incense all mixed together. She listened to the steady beating of his heart, like a pounding worship drum. She tightened her grip on her satchel, letting the presence of her mother's bones wash over her as well. Slowly, slowly, her heart rate calmed. The tingling in her fingers subsided as she took a deeper breath.

She pulled back from Ahkin, her breath hitching. She lifted her eyes to meet his, and something inside her cracked at the concern and desire that burned within them.

"Are you all right?" he asked, his voice deep and low. His breath mingled with hers, and her heart rate started to climb again for entirely different reasons. "I can go crush it for you if you want."

Mayana nodded vigorously. Ahkin's chest swelled at the chance to prove himself, and it almost made her laugh. She might have, if she wasn't so close to crying. He stepped toward the armored little demon and lifted his shield. She closed her eyes. With a sickening crunch that Mayana felt to her core, Ahkin obliterated it. An incredible rush of affection washed over her.

"Thank you," she said, her voice as wobbly as her legs.

He ducked his head. "It's the least I could do after you saved me from . . . well, pretty much everything else."

She reached up and placed her hand on the side of his face, rubbing her thumb along the line of his cheekbone. "I mean it. Thank you." She stood on her tiptoes and gently pressed her lips to his. Quick, and brief, but heartfelt nonetheless. Ahkin closed his eyes and made a sound deep in his throat, as if it caused him physical pain to restrain himself.

Mayana smiled and pressed her lips against his again, more firmly this time. Ona whined and pushed against her leg, trying to force his way between them, but she ignored him. Ahkin's chest seemed to tremble beneath her fingertips, and she deepened the kiss. Ahkin groaned and finally released whatever holds he had placed on himself. His good hand plundered her hair, her back, covering her skin with his fingers and trailing fire behind in their wake. Mayana pressed herself tighter against him. They may be opposites, but for a brief moment, they were entirely one.

Ona barked loud and sharp. They broke apart. The dog growled in impatience, not wanting to be ignored. Mayana giggled. "I'm sorry, boy. I still love you too."

"Too?" Ahkin asked her, fierce hope again blazing in his eyes.

Mayana sighed. There was no point in denying it. "Yes, I love him *too*. Because as much as I hate to admit it, he's not the only one I love."

Ahkin arched a playful brow and pulled her close again. "Oh really? And who else do you love?"

"Coatl. Obviously," Mayana said, rolling her eyes.

"Oh good. And here I was thinking that perhaps you loved me. It would be more convenient, though, considering I'm pretty sure I love you."

Warmth pooled inside her as she kissed him again. Once. Twice. The third one lingered enough that Ona barked to make them stop.

Mayana started to laugh, but then she noticed it—another scorpion crawling along after its fallen brother.

She jumped into Ahkin's arms again as the mist around them started to clear—not entirely, just enough to see the horror that lay before them.

The air emptied from Mayana's lungs. If she had been afraid of a single scorpion, her body could barely register what it experienced now. It was as if she had left her body entirely and was watching the scene from outside herself. It didn't feel real. Because surely nothing on any level of creation would be *this* evil . . .

Before them stretched another river, but instead of flowing with water or blood, the river teemed with black.

Black shells. Black claws. Black stingers.

They now had to cross a *river* of *scorpions*.

"Why can't I go down to the soldier training fields with you?" Coatl pouted.

"Because I promised Metzi to keep you busy with the remedies for the commoners. I'm sure she will be down there overseeing everything, and you need to stay away from her. For both of your sakes."

Coatl grimaced at the rows of tiny clay pots lined up across the stone tables. He picked one up and swirled its contents several times. Jars filled with herbs and mixtures lined the stone shelves of the High Healer's workroom. Yemania had spent hours smelling and inspecting every one. She felt like a child who had entered a marketplace stall full of toys and treats. Coatl groaned and dropped the pot with a clatter. "Can't we get a servant to do this?"

Yemania cut him a look.

"Fine." He lifted his hands in surrender and then flourished them in an elegant bow. "I'll get to work, most gracious High Healer."

"You're an irritating little gnat when you don't get what you want, you know that?" Yemania teased.

Coatl waved her off.

Yemania laughed to herself, grateful she'd found a way to make sure Coatl could stay with her. She didn't know what she would do without him here. Especially given the rising tensions in the capital.

The City of Storms had declared itself independent of the Chicome Empire—and promised swift retribution should Tollan attempt to take back control.

Metzi did not like to give up control.

With a sigh of determination, Yemania squared her shoulders and marched down the stone steps toward the training fields. She had set up a medical tent to see to the accidental injuries of the soldiers as they practiced. She also didn't want to be too far away from Metzi, who had insisted on overseeing the training alongside the other military advisors.

"An emperor is a warrior who understands the importance of protecting his empire. I don't see why an empress should be any different," she'd said, staring down the head of the Eagle warriors at the council meeting.

Yemania couldn't help but agree.

Ehecatl was an important asset to the empire, being the only city-state located on the coast. Yemania remembered her father trading with the city for fish and shells and other resources. Like every city-state, its inhabitants paid tribute to the capital with sacrifices. But it wasn't only Ehecatl's resources that the Chicome valued. It was also their responsibility to perform the rituals that prevented the world from succumbing to a great storm.

Their patron god, Ehecatl, was the wind aspect of the creator god Quetzalcoatl. In the age before their own, the sixth sun had been destroyed be a terrible storm. Quetzalcoatl, in the form of Ehecatl, descended to the realms of the underworld and retrieved the bones of humanity. With the sacrifice of his own blood, he brought humanity back to life in the caves of creation and set their current sun, the Seventh Sun, into motion. Legend said that he was the most-loved son of Ometeotl, and that his death had broken her heart more than any of the other gods and goddesses who had given their lives before him. The City of Storms believed that Ometeotl promised to bring her beloved son back from the underworld to rule the cosmos by her side. And then they—his descendants—would eventually rule the empire instead of Tollan.

And so they awaited his return, begrudging the other rituals the Chicome believed essential for their survival. If it weren't for the firm hand of Tollan ensuring their compliance, Ehecatl would forsake the rituals outlined in the codex entirely, focusing only on their worship of Quetzal-coatl and preparing for his return. Preparing for their favored treatment and eventual ascent to power over them all.

Yemania wasn't exactly sure what she believed about Ehecatl's role in the empire anymore, not now that Mayana had planted that seed of doubt about the rituals in the back of her mind.

Metzi and her advisors were absolutely clear in their stance. The call to arms had gone out the moment the storm lords declared war. Citizens of Tollan and the closer city-states to the capital—Atl, Ocelotl, and Millacatl—had been conscripted into service. Papatlaca requested not to send forces because of the distance, but instead supplied wagonloads of obsidian weapons they created at the volcano. The soldiers now arrived in droves, gathering in Tollan's garrisons for further training before making the march to the sea.

And now, thanks to Metzi, Miquitz would be contributing forces as well. Even the council had resentfully acknowledged the benefit of having the death demons fighting alongside them. And because of a tentative truce between the empires, Millacatl could shift its focus away from defending its borders to assist in the campaign.

Yemania had no doubt Ehecatl's rebellion would be crushed swiftly.

The training fields situated between the barracks of the various warrior cults had become a sort of camp. Most of the gathered army was being housed in the temple precinct, but the professional warriors rotated through their military exercises in groups. Almost every male in the empire received a basic form of training as a child, and in some city-states like Ocelotl and Papatlaca, every female as well. But for some, it had been so long that their skills needed to be sharpened before such a substantial campaign.

Yemania was nervous at first about having so many strangers from across the empire housed in the city, but she was surprised by the level of discipline. If a soldier was caught so much as stealing, he or she was executed immediately.

She hurried along behind the House of Eagles, the elegant gold-and-stone barracks and training facilities for Tollan's elite warrior force. When she emerged onto the training field that spread out between the House of Eagles and the House of Jaguars, she could see that the exercises were well underway. The field spread out as large as the plaza back in her home city, and though it had probably once been green with grass, thousands of feet had trampled it to a dusty brown. Her healing tent was set up beside another tent where Metzi watched from the comfort of a wooden throne lined with cushions.

Yemania couldn't help it; she scanned the field for Ochix. There were soldiers practicing with arrow launchers and bows, weavers preparing ceremonial battle costumes, weapons masters making repairs and organizing collections of shields, spears, clubs, and macana swords. All the while, Tlana priests in sweeping red robes wandered through the organized chaos, performing religious rites and rituals to bless the coming battle.

A glint of the Seventh Sun's light reflected off the long, dark hair of a warrior in a sparring pit, immediately drawing her attention.

Ochix.

He was directing some of the younger soldiers in blocking techniques. The young men stared at him with mouths agape, appearing to keep their distance from him. Likely the decades of tension between their empires prevented them from trusting him entirely. Yemania stopped where she stood to watch him, the thick bands of muscles along his arms and back tensing as he pretended to land a blow on one of the young men's upheld shields. He seemed so focused, so impassioned as he spoke.

"Yemania, come sit by me," Metzi called from her tent, indicating an empty cushion beside her. "You can heal if you are needed, but for now, come enjoy the shade."

Yemania did as she was commanded. She definitely didn't mind escaping the blazing heat. Her forehead was already sticky with sweat from the combination of the humidity and the unforgiving sun.

"When will the army depart for the coast?" she asked, settling on a cushion beside the empress.

"We don't know yet," Metzi said, her shrewd eyes narrowed at the warriors before her. "That's if they even have to go at all. We've sent negotiators to reason with Ehecatl, make them submit before they suffer worse consequences. I told them that if they offered me tribute, my forgiveness would be extended and Tollan would continue to protect them. We pointed out the many advantages for trade. They refused. So now we are trying to make them see that death and destruction are inevitable for their people if they do not submit. I offered to supply their rebel forces with fresh weapons, to show our confidence that we will not be defeated. The generals liked that idea. Hopefully it intimidates them into accepting a treaty. If not, we march and put an end to their little rebellion."

Yemania blinked several times. "That is a brilliant plan, Your Majesty."

"Of course it is. Everyone seems to be so surprised that I could possibly have a mind for strategy." Metzi tapped her fingers impatiently against her armrest.

"I'm not surprised in the slightest," Yemania said, her eyes again finding Ochix. He was now teaching the young soldiers ways to attack an enemy with the macana sword. His eyes lifted for a brief moment and found hers, a smile playing at his lips. Her stomach fluttered. "How are the warriors from Miquitz adjusting?"

Metzi sighed and rubbed her temple. Yemania made a mental note to make more tea for her persistent headaches. "The Chicome are still wary and generally keeping a safe distance. Not that I can blame them. But Ochix assures me they are well."

"Oh." Yemania clenched her hands together. "And how are things going with—with wedding preparations?"

Metzi closed her eyes and did not open them, continuing to rub at her temple. "We met with the matchmaker, Atanzah, this morning to discuss plans for the wedding festivities. Feasts, festivals, a separate celebration to be held in Miquitz itself. I guess it's actually happening." She didn't look remotely excited.

Yemania bit down on her lip to force herself to remain silent. She knew Metzi was acting on the orders of her advising goddess, that she didn't actually want to marry Ochix at all.

"And speaking of Ochix," Metzi said, jumping to her feet and looking concerned. "Are you all right, prince?"

Yemania wrenched her gaze upward to see Ochix limping toward them, a massive gash in his thigh oozing royal blood down the length of his leg. Footprints of blood trailed along behind him. A blade appeared to have cut right through the black fabric of his wrap and into his flesh.

"What happened?" Metzi scolded. Her eyes were already devouring the young men clustered in the sparring ring, probably wondering who she would have to punish.

"Don't worry," Ochix said through gritted teeth. "I'm sure your High Healer can patch me up right as rain."

"Um, yes. I can, let me—" Yemania scrambled to her feet as well, already reaching for the flap to enter the healing tent.

"Actually, do you have anything that can keep out infection before we heal the skin? I don't want to take any chances." Ochix winked at her, and Yemania immediately knew what he was trying to do.

"Yes, Yemania, take him back to the High Healer's quarters and make sure he's taken care of. The last thing I need to worry about right now is having to postpone the wedding to find another groom." Metzi frowned.

Yemania sighed, giving Ochix the nastiest look she could muster behind the empress's back. He only shrugged his shoulders in mock innocence and mouthed, *What?*

Yemania rolled her eyes. "Fine, follow me."

"With pleasure," Ochix said brightly, limping toward the palace alongside her.

This death demon was going to be the life or the death of her—Yemania just didn't know which yet.

Ahkin cursed the gods of the underworld for creating such a challenge. Of all the fears they could have created, they had to choose scorpions. He could see the blood slowly draining from Mayana's face.

There would be no wading across this river. Not unless they wanted to die extremely painful deaths.

Mayana's legs gave out, and she collapsed into him. He tried to steady her.

"That's not—that can't be—" she mumbled faintly. "You didn't say anything about a river of *scorpions*."

"I've never read about this," he said, breathless himself. How could the texts not have mentioned such a horrific trial? Maybe they did and he just forgot? How could he be so stupid to forget such a crucial piece of information?

"How can we get across it?" she asked, licking her lips.

"Can you float us across? With water from Atlacoya's amulet?"

Mayana tried to stand and wobbled again. Her breathing became quick but shallow. If she had been tortured by a single scorpion, how would she face a whole river?

Ahkin had seen soldiers suffer unseen injuries of the mind after facing battle. He himself struggled after Pech's death. Certain situations or sounds or even smells could cause perfectly brave men to suddenly curl into a fetal position. Their memories tortured them, and any reminder of what had scarred their minds brought them back to the place of terror they had known on the battlefield. Mayana seemed to be experiencing something similar. A scorpion had almost killed her during the selection ritual; then she spent days in a haze of poison and delirium. He could still see the scars of its barb marring the beautiful tanned skin of her leg.

But feeling that way didn't make her any less strong. She had overcome so much already. "You can do this," he told her.

Mayana nodded, only half listening. She absently reached for her knife and sliced into her palm. She opened her hand and closed her eyes, just as she had when the water had washed them clean of the river blood.

But this time, nothing emerged from the skull's mouth.

Mayana opened her eyes again, her chest heaving. She looked down at the necklace, her breathing growing more frantic.

"I—I can't. I can't find the will to summon it. It's like the waters are reacting to my fear." She turned to him with eyes wide and lost.

It stirred something primal within him.

"I'll find a way, Mayana. You've done so much already."

She curled into his side, hiding her face so that she couldn't see the river of terrors anymore. Ahkin wished he could do the same, but he couldn't let her down. Not this time.

What did he know about scorpions? He started to sort through everything he'd read, every lesson he'd had about nature from his tutors.

He could list off the colors of varying types. How to identify which ones were the deadliest. He knew about their habits. Scorpions ate other small insects. They liked water. They often hid in rotting leaves and wood . . .

And they loved darkness.

Scorpions often came out at night because they hated light!

Ahkin looked down at the shield of Huitzilopochtli, his smile widening. "I have an idea," he said.

He withdrew his blade and sliced into his ruined hand. He didn't need to crush them all. He needed a path forward. The river was not deep, only a layer or two of the creatures in a wide river ditch. Good. That would make this easier.

"Stay here with Ona," he said.

Mayana sank to her knees next to the dog, who cuddled into her and supported her with his weight.

Ahkin carefully inched his way closer to the teeming scorpions. He summoned light from the shield, from the faded light all around them, and pulled it all into one powerful beam. He directed the beam right into the scuttling blackness, burning and singeing as it made contact.

The scorpions instantly started to scuttle away from the light. He widened the beam, pushing them farther and farther until a path formed across the dirt.

"Mayana, there's a path. Come on!"

But Mayana remained where she was on the ground.

"You can do this, Mayana. I know you can. Think of everything you've survived so far. Everything you've done. You are the strongest woman I've ever met. And not just because of all you've faced, but because you have the courage to risk your heart over and over again. Caring and loving everyone and everything no matter the consequences. You have the heart of a warrior within you. Get up. You can do this!"

It was a speech he'd given new soldiers before battle, but he had never spoken them with as much conviction and passion as he did now.

Mayana met his gaze, terror warring with determination inside her eyes. "Go with me."

"I want to keep it safe enough for you. I'll be right behind you. If you want to save your mother, we have to escape. And we can't do that without crossing through."

At the mention of her mother, the determination in her eyes hardened. Her hand tightened on the strap of her bag and she rose shakily to her feet.

Ahkin's forehead dewed with sweat. He kept his focus on summoning the light. "You can do this. For your mother."

Mayana nodded once, firmly. Ona stood up too and leaned into her leg in solidarity.

"Don't look down at them, just run across. They hate light, and I'm keeping it hot enough that they should stay away, but it won't burn you. I'll hold them back, I promise."

Her feet pawed at the ground like a skittish deer, but her hand remained steady on the bag containing her mother's bones. She seemed to draw strength from them.

"All right," she said, her voice as hard as her eyes. "Join me on the other side as fast as you can."

"I will," Ahkin promised.

She took one more deep breath, and then sprang onto the path. He watched the muscles of her legs, the remains of her skirt flying around her. She was a glorious creation, inside and out. And after the kiss they had shared, he couldn't wait until when they were alone together again. He glanced down at Ona. Well, as alone as they could be here.

Ona's ears suddenly perked up and twitched. The hair on the dog's back raised as a growl rippled through him.

Mayana reached the other side and collapsed upon the sand, twisting around to see him, exhaustion and fear transitioning into a beaming smile of pride. She had faced her greatest fear and conquered it. Her hand motioned for him to follow, an invitation to join her.

Ona's growling beside him got louder, a defensive bark echoing through the mists around them. Mayana's smile slid from her face, replaced by a look of terror. She reached out to him across the distance. "Ahkin!"

Ahkin turned just in time to see the massive, spotted form of a jaguar materialize out of the mists behind him. It was unlike any creature Ahkin had ever seen. He had hunted the cats with his mentor, even killing one by himself as part of his training. Every Jaguar warrior had to prove himself by entering the jungle alone and returning with a pelt that would be used to create his warrior costume. But this jaguar was twice the size of the one he had killed in the jungles of Tollan. Typically, a cat would only stand as tall as his waist. This beast—now fixing him with its deadly yellow eyes—rose high above him. His own head only came to its shifting shoulders.

It opened its jaws and released a roar that shook the ground at Ahkin's feet. Even his bones rattled. Teeth as long as macana swords dangled within its maw.

The jaguar crouched, digging claws longer than Ahkin's knife into the black dirt. Its muscles bunched as it prepared to pounce.

Ahkin dodged to the side as the beast leapt, a clawed paw swinging around as it missed. Sharp points raked down his back, but he had moved enough that the cuts were not deep. He lost his focus. The path across the scorpions closed as his light faded, a mass of legs and claws and stingers flowing to fill in the space.

Ahkin cursed. His blood already exposed, he bent the light around himself. The cat let out a roar of frustration as it looked around, searching for the mouse that had suddenly disappeared.

It noticed Mayana on the opposite shore of the scorpion river. Mayana scrambled to her feet and bolted for the trees, hiding behind a dark, gnarled trunk.

The cat lowered onto its haunches, preparing to leap the distance across the river. Ona appeared out of nowhere, a mere beetle on the back of a wolf. Still, he dug his teeth into the leg of the jaguar, trying to pull its attention away from Mayana. The cat thrashed, swinging Ona free and sending him flying across the sand. Ahkin knew what he had to do.

He threw out his hand and opened the path across the river again. "Ona, go!" he roared at the dog. "Protect her for me."

Ona stumbled to his feet, searching for the source of Ahkin's voice before he darted across to the other side. Ahkin let the path close again.

He dropped his invisibility and waved his arms above his head, whistling to get the jaguar beast's attention.

The cat roared again. In the distance several more roars answered. There were more coming.

Ahkin looked across the space between them, to where Mayana's anxious face peered around the tree.

"I'll distract it away from you," he yelled. "Run!"

"No! Ahkin, I won't leave you!" she screamed back. "Don't you dare leave me alone while you try to be the hero!"

But he didn't give her the chance to argue further. The moment the cat's attention turned back to the easier target, he knew what he had to do to protect her.

"Ahkin! Don't! Please!"

He had to save her. If this was it, the moment where he could make sure she survived by sacrificing himself, he had to. He owed her that. The one thing he could do to rectify his sins.

Ahkin turned and ran into the forest, the sound of pounding paws on dirt behind him—and an unsaid goodbye still lingering on his lips.

CHAPTER

28

"I'm not leaving you alone with a death demon. Especially *that* death demon," Coatl hissed at her, eyeing the hanging curtain as though he could see through it to where Ochix waited inside.

"Coatl, it's fine. I promise. But I need to heal his leg before he bleeds out all over my workroom."

"Where am I supposed to go?"

Yemania clenched her teeth. She knew it was a bad idea, but . . .

"I actually need you to go down to the training fields. To have a healer close to Metzi—but don't you get any ideas about trying to convince her to take you back!" she added, seeing the joy that suddenly burst across his face, like the Seventh Sun breaking free from a bank of clouds.

Coatl launched himself down the hall, his long legs carrying him faster than Yemania could shout her warnings after him. "I mean it. You mess this up, I won't stick up for you when she sends you back to Pahtia!"

Unease settled in her stomach as he rounded the corner. Hopefully Metzi didn't bite his head off.

She pushed aside the curtain and entered. Her more pressing issue was the handsome death demon sprawled across the cushions on the floor of her workroom. Granted, he was bleeding all over them, but it still unnerved her to see him watch her the way he did. It made her acutely aware of how very alone they were. The memory of their kiss made her lips tingle.

She set to work crushing some alata leaves into a paste to prevent infection. "I can't believe you got an injury like this in training. Against inexperienced novices. How do you expect to hold your own on an actual battlefield?" She turned around and stuck out her hip—as her mother always did when giving a lecture.

To her surprise, Ochix laughed. "Oh, daughter of healing. I've seen more battlefields than you know. Believe me when I say you don't have to worry."

"Then what happened?" She perched a hand on her jutted hip.

Ochix shrugged. "I possessed one of the novice warriors and made him cut my leg to make it look like an accident."

Her mouth fell open. "Those poor boys had a right to be scared of you. Possessing them without their permission—"

But Ochix waved a dismissive hand. "He'll probably go back to the barracks and brag to all of his friends how he bested a demon prince. Trust me, I made the boy's day."

"But *why?*" Yemania picked up the bowl of alata paste and got down on her knees beside him. "Why would you make him cut you?"

Ochix lifted his wrap suggestively, exposing the butchered skin of his thigh. "I'll give you one guess, daughter of healing. You're a smart one. I'm sure you can figure it out." His smile was full of mischief.

Her cheeks raged with fire and she was tempted to slap him. "You're horrible."

"I like to think of myself as clever."

"Well, let's see how clever you think your little plan is when I start cleaning out your wound." She arched an eyebrow at him.

His smile faltered slightly.

To his credit, Ochix didn't scream when she slathered the alata leaf paste across his bloody gash. He did grit his teeth and groan as though he'd been stabbed again. Her fingers burned where they touched the skin of his leg.

"Not feeling so clever now, are we?"

"Depends. What can you do to distract me from the pain?" He reached up and twirled a lock of her hair around his finger. He tugged it gently, pulling her face toward his.

But Yemania pulled back. "No, no, no. I've got to stop the bleeding and then you're going right back down to the fields." She silently cursed the part of herself that wanted him to stay.

She pulled out her stingray spine and assessed the depth of the cut. She doubted a single drop of blood would contain enough power to heal such a significant injury. She reached for her small ruby-hilted dagger instead.

His eyes went wide at the knife. "It's that bad?"

Good. He should feel bad for making her waste her own blood for this dangerous little game he was playing. "Yes, it is. I can't heal it with a single drop. I'll need more."

Ochix's smile turned sheepish. "I'm sorry, I didn't mean to get hurt that badly. I just wanted a chance to see you again."

"You could see me fine from the training fields. From a distance."

"That's not enough for me," he said with a growl, making her pulse flutter.

Yemania cut a slice at the center of her palm and held her hand over the gaping skin. They were both silent for a moment as they watched the skin close back together. When she was finished, she wrapped a strip of cloth around her hand. She'd have Coatl heal it for her later.

"Where do you think this ends, Ochix? You're getting married in a little over a week. I'm not a servant that you can use on the side while you sneak around behind your wife's back. *That's* not enough for me. I am the High Healer of Tollan now. I deserve more than that."

Ochix dropped his gaze, his lips pursing tightly. "You're right. You do deserve more than that."

"No matter how much I don't want to say it, we can't do this"—she motioned her hand between them—"anymore. Whatever this is."

The tears were stinging her eyes again, but she forced them back. She had to appear strong in her conviction, before it crumbled into dust at their feet.

"What do you think would have happened? If I wasn't being forced to marry her?" he said wistfully, his dark eyes smoldering again.

Yemania's stomach clenched. "I don't know. You would still be in Miquitz. I'd be here. I don't think we were ever supposed to find each other." She folded her hands in her lap to stop them from trembling.

"I disagree. I think we found each other for a reason."

Yemania started to shake her head, but Ochix reached up and held her cheeks in his hands. "I'm a prince in my city as well, daughter of healing. I've had young women falling over themselves to impress me from the moment I picked up my first sword. Most only care about the title I carry, the power and influence they think they can get through some kind of match with me. Exactly what Metzi is using me for. But none of them, *none*, has ever held my attention the way you do. You don't care about my position. If anything, you despise it. I couldn't wrap my head around a young woman who would risk so much to save the life of someone she'd never met. Someone she had been trained her entire life to hate. And yet, all you saw when you found me was a soul worth saving. There's such purity in that, Yemania. Most would have run away and left me to die, but you didn't. I had to figure out why. I had to learn more about this curious sun worshipper that seemed to defy every one of my expectations. And then to see your passion for helping others, your beautifully wounded heart experiencing more in life than most should at your age, a heart that gives you so much tenderness and strength at the same time. I hated that you couldn't even see those things about yourself. I wanted you to see them." He swallowed hard. "I wanted to watch as you realized those things for yourself. Help you to see them if I could."

Oh gods, he would be the undoing of her. She couldn't tell him the reasons he had buried himself so deeply in her heart. His playfulness that made her want to laugh and scold him at the same time. The depth that allowed him to talk about things such as love and the purpose of life without shying away from such difficult questions. The strength that hung around him like an aura—the physical strength of a warrior, yes, but also the strength to stand up to his father for something he believed in, even to the point of jeopardizing his own life. The way he seemed to see her, *really* see her, when so many in her life had dismissed her for not living up to their expectations. He didn't make the fire for her that day in the jungles. He had let her struggle and encouraged her to do it herself, believing in her and telling her she could.

It was the kind of connection to another soul she only dreamed about, and she knew they were barely scratching the surface. What depths of the heart could they plumb together if they had the time to slowly learn and explore?

But they didn't. Not if they stayed here in Tollan. But where would they run? It was foolish to hope they were destined to be anything more than falling stars crossing paths before continuing on their separate journeys. She would remember him, though, remember the depths to which it was possible to feel connected to another human being. Perhaps if she was lucky, she would find it again someday.

But she couldn't put any of her thoughts into actual words. Not as beautifully as he just had, so instead, she said the only words she could think of. They were not her own—but they also were, in a sense. The words of her favorite poem had now become more hers than ever before . . .

> *"Because even a drawing cut in obsidian fades,*
> *and the green feathers, the crown feathers, of the quetzal*
> > *bird lose their color*
> *and even the sounds of the waterfall die out in the dry*
> > *season.*
> *So, we too, because only for a short while have you loaned*
> > *us to each other."*

Her voice broke at the end, and Ochix sucked in a shuddering breath.

She leaned toward him, the need to kiss him overwhelming her. It would be a kiss of goodbye, a kiss to release him back onto the path the gods had laid out before him.

He didn't stop her. The hands holding the sides of her face slid down to cup her neck as their lips met. Soft and sweet as the brush of a moth wing. But the taste of him ignited something within her, and Yemania wanted nothing more than to fan the feeling inside herself into flame. He pulled her onto his lap until she straddled him. She deepened the kiss, pressing herself against him in a way that felt entirely foreign yet achingly familiar. If she was going to say goodbye, she might as well do it properly.

Her fingers plunged into his long hair as his lips moved down her jaw to her throat. She pushed him back until he fell with a soft *flump* against the cushions, pulling her with him. Their lips met again with fevered intensity, his hands running trails of heat along the length of her back. He pulled at the strap of her dress and, with a rip, the fabric came apart to expose her bare shoulder. He pressed a kiss against the soft, tender skin at the nape of her neck and she shivered.

But then, a clatter of beads sounded behind them.

And Coatl's curse echoed around the small room.

CHAPTER

29

Ahkin did not stop running.

He wove through the trees like a night spirit, cutting back and forth to make it harder for the jaguar beast to follow him. His mind flashed back to his training under Yaotl on evading pursuing enemies. His eyes scanned the forest floor, the trees, looking for anything he could use to his advantage. But he couldn't see more than a few feet in front of him, the fog around him growing thicker the farther away from the river of scorpions he got. He wouldn't be able to outrun it for long, which meant he needed another option.

Something hard crunched beneath his foot. He looked down to find it trapped within the collapsed rib cage of a bleached white skeleton. All around him lay a graveyard of discarded bones, broken and jagged. Whatever jaws had devoured them had not been gentle.

"Ugh!" He shook his foot free, but an idea began to take shape. A trapping technique he'd seen hunters use for bigger game. It was all he had time to do. He gathered as many of the sharpest slivers he could find. Femurs splintered in half, ribs protruding like broken teeth. There wouldn't be time to dig a hole, but he didn't need to kill it, just incapacitate it enough for him to escape. He set his trap between two trees, ensuring the beast had no path forward except through. He jammed an armful of bones into the earth, where they stuck out like spearpoints waiting for flesh. Now all he had to do was make sure the beast ran across them. The sound of thudding paws grew closer.

He positioned himself on the other side and waited. When its spotted fur and golden eyes came into view, he raised his arms and yelled. The jaguar lowered itself into a hunting crouch and slinked toward him. Ahkin darted between the trees, knowing it would trigger its need to chase. Sure enough, the beast leapt toward him, but the moment its paws crossed the tree line, it suddenly drew back with a roar of pain. Ahkin didn't stay to watch the beast try and pry the bone shards from its wounded paw. He bolted back toward the scorpion river.

Another roar made his teeth rattle, and he swore his heart was trying to break free from his chest and run ahead of him. More roars sounded. The thud of multiple sets of paws.

The beast was no longer alone in its hunt.

Ahkin muttered a curse. He couldn't lead them all back to the river—to Mayana. He'd need to lead them in the opposite direction. So with a growing sense of dread, he turned and ran deeper in the heart of the forest instead.

The growling and pounding now began to engulf him, sounding all around instead of just behind. They were trying to corner him, surround him, and cut him off from escape. He thought of the broken skeletons littering the forest floor and a shiver of panic ran through him. If he did not figure out another plan fast, he would soon join them.

Something large and dark loomed through the mist ahead of him. He froze for the length of a breath, afraid it might be another fresh horror of Xibalba. But his moment of hesitation cost him. He turned just as one of the beasts pounced, claws raking across his chest and stomach. Searing pain overwhelmed his senses. Hot blood gushed down his torso. These cuts were not as shallow as those on his back. His flesh had torn apart to expose muscle and sinew. His good fist clenched, and a bright light shone from the shield of Huitzilopochtli, right into the jaguar's amber-colored eyes. It howled in pain and threw itself back, pawing at its face.

Ahkin pressed his hands against the wounds, knowing it would not be enough to staunch the bleeding. He stumbled, head swimming. He had to keep moving. What lay ahead remained a mystery, but behind him was certain death. He could not let these beasts rip his heart from his chest, though they had certainly come close.

A rocky outcropping materialized through the mist, jutting out of the ground and littered with boulders around its base. Ahkin headed straight for it. Perhaps if he could wedge himself into a space they could not reach . . .

He dodged between the bigger boulders, his eyes scanning for any crevice or hole big enough for him to squeeze himself into. A low fissure ran along the base of the solid black stone. It was tall enough for a small child to walk beneath, but definitely too small for the monstrous jaguars closing in around him. He counted one, two, three of them now. He threw himself beneath the ledge, dragging himself deeper into the crevice as claws raked against the stone opening, snapping jaws attempting to reach him underneath the rock.

He hit the back wall of the fissure and flipped onto his back, gasping for breath as the beasts continued to prowl outside. His hands were sticky with his own blood, which now coated him as thoroughly as if he had gone swimming in the River of Blood again.

The edges of his vision began to blur, and his pulse pounded inside his ears. His breathing increased. He had to calm himself before he went into shock and his body began to shut down.

But he couldn't.

There was no way out. The moment he left this crevice, the jaguars would consume him like a deer carcass. They would leave his bones to bleach upon the forest floor like the skeletons he'd stumbled across. The truth of his situation washed over him. *One of you will not survive.* He was going to die here. Bleed to death beneath the rocks.

He would never see Mayana again.

He hoped she had managed to get away. He slammed a fist against the dirt floor. He hadn't even managed to get her safely to the City of the Dead. Failed. He had failed her, again and again and again.

He deserved to die here, to rot in the underworld. His mistakes, his inability to handle his responsibilities. Everything came back to him. His shoulders that hadn't been strong enough to hold the burden of his birthright. The shame burned far worse than the flame of any fire. He was sick with it.

He curled into himself, a turtle trying to protect its fragile underbelly, and waited for the darkness to claim him as he bled out.

———

A cold hand touched his shoulder, and Ahkin jerked awake. Outside, the massive spotted paws of the prowling leopards continued to pace, long tails twitching with impatience.

He looked up, expecting to see the Lord of the Dead come to lead his soul away from his body. What he did not expect to see was . . .

His father.

Emperor Acatl sat beside him, the feathered headpiece he wore as translucent as the silvery tone of his skin. His face was just as Ahkin remembered it: lightly lined, wide and friendly, beads of jade inlaid in his front two teeth. Necklaces of ghostly feathers and beads hung around his neck.

Ahkin scrambled to sit up but hissed in pain at the wounds on his chest.

"Don't move so quickly, son, you'll do more damage."

"I'm not dead yet?"

Emperor Acatl fixed him with mournful eyes. "No, you are not dead yet."

"But I will be soon?"

His father did not answer, only smiled and drank in the sight of his son. "You have been so strong. I am proud of you."

Ahkin felt as though claws had sunk into his heart. He dropped his head. His father had come to welcome him into the realm of spirits. "You shouldn't be. I failed you. I failed Mayana. Everyone in the empire."

The emperor cocked his head to the side. "Why do you think that is?"

"So you don't deny that I've failed everyone?" The confirmation felt painfully hollow in his stomach. Of course his father agreed. It was obvious he had.

His father sighed heavily. "My son. There is still so much you have to learn—"

"I know, I was never ready to—"

"Let me finish, boy." Acatl smiled with teasing exasperation. "Do you know why I was such a successful emperor?"

"You were an accomplished warrior. You always knew the right decisions to make. You always knew exactly what to do, and everyone trusted you because they knew you would take care of them."

"No, Ahkin. You fail to understand. You have not been able to carry the burden of so much responsibility by yourself, because you were never meant to carry it *by* yourself."

Ahkin sucked in a painful breath. "I don't understand."

"Obviously." His father winked. "You think everything depends on you. Your choices, your actions. You take the weight of the world onto yourself. You try to study and plan and prepare and predict, and yet you fail because you still have not learned the most important lesson I wanted to teach you."

Ahkin's eyes stung. He tried to blink it away. He hadn't learned enough after all.

"The world is a terrifying place. Cruel. Unforgiving. But I was a great emperor because I learned I did not have to do it alone. I had a council of those I trusted. Advisors and delegates to help me make those decisions. You should know that yourself as a soldier. You can face the fiercest battles not because you aren't afraid, but because your brothers are by your side. They give you the courage to charge. But more than that, I felt whole in myself because I had found my true duality, and we ruled the empire *together*."

"Your duality?"

"Yes. My duality. The complement to my soul. Your duality is another human to connect with you on the most intimate of levels. To know you as no one else knows you, to accept you for who you really are. To teach you what no one else can teach you. A cord made of a single strand is easily broken, but a cord made with two is much stronger. If one falls, there is another there to lift them up. We as humans are not designed to be solitary creatures."

Ahkin nodded, lost in thought. "Mother was your duality?"

"Yes, your mother was and *is* the complement to my soul. I have not found her yet here in Xibalba, but her spirit calls to me, and I will not complete this journey until I have found her."

"So I must find a wife? Is that why our ancestors enacted the selection ritual?"

"Yes." But the emperor slowly shook his head, making the necklaces around his neck rattle. "And no. It is bigger than finding a spouse. What matters is finding the one who teaches you what you must learn, who challenges you, makes you the best possible version of yourself. They become the safe harbor your ship can return to no matter how intense the storms on the sea. Be that through love, or even friendship, or an advisory role. They are the second cord to your rope, the strand that makes you that much stronger.

"Our ancestors knew the best emperors led in communion with another soul, whatever that might look like. We are not meant to be alone in this world. The Mother created us to live as she exists, in communion, in duality. It is how we find balance. The original selection ritual was designed to help the emperor find *not* a wife, but his duality."

Ahkin swallowed hard and whispered, "Mayana."

His father smiled. "Yes, I like that one."

Ahkin made a sound somewhere between a laugh and a sob. "So do I."

"Then why have you not allowed her to be the duality she was created to be? You have tried to take all control and responsibility, and it has nearly been your downfall."

His father was right. Wasn't that what Mayana had been telling him all along? That he didn't have the control he thought he did. That he needed to learn to let go and trust her too. To overcome challenges together.

Ahkin felt the emotion rising in his chest, and he beat it back down. "But it's too late now. I'll never see her again. I'm probably going to join you in your underworld journey before nightfall." He looked down at the shredded skin of his chest and stomach. He could already feel his head getting heavier and his thoughts sluggish from the loss of blood.

"I think your duality will not let you fail. And you will make sure she does not fail either." His father winked again and started to drift toward the opening of the fissure.

"Wait! Father, don't go."

But his father continued to drift away. "I do not need to stay, my son.

Because this is not yet your end. You are not alone. You never were, and if you are smart, you never will be."

He smiled again, the warm, reassuring smile that Ahkin had known his entire life. The smile he would never forget.

And then he was gone.

A wave of emotion crashed over him. A few tears leaked onto his cheeks, but he swiped them away, likely smearing his face with his own blood.

Outside the crevice, one of the jaguars suddenly roared in frustration. A blast of water knocked it off its feet.

The darkness Ahkin had been fighting to press back finally clouded his vision.

CHAPTER

30

Her brother had seen them.

Yemania was suddenly filled with a different kind of fire, a burning, sickly shame that made her already flaming cheeks even hotter. She and Ochix scrambled apart, Yemania slipping slightly on the shifting cushions as she straightened herself. She lifted the corner of her dress to cover the bare part of her shoulder that was showing.

Ochix's chest was heaving, and she swore his fingers twitched toward the ruby-hilted blade left on the floor.

Coatl crossed the room in three long strides and yanked Yemania to her feet.

Glaring at Ochix, he snarled, "Is this how you behave in Omitl? Taking advantage of any woman you come across?"

"Coatl! No!" Yemania tried to get in front of him, to pull his attention away from Ochix.

"I knew you death demons were evil, the dregs of hell come to plague the good and honest people of this empire. You should all be sent back to the pits of the underworld you crawled out from," he spat. "I'll go to Xibalba myself before I let Metzi marry someone like you. Before I let you hurt my sister."

Ochix slowly stood, his hands up, palms exposed to Coatl. "This isn't what it looks like, sun worshipper. I wasn't taking advantage of her." He paused and swallowed hard. "I love her."

Coatl laughed bitterly. "Death demons don't know what love is. You aren't even capable of it." The crazed look in her brother's eyes sent a thrill of fear through her. She had to calm this down before—

Ochix's eyes hardened into cold, black stone. "I know more about love than you ever will, you termite. Letting your own sister be chosen as a sacrifice like some common beast? Maybe you should have spent more time acting like a true brother instead of being a princess's plaything. Don't think I haven't seen your jealous stares and sorry attempts to win back a woman who doesn't even want you anymore. You're pathetic."

Something in Coatl snapped. Her brother launched himself at Ochix and the two collided with the force of two warring jungle cats. Coatl swung his fists, making contact anywhere he could reach. Ochix blocked his blows over and over, seeming to be more concerned with containing him than fighting him back.

Panic flooded through Yemania, and she felt her heart pounding inside her skull. "Stop!" she screamed. "Stop it!"

Her brother's pampered palace life began to show as Ochix managed to grab one of Coatl's wrists and force his arm behind his back. Coatl screamed in frustration as the death prince forced him to his knees and wrapped a thick, muscled arm around his throat. Blood dripped from a cut along Coatl's chin, and a black shadow was forming under Ochix's left eye. Both of them were covered in tiny cuts and abrasions.

"Stop," Ochix commanded in a voice so fierce it actually made Yemania take a step back. "I will not fight you anymore."

"Good," Coatl panted, lifting his elbow and slamming into Ochix's stomach, right over the pinkish scar where he had been stabbed.

Ochix grunted and doubled over in pain. Coatl scuttled across the floor like a frenzied crab and closed his fingers around the ruby hilt of the obsidian dagger Yemania had left on the floor. He whirled, then charged toward Ochix with the blade raised high in the air.

Yemania screamed and did the only thing she could think of.

She threw herself in front of Ochix just as Coatl's hand came down . . .

A sharp, searing pain pierced her right shoulder. Yemania wanted to scream, but everything around her seemed to grow fuzzy at the edges, sounds beginning to muffle. She was dizzy, so incredibly dizzy. She slumped into Ochix's arms, and the pain in her shoulder began to build, cresting like a wave until it broke over her, bringing everything suddenly back into sharp, intense clarity.

She moaned low in her throat. The ruby hilt now protruded from her shoulder, the obsidian blade sank deep into her flesh. Hot, sticky blood poured down her arm and soaked her hand, pooling on the floor at her feet.

Ochix lowered her to the floor, his hands immediately pressing around the ruby hilt, trying to staunch some of the bleeding.

Coatl's eyes and mouth were open with horror, and he wobbled slightly before falling to his knees, tears streaming down his cheeks.

"Yem . . . Yem . . ." he whimpered.

A deep rumbling sounded in Ochix's chest as he lifted his gaze to meet Coatl's. Through the haze of her pain, Yemania's heart clenched again in panic at the deadly intent she saw burning there. For a moment, a shadow crossed Ochix's face and he truly looked the part of the death demon she teased him for being.

His eyes clouded over with the mist of possession, and immediately, Coatl's did as well. Her brother's arms went slack at his sides before his hands slowly inched their way up toward his throat. His own fingers closed around his neck and began to squeeze.

"Ochix, no! Stop! He's my brother!" Yemania shrieked. But Ochix did not stop. He was lost in his thirst for revenge.

She had to bring him back somehow. Her thoughts scrambled for any good reason Ochix might have for keeping him alive. The idea hit her like a burst of lightning striking a tree. "I need him! I can't heal myself!"

Ochix started and his eyes began to clear. Eventually, so did her brother's. Coatl pitched forward onto his hands and knees, gasping and choking for breath.

"I need him . . . to heal me," Yemania said again. She placed her bloodied hand against Ochix's bare chest, though she felt excruciating pain at the motion. Ochix shook his head like a dog clearing water from its ears. Coatl continued to sputter and suck in air on the floor.

"Heal her, now. Or your life will end faster than you can blink, son of healing," Ochix said, his voice quiet and dangerous.

Coatl eyed Ochix with disgust, as though he were a poisonous beetle he couldn't wait to crush beneath his sandal. But his eyes filled with concern when they took in the hilt of the dagger still in Yemania's shoulder.

Yemania panted from the effort of holding herself conscious, the blood loss and pain now threatening to pull her under. "I'll only . . . let him heal me . . . if you promise . . . not to kill him."

Ochix looked outraged. "What? Yemania, he just stabbed—"

"Promise . . . me!"

Ochix gritted his teeth, but nodded in agreement. "Fine. I won't kill him. I promise."

Coatl came toward them, glancing hesitantly at Ochix as though doubting his ability to keep his promise.

"*Death demons* do not go against their word, sun worshipper," Ochix growled at him. "I actually have honor."

Coatl's jaw tensed, but Yemania used her last remaining bit of strength to slap Ochix on his chest. "Stop."

Coatl knelt down beside her and used the tip of his fingers to prod and assess the damage. Yemania cried out with each touch, and she felt Ochix's arms tighten around her.

Coatl's eyes were swimming with tears. "I'm so sorry, Yemania, I never meant to—"

"I know," she said. "Just make sure . . . I don't bleed to death . . . and I'll forgive you." Then she looked up at Ochix and frowned. "I'll forgive you *both* . . . for being such prideful idiots."

Coatl and Ochix both tucked their heads in shame. *As they should*, she thought savagely.

Finally, after more prodding and poking—and on Yemania's part, cringing—Coatl sighed. "Okay, I don't think the damage is that bad. But I need to remove the blade so I can heal it."

"If you take out the blade, the bleeding will worsen," Ochix objected.

Coatl rolled his eyes. "Yes, on a battlefield you want to leave a dagger or arrow or spear inside the wound until you can find a healer, but when it is time to actually *heal*, it must be removed. Would you rather I heal her arm and leave the dagger there?" His voice dripped with sarcasm.

"He does . . . need to remove it . . . It's okay, Ochix." Yemania tried her best to assure him that as healers, they knew what they were doing.

Ochix rubbed her uninjured arm reassuringly. He did not respond, but nodded in acknowledgment. Through her pain, Yemania felt a twinge in her heart at the fear and concern she saw on his face.

"Hold her still," Coatl commanded. Ochix obliged, and Yemania gritted her teeth.

Even though she knew what was coming, it didn't prepare her for the agony of Coatl ripping the blade out. The blade quickly slid free, but she couldn't contain her scream.

Ochix's fist shot out and collided with Coatl's nose. There was a cracking sound and her brother's head whipped back, his hand protectively covering his face. Blood dripped from between his fingers.

"Sorry," Ochix grunted and then shrugged. "Reflex. I promised not to kill him, but I didn't like hearing you in pain. At least now his blood is exposed to heal you." Ochix's wicked grin was back.

Yemania made a sound somewhere between a laugh and a sob. "I'll heal your nose once I'm better," she said to her brother.

Coatl glared at Ochix again, his face a bloody mess thanks to his now-broken nose. He wiped some of the blood off and held his red-stained fingers over her shoulder.

Yemania couldn't see, but she could feel the wound closing, the muscle slowly weaving itself back together. It would definitely be sore for a few days to come.

"What in the nine hells were you thinking, Yem?" Coatl asked her, leaning back on his heels as soon as he was finished.

Yemania reached out and grabbed Ochix's hand, bringing it to her lips for a soft kiss.

"He already told you. He loves me. And I think I love him too."

CHAPTER

31

Ahkin was a fool if he thought Mayana would leave him behind. Had he learned nothing about her in their time together? They had to do this together. It was the only way to survive the horrors of Xibalba. She loved him, and if he was going to die beneath the claws of those beasts, then she would die fighting beside him.

She smirked to herself as she imagined what her family would say. *Your heart leads you into trouble.* Yes, it did, but it also led her out of it.

She followed the sounds of the echoing roars, Ona running swiftly at her heels. The moment Ahkin had disappeared into the trees, Mayana knew she had to follow him. She sprinted to the edge of the scorpion river, fighting the urge to retch as she beheld the mass of writhing black bodies sliding over each other.

"You have to do this," she told herself. She didn't tell Ahkin at the time, but one of the bodies she had beheld in "the place where bodies hang like banners" . . . had been his. Her eyes squeezed shut as she brought back the memory of his lifeless corpse hanging from one of those posts, a wound in his abdomen having bled him of all his life and power. It didn't take much for her to imagine what his body might look like after meeting the claws of those beasts. What it had almost looked like on the beach. What it had looked like when he collapsed from the snake's poison. A warm sensation solidified in her chest, wiping all fear from within her.

Even though he was not there, she could feel the ghost of his arms around her. Sometimes your greatest fears dissolve when you're called on to save someone you love.

She sliced into her hand, bringing enough blood to call forth the waters from her amulet once more. This time, her fear did not conquer her. She willed the waters to surround her and Ona. They slowly lifted into the air, the waters bolstering her courage, a reminder of the power contained within her. She threw out her hand and the waters launched them across the river of scorpions. With a crash that sent the volcanic black sand flying, she and Ona collided with the opposite riverbank. Ona shook himself off, and before she could say anything, he bolted into the forest after Ahkin.

Mayana sprinted after him, willing Ahkin to survive until they could reach him. Blood pounded in her ears as her feet pounded equally hard against the earth. Ona was a shadow darting between the tree trunks. She struggled to keep him within view. Soon the sounds of the roaring beasts grew louder, and she knew they were close. Breaking through another line of trees, she and Ona finally came upon a rock outcropping where three jaguar beasts paced around its base. She'd bet the bones in her bag that Ahkin was hidden somewhere within the strewn boulders. She sneaked closer, keeping her footfalls as light as a deer's.

There was no way to get to him with the cats guarding him, which meant only one thing. She would have to get rid of them somehow. She had no skills with a knife, and if Ahkin couldn't defeat them as a warrior, there was no way she would face them with only her hands and a blade. No, she had a far greater weapon hanging around her neck.

She wrapped her hand around the jade skull pendant, remembering how she had protected herself from a leaping jaguar on her way to Tollan for the selection ritual. She had summoned the river and turned it into a battering ram.

She could certainly do the same again.

To make sure she had enough blood for what she planned to do, she cut into both of her palms, dripping her life's essence into the dirt beside her. The more power of her ancestor that was exposed, the more she had at her disposal. The spirit of a man flitted out of the rocks like a wisp of smoke, and she prayed it was not Ahkin's. She clenched her bloodied hands into fists, ordering the water to emerge from the skull and obey her. The water rushed forth, surrounding her in a swirling mass of silver.

Mayana stepped out from behind the trees and threw her hands out. The water condensed at her command, forming a fist big enough to plow into the side of the nearest jaguar. The beast was tossed sideways, its spotted body spinning across the forest floor. It whimpered and ran into the trees.

Mayana stepped forward again, already summoning more water to take on the two cats that had now shifted their attention to her. They prowled closer, their yellow eyes close to the ground as they stalked. Mayana threw her arms wide, splitting the mass of water she had pulled from the necklace into two. She curled her upturned hands into fists, and the water condensed again into identical transparent spheres.

She opened her palms again and thrust them forward, sending the masses of water at the heads of the remaining cats. The water enveloped their heads, muffling the sounds of their terrified roars. Their heads thrashed back and forth, trying to dislodge the water slowly drowning them.

"Ona! Find him!"

The dog darted between the thrashing cats before ducking between the rocks. She prayed he'd find Ahkin quickly and heal whatever injuries he had sustained.

The first beast dropped to its side, its eyes sliding shut beneath the shifting crystalline surface. Mayana pulled the water away the moment it lost consciousness, making sure its side still rose and fell with breaths. She didn't want to kill them, just incapacitate them long enough to escape. Plus, she wasn't entirely sure beasts of Xibalba *could* be killed.

The second beast did the same, giving up in its attempt to dislodge the water and collapsing to the ground as its eyes closed. Mayana dispersed the water and its chest still rose and fell with strained, shallow breaths. Then she followed Ona into the rocks.

"Ahkin!" she screamed. "Ahkin, where are you?"

Ona barked urgently, and Mayana followed the sound. She wedged herself beneath a rocky overhang, a crevice formed between the stone and ground. Ahkin was there, his eyes closed, but still breathing. He must have lost too much blood. Ona was already working to lick the wounds closed, the skin healing beneath each pull of his pink tongue.

Mayana crouched down beside him, rubbing the short hair on his head with her hand and whispering, "Ahkin. Ahkin, wake up. Please." Tears traced their way down her cheeks and into his hair.

His eyes finally fluttered. He groaned, and Ona leapt between them, licking Ahkin excitedly across the face.

"Dog," he grunted, pushing Ona away, who only wiggled against him harder, licking more and more.

"I think he likes you now." Mayana chuckled, her voice thick with emotion.

His gaze focused on her face and without a moment's hesitation, he wrapped his arms around her neck and pulled her to him. Their lips came together, and this time, Ona let them be. His lips tasted like salt from both blood and tears, as he consumed her like a drowning man tasting air for the first time.

"You came for me," he said against her mouth, refusing to pull away.

Mayana cried and laughed as she kissed him. "Of course. You aren't doing this alone, Ahkin."

He made a sobbing sound in his throat and kissed her harder. "I know," he whispered. "I know."

He still seemed so weak, but he broke down and told her about his father's ghost visiting him, lecturing him on the foolishness of trying to shoulder everything by himself. Mayana raised an eyebrow at that, and Ahkin laughed. He seemed . . . so joyous. So light. Which was a miracle, considering where they were. She could sense that he really had let go of some burden that had been weighing him down since she met him. Even his smile seemed brighter, freer. He pulled her in for another embrace, kissing the top of her head. "You are my duality. And I am yours."

"The Mother told us that already," Mayana teased.

"Yes, but I finally understand what that means now. I don't have to do everything alone. It's safe to trust someone else to stand beside you. To accept help. It doesn't make you weaker. It makes you stronger, like a rope of many strands."

"About time you figured it out." Mayana laid a hand against his cheek.

He leaned into it, turning his face and kissing her bleeding palms. "Let's go before the jaguars wake."

Ona barked in agreement.

———

Ahkin seemed to hold his head a little higher as they stumbled back to the river of scorpions, back across the path burned through them by Ahkin's shield. This time, Mayana faced her fear with a greater strength. With Ahkin by her side, she felt steadier and lighter too.

The forest of dead trees began to thin, along with the mists. Mayana hoped they were finally reaching the end of such a horrific layer of the underworld.

"We should be close to the next layer, shouldn't we? The final river?"

"I think so. We are supposed to swim across it and then climb our way up to the City of the Dead."

"Where we will have to pleasantly negotiate with the lords of death and suffering to let us pass through and be home before dinner."

Ahkin snorted. "Yes. Though I doubt it will be as simple as that."

Their fingers twined together like a finely woven tapestry. The feel of his skin against hers made Mayana's stomach tighten with the memories of the kisses they had shared. "When is it ever as simple as that?"

She started to laugh, but it stuck in her throat as the last layer of mist finally cleared and revealed a stretch of marshland. The soggy landscape was comprised of low grassy plains interspersed with pockets of connected pools. Fat-bodied black-and-yellow spiders scuttled across the exposed dirt beneath low shrubs that looked brown and lifeless.

"What *is* that?" Mayana wrinkled her nose at the rotten stench washing over her. The pools' waters were not cool and smooth and clear. Instead, they were thick and even more sluggish than the blood had been. They swirled in eddies of a sickly yellow-green color. The smell reminded her of festering wounds mixed with mildew and wood rot. She covered her nose with her hand to stop from gagging.

"I think—" Ahkin stepped closer to the nearest pool to look, but then quickly backed away, retching. "It's . . . pus."

"*Pus?*" Mayana shrieked. Her stomach roiled at the thought. "We have to cross a marshland full of *pus?*" She thought she might prefer the scorpions. "This wasn't in your descriptions either."

Ahkin scrunched his eyebrows together. "Actually, now that I think about it, I do remember reading about rivers of blood, scorpions, and pus."

Mayana let out a breath. "*Now* you remember? Anything else we need to be prepared for before we reach the final river? Fields of rotting bones? Canyons of frogs and spiders?"

Ahkin grimaced. "Actually, it looks like there are plenty of spiders here."

Sure enough, spiderwebs glistened between the towering grass stalks, more bulbous black-and-yellow bodies wriggling across them.

Pus. And spiders.

A buzz sounded in her ear, and Mayana slapped at a mosquito that had landed on her neck.

Pus. And spiders. *And* mosquitoes.

Xibalba was truly a place of wretchedness, and it seemed determined to prove that it deserved its reputation.

"I don't understand . . . Didn't you meet last night?" Coatl frowned, testing his newly healed nose for soreness with his fingertips. Yemania had finished patching him up as soon as she had the strength to sit up again. Now that they had taken care of the physical damage done to one another, they all lounged on the floor cushions of the High Healer workroom, trying to repair the damage done below the surface.

She laughed softly. "No, actually. We met outside the jungles of Millacatl."

She could see Coatl putting everything together in his head. "The night you didn't come back," he said finally.

"Yes. I found him dying on a riverbank and I took care of him. It took me a while and we . . . spent a lot of time talking."

Coatl frowned. "You said you escaped a Miquitz raiding party."

"She did," Ochix cut in. "They wanted to take her, and I held them back so she could escape. We thought we would never see each other again. My father tried to have me killed the first time I refused to marry Metzi. The only reason I finally agreed is because I thought coming here might give me the chance to see Yemania again."

Coatl's eyebrows rose. He didn't seem convinced.

"Why did you come back to the workroom?" Yemania asked. "I thought you couldn't wait to get down to the training fields to see Metzi."

Coatl shrugged a shoulder. "Well, I thought about what you said, about what's best for both of us, and I realized the only reason she left me in the first place is because she was acting on . . . orders. So, I went to her room, knowing she wasn't there, to see what I could find out."

Yemania felt Ochix stiffen behind her. He wrapped a protective arm around her waist.

"I came back to talk to you"—Coatl spoke out of the side of his mouth to try and exclude Ochix—"about something I learned about her . . . friend."

"You know, if you're going to talk about me, you can at least address me by name," Ochix said.

Coatl sneered at him. "You know, *Ochix*, not everything is about you."

Ochix sneered right back. "That's funny, I was going to say the same thing to you."

"Both of you can knock it off," Yemania said, hands back on her hips. "By her 'friend,' you mean the Obsidian Butterfly?"

Ochix immediately hissed at the name, drawing both Yemania and Coatl's curious eyes.

"Are you familiar with her?" Yemania asked him.

Ochix's face darkened. He rubbed nervously at his chin. "Yes, unfortunately. I have no love for that deity. Itzpapalotl, the Obsidian Butterfly, resides in Tamoanchan, the heavenly paradise in the stars. She can be a benevolent warrior, but one of her aspects can also be treacherous and deadly. My father has been . . . consulting with her. I confronted him about it when we got into our fight. I told him I thought she couldn't be trusted."

His hand moved absently to the scar across his stomach. "My father has always been a bit . . . different. Obsessive when it came to unraveling the will of the gods, a little on the eccentric side. But when he started summoning her a few months ago, it was almost as though he fell off the ledge into madness. He'd stay up for days at a time, poring over ancient texts. Every wall in his room in the temple was covered in star charts and complicated drawings I didn't understand. He would talk to spirits that no one else could see. He even attacked and killed one of his servants for daring to interrupt him. He is not himself anymore, and it began when he started summoning *her*."

Yemania shivered. "How does he summon her?"

"It's a complicated ritual, but I've seen him do it. The lesser gods and goddesses cannot travel between the layers of creation except during times of cosmic instability. Only the creator, Ometeotl, can move however she wishes. In order to communicate with Itzpapalotl, you must sacrifice some of your own blood to a fallen star, a piece of the heavenly realms where she dwells."

"A fallen star," Coatl said quietly. He immediately started pacing the room, running his hands through his hair. "You mean like a meteorite?"

Ochix nodded gravely. "They are extremely rare and difficult to find, but we keep a fallen star in our temple in Omitl."

"We keep them in our temples here as well. They are regarded as holy gifts from the gods, tools used for certain rituals," Coatl said, still pacing.

"I didn't see it there, the last time I was in the library. I think I saw the shelf that usually housed it," Yemania whispered.

Coatl turned back to face them. He crossed his arms over his chest and rocked slightly. "Metzi has it. I remember her showing it to me. It was a gray stone as big as my palm, dark and jagged yet shining with something like stardust."

Ochix nodded slowly. "That sounds like a star stone."

"She must be using the stone to summon the Obsidian Butterfly," Yemania guessed. It might explain her constant headaches as well. If Metzi was expending so much of her energy to summon such a great power . . .

Coatl slammed a hand against the stone table beside him. "Why is she doing this, though?"

Ochix's face remained grave. "I'm less worried about Metzi's plans and more worried about whatever the Obsidian Butterfly is orchestrating. Metzi may think she is in control, but the goddess will use her. I feel like I'm a piece in a game I didn't know I was playing. And if that goddess can push my father into madness, I would hate to see what she could do to your empress."

Yemania squeezed his hand reassuringly. "Well then, we can't let her. Coatl, you said you had learned something when you went to her rooms?"

Coatl nervously rubbed the back of his neck. "I might have gone through some of her correspondences, messages she left out on her tables."

Ochix snorted in disgust, and Coatl shot him another nasty glare.

Yemania jumped in before either of them could say something inflammatory. "What did you find in the letters?"

"Mostly they were updates on the negotiations with Ehecatl, but I did find a letter from Tzom, head priest and emperor of Miquitz."

Ochix's eyes grew even darker at the mention of his father.

But Coatl continued, "It was a request for Metzi to visit Miquitz after the wedding. To join them for their eclipse ritual in a few weeks."

"What's unusual about that?" Yemania asked.

"It's how he signed it. At the end, it said, 'Thank you for your mutual service to our patron.'"

"Itzpapalotl must be the patron," Yemania guessed.

Coatl turned to Ochix. "No offense, death demon, but I don't trust you or your kind in the slightest. I trust this goddess even less. I'm worried Metzi is walking into some kind of trap set up by your father."

"*My* kind?" Ochix clenched his hand into a fist. "What is that supposed to imply?"

"This is your father, isn't it? Your crazy, bloodthirsty father scheming and making plans with some goddess and convincing Metzi to make these horrible decisions that—"

"That what? Take her away from *you*? I haven't known Metzi very long, but I'd be willing to give her much more credit than you are right now, and you are the one who supposedly loves her."

"I'm concerned about her! I don't want this Obsidian Butterfly influencing her! Driving her insane! What if this is all Miquitz's way of taking over the Chicome Empire, so you can be emperor of both!"

Ochix scoffed. "You're the insane one, son of healing, if you think that's the reason I'm here."

"Coatl," Yemania cut in. "Ochix has a point. Metzi is clever and I don't think she'd—"

"You don't understand! This was all her idea!" Coatl burst out. "Everything. From the beginning. Metzi asked me to poison her father, help her make Ahkin think the world was ending, and I did it all because—because I thought I was helping her escape from an arranged marriage. I thought she wanted to be with *me*. She told me the idea to steal the throne from her father and brother came to her from the gods, that she was acting out the divine revelation given to her . . . and now everything makes so much more sense. The idea must have been whispered into her ear by that mother of demons."

Yemania chewed on her lower lip as Ochix's chest heaved. She could see him barely managing to contain his rage. "Do you think that's something your father could be capable of? Influencing Metzi through the goddess?"

Ochix let out a breath. "I don't know. Like I said, he's been acting so differently. Before the sun prince died, he was obsessed with talking to him, of finding a way to get him to come to Omitl."

"Ahkin," Yemania breathed. Saying his name ripped open the scab that had been forming over her heart at the thought of him and Mayana.

Ochix continued, "If he wanted to kill him or take over the Chicome Empire, I don't see why he'd care about that. As soon as the prince sacrificed himself, my father's manic focus shifted to Metzi, hence the wedding proposal. He acted as if the world depended on it, and he was the only one that could find the answers. I put my foot down then, confronted him on everything I was noticing. And all it got me was a knife blade in the gut."

"But you finally agreed." Coatl narrowed his eyes. "You say it's because you love my sister and wanted to come to Tollan, but what if you're here for a different reason?"

Ochix rose to his feet and withdrew a long obsidian blade, its handle carved with the image of skulls. Yemania gasped, but before she could worry, Ochix flipped the blade over in his hand and offered the handle to Coatl.

"If I am such a threat, then end my life right here. I assure you I have no interest in your sun throne. I will take the throne and mantle of head priest in my own empire, I don't need another. The only thing about this place that holds any interest for me is sitting right here." He placed a hand on Yemania's shoulder. She reached up and put her hand over his.

Coatl didn't take the offered knife. "Then call off your wedding to Metzi."

"My father threatened to kill me and said I would never be welcome home if I didn't marry her. And with how you feel about my people here in the valley, where else would I go? I don't have a choice if I want any kind of life for myself besides living alone in the mountains."

"But what if Metzi called it off?" Yemania asked quietly.

Ochix opened his mouth to object, but then considered for a moment. "Actually . . . I don't think my father could blame me if she were the one to call off the engagement. But she isn't going to, especially not if the goddess wishes it."

Coatl's eyes grew bright. "I know I can convince her to call it off. If I could—"

"No," Yemania cut across him, already seeing where his head was going. "You aren't going to be able to convince her, not if the Obsidian Butterfly still has any influence over her decision. What we need to do, I think, is break off her connection to Itzpapalotl. *Then* maybe Coatl can convince her to end the engagement. I think she still has feelings for him. She told the Butterfly she did."

Ochix was following along with her. "Then we need to steal her star stone. If Itzpapalotl can't direct her, perhaps she would be willing to break the engagement. Which means"—he turned his gaze hopefully to Yemania—"I would be free to marry someone else."

Yemania's stomach flipped at the thought.

They had to do this. Find a way to convince Metzi that marrying Ochix wasn't the best idea. No one really wanted them to anyway, including Metzi herself. The only reason she had agreed was because the Obsidian Butterfly had told her it was how she could find freedom. And Metzi would do anything to secure her own freedom. Ochix's father obviously wanted to worm his way into Tollan like a maggot through a corpse. The council was nervous about the alliance—it was dried kindling waiting for a spark. Metzi didn't love Ochix, and he certainly didn't love her. Their hearts all belonged somewhere else. It seemed so perfect . . .

"But she keeps it locked in a blood chest in her room," Coatl said.

Yemania felt her hopes sweep away like a feather in a strong breeze. She swore under her breath.

"What's a blood chest?" Ochix asked.

Yemania sighed. "It's a stone box forged in the volcano at Papatlaca.

Only the blood of the chest's owner can be used to open it. And Metzi's blood is probably the most closely guarded resource in the empire." She rubbed her eyes. "So how are we supposed to get around that?"

Coatl's face split into a devilish grin. "I think I have an idea."

CHAPTER

33

Ahkin carefully stepped across the sickly pools of pus. He and Mayana followed a rough path through the thorny shrubs that separated the yellow pools. Every so often they heard the *glub* of a bubble forming and popping. He wanted to gag every time.

Then there were the spiderwebs. All around them, strings of webs floated through the air, suspended by the occasional gusts of wind sweeping across the marsh. Spiders dangled from the ends seeking places to land. He'd broken off a huge branch from one of the dead trees at the edge of the forest, and now he used it like a macana sword, slicing through his enemies. Granted, these enemies were smaller than those he'd faced on the battlefield, but the spiders were still larger than any he'd seen in the land of the living. They ranged from the size of his palm to the size of a man's head. The webs now stuck to the end of the branch like a ghostly white torch.

Mayana stuck close behind him, swatting at the incessant mosquitoes. They had both been bitten to the extent that they looked stricken with some kind of pox. And the itching? Ahkin wanted to rip his skin off, or at least run his arms through the thorny underbrush until they bled. The only comfort was watching the flying insects explode in little bursts of light or water, unable to handle the divinity within the blood they drank.

"I could really use one of Yemania's healing salves right now. Gods, I miss her so much." Mayana whimpered, smacking at another mosquito on her arm. It died with a little burst of water beneath her fingers. Ahkin scratched at his arms and suppressed the urge to scream. This layer was an entirely different form of torture.

A spider the size of his outstretched hand lowered from somewhere above their heads, its smooth black-and-yellow legs dancing toward his face.

Mayana screamed. Instinctively, Ahkin's arm shot out to strike it.

But he missed, and the stick connected with the silver thread above it. The spider jolted at the impact, jerking in the direction the stick pulled the web—until it landed on Ahkin's chest.

Mayana screamed again and stumbled back, tripping over Ona. She landed in the thorn-covered brambles. The thorns ripped into her skin as more black-and-yellow spiders, disturbed by the impact, emerged onto the path in a swarm.

The spider on his chest sunk in its fangs, and he ripped its body away. He didn't think it was poisonous. They looked like the orb weavers he'd seen in the jungles at home, only larger. Another piercing stab told him he'd been bitten on his foot. He looked down. The path now teemed with legs and hair and bulbous spider abdomens the size of his palm. He kicked out as Ona darted toward the bush where Mayana had fallen. Bodies crunched and burst beneath what remained of his sandals. He couldn't imagine Coatl ever surviving this layer of the underworld.

Mayana flailed, shrieking in terror and pain as the growing army of spiders began to overtake them. Ahkin lunged forward and yanked her upright. Blood oozed from the cuts covering her arms and legs. Angry, red swellings from spider bites now joined those from the mosquitoes. A clicking, hissing sound rose from the teeming mass of bodies. Webs began to cover their feet, entangling around their ankles as if . . . Oh gods. Did these spiders attack in packs and ensnare their victims in webs? Ahkin had a horrible vision in his mind of Mayana's legs wrapped in white silk as the army of spiders dragged them away from each other. That would never happen. Not when they'd fought so hard to be together in the first place. He wouldn't let *anything* come between them now. He kicked out harder at the webs, swinging with his stick, but he knew defeat when he saw it. There were too many, and reinforcements seemed to be swelling their numbers.

Mayana sobbed and clawed at her arms, frantically jogging her legs to keep them free from spiders. She was nearing hysteria. He didn't blame her in the slightest. Panic quickly clenched a fist around his own heart.

"Run! Don't let them get the webs around your feet!" He shoved Mayana ahead of him.

Ona snapped his teeth, but even he began to struggle in the tangle of webbing growing around his legs. Ahkin lifted him up and crushed another spider. Its abdomen popped beneath his foot. His stomach roiled. His injured hand throbbed, but he didn't loosen his hold on the dog.

He also knew he couldn't do this alone. "Mayana, use the water!"

She didn't argue. There was a sob, and then a rushing sound. The cool familiar waters of her necklace enveloped them and lifted them above the hissing and clicking spider mob below. But they did not stay airborne for long. Mayana was clearly weakened from fear and exhaustion, and soon, they crashed back to the ground in a small clearing in the brush. Not far, but thankfully out of reach of the spiders.

They both struggled to rise. "Do you think everyone in the overworld assumes we're dead?" Ahkin huffed, wiping water from his eyes.

"It's a miracle we aren't yet." Mayana's voice trembled as much as her hands. "And tomorrow is the last day of the Nemontemi."

They had to make it in time. They had to.

Ahkin stumbled back to his feet. There wasn't much time left. His body ached, his muscles seized, his skin stung and burned and itched all at once. He wanted to take out his obsidian blade and flay himself alive to stop the misery. Mayana's whimper told him she felt the same.

"I know it hurts, but we have to keep moving. I'm here. We can do this together."

"Together." Mayana nodded, tears of agony tracing her cheeks as he helped her back to her feet. Tiny yellow blisters had formed over some of her bites, matching the continued bubbling of the pus pools around them.

Ona licked as many of their wounds clean as he could, but his gifting apparently didn't extend to the itching poison of the bites.

"Come on," Ahkin said, resigned.

They continued to pick their way across precarious dirt paths and slippery footholds, beating away more spiders and mosquitoes as they went. Ahkin didn't think his stomach would be able to handle falling into one of the pus-filled pools. Eventually they passed a large green plant with protruding bladelike leaves, tiny points like teeth around their edges. Ahkin froze, recognizing the plant from somewhere.

"I've seen this before," he said, running his nails across the blistering skin on his chest. "Do you know what it is?"

Mayana studied it. "It looks like a bigger version of the plant Yemania gave you during the selection ritual."

"That's what I thought too. Do you remember what she told me when she presented the gift?"

Mayana tried to quirk her mouth into a smile. "For sunburns."

"Do you think it might soothe our skin?"

Mayana was already reaching forward to snap off one of the thick, fleshy leaves. The moment the leaf snapped in half, a clear, sticky sap oozed from within. Mayana smeared the sap across her arms, sighing in relief. Ahkin mimicked her, first in her movements and then in her sigh.

"It feels almost cool," Ahkin mused, starting down at his glistening arms.

"Thank you, Yemania," Mayana said, her tear-stained face tilted toward the overworld. "I miss you, wherever you are."

"You were close to the daughter of healing, weren't you?" Ahkin had seen Mayana with her on many occasions. She'd even helped the shy princess of Pahtia in her initial demonstration to display her healing abilities.

"Yes." Mayana sighed wistfully. "We didn't know each other very long, but you tend to bond quickly with someone when you both think your lives are in danger. She reached out to me, and my heart broke for her situation."

"Her situation?" Ahkin whacked another fat spider into the dirt and squished it. "What do you mean?"

"Her father sent her as a sacrifice. He purposely chose her, knowing you'd never pick her."

Ahkin turned back to frown at Mayana. "What kind of father would do such a thing? I mean, she was meek and insecure, but I don't see why he would disvalue her like that. She seemed kind and clever to me."

Mayana shrugged. "A father who didn't value her very much, apparently. Which is a shame, because she is an incredibly beautiful person. We initially agreed to die together so that neither of us had to do it alone."

"But I was going to pick you. What would have happened if . . . ?"

Mayana sucked a breath in through her teeth. "I wanted to try to find a way to save her. I even asked you about it, remember? You told me you didn't want to jeopardize your rule or our future together." She tried to sound as though she were stating facts, but Ahkin could sense the bitterness beneath her tone.

"I was being selfish," he said.

"You thought it was what the gods demanded." But she didn't meet his eyes as she said it.

"But you didn't think the gods demanded it. And you ended up being right."

Mayana sniffed and looked at her feet, shuffling them back and forth.

"Thank you, Mayana."

She looked up again, confusion pulling at her eyebrows. "Why are you thanking me?"

"Thank you for fighting for her. For showing me that the sacrifice of those beautiful daughters of the gods was unnecessary. I love that you don't back down from what you believe in. It shows incredible strength."

Mayana smirked. "If you are trying to get me to kiss you again—"

Ahkin pulled her toward him and cut her off with a swift kiss to her lips. Her skin was sticky and cool from the plant sap. "I don't need an excuse to kiss you. I can kiss you and still believe those things are true. It's the whole reason I picked you in the first place."

They shared a few tender moments before Ona barked to remind them that they didn't have time to waste kissing in the middle of the underworld, especially not with an army of spiders not far behind.

"Why did you pick me?" she asked as he jumped across a particularly wide pus puddle.

Ahkin held out his hand to help her across. She gagged, but thankfully managed not to throw up on him. "Because you filled my world with color. And passion." He gave her a wry smile. "And stubbornness."

"I'm particularly good at stubbornness." Mayana tilted her chin into the air.

Ahkin barked a laugh. "I've noticed."

"Why didn't you like the other princesses, though?"

Ahkin thought for a moment, wanting to be delicate in his answer. "It's not that I didn't like them. I cared about each of them, even if I didn't want to marry them."

Mayana snorted, and he knew she was thinking of Zorrah, the fierce animal princess of Ocelotl.

He brought to his mind the dark, deadly humor of the princess of fire. "The princess of Papatlaca honestly scared me a little bit. Yoli? She seemed to enjoy pain a bit too much for my taste. But she seemed to have a kind heart behind the, uh—"

"Black paint covering her eyes? The shard of obsidian she used to spear herself in the arm?" Mayana chuckled. "I was so intimidated by Yoli at first. But underneath her morbid style and humor, she fought for me against Zorrah. She was another true friend when I needed one most."

"Zorrah, well, I don't need to explain that one. I was half terrified she wanted to rip my heart out and eat it herself. I was more of a conquest to her than someone she actually wanted to share her life with."

"What about Itza?" Mayana paused, obviously remembering his jab he had made back in the caves. "Or Teniza?"

"Those were the matches the council preferred, obviously. But Itza . . . she was so lost in prayer and her obsession with Quetzalcoatl's return that I didn't think she'd make time for anything else. Plus, she seemed to have some kind of ulterior motive for being in the capital, which had me on edge. And Teniza? The thought of having to deal with her arrogant and controlling father . . ." He didn't need to finish. Mayana had met her and seen for herself how spoiled and superior the princess had been.

Mayana sighed. "I still didn't want to see *any* of them die, especially not for a ritual. Well, maybe Zorrah."

Ahkin narrowed his eyes playfully at her. He knew her better now. "You couldn't handle watching an enemy Miquitz soldier sacrificed. As much as you hate her, I'm sure you didn't want to see her sacrificed."

Mayana stuck out her tongue. "Fine, not even Zorrah."

"My father told me that the selection ritual wasn't intended to find a bride to continue the royal bloodline. It was originally intended as a way for the emperor to find a duality."

"You father told you that?"

He explained what the spirit of his father told him about the importance of not trying to lead completely by yourself.

Mayana nodded when he finished. "Ah. That's why you brought up that I'm your duality."

"You are," Ahkin said, wanting—*needing*—her to grasp the magnitude of such a thing. "You teach me what I need to learn, and you challenge me to be better. I hope I can do the same for you."

She gave him a shy smile. "You teach me a lot of things too, believe it or not."

Ahkin felt his pride inflating slightly. "Like what?"

"I've been wrestling this whole journey with the Mother's will. Trying to understand why she would have us make this journey instead of rescuing us. Why she's making us get the bones of Quetzalcoatl." She absently patted her bag with her mother's bones. "Now I know there was a reason. And you encouraged me to trust, when all I wanted to do was question her intentions."

"I'm honored to help you in your faith."

Mayana rolled her eyes. "I'll have more faith if she actually helps us get out of here alive."

"Don't give up hope just yet, daughter of water." Ahkin winked at her. He couldn't explain it, but he knew the Mother was watching them closely. He'd sensed her presence every step of this journey so far, felt her watching eyes or the gentle caress of her hand in the wind. Perhaps the vision and warning she'd given him was just a dream after all. He knew she'd see them through . . . somehow.

"Are you ready to go swimming again?" Mayana asked suddenly.

"Why?"

Mayana pointed ahead. Through the tall grasses, the glittering of water reflected like the surface of a gemstone. The sky around them was darkening, quickly tipping into their final night in Xibalba. "I feel the presence of water."

Ahkin parted the grasses and felt a thrill of both excitement and foreboding wash over him.

A vast, turbulent river stretched out before them. On the far shore, barely visible, the flaming lights of a city sparkled. They had reached the final river, and across from them lay their last stop before ascending back home—

The City of the Dead.

CHAPTER

34

"I'm not sure I like this idea," Yemania whispered to Ochix. "Why can't you possess her, and we can get some of her blood that way?"

While Coatl was supposed to be sneaking into Metzi's room to steal the chest, she and Ochix crouched hidden in the garden outside of Metzi's personal steam bath. Insects chirped and buzzed in the canopied trees, while moths fluttered low over the posted torches. The air was thick with the scent of night-blooming dragon fruit flowers. Metzi visited the baths every evening to cleanse her nerves, and it was one of the few times her guards were not immediately by her side.

"Being possessed doesn't mean you are unaware. You are fully awake, just unable to control any of your own actions. She'd know what was happening the entire time and remember."

Yemania huffed. "She'd probably break your engagement, at least."

Ochix gave her a crooked smile. "And have me executed in two heartbeats."

He slid a hand around her waist and pulled her closer to him, his fingers trailing suggestively down her back.

She rolled her eyes at him. "Will you stay focused? You have a job to do soon, prince of death."

"If this works, my only job will be to make you happy for the rest of my life," he whispered in her ear.

His words sent her heart beating like a worship drum—bolstering her faltering courage at what they were about to do.

"There she is," Yemania hissed, smacking Ochix's chest repeatedly with her hand.

Ochix chuckled. "I know, thank you, I can see her."

Metzi emerged from the flowing curtains of her suite at the far end of the garden and walked the short stone path to her private temazcalli steam bathhouse. Yemania blushed slightly at the empress's naked form. She was almost tempted to reach up and shield Ochix's eyes. She sneaked a peek in his direction to see how he would react, but to her surprise, he wasn't watching Metzi. His eyes were intently focused on her.

"Again, nothing I haven't seen before, daughter of healing," he teased. "Besides, I've seen better." He let his gaze drop suggestively to her chest, and she playfully smacked him on the arm.

"You are a beast."

Ochix pulled her toward him again and dug his face into her neck just below her ear. He growled and snorted like an animal as he tickled her with his nose. She smacked him again and shoved him off. "Shh, you're going to give us away!"

But she couldn't hide the wide smile that broke out across her face.

Ochix lifted his chin slightly and looked as proud as Coatl for making her smile.

Yemania squinted back toward the bathhouse. "Okay, I think she's inside. Are you ready?"

Ochix removed his skull-engraved dagger and pricked the tip of his thumb. A drop the color of cinnabar appeared, his eyes misted over, and he held it out in front of him, feeling for the closest servant's life force. Yemania deposited the small tray of tea she had prepared onto the path and rejoined Ochix, concealed behind the verdure.

"Found one," Ochix said quietly, his misty eyes distant and unfocused. "I'm bringing her to us now."

An elderly servant woman with a deeply wrinkled yet kind face slowly marched through the bushes. Her features were blank, and her arms hung limply at her sides over her white tunic dress. Her eyes matched Ochix's, filled with a fine silver mist.

"Direct her to grab the tray and take it to Metzi. Remember to make it seem like she's having a seizure so that Metzi doesn't punish her."

Ochix pursed his lips as he concentrated. The woman stooped down and swept up the tray before carrying it toward the bathhouse.

"What should she say?" Ochix whispered.

"Have her tell Metzi that I prepared an extra serving of her headache tea just in case she needed it tonight. And keep her face turned away so that Metzi doesn't notice the clouding in her eyes."

Ochix nodded. Yemania could barely hear what was happening over the trickling fountains and waterfalls of the private garden, but she did hear when the tray crashed to the floor and Metzi shrieked.

"Help!" Metzi cried, sprinting out of the steam bath and wrapping a towel around her waist. "Help!" she screamed again, louder.

Guards immediately burst into her room, some politely averting their eyes from her barely covered body.

"What's wrong, Your Majesty? Why are you bleeding?" barked one of the men wearing a jaguar pelt.

"I'm fine. But one of the servants, she's unwell. She dropped the tea tray on me, and the bowls shattered, it must have sliced my arm. But I'll be fine, just get . . . Yemania." Even from this distance Yemania could hear the strain in her voice, as though she were fighting the urge to summon Coatl.

"Your turn, daughter of healing," Ochix said, smiling at her. "It's up to you now. I'll meet you in your room later."

Yemania jumped up and trotted toward the side hallway. She'd pretend a servant had already found her and summoned her.

She ran into the empress's bedchamber, gasping for breath as though she had been sprinting a long distance. "Are you all right, Metzi? A servant told me to hurry to your room."

"Oh, thank the gods." Metzi grabbed Yemania's wrist and yanked her toward the steam bath. "One of the servants was taken suddenly ill, like she had a fit of some kind. You have to see to her."

Yemania was touched by the level of concern she heard in Metzi's voice. She actually cared about the elderly servant.

Yemania squeezed behind Metzi through the narrow doorway into the steam bathhouse. They found the servant already sitting up, rubbing at her forehead. She sat amidst the shattered remains of the tea bowls.

"W—what happened?" she asked, her hands trembling.

Metzi crouched down beside her and beckoned Yemania to follow. "Are you all right? You had a kind of seizure and then fell onto the floor. Do you remember anything?"

Her wrinkled eyes scrunched shut. "I remember bringing in the tea and then my hands seemed to act of their own accord. I—I felt as though I lost control of my body! I'm so sorry, Your Majesty, did I hurt you? The bowls just shattered everywhere."

"I'm fine." Metzi waved a dismissive hand. Blood dribbled from a small, jagged cut on her forearm, but nothing serious.

"A seizure can be frightening," Yemania said, making her voice calm and soothing. "I imagine it does feel like your body is acting if its own accord. If you are okay with it, Your Majesty, I can make sure this woman is all right before I tend to your arm. It doesn't seem to be serious."

"No, it's just a cut. I'll be fine. Make sure her health is not at risk first."

Yemania withdrew the clean strip of white linen she has stashed in her pocket. "Let me inspect it for just a moment to make sure it isn't more serious than I think."

Metzi held out her arm, and Yemania pressed the strip of cloth against her skin to clean it. "I need to clear away a little of the blood so I can see how deep it is," Yemania explained. "Yes, that will heal easily. Let me inspect the servant first and make sure things aren't more serious."

On cue, the woman's eyes misted over again. She tried to get to her feet but groaned, swaying back until Yemania caught her. The woman's eyes cleared again, and Yemania silently said a prayer of thanks for Ochix. As she steadied the woman on her feet, she discreetly slipped the strip of linen back into her pocket.

"Let me take her to my workroom to give her a full health inspection as quickly as possible. Are you all right if I send someone else to heal your cut, since it's so minor?"

Metzi ground her teeth together. "Isn't Coatl the only other healer in the palace?"

"He is, but I promise you he will be quick."

Metzi looked uneasy, but Ochix forced the elderly woman to wobble once more.

"I'm sorry, Metzi. Let me make sure she's all right first."

Metzi let out a little groan of frustration but eventually conceded. "Fine."

———

Back in her workroom, Yemania pretended to inspect the servant, eventually giving her a clean bill of health and encouraging her to enjoy a night of rest with her family.

"Thank you, High Healer. You are such a gift." The old woman ran a hand along Yemania's cheek before she left.

Yemania lifted her own hand to touch her warm cheek. The woman had called her a gift. Something to be cherished. She didn't know why, but such a simple gesture brought tears to her eyes.

"She's right, you know." Ochix appeared in the doorway, crossing his arms and leaning against the golden frame. "You are a gift."

"I don't feel like one sometimes." Yemania dusted off her hands and started putting away the little stone vials and pots she had taken down from her shelves.

"Just because you don't feel like it, doesn't mean you aren't." He pushed himself off the doorway and moved to stand directly behind her. His hands slid around her abdomen and pulled her back against his chest.

Yemania sighed and leaned her head back against his shoulder. "Too bad you're the only one who thinks that."

"That's not true." Ochix leaned down and ran his lips down the length of her neck, sending shivers down her spine. "I imagine your brother would have something to say on that matter. And the commoners that will be receiving the remedies you made for them."

Yemania scoffed.

"No one can tell you your worth, Yemania. It's something you have to discover for yourself. I can say it a thousand times, but until you believe it in your heart, it won't be true."

"If only it were that simple," she replied.

"*It is only by my hand, by my face, my heart, my spirit that either I will wither, or I will bloom,*'" Ochix chanted.

"That's beautiful, did you make that up?"

Ochix chuckled. "No, I wish I did. It's from another of my favorite poems."

Yemania turned her body to face his, snaking her arms up and around his neck. "I didn't know you were such a poet."

Ochix's mouth twisted into a half smile. "There's a lot you don't know about me, princess of healing. But you'll have plenty of time to learn." Without warning, he lifted her up until she was sitting on her stone worktable. Yemania squealed in surprise.

His eyebrows scrunched together at a sudden thought. "I forgot to ask you when I first came in. Were you able to get some of Metzi's blood?"

Yemania smiled conspiratorially and reached into her pocket to remove the bloodstained strip of linen. She held it up. "I was. I hope it's enough to open the blood chest when Coatl returns with it."

"How does that work?" Ochix stepped closer and pulled her hips toward him.

Yemania wrapped her legs teasingly around his waist. "I'll touch it to the lid and the specially forged stone will register the magic in her blood. It should make it open. Then we can get the star stone and hide it somewhere she can't find it. I can't believe the plan worked that well!"

"I never doubted you for a moment," Ochix said, lowering his mouth to hers. Yemania arched up and pressed herself into the kiss.

A throat cleared from the doorway.

Yemania broke away from Ochix's lips and leaned around him to greet her brother. But it wasn't Coatl standing before them with crossed arms and eyes burning with rage.

It was Metzi.

CHAPTER

35

Mayana loved swimming.

Being from Atl, city of water, that was her joy as a child. When they weren't studying the codices or playing ball games in the temple plaza, she and her brothers would spend hours swimming through the city's canals or venturing into the jungles to find secluded cenotes.

Mayana did *not* love swimming in the frigid waters of the final river separating them from the City of the Dead.

When she first tested the turbulent black waters by dipping her toes in, the cold seemed to sink deeper than her skin. She felt as if her very bones were freezing. She knew from experience that it was better to dive in than torture herself by prolonging the inevitable. She angled her arms in front of her and jumped.

Her head submerged, the cold water filling her ears and caressing her skin with icy fingers. When she surfaced again, she kicked out after Ona, who paddled ahead of her with frantic little strokes. Night had fallen, and darkness surrounded them.

"Come on, Ahkin. We have to swim across now. Tomorrow is our last day to escape." She motioned with her hand. They left behind the cloaks they'd worn ever since the crashing mountains, knowing they'd never be able to swim in them once they became waterlogged.

The prince of light frowned at the water, but finally threw the longer strap of his shield over his back and inched his way in. He had wanted to wait until morning to make the swim, but they both knew their time was precious. His body began to shiver as he slowly let the water creep up his skin, first to his knees, then to his waist, the prince hissing and groaning with each step he took forward.

"Dive in and get it over with," she called.

Ahkin cut her a look. "It's easier this way."

Mayana chuckled. "No, it isn't. Trust me."

His voice grew high-pitched as the water covered the plane of his stomach. But then he stopped.

"What's wrong?" Mayana called to him, swimming closer to shore.

Ahkin crossed his arms across his chest to suppress his shivering. "I, um"—he cleared his throat—"I can't . . . swim."

Mayana choked on some of the frigid water. "You can't swim?"

His jaw tensed. "No."

"But we spent all that time together in the pools of the pleasure gardens. I thought you could."

"I can stand up in the shallow water of a pool. But that's different from swimming across a river that's as wide as a lake. And likely as deep as one too. All with a bad hand." He lifted his oddly bent fingers for emphasis.

Mayana thought back to the Sea of the Dead. How had he survived that swim, as they outran the monster crocodile Cipactli? She smacked herself on the forehead. Of course. He had been nearly unconscious, bleeding out, and she had propelled him through the water with her abilities.

He dropped his eyes and hugged himself tighter. His pride was as shriveled as other parts of him likely were in the freezing water.

"Do you want me to help you? I can use some of my blood to—"

"No." Ahkin rubbed his arms. "It's fine. I just—maybe Ona can help me? I can hold onto him if I start to struggle. Save your blood for now."

Mayana's face must have shown her suspicion because he added, "I'm not saying that because I don't want you to help me this time. I mean it. I want you to save your blood to help us later. I have a feeling we are going to need it. Let me at least try this first, and if I need your help, I promise I will ask."

Mayana dipped her head in the water and smoothed back her hair. "Fine. But you have to ask."

"I will," Ahkin assured her.

She continued to tread water, and he whistled for Ona. The dog yipped in excitement and paddled back for him. Ahkin wrapped his injured arm around the dog's smooth-furred back and with a deep breath of determination, left the safety of the shore.

Mayana felt a surge of pride. She knew how scared she was to swim a river this large with no idea what lurked below them. And she was comfortable in the water. Ahkin would be fearing the water itself as much as whatever lived within its depths.

"Do you think there will be any beasts or creatures in it?" Ahkin asked, voicing her thoughts.

He and Ona reached her, and they slowly made for the distant lights flickering against the night.

"There will likely be something that tries to stop us. The trial can't just be the swimming itself."

Ahkin grunted. "It should be."

Mayana smiled and dipped her head below the surface once more. She propelled herself forward like an otter gracefully dancing through the currents.

"Show-off," Ahkin muttered, but his smile was teasing. She splashed at him and dove below again.

Her ears began to throb from the cold, and she decided it was probably safer to keep her head as dry as possible.

They swam for what felt like hours. The lights in the distance barely felt any closer. As the shore behind them grew farther and farther away, the waves of the river began to grow more turbulent. Darkness seemed to envelop them entirely. Ahkin clung to Ona, coughing up water each time a rough wave slapped him in the face. Her own arms and legs were beginning to burn with exhaustion.

"This is the reason they bury dogs or the effigies of dogs with the dead," Ahkin said, his voice straining with effort.

"Why?" Mayana panted.

"Dogs are supposed to guide you across the final river. And I'm sure grateful for him right now."

Ona, who appeared to have more energy left than either of them, looked smug.

"You should come swim closer to us," Ahkin added. "His body is so warm, and I can tell it's making a difference for me."

"I'm okay for now." Though her teeth rattled together.

The cold began to seep its way into her thoughts as well as her skin. *Why do you keep fighting?* whispers in her ears began to say. *Just give up. You will never make it.*

But she fought back. *I will make it. If anyone can swim across this river, it's me.*

But then another hour passed.

Her lungs struggled to suck down air. Her muscles began to scream as much as her mind, wanting to push away from the cold and the exhaustion but having nowhere to go. Infectious thoughts began to spread, festering and feeding on her strength.

The Mother goddess never prepared you for this, the whispers insisted.

No, she let me find the bones of my mother. She has given me a great gift.

No, she took your mother away from you in the first place. She never should have died.

It was an accident. The steps of the temple are impossibly steep. She was not the first to fall, nor the last.

The harder she fought the voices, the angrier they seemed to become that she did not believe them. She began to lose the strength to challenge them. The waves themselves even began to look like faces, demon faces with black, soulless eyes, as the whispers in her head crescendoed unbearably.

You will die here, daughter of water. You are not strong enough. You will never make it.

You think that prince has learned his lesson? You really think he trusts and accepts the real you? He called you a lying heretic.

Why fight to return to a family that doesn't want you anyway? You are a burden to them.

The empire will never accept you or your beliefs. They will not believe you. You will be sent back here the moment you return.

Mayana couldn't take it anymore. *Stop it. Stop it!* STOP IT!

Mayana clawed at the water, almost as if she could dispel the voices if she could drown them out. If she pushed herself hard enough, maybe she could escape them. Outrun them. Ahkin's warning cry sounded somewhere far behind her.

You are too sensitive. Too emotional. You think your passion is a gift, but it is a curse. You are too much for anyone to handle. You think the prince of light will marry someone like you? He will eventually see you for what you are. Unstable. Unpredictable. Unsafe. You are not worthy of being trusted, because you are selfish.

No. I'm not. Her own voice was barely a whimper in her mind.

The whispers smelled the blood of her greatest fear. Her greatest wound.

You are selfish! they taunted. *You think you care so much, but you only care about yourself. Your own comfort, your own feelings. You care only to protect yourself! You do not believe in the sacrifices because you do not understand the selflessness required for such an act of love. You only love yourself because you secretly fear that no one else ever will . . .*

"Stop!" she screamed, pressing her frozen hands against her ears. Where was Ahkin? She couldn't see him or Ona above the turbulent surface. She was alone in the waves, in the middle of this endlessly dark river.

The Mother goddess did not save you, because she doesn't really care about you. She wants you to die here. You are nothing to her. No more than an ant under the sandal of an emperor. She will not save you . . .

She screamed again. She couldn't tell if the water blinding her was from the waves or from her own tears. Another wave crashed into her, forcing water down her throat. She sputtered. Her muscles burned with fatigue. She couldn't keep going like this. Another wave choked her before she even got the chance to catch her breath.

Stay with us, daughter of water. Stop fighting and stay here. Give up. Life has never been fair to you and it never will be. What is there even to return to up above? No one there loves you. You don't deserve to live . . .

The next wave pulled her under completely.

And she couldn't pull herself back up.

Metzi looked at Yemania as though she had never seen her before, and the shame of it made Yemania want to curl into a ball on the floor.

She shoved Ochix away from her and exposed her palms to Metzi. "Your Majesty, I can explain . . ." But she couldn't. There were no words to explain away what Metzi had just witnessed.

"I'd be fascinated to hear what your explanation is. Because to me, it looks as though you and my betrothed have been sneaking around behind my back. And not only are you trying to break my engagement, you want to steal my fallen star?"

Yemania opened her mouth, but no sound came out. Her shame boiled like a hot spring inside her stomach until she thought she was going to be sick.

"Why?" Metzi suddenly demanded. She clenched her teeth and spat the words at Yemania like poison from a snake. "After everything I did to raise you up? I made you High Healer. I thought you understood what it felt like to be treated like nothing. And now you betray me like this? Was it to humiliate me? Prove something to yourself?"

"No," Yemania sobbed, finally finding her voice. "It's nothing like that. Please, Your Majesty. Ochix and I met before you ever—"

Metzi backed away from her, shaking her head in disbelief. "He was right. Everything he told me. I should have listened . . ."

And then she saw Coatl, half hidden in shadows in the hall. "I didn't want to hurt you like this, but I thought you needed to know the truth. About both of them." His voice made Yemania's knees give out. They hit the ground with a sickening crack, but Yemania didn't even register the pain radiating down her legs.

Coatl stepped into the candlelit room and put an arm around Metzi's shoulders. Metzi did not push him off, but embraced him back as though he were the only solid thing to be found in the world.

Coatl's lip curled as he eyed Yemania with a look of deepest disgust. "I couldn't believe it myself when I discovered them half naked together in the High Healer's workroom. But I knew you needed to know the truth. I knew you wouldn't believe me until you saw and heard every-thing for yourself."

A sound like rushing water filled her ears and her arms began to trem-ble. No. Coatl couldn't have betrayed her. *No . . .*

Metzi reached forward and ripped the ruby pendant from around Yema-nia's neck. She barely registered the sting of the chain cutting into her skin. Not as she watched Metzi hand the High Healer's amulet back to Coatl.

"You thought you could control me? Make me do what you wanted?" she seethed. "I've proved it once and I will prove it again, that *no one* makes my decisions for me. No one takes that power away from me. *Ever!*"

Her hand collided with the side of Yemania's face, and pain exploded across her cheek. Yemania fell sideways onto the floor as Ochix jumped between them.

"Please, this is my fault. She's innocent. I seduced her, tricked her into helping me—"

Metzi fixed Ochix with a look terrifying enough to make him flinch, stopping him midsentence. She took several heaving breaths, and her voice became deadly calm. "You got your wish, prince of death. This engage-ment is canceled. I will not be marrying you. I think we will be having a ritual sacrifice instead."

"Metzi, please—" Ochix started, but Metzi screamed him down.

"I am an empress! You will refer to me as 'Your Majesty.' I am the one with the power here, not you. Guards, seize them!"

Several Eagle warriors marched into the room and seized Ochix's arms. He tried to pull himself free of their grip, fists pounding at faces and stomachs, but he was quickly overpowered. One soldier grabbed his long hair and forced his head back, and another quickly deprived him of his skull-engraved knife. He tried to arch toward Yemania, her name on his lips, but found his own knife pressed against his throat.

"Go ahead, spill my blood now. Why wait for a formal ritual?" he hissed at Metzi. His eyes shifted to Coatl with a look that clearly said, *I will kill you for this.*

Metzi's mouth curved into a wicked, taunting smile. "Oh, I won't be sacrificing you, prince of death. I'm not foolish enough to bring on the wrath of your entire empire. I will be sending you and your delegation back to Miquitz. I want you out of this city before sunrise. You can tell your father our agreement is over. He can deal with the consequences of disappointing the gods."

Ochix's eyes went wide with realization just as Yemania's did. Metzi would not be sacrificing Ochix. Which meant . . .

"No!" Ochix screamed, straining against his captors. His desperate eyes found Yemania, still sprawled on the floor. He fought to get to her. "No! Take me instead!"

"Take him away." Metzi dismissed them with a jerk of her head.

"No! Yemania! Yemania!" Ochix continued to scream as he was dragged forcefully from the room, his screams echoing down the hall and fading with each passing second. Until he was gone.

Until she was alone.

Metzi stalked over to the stone tables, where the remedies Yemania and Coatl had been preparing for the commoners lay spread out in neat rows. They were organized according to the ailment they would treat, some even containing precious drops of Yemania's or Coatl's blood.

With an almighty sweep of her arm, Metzi wiped the tiny clay pots off the table and onto the floor. Yemania felt her heart shatter with every crashing pot, her soul bleeding out with every mixture and concoction now spreading across the wreckage. All her work . . .

Yemania couldn't find the strength or will to push herself off the floor, so instead she curled in on herself, tears burning their way down her cheeks. She wanted to dissolve into nothingness. To stop existing at all.

An Eagle warrior wrenched her to her feet, but Yemania felt as though her legs no longer functioned. Another soldier lifted her other arm, until she was suspended between them. It was probably for the best. She felt so disconnected from her body it was as if she were an observer watching herself being carried toward the hall.

"Take her to the sacrificial victim chamber in the temple. Come sunrise, I will show the empire exactly what I plan to do to people who betray me." Metzi's voice was as cold and inhuman as her patron's.

Yemania found one last scrap of strength as she passed by Coatl. Enough strength to give him a look that said, *Ochix will only kill you if I don't get there first.*

Coatl blinked in fear and took a step back. *Good,* she thought savagely. That scheming snake. She couldn't believe he had done this to her, set her and Ochix up so that he could worm his way back into Metzi's good graces.

But at the same time, she felt like a fool for not seeing it sooner. They had finally been repairing the breach their relationship suffered when he left for Tollan all those years ago. He had been one of her sources of comfort in this new and foreign place, and she had comforted *him* when he lost the woman he loved.

Perhaps it had been real, the bond they were rebuilding. But now she saw he was still the selfish little boy who'd abandoned her to run to the capital. He cared about her when it served his best interests, but he still cared more about himself than anyone else. The moment an opportunity arose for him to get what he wanted, he took it—their relationship be damned. Whatever it took to get Metzi back. What was his sister compared to the empress of light, the love of his life?

Could she blame Coatl for making such a choice? It was the same choice her father made when he sent her as his tribute. The same choice Ahkin made when he chose Mayana over her. She was the easiest to sacrifice. Exactly as her father had said that day. The one it hurt the least to lose.

Perhaps sacrifice had been her destiny all along. It was time she embraced it. She was a fool for thinking, or even hoping, for anything more than that. For thinking she mattered enough to the world to be worth staying in it.

Now she'd never see Ochix again. She'd never fulfill her dream of healing those who also felt they didn't matter.

At least she would get to see Mayana again soon.

CHAPTER

37

Ahkin searched the waves for Mayana, but the dark tint of her hair blended so well with the blackness of the water that it was like trying to find a grain of sand on a beach. She had been swimming beside him and Ona a few moments ago, and then suddenly, she was no longer beside them. He tried to see over the jagged peaks of the choppy waters, but nothing.

She was gone.

"*Stop it!*" he had heard her scream.

Panic clenched his heart. Something was attacking her. He clung to the warmth of Ona's body and scanned the waves. Where was she? *Where was she?*

He threw his prayers toward the suffocating clouds. *Mother, please help me find her.* A tug on his heart pulled him to the right, and he looked, just as a hand slid below the surface.

Ahkin didn't think. He dove after her.

He realized the moment he did so that it wasn't the smartest of ideas, especially considering the fact that he didn't actually know how to swim. Ona barked and followed him.

His lungs stung at the loss of air. Still, he pushed himself forward, more flailing than swimming. But at least he was moving. He opened his eyes, and the water burned as much as the ice had in the crashing mountains. He reached out into the darkness. Feeling. Searching. Hoping.

He'd never find her like this, never . . .

The fingers of his good hand brushed against something and he grabbed. He would not miss her this time.

He pulled her toward him, wrapping her up in his arms as he kicked for the surface.

They broke through, the air pricking at his face like a thousand bone needles. He pulled back to assess her condition. She wasn't breathing. He kissed her, forcing air into her mouth, and slapped her back roughly. Then Ona was there, licking and barking and wiggling against them both.

Her eyelids fluttered. The dog's heat seemed to make a difference.

"Ona, keep licking her!"

The dog obliged, nuzzling against her head, neck, chest, until finally her eyes flew open.

He hugged the dog, cradling him between them as Ahkin fought with his legs to keep them all afloat.

Mayana seemed to realize this because she pulled him toward her too, pressing her frozen lips back against his as she combined her kicking with his. They supported each other in the water.

"What happened?" Ahkin panted between gasping breaths.

Ona began paddling again too, this time with both Mayana and Ahkin pressed tightly against his body on either side.

Mayana shook her head as though she was dispelling more than water from her ears. "There were voices. Horrible voices . . ."

She explained what she had heard, what they said to her. How they ultimately pulled her under. Ahkin's temper rose with each phrase she repeated. Was it possible to beat up a river?

"I don't understand. Why didn't the voices affect you?" There were dark crescents beneath her eyes, and she looked as exhausted as she sounded.

Ahkin remembered how the dog's body heat had sustained him through the swim, how she had revived when Ona had pressed his body against hers.

"The dog," he said quietly. "There is a reason the ancient texts say a guide dog is essential to join you as you cross the final river. They must protect you from whatever power this river possesses."

Mayana leaned her head against the nearly hairless back of her child-hood friend. Her voice cracked with emotion as she said, "Dogs are a gift from the gods."

———

With Ona as their guide and source of strength, they kept swimming. The lights in the distance began to grow larger and larger until finally, Ahkin saw massive stone bowls, as big as a house, burning with flame. They stood on either side of a black sand beach, flanking night-dark stone steps that led up the side of an obsidian cliff. More light glowed from atop a low cliff above their heads.

Beacons to welcome souls to the City of the Dead.

Xibalban morning had begun to dawn by the time they crawled onto the beach. Ahkin could barely speak from exhaustion, and judging from Mayana's silence, neither could she. Though Ona was usually as excited and energetic as a squirrel from the overworld, the moment they dragged themselves out of the water, his ears went back and he assumed a submis-sive stance. Something about this place terrified the dog. And Ahkin didn't really blame him.

In the light of the flaming stone beacons, he could see that the bottom of the cliff was littered with bones. Skulls, femurs, rib cages, all piled into mounds like the carefully crafted nest of a jungle bird. He assumed they were the bodies of souls that had not survived the crossing of the final river. There were thousands of bones piled there. The thought raised the hair on his arms.

They were blessed to have made it so far.

Mayana had been incredibly quiet since her near-drowning incident. Ahkin assumed it was difficult for her to accept that the daughter of water had almost died in . . . well . . . water. As if a friendly companion had turned suddenly vicious and attacked.

He also couldn't believe some of the things the river had whispered to her. Were those really the deepest fears and insecurities that festered within her heart? Were they really so different from his own? That no one would love and accept her? They were whispers she would have to continue to fight to keep them from dragging her under.

"Are you okay?" he asked her, knowing it was a foolish question.

"I'm alive," was her only answer. She sat on the edge of the water, her arms wrapped around her knees. Her bag lay beside her on the sand.

He looked down the long beach at the base of the obsidian cliffs. "I know it's morning, but we have to rest. It's the last day of the Nemontemi here in Xibalba, and I think we need to go in to meet the Lord of Death as alert as possible."

"Okay," she whispered.

Ahkin led them to hide behind one of the mounds of bones. He didn't want to attract any attention to their arrival, so they couldn't light a fire, but his shield could at least provide heat. He took it off his back and pricked his finger, allowing the golden face of the sun etched into its surface to warm and glow. Mayana rubbed her hands together above it and then set to work making some maize mush for them.

"I can do that," Ahkin offered. "If you want to rest for a moment."

"It's okay," she said, her voice sounding hollow and empty. "I want to keep busy so I don't have to think."

Ahkin respected her wishes. When she was finished, he took the maize mush from her gratefully, but he was still worried about her. He wanted to wrap his arms around her and hold her together, but she seemed to need some distance to put together her thoughts.

"You sleep," he insisted. "I'll keep first watch."

"And you will need sleep too, so don't be a hero. Make sure you wake me up at some point." She eyed him warily.

"I know. We are a team in this now, not just me trying to make up for being an idiot."

A ghost of a smile tugged at her lips. Seeing it warmed Ahkin as effectively as the shield.

She scooted closer to him and leaned into his shoulder. Ahkin draped an arm around her and hugged her tighter.

"Sleep," he said.

Mayana dropped her head and let her eyes slide shut. Soon her breathing slowed, and she snuggled in tighter against him. Ona curled up at their feet, not wanting to be far away from them. The dog's skittishness set his own nerves on a blade's edge.

He tried to think about what the day would bring, but everything he had read about the City of the Dead was not encouraging. They would want to find the council chamber of the lords of death and ask to speak to Cizin directly. He knew the lords loved to humiliate any who dared to enter their realms alive. He also doubted Cizin would let them leave without first proving their worth. They also needed to find and save the bones of Quetzalcoatl.

After a few hours, Ahkin felt sleep threatening to pull him under. He kept his promise to Mayana and woke her gently with a little shake to her shoulder.

Mayana jerked awake. "What? Is everything okay?"

Ahkin chuckled. "Yes, we are fine. You told me to wake you up so I could get a chance to sleep."

Mayana stretched as sinuously as a cat, and Ahkin felt the back of his neck heating again.

"Thank you for actually waking me," she said. She smiled at him with genuine pride.

Ahkin would make it his goal in life to see her smile like that every single day. "I promised I would."

She seemed to be in a much better place after getting some rest. She pressed a light kiss against his lips and ran her hand lovingly across his cheek.

Ahkin sighed in contentment and rested his head in her lap, her fingers dancing absentmindedly through his hair. The warmth of her thigh beneath his cheek made him squirm, but not in an unpleasant way. Between the gentle tracing of delicate patterns her hands made in his hair and the feel of her skin so warm and close, he actually felt at peace.

At least as much at peace as was possible sleeping behind a pile of bones on the outskirts of the City of the Dead.

CHAPTER

38

The temple's holding chamber for sacrificial victims was much bigger than Yemania expected. The low stone room, lit by a single sputtering torch, could fit several small houses inside, though it was barely tall enough to stand. It was usually used for housing hordes of captured enemies from Miquitz. Now, besides her, there was only one other victim, buried beneath a bundle of rags in a corner. Probably another criminal awaiting execution.

Because that's what she was now. A criminal. A traitor. She had betrayed the empress, the gods' chosen vessel to lead the empire. To challenge her word was to challenge the word of the gods, and now Yemania would be paying her penance for that sin for the rest of her afterlife through the layers of Xibalba.

The inner bowels of the temple were still warm and humid, heated by the jungle air seeping in from above. Yemania felt as if she were sitting in the mouth of a great beast, waiting for it to swallow her whole. She pulled her knees in tighter against her chest, hugging them for comfort.

"Why do you just accept your fate?" rasped a voice from the bundle of rags. The figure within them shifted and slowly sat up.

"What choice do I have?" Yemania said, her voice thick from crying. Something scuttled in one of the dark corners of the room and she flinched away from it.

"You seem like the type to have more fight in you, that's all." The rags shifted further, and Yemania saw that the other prisoner was an elderly woman. Her face was deeply lined, and her dark hair swirled with white into a bun on the top of her head. What could an older woman have done to deserve such criminal treatment?

"Why are *you* here?" Yemania asked.

"I'm here because I want to be. But I'm thinking I'll leave soon." Her voice was still raspy, but Yemania sensed a tint of madness. Perhaps the old crone was insane and a danger to herself and others.

"Well, I'm sorry to disappoint you," Yemania said, "but I don't think either of us will be leaving until they lead us to the sacrificial altar." Her eyes darted to the thick stone rolled across the entrance to their chamber. There weren't even any windows, so she had no idea how close to morning it was. The only indication of time passing was the torch burning lower and lower.

The old woman fiddled with something in her hands, and Yemania stretched her neck to see what it was. A tiny red dress. A small humanoid shape.

"How do you have a doll?" Yemania asked. "Did they let you bring it with you?"

"No one *lets* me do anything, daughter of healing. I do as I wish."

"Mm-hmm." Yemania knew better than to argue with someone whose mind was obviously lost.

"Do you want to see what I've made?" she croaked, a glint in her dark eye.

"Um, sure." Yemania couldn't see any harm in entertaining her. She imagined she would be strong enough to fight her off if she needed to. But so far the crone seemed harmless.

The woman hobbled toward her on spindly legs. As the rags fell off completely, Yemania noticed her dress was woven in an intricate geometric pattern of white and black. How could a woman like her afford such a beautiful garment?

She stopped right in front of her, and Yemania instinctively leaned back. The woman held out the doll for Yemania to take, and she did so with shaking fingers.

The tiny red dress, a tunic dress, was cut exactly like her own. The doll had long dark hair, a puckered little mouth, and sad slanting eyes of thread. Its nose seemed slightly too large for its face, and there were red whorls of paint across the cheeks. A tiny red pendant even hung around its neck.

Yemania frowned as she studied it, a thrill of unease raising the hairs on her arms. "Is this—is this supposed to be me?" She locked eyes with the old woman.

The wrinkled face split into a wide-toothed grin. "Indeed, daughter of healing. I've been working on it for some time. I think I've almost got it right."

"I don't understand. Why would you make a doll of me? I've never met you before." The unease was solidifying into full-blown fear. She threw the doll on the ground at the old woman's feet and scooted away from her.

The woman bent down and retrieved the doll from the grime of the chamber floor. She brushed it off gently with loving fingers.

"You should treat yourself with more care," she cawed like a crow, her face crumpling into a frown.

"I don't know who you are or what you—" Yemania started to say.

"You know, Mayana had a very similar reaction when she met me. She didn't trust me in the slightest."

"Mayana? You knew Mayana?"

"I *know* Mayana." The old woman jutted her chin into the air.

"Then I'm sorry to tell you, but Mayana is *dead*. She's gone. Like you and I are going to be in the morning."

But the wide-toothed grin was back. "I don't think either of us is going to die tomorrow. Because you see, my child, I cannot die. And I don't think I'm going to let you either. Not tomorrow, anyway."

"You are insane." Yemania huffed, burying her face into her knees.

"You would really call the Mother of creation insane?"

Mother of—? Yemania slowly lifted her head, her eyes wide in disbelief. No. That wasn't possible. This old woman was not—

"You may call me Ometeotl. Mother, and technically Father, of creation. I am the duality, the light and the dark, the earth and sky, the sacred two energies."

A soft glow surrounded her, filling the chamber and chasing the shadows away until every stone in the wall seemed to shine with golden light. It was almost too much for Yemania to behold. She felt her mouth gape open, and without hesitation, she prostrated herself on the floor in front of the goddess.

"No, no, no. None of that. We don't have time." Ometeotl reached down and lifted Yemania's chin. "Get up, my child."

"Wh-wh-wh—" Terror and awe mingled inside her with such intensity that Yemania couldn't decide which emotion to feel. Nor could she apparently decide what to say. What does anyone say to *the creator of the universe*?

"I am here because I needed to give you this." Ometeotl again handed her the doll.

"You came to me to give me a doll?"

Ometeotl chuckled. "I came to give you *yourself*."

Yemania frowned even deeper, causing the goddess to sigh in exasperation. "Humans," she muttered. "Let me try another way. My daughter of healing, do you think I make mistakes?"

Yemania shook her head. "No, of course not, great Mother."

"Then why do you question what I made you to be?"

Yemania opened her mouth. Closed it. Opened it. Closed it again.

Ometeotl smiled warmly at her. "You think you do not matter, that you have no value. That everyone is willing to toss you aside like a husk of maize."

Tears swam behind Yemania's eyes, and she swallowed hard to hold them back. She did not answer.

"You, Yemania of Pahtia, are *my* treasure. I made you. I designed you exactly as I meant you to be. And as we both agree, I do not make mistakes. You have an important role to play in the coming weeks. A role that you and you alone can fill. I need you. And Mayana will need you."

"Mayana is still alive?" Yemania gasped.

Ometeotl scrunched her face in concentration, as though she was trying to see something far away. "Hmm, yes, for now she is still alive. I'm hoping she remains that way. But I have faith in her, as I do in you."

Yemania fell silent for several moments, trying to collect her thoughts. But there was still something she wrestled with. "How am I supposed to believe I have worth when everyone around me treats me like I don't?"

A shadow crossed Ometeotl's ancient face. "Sometimes my creations can be cruel to each other. You cannot let your own worth be determined by others. You and you alone decide that. Your worth comes from the fact that you are my creation. Uniquely gifted. No one gets to take that away from you. What is it that darling boy of yours said? '*It is only by my hand, by my face, my heart, my spirit that either I will wither, or I will bloom.*' It was the truth you needed to hear, Yemania. You alone will choose whether you wither or bloom."

Yemania let out a small sob at the mention of Ochix. "Is he . . . ?"

"He's fine, dear child. And if I know him, which I do—I did make him, after all—he is fighting to find a way back to you. So, are you going to fight to find a way back to him? Can you believe that you are worth it? I think if you look close enough, you will find there is much for you to be proud of."

Could she? Could she believe she mattered? Not because her family thought she did, or because a prince chose her above all others, but because she was created to be exactly herself? Her gaze fell to the tiny doll in her hands, to its sad-looking eyes. She was a gifted healer. She had a heart of compassion and love for everyone, no matter their status or nationality. She was a kind sister, even when her brother did not deserve it. She was clever and full of passion for helping others. A smile tugged at her mouth—she could even start a fire with her own two hands.

And she could decide her worth for herself.

Ochix had loved her not because she was the most beautiful, the most powerful, the most influential princess in the empire. He had seen her. *Really* seen her. He had noticed her because of her heart, and he had found her to be beautiful. The question was, could she see those things for herself?

"Yes," Yemania whispered.

"What was that, dear?" Ometeotl leaned in, her thin lips curving into a smile.

"Yes, I can believe I'm worth it," she said louder, her voice echoing around the stone walls.

"Good, because like I said, I'm going to need you. So let's get you out of here, shall we?" Ometeotl rubbed her hands together. When she opened them again, a bulbous black-and-yellow spider was sitting on her palm.

"Here," she said, offering Yemania the spider.

Yemania arched an eyebrow. "Um, how is a spider going to help me escape?"

The Mother goddess snapped her fingers and a walnut shell appeared in her other hand. She pushed the little insect into the shell with a nudge of her finger and closed the lid. "Trust me, this will be all you need to escape. And when you do, head for Omitl. You will know what to do when you get there. Ochix will find you on the way."

Yemania had no idea how the spider would help, but she took it anyway. Who was she to question the goddess? "I—um, okay. I'll trust you."

"Good. Do me a favor and if you see Mayana, tell her she could learn a lesson from you," she said with a wink. "And keep the doll. I think it's finally finished."

Yemania blinked, and Ometeotl was gone.

All that was left were the little walnut shell containing the black-and-yellow spider and the tiny doll version of herself.

Yemania smiled as she looked down at the doll. Its eyes were no longer slanting down in sadness, but quirked up, as if the doll itself were smiling too.

CHAPTER

39

It was the last day they had to escape Xibalba, and Mayana anxiously wanted to get moving. The morning had already turned into afternoon, but still she let Ahkin sleep. She knew they would never make it through whatever trials the city held if they did not have their full strength. Finally her anxiety got the better of her, and she tapped him gently. Ona licked his face too, which definitely helped.

Ahkin jerked awake, his hand darting to the knife on his waistband.

"We need to get moving. The day is already half gone, and if we don't escape by tonight . . ." She didn't need to finish that thought.

Together, they finished off the last of the maize kernels in the bag the Mother goddess had given them. Now all that remained were the bleached white bones of her mother and the walnut shell containing a tiny worm. Mayana still didn't know the purpose of the worm. Perhaps it had been the goddess's idea of a joke.

"Since I know you like plans so much, what's ours?" she asked him.

Ahkin tried to smile. "I know we need to find the council chamber of the lords of Xibalba. We will need to ask to speak to Cizin, the Lord of Death himself. The legends say that the council will try to humiliate any who enter."

"You don't know how?"

Ahkin shook his head, looking disappointed with himself.

Mayana perched her hands on her hips. "We will need to be careful and clever and quick."

"My specialty." Ahkin gave her a roguish smile.

Mayana rolled her eyes with a good-natured sigh and started walking toward the obsidian stairs.

Ahkin scrambled to his feet after her.

The cliff above them was not tall, but the obsidian stairs snaked their way up, lined on either side by flaming torches. At first, Mayana didn't think anything of the torches—and then she noticed them burning in human skulls.

How in the nine hells were they supposed to survive a place that lined its welcoming steps with skull torches?

They crested the final steps and emerged onto a great plaza. And what Mayana saw ripped the air from her lungs and turned her legs to stone. She could not force herself to move forward.

The city was surrounded by volcanic mountains, their peaks glowing like embers and oozing liquid fire down their craggy sides. Because the mountains were so tall, it seemed to be cast in shadows, yet everything was tinged with red and orange light that reflected off the smooth glass of the numerous tiered pyramids. The entire city seemed to be consumed with fire.

But it was indeed a *city*. There were seven large pyramids, three on each side of a main plaza, with the largest pyramid at the head, almost too far away to see clearly. Around each pyramid clustered gardens and smaller structures. The main pyramid appeared to be shaped like the flaring roots of a massive ceiba tree, complete with spikes that looked longer than Mayana's entire body. The underworld was said to contain the roots of the great tree that spanned creation, so she immediately understood the significance of the main temple's structure. She had a feeling that was their destination if they wanted to reach the overworld.

Also like a city, the main plaza and avenue buzzed with activity, like an active beehive. Except that these were not bees—or even humans—that bustled about.

They were demons.

Mayana had never seen demons before, and now she wished to never see them again. They were as varied in color as the flowers in the jungles of her home: deep red like the color of a muddy riverbank, vibrant green like a freshly cut vine, as yellow as a snake's eyes. And their shapes were just as different. Some stood barely to her knees, stocky and rounded as they waddled down the street. Others were thin and as tall as trees, dragging long, spindly fingers along the ground. Some had legs or feet that faced the wrong way. Some were missing eyes or had far too many. A few even looked like children, but with bone-like horns projecting from their smooth heads and blood dripping from their pointed teeth.

Mayana's palms were slick with sweat. She tried to wipe them against her legs. She found herself so close to Ahkin that she imagined she could hear the frantic beating of his heart. Her hand reached out and clenched his arm, while he moved the shield from his back to a ready position in front of him. Her stomach was so tight she feared it might reject the last of the maize she'd eaten. Ona would not move from between her legs. His whimpers of fear intensified her own feelings of dread.

"What are they?" she whispered in Ahkin's ear. "Why do they all look so different?"

Ahkin snaked his bad hand behind her waist and held her close. "They serve the different lords of Xibalba. They are sent above to wreak havoc and to bring ailments and torture to anyone unlucky enough to come across them. They roam the jungles at night."

Mayana swallowed hard. She'd never be tempted to break curfew again if those things roamed the jungles. No wonder the Chicome were so strict about staying inside at night.

"Will they let us pass?"

"I doubt it. They take pleasure in torturing humans." Ahkin lifted his shield higher. "Best to stay hidden, I think."

Mayana assumed that he had cut his finger at some point, because when she looked down at her hand, she could no longer see it. He was bending the light around them to hide them from view.

"Let's hope they can't sense us in other ways," he said.

They carefully stayed off the main avenue, avoiding contact with any of the passing demons. They hugged the walls of various structures littering the bases of the smaller temples, stopping every so often and holding their breath if anything came too close. Each demon they passed seemed even more terrifying than the last. After passing a tall, sickly yellow demon with human hands and feet impaled upon long spikes along its back, Mayana decided to keep her eyes trained on her feet to keep herself from vomiting.

Ahkin slowed them to a stop and pressed them against another wall. A bat-winged demon that looked as though it had been carved from angular obsidian turned its burning red eyes toward them as though it could see. It released a forked tongue from its snakelike face, and Ahkin quickly rushed them on. Ona nearly tripped her as they ran, the poor dog refusing to leave the shelter of her legs.

There were so many close calls, Mayana was sure they'd be caught. All too soon, and yet not fast enough, they reached the narrow steps of the main temple pyramid. It had taken almost the entire afternoon to sneak across the city unseen, slowly inching their way through crowded marketplaces and streets. By the time they reached the temple, night was already starting to fall. They didn't have much time left to escape. The steps were as impossibly narrow as the steps of her temple back home, the same steps her mother met her death upon. Mayana squeezed her bag for comfort, reminding herself that if they could escape, she could correct that grave mistake.

And so they began to climb. Ahkin kept them hidden from view so that none of the demons rushing up and down the steps would notice them. Mayana bent forward to climb up the massive stairs, wondering if they had been built to be so tall on purpose. She felt as though she were groveling at the Lord of Death's doorstep. The gathering darkness of night unsettled her stomach. They had to hurry. And they would have to reveal themselves eventually if they wanted an audience with Cizin—though part of Mayana wished they could remain hidden forever.

It took them almost an hour to climb the pyramid stairs. At the top, a black stone building with columns made of more piled human bones greeted them. The walls were smooth and reflected the flickering light of the volcanoes around them. Mayana briefly thought of Yoli and wished the princess of fire was here with them. Her odd sense of humor would be a welcome distraction. But the building seemed to have no doors. The demons walked right through the smooth stone wall as if it were a curtain. Ahkin pressed his hand against the stone, but it remained solid and immovable. Apparently, humans were not allowed to enter as easily as the demons doing their masters' bidding.

"If you wish to enter, you must first pass a test," said a voice as cold and ancient as a star demon.

Mayana whipped around, looking for the source of the speaker. But instead of a demon standing nearby, a skull appeared within the wall itself, as if the bone-white face was trapped within the fire glass. It was completely fleshless, no eyes in its inky black sockets.

"If you wish to enter, you must first pass a test," it repeated. Fingers of ice reached their way down Mayana's back.

"Hasn't everything here already been a test?" Ahkin grumbled.

The skull smiled—well, Mayana supposed it smiled. At least, it opened its mouth and did not speak again.

"Wh-what is the test?" Mayana asked.

"You must play the conch."

"Conch?" Ahkin said. "What conch? I don't see a seashell any—" but a clatter sounded at their feet. Mayana and Ahkin both looked down to see a beautiful conch shell, bone white and pink, waiting as if it had been there all along.

"Prove you are clever enough. Play the conch," the skull repeated. "And then you shall be allowed to enter."

Ahkin strapped his shield onto his back, stooped down, and lifted the shell. He turned it over in his hands. There were no holes to play the shell like a horn.

"How am I supposed to play it if there is no hole?" he asked the skull.

Again, it did not answer.

"I remember this story," Mayana said quickly. "Quetzalcoatl had to play a conch shell when he came to rescue the bones of humanity. But there were no holes in it!"

Ahkin waited with wide eyes. "And? How did he do it?"

Mayana chewed on her thumbnail for a few moments, trying to

remember the story she had heard as a child. Then it came back to her. "He put bees in it!"

Ahkin swore. "We don't have any bees!"

"But we do have a worm! A worm that likes to bite, remember?" She was already digging in her bag for the walnut shell. When the Mother goddess had given them the tiny white worm as one of her odd gifts that day on the beach, Ahkin had opened the walnut shell. The worm had bitten a perfect circle into his palm before Ona healed it.

Ona sniffed at the shell and sneezed when Mayana held it out on her palm.

"The shell may not have holes to play it like a war horn yet, but drop this worm on it and I guarantee it will have holes within a few heartbeats."

Ahkin held the shell out to her. Mayana opened the walnut and released the tiny, wiggling worm onto its surface.

The little worm lifted its head and immediately arched toward the shell, taking a tiny bite with a surprisingly loud crunch.

"Have it bite the end here." Ahkin indicated the pointed tip of the conch. "We use conch horns on the battlefield. I've seen where they drill into them with tools."

Mayana scooped up the worm back into the walnut shell and moved it to the pointed top. With another loud crunch, the worm bit the point clean off. Back into the walnut shell it went and safely into Mayana's bag.

She tried to mimic the skull's eerie voice. "Go ahead. Play the conch, Ahkin."

"Play the conch," the skull repeated, as though unsatisfied with Mayana's attempt to be eerie and needing to upstage her. ·

Ahkin lifted the shell to his lips and took a deep breath. He blew.

The deep, resonant sound echoed around them, loud enough that it carried down the steps of the temple and back toward the main avenue. Every demon they could see froze and turned its eyes expectantly to the top of the temple. They all knew the horn meant one thing.

Humans were here to see the lords of Xibalba.

CHAPTER

40

Yemania dozed in and out, confident in the Mother's promise that she would not die come sunrise. Finally, when the torch's light was close to burning out entirely, there came a scraping of stone at the chamber's entrance.

Yemania straightened up, tightening her grip on the doll and walnut shell.

"Yem? Yem? Are you in there?"

Bile rose up in her throat at the sound of Coatl's voice.

She didn't even bother getting up off the floor. "Yes, I'm in here. Do you really think I'd be anywhere else?"

Coatl whispered to the guards outside, and the fading slapping of several pairs of sandals on stone told her he'd asked the guards to give them some privacy. She snorted. He probably didn't want them overhearing whatever she was about to scream at him.

Always protecting himself.

"What do you want, Coatl? Come to say goodbye before your girl-friend rips my heart out?"

"You can't be mad at me, Yem." He stepped into the dimming room. The fading torchlight glinted off the ruby pendant hanging against his bare chest.

"Oh, I can't be mad at you for selling me out? For using me and Ochix to get what you wanted at the expense of *my life*?"

"You're being so dramatic." Coatl sniffed.

"I'm not being dramatic. I have a right to be upset about what you did to me. I have a right to beat your face in too, come to think of it."

Coatl stopped coming toward her. He threw his hands in the air in frustration. "What was I supposed to do? I was losing her, Yemania. It was the only way to—"

"And you were okay with losing me? Sacrificing me for the sake of getting what you want? You used to stand up for me, protect me from Father when he was in his rages. What happened to that Coatl? Did our father eventually break him so completely that he forgot how to care about anyone but himself?" Yemania got to her feet and stalked toward her brother.

Coatl held his ground. "You're twisting what happened. You're the one who went behind everyone's back with Ochix. He didn't even care about you, he was using you because you were desperate enough for someone to give you any scrap of attention."

"No," Yemania said, standing almost nose to chest with him. She tilted her face up to glare at him. "You're wrong. He loves me because he knows what an incredible healer I am. He sees my heart and my cleverness. He thinks I'm *beautiful*. And I will not let you or Metzi or our parents or anyone ever make me doubt myself and my own value ever again. You don't get to decide if I'm worth sacrificing or not." She jabbed her finger into the glistening ruby of the amulet on his chest. "A true healer does not harm others, especially for their own selfish desires. You are *not* a true healer, Coatl. Not anymore." She took a deep breath. "But I am. I am the true High Healer of Tollan, whether I wear that amulet or not. And I hope you never forget that."

Coatl stared at her in disbelief, his eyes wide with terror. He'd never seen her lose her temper like this before. The only time she'd seen him look this afraid was when they were children and he had been bitten by the . . .

Yemania gasped in realization, and her attention drew to the walnut shell hidden in her closed hand. Ometeotl had said the spider would be the key to her escape, and now she knew exactly how.

"Where are the guards?" she asked quietly.

Coatl rubbed his face, obviously relieved that she had calmed down. "I sent them to take a break. I told them I would make sure you didn't escape."

"Why?"

"Well, I couldn't have them hearing if you started talking about how Emperor Acatl really died."

Perfect. Yemania pretended to sniff. "I'm sorry, brother. I understand why you chose Metzi. I saw how much losing her destroyed you."

"Aw, Yem . . ." he said, reaching out and drawing her toward him for an embrace.

Yemania let him. Pretending to shake with sobs, she threw her arms around his neck and embraced him. "I'm going to miss you, brother," she said, adding a small choking sound for emphasis.

Coatl embraced her back. "I wish there were another way."

"Actually, there is," she whispered in his ear, just as she opened the walnut shell over the back of his neck.

She pulled away, and it took about two seconds before Coatl's eyes went wide. She imagined he felt the awful sensation of tiny legs scuttling over his skin. His back arched and his hand flew to his neck. He let out a panicked scream as he began to throw his shoulders back and forth in a terrible dance to try and dislodge his worst nightmare.

Yemania didn't wait to see if he managed to get the spider off—she sprinted for the chamber's entrance.

With no guards standing outside, there was no one to stop her from bolting down the long, labyrinthine hallways. Dawn was quickly approaching, and through the stone slit windows she could see the Seventh Sun's glow beginning to lighten the inky blackness of the night sky. The city would be stirring awake. Yemania raced toward the exit, knocking over a Tlana priest carrying a stack of codex sheets as she barreled past.

"I'm sorry!" she threw over her shoulder, but she did not stop.

Sweat clung to her skin as she finally burst into the open air. Her feet raced down the narrow temple steps, her eyes focused on the distant city gate that led down the plateau's steep cliffs and into the jungles beyond. Shouting sounded behind her when she reached the bottom of the steps. A handful of Eagle warriors appeared above her, pointing and beginning their own descent down the side of the massive Temple of the Sun.

Yemania panted for breath, and a painful stitch in her side almost made her double over. But if she stopped now, she'd never make it out of Tollan. She focused her attention on the marketplace that sprawled out on the plaza in the temple's shadow. It wasn't crowded yet, but the earliest risers were already teeming through the stalls. If she had any chance to lose the guards, it was there.

The plaza in Tollan was the largest in the empire. Tens of thousands of Chicome citizens were said to visit the sprawling marketplace in a single month. Each city-state had its own local market, but Tollan was where foreign traders convened to sell luxury items in addition to the daily necessities. Here you could find produce ranging from bulbous red tomatoes to shining green peppers, ears of maize in every color imaginable, bone needles and wool for weaving, blankets and clothing, dyes and herbs from various jungle plants, basic clay pottery and delicate ceramic vessels too expensive for the common citizen to afford. There were baskets overflowing with freshly caught fish, animal pelts from deer and wolves, and cages containing live monkeys, birds, and dogs. Jewelry and brightly colored feathers from exotic jungle birds hung from racks to tempt the wealthy merchants and nobility. Finally, meandering throughout the masses of people and goods were government officials, clothed in golden cloaks. They were responsible for collecting taxes and ensuring the quality of the goods offered, and, in Yemania's case, would need to be avoided at all costs.

Just as the sun's face made its appearance and bathed the plaza in fresh yellow light, Yemania ran down a row of stalls. The calls of sellers, hagglers, and animals alike drowned out the sound of her pounding feet. Metzi must have performed her daily sun ritual. She wondered briefly if Coatl had managed to make it back to her side. The empress would be hearing about her escape soon.

She ducked behind a tent selling animal skins, gasping for breath. How was she ever going to make it to Tollan's front gate and down to the jungles? Soldiers would be monitoring every visitor in and out of the capital. The Mother goddess hadn't mentioned *how* she was supposed to find Ochix and make it to Miquitz.

"Mother, help me . . ." she whispered to herself. A stall with dresses of every color imaginable drew her eye. She looked down at her own.

Bright red. The mark of a healer. She needed to change and blend into the crowds. She stripped off her bracelets and bangles and slipped her feet out of her golden anklets. Jewelry as fine as this would more than cover some necessities, if she was quick and careful.

The dress stall was happy to accept her red tunic dress in exchange for one of simple white. The fabric quality alone had the merchant drooling like a wolf over a fresh deer carcass. Yemania quickly changed into the inconspicuous attire and purchased a small bag, some herbs and fruits, and a small loaf of flatbread. Her heart threw itself against her ribcage any time an official strolled past, their keen eyes assessing for anything suspicious. Yemania tried to act friendly and smile with each merchant, to curb any sense of unease. Only yesterday she had dreamed of being able to distribute remedies here.

It wasn't until she was trading her last bracelet for a simple obsidian knife that she finally heard them. The Eagle warriors were spreading out through the market, in search of "the runaway healer." She prayed the merchant who bought her tunic dress had a tight lip.

"This is such a fine bracelet," said a young man with teeth inlaid with jade, admiring the shine of the gold in the freshly risen sunlight. "Are you sure you'd like to trade it for such a simple knife?"

"Maybe two?" she said quickly, tapping her foot against the tiled floor of the plaza. Two would come in handy if she needed to make fire again, and she didn't want to seem too desperate to complete the trade.

The warriors were still at the end of this row of stalls, but she needed to get moving.

"That still seems like too good of a deal. What's the catch? Is there something wrong with it?" The merchant narrowed his watery eyes at her.

"No, no catch. I just need two knives." She nervously glanced down the row of stalls as the Eagle warriors came ever closer.

"All right, then." The man shrugged his shoulders. "You want them wrapped up?"

"What?" Yemania jerked her head away from the warriors and back to the merchant's face. "No, no thank you. I'll put them in my bag like this."

"Wonder what they're looking for," the merchant nodded his head in the direction of the warriors. "Or who."

Yemania busied herself with putting the knives away, face burning. "Yes, well, I'm sure they'll find whatever it is."

She threw the bag over her shoulder and ordered herself to walk naturally in the opposite direction from the warriors going stall to stall. They had no reason to suspect her if she didn't give them a reason to. *Calm. Stay calm*, she chanted over and over in her head. Her heart didn't seem to be heeding the command, frantically thrashing inside her chest. She finally neared the end of the row, but as she did, another group of three Eagle warriors turned the corner.

And she was now trapped between them.

CHAPTER

41

Ahkin had read several codex sheets describing the council chamber of the Lord of Death, but none had prepared him to experience it for himself.

It was a long hall, lined on either side by pillars carved with the most disturbing images. The hieroglyphs painted in blood depicted every form of death and torture imaginable, some that Ahkin had never even thought to imagine. There was no ceiling. Instead, the hall opened to the swirling clouds above and the molten peaks of the surrounding mountains.

The center of the long hall was sunken like a pleasure pool, but it was not filled with water. Instead, it was filled with hundreds of statues. At least, Ahkin thought they were statues. As he and Mayana crept closer, the figures appeared so lifelike that he couldn't tell if they were real or not. They depicted the twelve lords of Xibalba themselves, more cruel and vile than their demon servants. They appeared just as he had imagined them from the texts. They varied in appearance, from the dripping, grotesquely swollen form of Ahalpuh, Pus Master, the lord that afflicted humans with infection, to the flayed, bloody form of Cuchumaquic, Gathered Blood, who sickened people by making them cough up blood. He recognized Chamiabac, Bone Staff, and Chamiaholom, Skull Staff, the twin demon children responsible for starvation and decaying dead bodies into skeletons. They were easily identified by their staffs, which were constructed of human femurs and tipped with human skulls. Mayana seemed most terrified of Ahaltocob, Stabbing Demon, whose razor-sharp claws and teeth dripped with blood that matched the eerie red tint of his skin. His humanoid body was topped with the face of a monkey, though his limbs seemed to be on backward.

But there were many duplicates among the hundreds of statues, sitting in thrones of various substances. From thrones made of bones or teeth to thrones made of excrement or mud.

There was no way through the hall except through the throngs of gathered statues. The thought of passing so close to them, seeing them in their gory detail, made Ahkin wish he had been eaten by the jaguars. He didn't want to admit to Mayana how terrified he felt, not when she seemed so close to fainting herself. He had no choice but to press on.

At least he did not have to walk through the statues alone. He and Mayana clung to each other, neither walking in front of the other. They would face this obstacle as the Mother goddess intended them to: together.

"Which statue is Cizin?" Mayana whispered out of the corner of her mouth.

Ahkin forced himself to look around until he spotted it: a statue in the likeness of the Lord of Death himself, Cizin, the Fetid One. He was tall and thin, his ribcage protruding from his skeletal form. Dying gray flesh clung to the bones, riddled with black spots of decay. His head was that of a rotting skull, and upon his head sat a headpiece made of owl feathers. Around his neck hung a necklace of human eyes, still dangling from their nerve cords.

"Gods, he's horrible." Mayana quickly turned her eyes away. "I can't even look."

Ahkin's nerves were stretched as taut as a bowstring. Something about these statues did not feel right. Their eyes seemed to follow Ahkin and Mayana as they passed. Just when Ahkin was sure he saw one of them move, the closest statue of Xic, Winged One, responsible for stealing lone travelers on roads, literally came to life. His black-furred body was humanoid, but instead of arms, bat wings stretched out from his torso, while the head of a wolf smiled at them with pointed fangs.

"Welcome, humans. You have survived much to make it this far. But you must play a game before you can be allowed to speak to our master, Cizin." Xic's voice was high pitched and breathy, as though the wolf's head was wheezing out his words. "Would you care to take a seat while I explain the rules?" Xic motioned to an empty bench behind them.

Ahkin didn't trust the glint in the Winged One's eyes. Ona, who still cowered beneath Mayana's legs, growled at the bench, confirming his suspicions. "No, thank you, I think we would prefer to stand."

"Shame," Xic complained. "That is always my favorite trick to play. You see, the bench is as hot as a cooking stone. You humans are so funny to watch when your buttocks are burned to blisters." He coughed a wheezy laugh.

Mayana stiffened beside him, reaching for her dagger. "What are the rules of your game, Winged One?" she said.

Ahkin wanted to kiss her for how strong and confident she sounded. He could feel her pulse fluttering like a hummingbird's beneath his hand, and it made his heart swell with pride.

"The rules are simple. You must find Cizin. The real Cizin. There are many representations of his likeness scattered around this hall, but only one of the statues is the true Lord of Death. If you can identify him, you will be granted an audience. If you choose incorrectly"—Xic's wolfish smile widened—"we will take turns torturing you until Cizin finally rips your souls from your mutilated bodies."

Hundreds of wicked laughs, from high pitched and wheezing to as deep and ancient as the earth, surrounded them in a cacophony. It was as if every lord of Xibalba was mocking them.

"We will play your game," Mayana said.

Xic howled and flapped his massive wings, taking to the skies to observe them in their quest to identify the true Lord of Death.

Ahkin's blood was pounding in his ears. "How are we going to find him?"

Mayana licked her cracked, dry lips. "What do you know about Cizin? What have you read?"

Ahkin racked his brain. "He goes by several names. Cizin, Ah Puch, One Death, Yum Cimil. But he is always the Lord of Death. His symbol is the owl. He sometimes tortures souls by burning them and dousing them with water repeatedly until they dissolve completely."

Mayana made a sound of disgust, but she let him continue.

"His name means 'Fetid One.' Stinking . . . as in flatulence."

Mayana actually giggled at that. "His name literally means—?"

"Yes, as in gas. Stench." Ahkin couldn't help it, he snorted a laugh too.

"I wonder what the Mother was thinking, naming him *flatulence*."

A grumble of discontent rumbled from somewhere close by.

"I've also read that it is essential for mourners to scream loudly when someone dies, to scare him away so he doesn't take more than one soul with him when he goes back to Xibalba."

Mayana nodded in acknowledgment. "Okay. Now that we know that, I think we can make a plan from there."

"Make a plan?" Ahkin arched an eyebrow at her.

Mayana sighed in frustration. "Yes, a plan. But you need to promise to trust me if my intuition leads me away from the plan, all right?"

Ahkin could feel the war raging within him. Making a plan is exactly what he wanted to do. Find some kind of systematic way to rule out the least likely statues and use logic to narrow down the rest. Mayana wanted to start out with a plan but be allowed to follow her heart if she felt led to do so. It went against everything he'd ever been taught, but then he looked at the determined set of her jaw, the smoldering passion in her eyes. *You need to promise to trust me*, she'd said.

She had been right so many times on this journey, and even before they leapt into the underworld. Her heart had led her to the truth about how the Mother goddess really wanted to be worshipped, the truth about his sister's evil intentions. She thought quickly enough to make a weapon to kill the snake, saved him from rock monsters with her water power, knew how to appease the demon guardians on the mountain. She even knew to comfort the spirit of a weeping woman and had been rewarded with the bones of her mother.

And she had saved him from the jaguars when he had been about to die.

Mayana was stronger than any woman he had ever known. Not because she could wield a spear or a knife, but because she could wield her heart with deadly accuracy. Though everyone around her challenged her and accused her of being selfish for following it, it was a heart that Ahkin knew and trusted in the deepest parts of himself. Yes, yes, he could trust her to know the truth. Hadn't she been doing that all along?

"Yes," he breathed, pulling her toward him for a fierce kiss. "I will follow your heart to the place where smoke has no outlet, if I need to."

Mayana kissed him harder, clutching at the hair on the back of his head. A soft sob of gratitude escaped her throat. "Thank you. Then let's work together to find—to find—" Her eyes went wide and distant, as if a thought had just occurred to her. "Ahkin, I have an idea!"

Ahkin grabbed her hand and squeezed. It was difficult to let go of the control, to let the responsibility of such an important choice fall onto someone else's shoulders. But he also knew he had to. "I trust you."

And he smiled, realizing that in the depths of his own heart, he really truly did.

Yemania froze in place. The Eagle warriors on either side of her stalked closer, unaware their prey was mere yards away. Should she try to run? Hide? Beg? She didn't really know what she should . . .

"You there," one of the warriors called to her. He stepped closer to get a better look at her face. Yemania ducked her head, trying to obscure his view. *Run,* a voice inside her head screamed at her. *Run!*

But they would catch her. She knew she was no match for some of the most elite warriors in the empire.

A hand closed around her wrist and the warrior wheeled her around to face him. "You . . ." the warrior began, recognition washing over his features. But then his eyes misted over with a silver sheen, and his features went oddly slack. "You . . . you . . . are free to go, miss. Please let us know if you see any sign of the escaped healer." He dropped her wrist, and Yemania stepped back. Surprise and understanding sending her pulse fluttering.

"Thank you, I will," she said. Then she lowered her voice so that the other warriors could not hear her. "Where can I find you?"

The warrior lifted a finger and pointed north, back toward the temple itself.

"Thank you." Yemania rushed past the warriors, some frowning as though they weren't sure their companion's decision was the best. But mercifully, none of them stopped her.

When she rounded the end of the row, another hand found her wrist and yanked her toward the darkness between the two stalls. Her hands flew up and she found them splayed across a tanned, well-defined chest, a necklace of human finger bones beneath her fingers.

Yemania let out a small sob of relief and threw her arms around Ochix's neck. His own arms tightened around her, his face burrowing into her neck as he embraced her.

"You found me," she breathed, pulling back and drinking in the sight of his face.

"I always will," he said, pressing his lips against hers for a swift kiss. "But we need to get out of here."

"I know. We need to go to Miquitz. To Omitl."

Ochix frowned. "Why? My father is there, and he'll be furious I ruined his plan. That's the *last* place I should go."

"It's hard to explain, but will you believe me if I say the Mother goddess told me to?"

He studied her face for a moment and must have read the conviction there, because he finally responded, "I will. If that's where she told us to go, then go we shall."

Yemania squeezed his hand. "Thank you."

But Ochix arched an eyebrow. "You have to explain to me on the way how you escaped—and with directions from the Mother goddess herself."

Yemania smiled. "It's a long story, but I have a feeling we have a bit of a journey ahead of us, so there will be plenty of time."

———

Ochix showed Yemania how he had sneaked back into the capital city the previous night, and her jaw fell open.

"You scaled the cliff? In the dark?" Yemania stared down the edge of the volcanic plateau into the jungles below.

"I couldn't exactly walk back in through the main gate." He gave her an exasperated look.

"You could have *died*," Yemania scolded.

"Well, you were going to die if I didn't, so I didn't think too much beyond that."

Yemania's heart swelled at his determination to come back for her. "Thank you," she said.

"Don't thank me just yet, we still need to get back down if we truly want to escape. And then I have an idea that might get us safely into Miquitz, but you may not like it."

"Let's talk about that if we survive this climb down the cliff. How did you find me, by the way?" Yemania secured her bag on her shoulder so that she wouldn't lose her supplies in their descent.

"I was watching the temple, waiting for when they'd bring you out for the sacrifice, and then you appeared, bolting down the steps like a spirit from Xibalba was after you. I saw you run into the marketplace and I followed."

Yemania blanched. "What were you going to do when they brought me out to sacrifice me?"

Ochix shrugged. "Again, hadn't really gotten that far. I was ready to fight my way to you and then . . . make it up from there?"

Yemania leaned forward and pressed a kiss against his nose, trying not to laugh. "And you would have gotten yourself killed right along with me. Thank goodness my plan worked before you got the chance to enact yours."

Ochix boomed a laugh. "As much of a pleasure as I'm sure it would have been to travel the layers of Xibalba together, I must say I prefer maneuvering the land of the living."

"Me too. And let's keep it that way. I'm not a climber, so I'll need you to show me the safest way down this thing, all right?" She eyed the long distance to the jungle floor.

"Just keep your eyes on your feet and focus on the present moment. Don't get too ahead of yourself and don't look down." Ochix pulled out a length of rope and tied it around his waist before tossing her the other end. "Picked this up in the market while you were flitting around the stalls like a busy little bee visiting flowers."

Yemania turned up her nose. "Well, if we need any of my remedies you will be grateful I was a busy little bee."

Ochix chuckled and helped her tie the other end around her own waist. "If you fall, I will catch you."

Yemania swallowed hard. "Are you anticipating me falling?"

"No, but sometimes having that extra assurance of someone there gives you the boost of confidence you need. I think you can do this without me, but I want to be there to support you if you need me."

"Thank you," she said quietly. She pulled out the little doll Ometeotl had given her and studied the doll's now joyous face.

He took a steadying breath and said, "All right. I'm ready. Let's go."

———

Yemania and Ochix were both drenched with sweat by the time they reached the base of the cliff. Yemania gasped for breath and wanted to kiss the dirt of the jungle floor. She would never climb another cliff for the rest of her life.

Ochix untied the rope from around their waists and motioned for her to follow him into the safety of the trees.

"You are absolutely sure we need to go to Omitl? You wouldn't rather run to Ehecatl? The Miquitz Mountains are in the opposite direction."

Yemania clutched at a stitch in her side. "Yes," she gasped. "Ometeotl was extremely clear."

Ochix's eyes went wide with wonder. "I still can't believe the creator goddess herself appeared to you. That is such an unbelievable honor."

"Well, she's fond of you, so take that as a compliment."

Ochix stumbled back a step. "She said she's fond of *me*? Really?"

Yemania giggled. "She called you darling, so I imagine that's a good thing."

Ochix smiled as though he'd had too much pulque to drink.

"But on a more serious note, how are we supposed to get back to Omitl?" She eyed the dense expanse of jungle that spread out before them. "Will they even let us in?"

Ochix rubbed the back of his neck. "I have an idea to get us in, but I warned you before, I don't think you're going to like it."

Yemania narrowed her eyes. "Why?"

"I left my delegation on the road not far from here. They are waiting for me to return. If I go with them, I can enter the city with no issues. My father will likely be furious when I return a failure, but there is no way they will let you join us on the journey home unless . . ."

But she already knew where he was going in his line of thought. "Unless I'm your prisoner?"

Ochix gave her a sheepish smile.

Yemania let out a heavy breath. "All right. I think that will work."

Ochix arched an eyebrow. "You want to go as my prisoner?"

She shrugged. "I don't see any other way to make it there safely. And you won't let anything happen to me once we get there, right?"

Ochix's face went suddenly intense, as though flames burned within his dark eyes. "I would die myself before I let any harm come to you."

"The Mother goddess obviously likes you, so that is a good recommendation for me to trust you." She arched an eyebrow.

Ochix laughed and kissed her. "All right. Then we know how to get back inside Miquitz."

He cut a length of rope from the one they used to climb down the cliff and wrapped it around Yemania's wrists.

"I've made it loose enough that you can wriggle free in an emergency," he assured her.

Yemania nodded. Now that they were actually going through with their plan, she was a little more nervous about it.

She chewed the inside of her cheek. "They won't kill me before we get there?"

Ochix shook his head. "Absolutely not. You will be revered as a divine sacrifice. No one will want to waste a drop of your blood. We will take you to the capital and you will be housed in the temple until the final day of the Nemontemi—so the end of tomorrow. That's when we gather at the entrance to the underworld and wait for Cizin to emerge. If he does, we offer him a selection of the finest sacrifices we can gather, human and beast and luxury goods, to persuade him to spare the city."

"Then I will be offered to Cizin as a sacrifice?" Yemania was sick of everyone trying to use her divine blood to save themselves.

"Cizin hasn't emerged in the last hundred years, so I am not worried about that. Besides, I will set you free before it gets to that point. I promise. I know my way around my city and have many loyal friends willing to help me if I need a quick favor." He winked at her.

"All right." She hoped whatever the reason the Mother goddess needed her there was an important one. Ochix secured her mouth with a gag, tying it loosely like the ropes so she'd be comfortable.

They stepped out of the underbrush and back onto the main dirt road. After walking for a while, they finally came across the delegation Ochix had come to Tollan with. They waited for him on the side of the road.

The minor priest that had accompanied them leapt to his feet. "My prince, you return with a captive?"

Ochix's voice went hard and cold. "Yes. If they mean to insult us by breaking our alliance, then we might as well take a consolation prize." He lifted Yemania's tied hands.

The thin priest walked around her, assessing. Yemania knew her white dress would make her appear to be commoner. "Is she a peasant?"

"She is a healer, descended from the god Ixtlilton."

The priest frowned. "Why is she not in red? I thought all the Chicome healers wore red?"

Ochix shrugged. "I think she was a criminal of some kind. I found her trading her red dress for this white one in the marketplace. Guards were tracking her and she was distracted. It made her easy to capture."

"We can test her abilities for ourselves when we get back home. I am sick of this place and want to get back to our mountains. If she does prove to possess divine blood, your father should be happy with such a precious captive."

"My thoughts as well," Ochix agreed.

The priest motioned for the four other members of their delegation to get moving. "We will be there by tomorrow afternoon if we leave now and hurry. I would like to arrive before the end of the Nemontemi to make sure she is part of the offering."

"I will keep guard over the captive. I can use my ability if she makes an attempt to escape." Ochix tapped the side of his head, right next to his eyes, for emphasis.

"Excellent idea, my prince." The priest led the way toward the dark mountains in the distance.

The moment everyone's backs were turned, Ochix lifted her bound hands and pressed a fleeting kiss across her fingers. "Let me know if the gag is bothering you at all. I'll adjust it."

Yemania nodded. Though it wasn't her bound wrists that bothered her most now. It was the nervous fluttering in her stomach.

She was going to Miquitz.

CHAPTER

43

Mayana couldn't tell Ahkin her plan in case the lords of Xibalba were listening. She couldn't give away her one advantage.

She patted her leg for Ona to follow her. The dog perked its ears, eager to help.

She began to slowly walk between the hundreds of statues, Ona at her heels, passing horrific figure after horrific figure. They were so life-like. She couldn't even stand to look at Ahaltocob. He had been one of her greatest fears, a clawed demon that lurked in unclean areas of a house. As a child, Mayana frantically cleaned her room in the stone palace of Atl, convinced that any little pile of dirt would summon the Stabbing Demon, who loved filth.

There were dozens of statues of Cizin, each indistinguishable in appearance. The details were grotesquely exquisite, from the identical spots of decay scattered across his mottled skin to the protruding ribcage. Each headpiece of dark-gray feathers had two large wooden eyes like an owl. Visually, they were all identical.

But Mayana wasn't studying them for their appearances. She carefully approached each one, inspecting as if she was, but in reality, she was getting close enough to *smell* them. Ona had a much better nose than she did, and she watched him carefully for signs. Four, five. Eventually ten, eleven, twelve. She pretended to inspect each Cizin statue, waiting for

Ona to detect the one difference that would mark the true Cizin—his stench. He was known as the Fetid One for a reason, and she doubted it was something he would be able to hide completely.

Finally, after at least thirty different statues, she and Ona approached one along the edge of the group that made Ona take a step back. The dog's nose scrunched in discomfort, and as they got closer, even Mayana could smell it—an unpleasant odor of sulfur and rotting meat. She inspected the statue as she had all the others, and this time she had no doubt. The stench was subtle, as though the Lord of Death was attempting to mask it but could not eliminate it entirely. Plus, something about this one felt right. She couldn't exactly put it into words, but she knew all the way down to her toes that this was him.

She turned to find Ahkin, a smile spreading across her face. "I found him."

Ahkin came to stand beside her. "You're sure?" His eyes raked up and down the statue. "It looks exactly like all the others to me."

"I'm positive."

Ahkin took a deep breath. "All right. Xic, we have made our choice."

The Winged One flapped down beside them, his wings beating the air like drums. He turned his wolfish face toward them. "You are confident in your choice?"

"Yes," Mayana breathed.

"Should I remind you what will happen if you choose wrong?"

Ahkin widened his eyes in fear, as though to ask, *Are you absolutely sure?*

"He's trying to make you doubt my decision," Mayana hissed at him. "I know my choice. I am literally betting my life on it. Can you?"

Ahkin chewed his lower lip, gaze darting from the statue, to Xic, back to her. Mayana kept her face straight and confident. Together. This decision to trust her had to come from him.

He fixed his hardened gaze upon Xic. "That is our choice."

"Very well," Xic wheezed.

There was a crashing sound as one of the statues beside them collapsed into rubble. Mayana jumped and screamed. Then another crash, and another, and another. Ahkin flinched with each crash, his arms protectively encircling her. The deafening sound of collapsing statues filled the council chamber, until Mayana, Ahkin, and Ona were covered in dust. Xic flapped his wings harder and a great wind swept through the hall, surrounding them in swirling cyclones of dust and shards of clay. Mayana clutched Ahkin's arms, digging her face into his chest and squeezing her eyes shut. Finally, it was silent. The winds died completely.

When Mayana lifted her head and looked around, they were no longer standing in a sea of statues, but in the center of a circle of twelve thrones. Each throne was comprised of the same materials some of the statues had been sitting in: mud, excrement, bones, teeth, and even one that looked to be covered in human flesh. Seated upon them were the living, breathing forms of the eleven lords of Xibalba. They were even more terrifying to behold alive and moving than they were frozen as statues. The largest of the twelve thrones, a massive chair of jade bones and skulls, remained empty. The statue beside them, the last one standing, the statue they had declared was the real Cizin, suddenly dropped its jaw. Life flickered within the lidless sockets as bloodshot eyeballs rolled forward to face them.

The skull-like face of Cizin, Lord of Death, smiled at them.

"You have chosen well, humans. Unfortunately for me, we will not devour you today. You will be allowed to safely venture back to the land of the living." His voice was not what Mayana expected from a figure so skeletal and thin. His voice boomed deep with power and authority, how Mayana imagined a mountain itself might sound if it had a voice.

Mayana's legs wobbled and she almost collapsed to her knees in gratitude. Beside her, Ahkin released a long breath he had apparently been holding. He squeezed her tighter.

"Just like that? We are allowed to go?" Mayana wanted to elbow him in the ribs for questioning their permission to leave.

Cizin slowly paced toward his jade-bone throne, settling onto it while a gray owl three times larger than any she had seen in the jungles settled on his backrest. "You have proved your worth. You can choose to stay if you wish, or you may take the tunnel passageway through the mountain of fire back into the overworld. But if were you, I would not linger. You have very little time before the passageway closes."

"Thank you, Lord of Death." Ahkin bowed his head.

"You are welcome, prince of light. I am curious to see if you have the strength to face what lies ahead of you, should you choose to return home."

Ahkin stiffened. "What do you mean?"

The Lord of Death ignored him. "Daughter of water, I can see there is something you still wish to ask me? I can sense the question hovering on your tongue like an arrow waiting to be loosed. You better ask quickly, as your window to escape my realm quickly closes."

Mayana swallowed and took a step forward. "Lord of Death, we do not come only to pass through to the overworld. We have a very specific request to ask on behalf of the great creator Ometeotl."

Cizin's bloodshot eyes seemed to go redder, and every eyeball hanging around his neck swiveled to look at her. His skeletal fingers tightened on the armrests of his jade throne. "You ask for more than your freedom?" His voice remained even, but Mayana could sense the ire hiding just below the surface. They had insulted him by daring to ask for more beyond their lives.

"Ometeotl has sent us to request the bones of her son, the god Quetzalcoatl. He sacrificed himself to bring about the Age of the Seventh—"

"I know who he is!" Cizin boomed, rising to his bony feet.

Mayana flinched back, praying to the Mother to protect them from his fury.

He cocked his skull head to the side, considering them. "The jade bones of Quetzalcoatl are my most prized possession, daughter of water. They represent my conquest over the favored son of our mother, the foolish wind god who sought to humiliate me by stealing the bones of humanity after I claimed them. The sixth sun had been destroyed by great storms, and the souls that perished belonged to *me*."

Mayana tried to explain. "I'm sorry. We don't want to insult your generosity. We are merely doing as the Mother—"

"I will give you the bones of Quetzalcoatl, daughter of water," he interrupted.

"Y—you will?" Mayana blinked in wonder at the putrid Lord of Death. Hope blossomed within her. Perhaps he was more benevolent than the legends claimed.

"In exchange." He rapped his fingers against his throne, seeming satisfied with his idea. Several of the lords hooted with glee, their excitement rising.

Mayana's hope withered like a fragile flower. "In exchange for what?"

"You are asking me to make a great sacrifice. In order to grant your request, I must lose my greatest treasure."

Mayana waited, her pulse pounding in her ears and fear tingling in her stomach.

He leaned forward. "I will give you the bones you seek in exchange for the bones you carry in that little bag of yours. The bones of your mother."

The other lords around them cackled and howled.

A rushing sound filled Mayana's ears as sour bile coated her tongue. Their laughter felt like a weight pressing down on her chest. She wanted to collapse underneath it.

"No." She lifted the bag and hugged it to her chest. The bones of her mother. The last hope she had to ever see her again. "No. Anything but that."

Cizin sat back in his throne, laughing cruelly along with his deadly companions. "You have my price, daughter of water. Now the decision is yours. And I advise you choose carefully and quickly. More than you realize hangs in the balance. The foolish daughter of light brings the next apocalypse upon us, and I look forward to flooding my lands with the souls of your people."

Mayana's head snapped up. The hollow feeling inside of her deepened. Her choice?

Before your journey ends, you will have to make a choice that will destroy your world or mine.

The Mother goddess had spoken those words to her on the beach a lifetime ago. Had it really been only five days?

This was that choice. Mayana knew it as certainly as she knew which statue had been the true Cizin. If she didn't give up her mother's bones, Ometeotl would never get the bones of her son, destroying whatever plans she had for them. But if Mayana did give up her mother's bones, then it was Mayana's world that was destroyed. She'd have to give up the chance to ever see her mother again. It was an impossible choice.

And she raged against it.

"Mayana?" Ahkin's voice said, but it sounded distant and far away as she spiraled into herself.

An anger unlike any she had ever felt before burned inside her chest until she thought the flames might consume her entirely. She had known. The Mother goddess had *known* that Mayana would have to make this choice. Which also meant, she gave her that doll on purpose. She made sure Mayana had what she needed to retrieve the bones of her mother. Not as a reward, not as a gift, but as the payment to get what the goddess really wanted. How could the Mother goddess have done this to her? Had she even considered what something like this would do to Mayana's heart? Did Ometeotl even care?

Mayana's anger consumed her until her eyes themselves burned, burned with tears that now traced their way down her blazing cheeks. Mayana wanted to turn her face to the heavens above and scream her rage at the sky.

She had a chance to bring her mother back—the mother that never should have been taken away in the first place. Ometeotl hadn't protected her. It was *her* fault she had even died! This gift was supposed to right that grave wrong. And now, Mayana couldn't believe she had been foolish enough to think the Mother goddess had given her such a miraculous gift. Of course not. Her mother's bones were to be used to serve the greater purpose, just as Mayana herself was being used as a servant running errands for Ometeotl.

Did the goddess even love her at all? Were her own dreams and desires pointless compared to whatever greater plan the creator was orchestrating?

Mayana hugged the bag against her chest even tighter, sobbing harder than she'd ever sobbed in her life. She sank down to her knees and cradled the bag, not unlike her mother had cradled her as a child. She rocked back and forth, releasing her agony at having to say goodbye to her mother *again*.

The lords of Xibalba laughed and relished her pain, which seemed to drive the obsidian knife even deeper into her back. Curse all of these gods. These beings that sought to torture humans for their own pleasure. Or worse, pretend they love them, only to use them to serve their own selfish purposes.

Selfish. Selfish. Selfish. Wasn't that what the voices had whispered in her ears in the freezing waters of the final river? That *she* herself was selfish? Unwilling to submit and trust the will of the gods? It was the same whisper she'd heard in her ears from her family. Selfish for not wanting to follow the rituals. Selfish for caring more about her own heart than the lives of the people in their empire.

She turned her gaze to Ahkin. The prince of light had collapsed onto his knees beside her, palms open and pleading and exposed to her. An invitation to let him help.

"What do I do, Ahkin?" she sobbed.

"I can't make that decision for you. It's your choice to make, not mine. I know that *I* trust the Mother goddess. Whatever reason she has for bringing us here, it is for our own good. Even if I can't see what that good is yet."

She took in his handsome face, his beautiful dark eyes turned down in concern. He always trusted the gods so blindly, so devoutly. To the point of doing nothing while his mother stabbed herself in the chest. He had faith. A faith that she obviously lacked. His faith had been misguided, placed in the rituals instead of the gods themselves, but he had a conviction that was admirable. A dedication that she had never been able to muster herself.

Could there be a greater purpose Mayana could not see yet? Even if she didn't entirely believe that, could she believe it enough?

Mayana thought back to all the times she had questioned the Mother's will over the course of their journey through Xibalba. How everything had come together for a purpose. The doll, the worm, even Ona. Everything the Mother had given them served an important role in getting them here, even when Mayana could not see their purpose beforehand. She and Ahkin were dualities, gifts to each other, teaching and challenging the other's deepest weaknesses. Ahkin needed to let go of his twisted sense of responsibility. But what did she need to learn? What had he been meant to teach her? Faith? Trust?

Ona slinked up to her and ran his tongue along the side of her face, licking up her tears as he did so. He curled up against her, looking up at her with doleful eyes. The Mother could have sent any dog to help them, but she had sent Ona. Mayana's dearest friend. She knew it would be an encouragement, a gift. She had to trust that the Mother goddess loved her, even if half of her heart raged against that choice. There was no time left. They needed to leave now.

Before your journey ends, you will have to make a choice that will destroy your world or mine.

"I've made my choice," Mayana said, rising to her feet once more.

CHAPTER

44

Ahkin watched as Mayana forced herself back to her feet. He could not imagine the magnitude of the choice she was about to make. To give up the bones of her mother to save the bones of Quetzalcoatl. It was brutal. Cruel. But he did believe the Mother had a reason. He couldn't explain how he knew, but he did.

He also knew that Mayana would make the right choice, whatever that was. The Mother goddess had faith in her. And so did he.

She tilted her chin in the air, a small act of defiance and pride that Ahkin couldn't help but admire her for. Stubborn and passionate until the end. How he loved that about her. "I will make the trade."

The wolf-headed Xic howled from his throne made of teeth, while the other lords of pain and suffering guffawed and stomped their grotesque feet or claws against the tiled floor of the council room.

"Very well," boomed Cizin. The skeletal demon was truly a monster for doing this to her. Ahkin wished there was some way to rip that mottled flesh right off his bones. "Keep your thoughts respectful, prince of light, or perhaps I will not let you leave so easily."

Ahkin bit his lip to keep from responding.

Mayana marched forward and held out her bag to the Lord of Death. He took it in his pincerlike grip and opened the flap. With a snap of his fingers, the bones within the bag rose, floating and hovering like white birds. The bones then flew, whirling around Mayana in a taunt that made her slam her eyes shut to stop from seeing them.

More howling laughter from the lords of Xibalba.

Finally, Cizin snapped again, and her mother's bones flew to join those that comprised his throne—the bones that were his most cherished possessions. The white bones melded with the jade, making the throne now look as mottled in color as his rotting skin.

"The Lord of Death keeps his promises," he said. He snapped a third time and several of the jade bones ripped themselves off his throne with a sickly crunch, hovering in the air like jade birds instead of white. He pointed to her bag, where the jade bones settled into their new home. "You now have the jade bones you asked for, daughter of water. Are there any other deals to be struck, or are we finished?"

Mayana made a sobbing sound, but kept her chin held high. "We are finished."

He dismissed them with a wave of his hand. "Very well. My wife, Ixtab, will show you to the passageway home. I advise you to hurry." But something about his grotesque smile unsettled Ahkin's stomach. It shouldn't be this simple. Not that Mayana sacrificing the bones of her mother had been *simple* . . .

From beside Cizin rose a terrifying figure that Ahkin had not focused his attention on before. The woman was incredibly beautiful. Her long, flowing white skirt fell to the floor, exposing her thighs along the sides. Her ebony-black hair was plaited down her back with golden ribbons. Ahkin averted his gaze from her uncovered chest to the white paint that covered her beautiful face, with black lines of paint arcing out from her mouth and surrounding her eyes. But what was most disturbing of all was the length of black rope that looped around her neck and dangled into her hands, wrapping around her arms like snakes. A noose, he realized. Ixtab was the deadly Lady of Suicide and Sacrifice.

"Follow me," she said in an elegant, mournful voice.

Ahkin reached out a hand to the small of Mayana's back as they followed Ixtab out through the doorway from the council room. Ona trotted in their wake. Behind the council room was a dark chamber lined with black stone pillars that disappeared into the darkness above. It reminded Ahkin of being back in the caves. At the center of the chamber stood a pure-black altar carved from obsidian. Vivid scenes of dismemberment and beheading adorned its surface. The sight of it sent a wave of cold over his skin. He had no desire to know what that altar was used for. Their footsteps echoed off the stone floor as they walked around it.

Cizin's temple backed against one of the fiery mountains. A cave entrance at the end of the chamber contained roughly hewn steps that spiraled upward. It was lit with more flaming skulls.

"What is the altar for?" Mayana asked, looking back at the large blade sitting upon it.

Ixtab faced them with black, whiteless eyes. "Let us hope you do not have to find out. This passage will take you back to the overworld. Do not linger here. The passage will soon close." She bowed and dismissed herself back to the council chamber.

"We made it," Ahkin said, hugging Mayana against him. "We survived Xibalba. And rescued the bones of Quetzalcoatl."

A rush of joy flooded through him as he realized they would both escape. The warning he had fretted over for days was for nothing. They would *both* survive.

But Mayana looked as though she had left her spirit back with the lords of Xibalba. "At what cost?" Her voice cracked with emotion. Tears flowed down her cheeks once more.

Ahkin embraced her again, his heart aching. He wished he could take her pain onto himself instead. "I'm so sorry, Mayana."

She cried for a few moments into his shoulder. When she finally hiccuped herself into silence, they began their ascent up the winding stone staircase.

The farther they climbed, the hotter the air around them grew. It felt as though they had entered a temazcalli steam bath, but the air was dry instead of moist. Soon Ahkin's lips were cracked, and he had to ask Mayana to summon some water from her pendant. She did, offering some to him and Ona, but refusing to drink some herself.

A loud screech echoed through the cave stairwell.

Ona barked a warning.

Ahkin turned and braced his shield on his arm just in time to see a giant gray owl descending upon him, black talons reaching for his face. He blocked the impact, but the force of it threw him to the ground. Mayana screamed as the bird dove at her next, its talons ripping at the canvas of her bag.

"No!" Mayana withdrew her knife and slashed at the owl.

Ahkin realized what the bird was after. "It's trying to steal back the bones of Quetzalcoatl! That lying, stinking—"

SCREECH! A glisten of jade appeared in a hole the owl had managed to rip. Mayana slashed again with her knife, making contact with the bird's scaled foot. It shrieked in indignation.

Mayana cried out as the bird sank its talons into her skin, her blood flowing down her chest in small red currents. The passage around them began to rumble ominously.

Ona launched himself at the owl. His jaws clamped around the bird's leg until it released Mayana from its grasp. Ahkin lurched toward her, lifting her in his arms right as the owl sunk its blade-sharp beak into Ona's side. The dog howled but refused to release his grip on the owl. He locked eyes with Ahkin, a look that clearly said, *Take her and go.* Then, the beasts both fell to the ground, the dog and bird tumbling down the staircase and out of sight in a flurry of feathers and fur.

"Ona! No! ONAAA!" Mayana screamed, reaching over Ahkin's back to where her best friend had sacrificed himself to give them a chance to escape.

"He wants us to run," Ahkin yelled, throwing Mayana over his shoulder and starting back up the staircase. Her blood coated his chest, making it slippery to hold her. He tightened his grip. She raged against him, clawing at his back with her nails and drawing his own blood.

"No! Take me back! TAKE ME BACK! ONA! ONA!"

"Mayana, we have to escape now! The passageway is going to close, and if we don't go now, we will be trapped here forever!"

"I don't care!" she sobbed, beating his back. "I won't leave him here. I can't!"

"He gave us a chance to escape. You'll waste his sacrifice if we don't go now!"

The tunnel around them began to shake, as if the earth itself was trembling. Fissures and cracks formed in the walls. Steam leaked from the cracks with a hiss. The layers of creation were shifting.

Mayana kicked against his stomach. Ahkin grunted in pain. He loosened his grip—just enough for her wiggle out of it. Before he could stop her, Mayana bolted back down the stairs. Blood coated the ground behind her.

"MAYANA!" After everything he'd done to keep her safe, to make sure she didn't pay the ultimate price for his mistake . . . She would not die here. He wouldn't let her.

The image of her dead body hanging from the post flashed behind his eyes. He would not return to the overworld without her.

With a quick glance back at their only way out, Ahkin sprinted after her.

He skidded to a stop at the bottom, emerging into the lower chamber just in time to see Mayana standing above Ona's barely stirring form. Blood pooled on the stone beneath the dog's skin.

With arms stretched out, her eyes glowed with a faint hint of blue light and her teeth were bared in a growl. The intensity of her face pulled the air from his lungs. For a moment, Ahkin swore she radiated the energy of a full-fledged goddess. Nothing and no one would stop her. The owl shrieked and fluttered into the darkness. Water swirled around her, lifting her hair to float above her head. The glowing in her eyes grew brighter, and she unleashed her fury upon the owl. The feathered figure swirled within a cyclone of Mayana's making, thrashing and fighting against the currents. But when she opened her hands, the cyclone hurled the owl back into the council chamber behind them.

"Maya—" Ahkin started to call, but he didn't get the chance to finish.

The ground beneath them shuddered, sending more cracks splintering up the back walls of the chamber. There was a crashing sound, so loud Ahkin swore the whole room was collapsing. He turned to see the doorway to the stairs collapse, covering their only escape with stone. From somewhere in the distance, the lords of Xibalba cackled with glee.

The Nemontemi was over. The layers of creation were closed.

And they hadn't escaped in time.

Miquitz was unlike anything Yemania had ever experienced before. It took them hours to climb the steep mountain trails, at times skirting ravines so steep that it made Yemania's head spin to look down. But the Miquitz soldiers and Ochix seemed perfectly at ease, like a bunch of mountain goats hopping along paths they'd trekked their entire lives. Which, she supposed, they had.

Yemania was terrified she'd tumble to her death into one of the gorges. Far below them gushed a young river teeming with rapids, while beside her rose towering rock walls of various shades of gray, brown, and black. Stunted trees and slick green grasses grew in patches across the mountains' many faces. She was surprised by how much green there was. Her assumption had always been that the Miquitz Mountains were dead places of stone, not bursting with bunches of wildflowers and scampering rabbits and squirrels. Even glorious birds of prey soared on currents of air rushing up the mountainsides. Mountain fields were impossibly steep and sloping, and yet crowded with livestock and llamas. Waving hands greeted them from inside stone cottages with thatched roofs. For the empire of death, it seemed to be teeming with life.

"This isn't what I expected at all," Yemania whispered to Ochix.

He grinned. "What were you expecting? Cold buildings of stone without a blade of grass to be seen? Perhaps bones and skulls littering the desolate landscape like a grave?"

She snorted a laugh.

"Wait until you see the capital, Omitl. You will be amazed."

Yemania smiled at the pride that seeped into his every description. She could tell how much he loved his home. And it made her love him that much more.

"You will be an amazing emperor here someday," she told him.

Ochix strutted ahead. "Of course I will. I will be the most handsome emperor Miquitz has ever seen."

Yemania rolled her eyes. "And the most modest as well."

"I will be the humblest emperor Miquitz has ever had too. None before or after will be able to match my humility." Yemania giggled, and one of the soldiers glanced back at them through narrowed eyes.

"Stop having so much fun. Act more captive-ly," Ochix whispered out of the corner of his mouth, though he couldn't stop his teasing smile.

Yemania fought to keep her face straight. "Sorry, more terror and less giggling. Got it."

They continued up the mountain trails until they crested a final peak. Her first view of Omitl took her breath away. The city stretched between pointed peaks, four of them jutting up like thumbs. Their rocky faces were covered in plants, and the terraced fields of crops and gardens were green enough to rival the jungles outside of Tollan. The city itself was made of stone but bustled with life. Streets wove their way across the steep slopes, stairs snaking around the city's many terraces. Precarious rope bridges spanned the gaps, while pearly white mists clung to the peaks and lingered in the canyon gorges below. The air smelled crisp and cold and clean, hinting at the scent of wildflowers and wet rock. A crashing waterfall fell from the highest of the mountain peaks, silhouetting the entire stone city against a backdrop of rushing water.

It was absolutely beautiful.

There were so many plants and herbs in these higher altitudes that she was unfamiliar with, and she itched to discuss their properties with the locals, to see if new remedies were to be discovered. Though that would have to wait until Ochix had broken her out of the temple.

The Temple of Omitl was by far the largest structure in the city. The pyramid of stone was not tiered like those in the Chicome Empire, but smooth. It backed up against one of the highest peaks, where beside it a cave opening led to a massive amphitheater.

"Is that where . . . ?" She nodded toward the cave.

Ochix furrowed his brow and nodded. "The whole city gathers for the ceremony."

"When does it take place?" She swallowed.

"At sunrise tomorrow. Those are the final moments the opening between the levels of creation can be accessed."

Yemania's eye was drawn to the gaping dark tunnel that appeared to lead into the mountain itself. It was ominous in its bleakness, and even from this distance, Yemania swore she could hear the whistling of winds carrying the whispers of tortured souls trapped below.

They marched her through the city, where the Miquitz people dressed in thick cloaks of black and green watched her progress with an excited gleam in their eyes. Children carrying dolls or sticks followed along after their little caravan, chanting songs and chattering excitedly about the newest captive.

The Seventh Sun was already starting to set in the sky, casting the mountaintop city in eerie purple shadows. They marched up to the temple itself, which Yemania assumed was also the emperor's palace.

"The palace is built into the mountain," Ochix said quietly. "It looks smaller on the outside, but it is much larger than it appears. And much grander."

For a brief moment, Yemania wondered if this would become her home, if she and Ochix did marry and he became emperor . . .

Soldiers lined the stone bridge that spanned a gorge and separated the temple from the rest of the city. Their bone-tipped spears were honed to be impossibly sharp. They watched her pass with dark eyes matching the equally dark cloaks which fastened at their shoulders.

They entered the temple, and Yemania immediately saw what Ochix had meant. The inside stretched high above their heads in a massive cavern supported by carved pillars along all four walls. The pillars were carved with hieroglyphs that Yemania couldn't quite make out, and the sunken stone floor was polished to an impossible shine. Rubies and jade glistened from hanging weavings that depicted images of the gods. Hallways led off from the main chamber into what Yemania assumed were council chambers and storage rooms, and likely the residences of the royal family.

Before her, on a throne carved entirely of jade, a man with a perfectly smooth head painted white as a skull, and decorated to resemble one, sat poring over codex sheets he fumbled in his hands. His black robe was open to reveal a bare chest, where a necklace of bone and black toucan feathers hung. Upon his head sat a small crown of black feathers.

"Father," Ochix said, approaching the emperor and high priest of Miquitz. "We have returned with some good and bad news."

Tzom, as Yemania knew he was called, did not look up from his papers. "What do you mean, bad news? Shouldn't you be in Tollan preparing for your wedding?"

"There will be no wedding, Father. At least not between me and the princess of light."

Tzom slowly lowered the papers, his face deadly calm. "And why is that?"

Ochix kept his chin high, but he would not meet his father's direct gaze. "She has called off our engagement in her desire to marry another. There was nothing I could do to remedy the situation. I did, however, bring a tribute to you in my apology for failing you."

Tzom's eyes snapped to Yemania and narrowed. "A tribute? I do not need another wife."

Ochix's jaw tightened. "No. Not as a wife. She is of Chicome royal descent. A healer, descended from Ixtlilton. I bring her to add to the offering."

Tzom's eyes, painted black within their sockets to enhance his skull-like appearance, widened in surprise. "You bring divine blood for the sacrifice? Well, that is a fine tribute indeed."

When he turned back to face his son, his face split into a smile, made even wider by the black paint stretching out from the corners of his mouth. Yemania could see the madness in that moment, a gleam of manic insanity that lurked beneath his father's eyes.

"I will need to consult with my patron as to how to proceed." Tzom rose to his feet and swept from the room. "I will wait to decide whether or not to kill you, son, based on her guidance. I recommend you make yourself at home until I return."

Ochix turned back to her and frowned. He pulled at her ropes and led her out of the main throne chamber. "I'll take her to the sacrificial holding rooms with the others," he called out to the guards.

They let him pass without incident into the darkened halls lit with torches.

"Will he really kill you?" Yemania asked now that they were temporarily alone.

"Well, I guess if the Obsidian Butterfly decides I can live, then I live."

"Do you think she will?"

"Doesn't matter." Ochix smirked. "Because I'm not giving her a chance to decide. You and I"—he pulled her close and slipped a blade out from his waistband—"are going for a little walk in the city, what do you say?"

"A walk?" Yemania asked flatly.

"I was actually thinking more along the lines of *hiding out* in the city. I know an innkeeper who will let us stay there until we figure out what to do next. She is a close friend of mine and will let us hide there for a little while."

Yemania bristled for a moment at *she*, but then quickly let it go. She didn't have time to worry about that. "If it keeps me away from any sacrificial altars, then lead the way."

Ochix grabbed her hand and pulled her to the labyrinthine halls of the palace. They reached a crevice in the stone concealed behind a small wooden door. There was no hallway behind it, only a roughly hewn cave. "I know a secret way out. I used to use it to sneak out and meet"—he paused, looking embarrassed—"meet, uh, people. When I was younger."

Yemania's cheeks went hot. He sneaked out to meet with *girls*, he was probably going to say. Maybe a little jealousy was called for.

Ochix must have read the look on her face. "It doesn't matter what I've seen before, daughter of healing, you are the only one I see now and will ever see." He pulled her close and kissed her deeply. Yemania melted within his arms.

"All right," she conceded, though she still gave him a playful smack on the arm.

Ochix beamed at her and pulled her into the dark interior of the mountain. Yemania didn't know what the Mother goddess's purpose was in bringing her here, but she trusted she would find out soon enough.

The water swirling around Mayana crashed to the stone chamber floor. She fell to her knees beside Ona. The wounds on his abdomen gaped, blood rushing out of him and coating her knees. She placed her hands on his sides, feeling his frantic, shallow breaths. He was in so much pain.

"Ona, I'm sorry, I'm so sorry . . ." she cried into his fur. Ona tried to lift his head, but whined and lay back down, panting heavily.

Ahkin's hand gripped her shoulder. She wanted to jerk away, but she couldn't. His touch steadied her.

Ahkin sank to his own knees beside her. His grip on her shoulder tightened. "Why?" was all he said through gritted teeth.

His suppressed rage ignited her own. "He saved us! So many times. I couldn't leave him down here to die alone."

She glanced up at his face, at the rage and despair he was trying so hard to hold back. But even Ahkin couldn't be that strong. He released her and fell forward, his hands digging into his short hair. "We were so close. So *close*."

Mayana flinched and turned back toward the stairwell. The doorway was sealed in stone. The Nemontemi was over. They had failed.

Ahkin's huddled form began to shake. He beat against the ground with his fists. He was furious, but Mayana knew that fury was only masking his fear. Perhaps she should feel more afraid, but she couldn't find anything to feel. She was numb. Numb with disbelief that their journey had brought them here.

"We did the best we could," she offered. Her voice sounded flat in her own ears. Cold, emotionless. But it did nothing to help.

"I promised to get you out. It can't end like this," he yelled, beating against the stone.

"It does not have to, prince of light," came the melancholy voice of Ixtab.

The Lady of Death stood before them, her hands folded neatly in front of her long skirt. A wicked smile pulled at her black lips.

Mayana's gaze connected with the goddess's. "What do you mean? Is there another way out?"

Ixtab gently caressed the black rope around her neck. "Of a sort." She seemed to be enjoying this far more than she should. A sour taste coated Mayana's tongue.

She stepped aside, giving Mayana full view of the black obsidian altar that rested in the center of the chamber. Upon it sat a stone bowl and a single obsidian blade. Mayana studied the glyphs carved into its sides, the glyphs depicting gruesome forms of human sacrifice.

A sickened feeling swirled in her gut.

Ixtab slowly walked to stand beside the altar. She ran an elegant hand across its surface, gazing lovingly at the tools. "For most, the way to enter Xibalba is death. But it is also the way to leave. The Nemontemi destabilizes the layers of creation, but so does releasing the power housed in one's lifeblood. So yes, escape is still possible . . . but not for one of you."

Realization washed over her. Of course. One of them would have to die to allow the other to escape.

Ahkin rose off the floor and back into a seated position. His eyes met Mayana's, and the intensity swirling within them told her everything. He was already planning to give his life for hers.

"No, Ahkin. No. I know what you're thinking and—"

"The Mother goddess warned me this might happen in a dream. In a way, I've been preparing for it all along. We both don't have to suffer for my mistakes."

"I'm not leaving here without you." She glanced down and rested a hand on Ona's still-panting side. "Either of you."

Ahkin rose to his feet. "I made the mistake of sacrificing myself, and—"

"And so you're going to do it again?" Mayana stood. "Ahkin, think about it. If you don't return, who will become emperor? Metzi cannot rule, she killed your father! She tricked you! And she is the only sun child left. The empire needs *you*. It can survive without me."

Ahkin's eyes went wide with horror, ghosts of memories she couldn't see torturing his mind. Perhaps he was picturing her form hanging from the post in the desert. She couldn't shake the image of his dead body from *her* mind. "I'm not saying I want to die. I just can't . . . let you die, either. We can find another way. There has to be another way." He shook his head as if to dispel the memories plaguing him.

He took a step toward the altar, and Mayana stepped in front of him. "This isn't about me and you anymore, Ahkin. You are the emperor. Your people need you. There's no other way to open the doors." Her calmness surprised her. Here she was, convincing the boy she loved to let her die in his place.

"Give me time to figure out another option." He reached around her for the dagger.

Mayana's hand snapped out to grab his wrist. She narrowed her eyes at him. "We don't have time."

Ixtab's smile widened, a shark sensing blood in the water.

Ahkin's own eyes narrowed, and he made to reach for the blade again. Mayana tugged his wrist away.

"Mayana, please. Don't make me—"

"What? What would you do?"

Ahkin roared in frustration. "I will not let you kill yourself for me. I already watched my mother die for my father, and I won't let you do the same!"

Tears began to burn behind her eyes. She had been afraid it might come to this. "I'm not making this decision for you. I'm making this decision for *us*. For the empire." This time, she reached for the blade, and Ahkin's hand captured hers.

Mayana had not come this far to let her empire fall into the hands of a manipulative power freak like Metzi. One of them still had to return the bones of Quetzalcoatl to the Mother. Her hands flew out and pushed against Ahkin's chest, knocking him back. Perhaps he could strategize against his enemies, fight battles against flesh, but this was different. This was not a battlefield. They were playing by the rules of the gods now, not the rules of men.

She reached for the dagger, but a flash of light blinded her. She yelped and covered her eyes. When she opened them again, Ahkin was facing her, bloody palm outstretched. "Not yet! Let me figure this out."

Mayana withdrew her own blade. "There's nothing to figure out. This is the only way."

Quick as a flash, she sliced into her own palm and released a jet of water from her necklace. The water knocked the blade from Ahkin's hand, sending it skidding across the stone floor.

He dove for it, but Mayana was done arguing. If he couldn't do what was best for their empire, then she would have to do it for him. Tears trailed down her cheeks as she willed a wall of water between him and the knife.

Ahkin screamed in frustration and pushed against it, clawing at the water as though he could force his way through. But she held it firm, rushing it back into place where his hands scooped it away. Finally, his arms flopped to his sides as he gave up, obviously deciding to try another tactic. He faced her, chest heaving and his eyes wild. Mayana let the water crash to the floor and cover his feet.

He reached toward her. "Mayana." His voice trembled as he read the determination on her face. He took a step forward. "Don't—"

It broke her heart to do what she did next, but he left her no choice. He might be physically stronger than she was, but her magic was stronger. Light couldn't hold someone back the way water could . . .

"I love you, Ahkin. Please tell my family how much I love them too."

"Mayana! Stop! Please, wait—"

But she unleashed even more water from her pendant, the pendant her ancestor had used to save the world. Now, it was her turn to save it. She would make sure they had an emperor to raise the sun. Ahkin ran toward her, but she forced the water around him, engulfing him as he thrashed and fought against it. His arms punched and pulled at the water, but she made sure it held him firm.

"NOOOOO!" he screamed. "MAYANA! NOOOO!"

It was too late. Mayana knew what came next. She lay back on the black stone altar and lifted her knife above her chest. How ironic she would never raise a blade to hurt an animal, and yet she could raise one on herself so easily. She turned her head for one last glimpse of Ahkin, to make sure his face would be one of the last things she saw.

Her grip tightened and she took a deep breath.

Ahkin screamed, and Mayana drove the dagger toward her heart.

A blur of black flashed in the corner of her vision. Just as the blade came down, a warm body leapt between her arms. The blade sank into flesh that was not her own. There was a howl, and hot, burning blood flowed over her arms and chest. Mayana leaned her head back to see what had jumped between her and the knife. A sob ripped out of her, and then a scream.

It was Ona.

The dog had jumped into her arms to take the blade instead.

Mayana scrambled to sit up, just as the water holding Ahkin collapsed around him. She ripped the blade back out, but it was too late, the light was already fading from the dog's eyes. Just as it had when he was sacrificed by her father. When he'd forced her to watch.

But this time, his blood coated *her* hands.

"Ona! No!" She sobbed, hugging him to her chest as she rocked. His body finally went limp, and a renewed wave of grief washed over her. Ona had loved her so much. Truly the greatest love was the willingness to lay down one's life for another.

Ahkin's arm came around her as he embraced them both, kissing the top of her head fiercely, his tears falling into her hair. He laid a hand against Ona's face and closed his eyes.

"*One of you will not survive.* Thank you," he whispered, his voice cracking.

Blood flowed from the edges of the altar into carved grooves around its base. The room began to shake once more, the black columns vibrating as though the volcanoes around them were erupting. The crunching of shifting rock sounded from the stairway.

"The price has been paid. If you wish to leave, you must do so now," Ixtab said.

Ahkin didn't want to be insensitive. But he also didn't want them to *die*. "Mayana, come on, we have to go."

She ignored him and continued to cradle the body of her beloved Ona.

"The passage will not be open for long," Ixtab warned, her tone mournful. She seemed disappointed that both Mayana and Ahkin had survived her little game.

"Mayana!" Ahkin's voice turned sharp. "Do not waste his sacrifice! We have to go now!"

Mayana pressed one last kiss against Ona's muzzle and rose to her feet.

The walls around them began to shake wildly. Was the passageway starting to close again already? There was no way Ahkin was wasting this second chance they had at life. With his good hand, he yanked her toward the stairway.

"Can you run?" he yelled. It was hard to hear over the rumbling of the mountain around them. If the passageway between the layers collapsed with them inside it, they wouldn't just be trapped in Xibalba, they would be crushed. Ahkin already knew what it felt like to have his hand crushed, and he wasn't looking forward to experiencing that with his entire body.

"Yes," Mayana sobbed. She gave one last wistful look at the altar and wrenched her gaze away. "We can't let his sacrifice be for nothing."

They reached the doorway to the stairs, and Ahkin turned back for the briefest moment. Ixtab stood still, her hands again folded in front of her skirt, but the translucent form of a spectral dog now sat beside her. Its tail wagged as it watched Mayana with expectant eyes, as though to say, *I'll wait for you to come home.*

Ahkin's heart nearly cracked in two. They would see Ona again, someday. He knew it deep inside his bones.

And then they ran. Harder than Ahkin had ever run in his life. One hundred steps. Two hundred. Ahkin stopped counting as the muscles in his legs raged in protest. The stairs beneath them began to shift and roll, as if they were running up the back of a large snake. Mayana fell, and Ahkin lifted her to her feet. She clutched at the wound on her shoulder from the owl's claws.

Ahkin threw her arm over his shoulders and half carried her. Up ahead, a glimmer of light reflected off the smooth dark stone. They would escape. Together.

"We're almost there! Keep going."

Mayana's nearly bloodless face was soaked with tears. He could not imagine the pain she was in, having just lost her mother and dog all over again. The fact that she even tried to continue was a testament to her strength. They had supported each other so much through this journey. He knew they never would have made it without each other. Blood pounded like drums inside his ears.

The light ahead grew brighter and brighter, blinding him with its brilliance and purity. Mayana pushed herself with a renewed strength, rocks tumbling down around them. More pounding in his ears, like the increasing tempo of a worship dance. They had to make it. They'd come too far not to . . .

Ahkin threw himself the final few feet as the cavern collapsed entirely behind them. He and Mayana sprawled across the dirt, gasping for breath. Cool, clean air whipped across his face. But the pounding drum in his head did not stop.

Ahkin opened his eyes, blinking against the brilliant orange sky. Above him clouds swirled, but not the same dark clouds that had suffocated them the entire journey through Xibalba. These clouds were thinner, lighter, stained with the colors of sunrise. The Seventh Sun appeared over a distant mountain range.

They had made it back to the overworld.

Ahkin rolled onto his stomach and pushed himself into a sitting position, too exhausted to stand up. He lifted his good hand to his aching head. Why wouldn't his ears stop pounding?

He looked up, and as he did, the pounding suddenly stopped.

Mayana gasped beside him—as did hundreds of faces that surrounded them, an audience sitting in the stands of some kind of amphitheater.

The pounding in his ears hadn't been from blood. The pounding had sounded like drums because it *was* drums—drums that had stopped at their sudden appearance out of the cave and onto the floor of the amphitheater.

Mayana scuttled toward him like a crab, leaning into him and clutching at her bleeding shoulder. Her eyes were wide with terror, her chest heaving with heavy breaths.

And he didn't blame her.

Ahead of them, on a raised platform in the middle of the stone amphitheater, stood a figure Ahkin had seen only once before in his life. But it was a figure he would never forget. The painted, skull-like face of Tzom, the head priest of Miquitz, was standing before them with his arms spread wide. He was dressed in elegant black robes with a matching headpiece adorned with toucan feathers. The bones of his necklace rattled against his chest. But as soon as he saw them, his face fell, eyebrows pulling together in confusion, as if Mayana and Ahkin were not the ones he was expecting to see. Beside the platform was a group of about twenty people on their knees, hands tied and gags stuffed into their mouths. Sacrifice victims.

Ahkin let his gaze wander to the mountain peaks surrounding them, stone shrouded in mist. A terrible realization crashed into him, and he pulled Mayana closer.

They had escaped the underworld . . . and emerged right in the middle of a Miquitz Death Day ceremony.

The death priest stepped closer. The surprise on his face hardened into something more like triumph.

"My dear prince of light." Tzom smiled like a skull. "Welcome to Omitl."

I must admit we were not expecting you, but your timing could not be more divine. We are about to partake in one of our most sacred ceremonies."

He motioned around the amphitheater. Hundreds of faces blurred against the backdrop of their black attire splashed in vividly colored decorations and adornments. Terror slowly crept its way up Ahkin's spine. His heart thrashed inside his chest.

"After you threw yourself into Xibalba, my plans shifted to your sister, but the goddess has blessed the mission she entrusted to me. What fortune. She has brought you to me after all!"

Ahkin's memory flashed back to the battlefield outside Millacatl. The battle where he had failed to save the kidnapped peasants—the same peasants who now appeared to be tied before him. He remembered how determined Tzom had been to find him, to "speak" with him. The death priest had told his soldiers that his purpose was to save the sun . . . but the sun had not really been dying. So what had his true motive been? He obviously wanted Ahkin for another reason.

"What do you want with me?" Ahkin's voice scratched against his raw throat.

Tzom ignored him and motioned to the contingent of guards beside him. "Secure our guests. I want to make sure they don't miss this momentous occasion."

Ahkin jumped to his feet, his hand already on his knife. But his muscles screamed in protest, the breath coming into his lungs in sharp bursts. He cursed the exhaustion leaching away his strength. A blow to the back of his knees sent him flying to the ground, and the guards plucked Mayana away from him as easily as a doll ripped out of the hands of a child. One of them pressed a bone-white blade against the fragile skin of her throat. His gaze flew to her face, and her dark eyes were clouded over with the mist of possession.

"Leave her alone!" Ahkin roared, lurching back to his feet.

Tzom leered at him with a sinister smile. "Unless you want your companion's blood needlessly spilled, I recommend you drop your weapon."

Ahkin's chest heaved, but a drop of blood dewed beneath the blade pressed against Mayana's throat. Her clouded eyes remained distant and unfocused. Ahkin lifted his hands in surrender and the blade dropped into the sand.

Something like madness glittered within Tzom's eyes. "Wonderful! You see, I need your blood, son of the sun. My goddess has promised me that it is the only way to save my people. I will help her bring about the darkness that will allow them to descend! They will feast on the flesh of sun worshippers—and in return for my service, spare the Miquitz!"

"What are you talking about?" Terror rose inside Ahkin's chest. "Who will descend?"

Tzom smiled a savage smile. "The Tzitzimime! The star demons! The followers of the great Obsidian Butterfly! She will rule the new earth and spare us as her loyal servants. They can descend only during an eclipse, and now that I have the blood of one who controls the sun, I can ensure the eclipse will never end!" He paused, as though expecting Ahkin to celebrate with him. "You will be my guest of honor, son of Huitzilopochtli, as we usher in the age of the *Eighth* Sun!"

Although this world is a fantasy and not based on any one historical group, it was heavily inspired and influenced by diverse Mesoamerican mythologies and traditions, many of which do share some similarities. I take my research very seriously, but I also do take some artistic license for the sake of the story.

Xibalba is the underworld in Maya mythology and the name literally translates to the "place of fear." There are different versions of the mythology, but I tried to incorporate various aspects mentioned in the *Popol Vuh* into the fantasy version that Mayana and Ahkin must transverse. One consistency across many underworld mythologies is the presence of various trials and obstacles to overcome. The number nine is also very symbolic. Because there are nine months of gestation to enter the world, many cultures embraced the idea of nine levels of the underworld. It is also thought to be why many burial temples have nine levels, such as Temple I in Tikal, Guatemala. The various trials often include a crossroads of paths meant to confuse travelers and rivers of blood, scorpions, and pus. You will recognize many of those elements incorporated into the story. One example of a change I made was to change the third river of pus into a swamp because I wasn't sure I could stomach making them swim through a river of pus (sorry, not sorry? Haha!).

Many descriptions of Xibalba also include a council place of the Lords of Xibalba. The Lords loved to humiliate human visitors by creating realistic mannequins of themselves to confuse them or by tricking them into sitting on a hot cooking surface. The main Lord of the Dead can go by many names, as Mayana and Ahkin mention when they are trying to identify which mannequin is his true form. There are also aspects I incorporated from Mictlan, the Mexican version of the underworld, including the throne made of jade bones and the trial of playing a conch shell with no holes. In Mictlan, the number nine is significant and some of the levels include mountains that crash, bodies that hang like banners, wind that cuts like knives, and jaguars that devour your heart. Like Mayana and Ahkin with Ona, many spirits that descend into Mictlan are aided in their journey by a spiritual guide dog.

I hope the story has inspired your curiosity to learn more about the ancient civilizations and cultures of South and Central America. As always, I encourage you to do your own research too! A great place to start is *Handbook to Life in the Aztec World* by Manuel Aguilar-Moreno or national museums such as the National Anthropology Museum in Mexico City.

Lani

ACKNOWLEDGMENTS

I first want to thank my readers. I have been blown away by how many of you fell in love with Mayana and Ahkin's story in *The Seventh Sun*. I hope book two was able to deepen that love before the heart-wrenching conclusion waiting for you in the final book of the trilogy!

A huge thank-you to everyone who played a role in bringing *The Jade Bones* to life. So much work goes into creating a book, and I know I couldn't have done this without you. Samantha Wekstein, I'm still in awe that I am lucky enough to have you for an agent. Thank you for believing in this story and being my guide through the (under)world of publishing. I'm certain I'd be stuck wandering endless winding paths of confusion without you and the rest of the team at Thompson Literary! To Betsy Mitchell, Courtney Vatis, and Kathryn Zentgraf—you polished this story into the gem that it is. Your enthusiasm and passion for the story has helped me hold on to my own when I forgot to look up and see the light filtering down through the clouds overhead. Thank you to the entire Blackstone team for championing this series. To Josie Woodbridge, Lauren Maturo, Jeffrey Yamaguchi, Mandy Earles, Rick Bleiweiss, and everyone else at Blackstone Publishing, I was so fortunate to have you all working alongside me to bring this series into the world, and your support and partnership has been priceless!

An author never operates in isolation, so I absolutely want to thank all of my family, friends, critique partners, and early readers for lending me your perspectives, your hearts, and your time. There are honestly too many names to list, so please know that I love each and every one of you so much. You know exactly who you are!